Rosie Goodwin is the author of a number of bestselling historical fiction novels. Having worked in the social services sector for many years, she is now a full-time novelist, becoming one of the top 100 most borrowed authors from UK libraries. Rosie lives in Nuneaton, the setting for many of her books, with her husband and their dogs.

Visit www.rosiegoodwin.co.uk to find out more about Rosie and sign up for her newsletter. Or follow Rosie on twitter @rosiegoodwin

Rosie GOODWIN
A Mother's Shame

corsair

CORSAIR

First published in Great Britain in 2013 by Canvas
This edition published in 2016 by Corsair

7 9 10 8

Copyright © Rosie Goodwin, 2013

The moral right of the author has been asserted.

A CIP catalogue record for this book
is available from the British Library.

ISBN: 978-1-4721-0170-9

Printed and bound in Great Britain by
CPI Group (UK) Ltd., Croydon, CR0 4YY

Papers used by Corsair are from well-managed forests
and other responsible sources.

MIX
Paper from
responsible source
FSC® C104740

Robinson
An imprint of
Little, Brown Book Group
Carmelite House
50 Victoria Embankment
London EC4Y 0DZ

An Hachette UK Company
www.hachette.co.uk

www.littlebrown.co.uk

Welcome to the world Layla Rose, born 5 May 2013. A very welcome, long-awaited and precious little granddaughter!

Chapter One

Nuneaton, Warwickshire, January 1857

'I feared as much. Is there something you need to tell me, Maria?'

The girl's startled eyes flew to the doorway of the outside privy, where her mother stood wringing her hands together.

She forced a smile in the woman's direction.

'No, no, I'm all right, Mother . . . honestly. I think that rabbit stew you did us for tea last night must have disagreed with me, that's all.' Swiping the back of her hand across her mouth, Maria lurched unsteadily to her feet.

Running her hands down the front of her plain calico apron, Martha Mundy frowned. The girl looked dreadful. The bags beneath her eyes were so large that Martha thought she could have done her shopping in them, and her face was the colour of bleached linen. She seemed to have been in and out of the privy being sick for days – but then,

1

Martha told herself, her suspicions must be wrong, Maria was a good girl. She had never been any trouble to her. Not like her younger brother Henry, who was always up to some mischief or another.

'Well, if you're quite sure that's *all* it is.' Her voice was still heavy with doubt. Nobody else in the family seemed to have suffered any ill effects, and they had all eaten the same the night before. Maria pushed past her into the tiny yard, nearly colliding with the tin bath that hung on a hook outside the back door.

'Of course I'm sure.' Maria's voice carried across the yard, before it was whipped away by the biting wind. Then: 'Come on, Mother,' she urged lightly. 'Let's get in out of the cold, eh? Father will be home from chapel soon and all hell will break loose if his dinner isn't on the table, as well you know.'

Sighing deeply, Martha followed Maria into their tiny cottage. Wet washing was strung on lines suspended from the ceiling from one end of the beams to the other and Maria had to duck her way through it to get to the easy chair at the side of the roaring fire.

'I'll just put my feet up for a few minutes and then I'll help you dish the dinner up,' she promised.

Once her mother had bustled away to stab at the cabbage that was bubbling in a pan on the range, Maria screwed her eyes tight shut to stem the tears that were stabbing her – like sharp little needles at the back of her eyes.

She felt so ill that just to stand was an effort, but worse than that was the fear that was growing daily. Her monthly course was way overdue, and with each day that passed she felt worse. Even now, the smell of the meal that was cooking was making her stomach revolt. Thankfully, Emma, her little sister, who was playing with her peg dolls on the rug, took her mind off her predicament for a second.

'Maria, will you make me some more new clothes for my dollies soon? Mother's got some scraps of material left over from the dress she made me for Sunday school and I was thinking you could perhaps use them?'

Maria smiled fondly as she stroked the girl's fair hair back from her pale face. Emma had never been a robust child, in fact, she might have been termed sickly, but Maria had doted on her from the moment she was born. She could still remember that day eight years ago, and the terror she had felt as she huddled in the kitchen listening to her mother's screams as the doctor battled to bring the child into the world in the bedroom above.

Now she promised, 'Of course I will, sweetheart. At the weekend when I have more time we'll set to, eh?'

Contented, Emma turned her attention back to her dolls as Maria flashed a glance at the tin clock that stood on the mantelpiece. It was almost six thirty, which meant that at any second, her father would be back from the chapel in Chapel End where he was a minister. Heaving herself from the chair, she dragged the table from the wall at one side of the kitchen across the red quarry tiles, and after lifting the wooden slats to open it out, she threw a snow-white tablecloth across it and began to set out the cutlery.

Just as she finished, the door banged inwards, making the fire roar up the chimney – and Edward Mundy barged into the room, large as life and twice as nasty.

Thankfully, tonight he seemed to be in good spirits and they all heaved a sigh of relief as he sniffed at the air appreciatively. 'Is that a steak and kidney pie I can smell?'

Martha nodded as she wiped a strand of faded fair hair back from her face. She had been a good-looking woman in her day, but living with a bullying husband and sheer hard

3

work had made her old before her time. Although she was only in her mid-thirties she could have been taken for fifty at least. Turning away from the stove, she wearily poured the kettle of hot water she had ready into a tin bowl for him to wash in.

Slinging his coat across the back of a chair, Edward, a great bear of a man, placed his Bible down on the sturdy oak sideboard and plunged his huge hands into the water.

'Have you had a good day, dear?' Martha ventured timidly.

'Huh! How good can a day be when my parishioners are dropping like flies?' he retorted. 'The flu epidemic that has spread from London is getting worse by the minute. Word has it that fifty a day on average are dying there. Three little ones drew their last breath here today *and* two more men from the pit cottages in Chapel End. The undertaker is having to work through the night to keep up with the demand for coffins.'

Martha chewed on her lip as she handed him a rough towel that no amount of boiling would ever get white again, then turned away to drain the cabbage into the deep stone sink.

When Edward had finished his wash and was drying himself he glanced around the kitchen before asking, 'Where is Henry?'

'Oh, he er . . . just ran an errand for old Minnie Hickman,' Martha lied glibly rather than tell the turth and provoke his wrath, but underneath she made a mental note to give Henry an earful when he did finally put in an appearance. Their son had been working down one of the local pits for three years now and hated every single second of it. Martha wished there was some other job he could do that would allow him to be out in the open air, but jobs were scarce and the whole town relied on the ribbon-weaving factories and the pits for their survival. It was mainly Henry's wages that kept their home afloat. Edward's stipend as a preacher was barely more than a pittance, augmented by modest donations from his parishioners. Sometimes she despaired, wondering how they would ever manage when Henry was of an age to wed. Even now he was certainly never short of admirers. Still, Martha had decided that that was a problem she would face when she came to it.

Henry was never on time for anything, and his mother feared he would be late for his own funeral – an event that would come sooner than he expected if his father ever got to know of even half of the pranks he got up to. Henry would sneak off and go poaching on the local squire's land when he finished his shift down the pit each evening, and Martha was painfully aware that should he ever be caught, they would be thrown out of their cottage. But then the rabbits and pheasants he caught came in more than handy. And at least Edward seemed to be in a good enough mood tonight, so she quickly carried the pie to the table as he took a seat, and thanked the Lord for small mercies.

Once everyone was seated, Edward clasped his hands and bowed his head as a hush fell on the room. 'For what we are about to receive, may the Lord make us truly thankful. Amen,' he muttered, and then he fell on his food as if he hadn't eaten for a month. Maria kept her eyes averted and tried desperately to swallow something, aware that her mother was watching her like a hawk. Luckily, Henry barged in only minutes later and Martha's attention turned to him as she flashed him a warning look.

'Did you manage to get what Minnie wanted from the shop, son?'

'What? Oh er, yes I did, Mother.' As he slithered onto a

seat he gave her a grateful smile, glad that his father was too intent on eating his meal to have noticed his hesitation. At fifteen, Henry was a tall lad with huge brown eyes and hair as black as coal, and his mother adored him – although the same could not be said for his father. The two were as different in nature as chalk from cheese. To the outside world beyond the cottage walls, Edward Mundy was a fine, godfearing man. But within the walls he was a domestic tyrant, ruling his wife and family with a rod of iron. Henry on the other hand was gentle-natured, if somewhat mischievous, with a heart as big as a bucket. Many a time he had stepped between his parents when his father raised his hand to his mother, and Martha had long since given up hoping that the two of them would ever get along, although Edward was far more lenient with his son than he was with Maria. The two girls took after their mother, being blonde and blue-eyed, though Martha's hair was now prematurely streaked with grey. Sometimes when Martha looked at them, particularly Maria, she could see herself as she had once looked: young and light-hearted in the days before family life had taken its toll on her.

Her life with Edward Mundy had not been easy, yet for all that she still tried hard to be a good wife to him. Deep down she knew that she had never truly loved him, but she had envisaged a life of ease when she had married him. After all, how hard could the life of a minister's wife be? At first, she had felt fortunate – but she had soon learned differently. In many ways it was true: they were better off than most of the village people. They had their own small terraced cottage in Coleshill Road for a start, and woods and fields surrounded them rather than the tiny cramped yards that many of Edward's parishioners were forced to share. But money had always been short, and with five young children to feed it had been hard to make ends meet, which was why she had begun to take in washing some years back from the wealthier folk who lived on the outskirts of the town.

Sadly, only three of the couple's children remained alive. They had lost their four-year-old old twins, Samuel and Daisy, to a measles epidemic that had swept through the village some years back. Following their deaths, the financial situation had eased. But not so Martha's heartache, and anyone who knew her would have said that she had never been the same since. The twins had been just a year younger than Maria, and were the apple of her eye; even now, not a day went by when Martha didn't still feel their loss.

That was probably part of the reason why she was so protective of the three children she had left. Many was the time she had stood in the way of the belt and taken the brunt of the beating their father was administering to them. Like Henry, she could not tolerate his cruelty.

Now, as she glanced across at Maria picking at her food, every maternal instinct she had was screaming at her. And if the suspicion she had should prove to be correct . . . then she shuddered to think of the consequences. Unconsciously, she peered at Edward and a ripple of pure terror flowed through her veins, robbing her of her appetite.

Maria was just seventeen years old – young, beautiful and spirited. Unbeknownst to her father, a boy from the village had been trying to court her for some months now, but as far as Martha was aware, Maria had flatly refused to walk out with him up until now. And even if she had relented, surely she wouldn't have been foolish enough to let him put her in the family way? She had always been such a sensible girl.

Throwing his knife and fork down onto the empty plate, Edward brought her thoughts sharply back to the present as he demanded, 'So what's for pudding then?'

Scraping her chair back from the table, Martha answered, 'Spotted Dick and custard. It'll take me but a few minutes to dish it up.'

Sighing with satisfaction, the man ran his hands across his bloated stomach, but then as his eyes came to rest on Maria and he saw her pushing her food around her plate, he snapped: 'What's the matter with you then, miss? That meal cost me hard-earned money, as well you know. It's a sin to leave good food when there are starving people in the village. Are you sickening for something? I hope you haven't been in contact with anyone who has this flu.' Edward took every opportunity he could to pick on Maria.

'Sorry, Father. I'm not feeling too well at present but I'm sure it isn't the flu,' Maria blustered. 'Could I be excused? I think I might go up and have a lie-down for a while if you have no objection.'

Pulling her plate towards him, he intoned: 'Waste not, want not. That's what my dear old mother always used to say, God rest her soul. The trouble with you is you've had it too easy. Go on – away with you. But I shall expect you down in time for your Bible reading. Is that understood?'

'Yes, Father.' Scrambling away from the table, Maria lifted her drab calico skirts and headed for the stairs door, beating a hasty retreat whilst the going was good. She clattered away up the threadbare carpet runner and didn't stop until she had closed her bedroom door firmly behind her. Then, sinking onto the end of the bed that she shared with Emma, she dropped her face into her hands.

Eventually she rose and crossed to the small window that looked down onto the Coleshill Road.

Why hadn't Lennie been waiting for her for the past few weeks when she finished her shift at the post office in Chapel End? For months he had been there as regular as clockwork, the second she set foot out of the door, but now it was as if he had vanished off the face of the earth, ever since the night he had taken her.

Her mind raced back to the night he had led her into the churchyard behind the chapel. Her heart had been in her throat. What if her father was to find them there? But then Lennie had chased all her fears away when he told her that she was the most beautiful girl he had ever seen and how much he loved her. Her heart had soared. This was Lennie making a promise to her, surely? Why would he have said those things otherwise? And life with him would be so different from the humdrum life she had known so far. There would be no scrimping and saving and having to make every penny count with Lennie. He always had money aplenty and was not afraid of spending it. And then he had kissed her – but the kiss tonight was different. There was an urgency about it and she had become alarmed when his hands began to wander to places they should not go.

'It's all right,' he had told her as his large hand found its way beneath her blouse and squeezed her nipple. Before she knew it he had her pressed against the church wall and then his fingers were stroking her thigh and pulling her drawers aside. 'I love yer, Ria,' he had gasped as he hastily undid his breeches.

It was then that she had begun to struggle. As much as she loved him she knew that this was wrong. Kisses and cuddles were one thing, but this was something that only married couples should engage in.

'Lennie . . . *no!*'

His hand clamped across her mouth and now she was terrified. But it seemed that the more she fought him, the more determined he became to have her, and suddenly, as he forced himself into her, she knew a pain the like of which she had never imagined. It felt as if he was ripping her apart and she was helpless to stop him. After it was over she could remember crying softly and the tender way he had held her.

'Don't worry,' he had told her. 'You're my girl now. I was only gettin' it out o' the way. You'll grow to like it, you'll see.'

Thoughts of him lifted the corners of her mouth into a rueful smile. She knew that her mother didn't approve of him, but she loved him so much she could even forgive him for forcing himself upon her. He was so different from anyone else she had ever known. Oh, she knew he had a reputation for being a bit of a Jack the lad. But then who could blame him for not wanting to work down the pit like most of the other men in the village? As Lennie had told her, he wanted better, and if doing business deals here and there got it for him, then so be it. *'You stick wi' me an' you'll have it all, gel,'* he had told her, so where was he now when she needed him most? He had avoided her like the plague ever since the night in the churchyard, although she had looked out for him every single day. He must have been busy, that was the only explanation for it. He loved her, didn't he?

Suddenly she knew that she must see him and a plan born of desperation began to take shape in her mind. She would wait until everyone was in bed then she would sneak out and go and see him. Glancing at the rain-lashed window she drew her shawl more closely about her slim shoulders. But it wasn't the thought of the weather that made her flinch; it was the realisation of what would happen if her father caught her. She could clearly remember the last time she had displeased him, and the cruel sting of his cold leather belt on the back of her bare legs.

Her chin suddenly jutted with defiance. Desperate

situations called for desperate measures, and as far as she was concerned, if her suspicions proved to be correct, then this situation was desperate indeed.

She sat in the chilly bedroom for another hour then slowly made her way downstairs to sit through her father's Bible-reading. The reading seemed to take twice as long as it normally did this evening, but at last he closed the Bible and peered at his children over the top of his gold-framed glasses.

'You may all go to bed now,' he told them, and one by one they formed a line and dutifully planted a peck on his cheek before climbing the stairs.

Once in the privacy of their little room, Maria helped Emma to get undressed and slipped a faded cotton nightgown over her head.

'Aren't you going to get undressed too, Ria?' the child asked as her arms snaked around her sister's neck.

'In a minute, sweetheart. I'm a bit cold right now, so I thought I'd get in and you could give me a cuddle and get me warm.'

Emma giggled as Maria lifted the blankets and snuggled down beside her fully clothed.

'Mother will be angry if you get your clothes all creased,' she warned.

Maria kissed her soft cheek, whispering, 'Mother won't notice if we don't tell her. Now you close your eyes and think of nice things.'

Emma immediately screwed her eyes tight shut and soon the sound of her gentle snores echoed around the room. Once she was sure that the child was asleep, Maria disentangled her arms and carefully rolled to the end of the bed. Downstairs, she could hear her mother pottering about as she banked down the fire and locked the doors, then seconds later she heard her father's heavy footsteps on the stairs followed by her mother's lighter ones.

She heard them walk down the long narrow landing and the sound of the bedroom door closing behind them, then she waited for what seemed an eternity until the only noise that could be heard was the wind flinging the rain against the windows.

Gingerly, she got off the bed and padded to the door. Inching it open, she peered along the landing and was rewarded with the sound of her father's guttural snores. With her shoes in her hands, she tiptoed down the stairs. Her heart was hammering in her chest and every second she expected to feel the clamp of Edward's steely fingers on her arm, but at last she made it to the back door. Quickly snatching up her coat, she quietly turned the key.

Once outside, the biting wind made her gasp and she struggled into her coat and slipped her shoes on before hurrying away.

In no time at all she had left the cottage behind and was battling against the wind and rain as she climbed the steep Chapel End hill. The full moon cast an eerie glow along the deserted road as she finally turned into Chancery Lane and paused to get her breath. Ahead of her she could see Lennie's mother's small house on the bend in the lane, and was relieved to see a light faintly shining through a gap in the curtains. That meant that they were still up. Perhaps Lennie had gone down with the awful influenza illness that was sweeping through the village at present? That would explain his absence for the last few weeks. The thought lent speed to her feet and she hurried on, eager to see him again.

Once she reached the front door, which opened directly onto the street, she did her best to flatten her damp windswept hair with the palm of her hand before tentatively tapping.

Almost immediately she heard the sound of a bolt being drawn back. A plump middle-aged woman with tight frizzy hair peered out into the darkness. This was Lennie's mother then. Maria had never actually met her before, apart from glimpsing her in the post office, and she was momentarily at a loss for words.

'I er . . . Hello, Mrs Glover.'

'*Whadda yer want?*' the woman barked.

Maria gulped and went on, 'I'm er . . . a friend of Lennie's. I was wondering if I might have a word with him, please. If he's in, that is . . .'

Maria's voice trailed away as the large woman glared at her – and then suddenly the door was slammed in her face.

She hovered uncertainly and was just about to turn away when she heard the woman shout, '*Lennie!* There's one o' yer fancy pieces at the door askin' to see yer! Right bloody time o' night to come callin', this is. She wants her arse kickin' if yer ask me.'

Once again the door was flung open, and Maria's face flushed with pleasure as Lennie peered out at her.

He looked slightly nonplussed to see her, and a shifty expression crossed his face. 'What brings you here at this time o' night then?' he asked. 'I thought yer dad didn't like yer out after dark?'

'He d-doesn't,' Maria stuttered. 'He doesn't know I'm here.'

'So why are yer then?'

Maria was suddenly glad of the darkness that would disguise the burning in her cheeks. 'I had to see you, Lennie. There's something I have to tell you. Is there anywhere we can go where we can talk?'

'*What* – at this time o' night and in this weather?' He scowled, but then seeing that she was upset he snapped,

'Oh, all right. Wait there. I'll just go an' get me coat an' me boots back on.'

Once again the door was shut in her face and Maria glanced fearfully up and down the lane. There would be ructions if anyone saw her here and word got back to her father. Thankfully, Lennie reappeared within seconds, buttoning up his coat. Grabbing her elbow, he began to guide her none too gently down the lane across the uneven cobblestones.

'Me Mam ain't none too pleased, I don't mind tellin' yer,' he muttered peevishly. 'She were just about to lock up an' go to bed, an' I'm dead on me feet. I've bin fer a game o' dominoes in the Salutation wi' me mates an' I were lookin' forward to a good night's sleep. Another ten minutes an' I'd have been abed.'

Maria's stomach sank into her boots. Lennie didn't seem pleased to see her at all, and no doubt he would be even *less* pleased when he heard what she had come to tell him.

'*So*, come on then. Spit it out – whatever it is yer need to say to me. I ain't got all night to be walkin' the streets in the rain, yer know.'

Stopping abruptly, Maria sought for the right words to convey her fears to him. Finally deciding that there was no easy way, she blurted out, 'Lennie . . . I think I might be with child.'

Even in the dim moonlight she saw the shock register on his face. He took a step away from her as if he had been stung before gasping, 'So what yer tellin' *me* for?'

Hurt made the tears that had been threatening spill from her eyes and stream down her cheeks. 'I'm telling you because it's your baby, of course, Lennie.'

He shook his head and held his hand out to keep her at a distance. 'Fuck off. Yer needn't try pinnin' it on *me*. The flyblow could be anybody's.'

'Oh, Lennie, how could you even say that? I've never . . . You were the first and I've never been with anyone else. You know that.' She was sobbing now but Lennie was unmoved and wishing that he was a million miles away.

'Huh! I bet every girl in your position says that. I weren't born yesterday, yer know. An' anyway – we only did it the once. I never meant fer it to get serious.'

'*You* only did it once – and you said you loved me.' Her voice was thick with raw pain and she suddenly felt as if she was caught in the grip of a nightmare. For weeks Lennie was all she had thought of, every waking minute. She even dreamed of him at night, but now here he was telling her that he hadn't meant any of the things he had said to her.

'But . . . but what shall I do if you don't stand by me?' she faltered. 'My father will kill me when he finds out – and you too! You know what a temper he has. There's only one solution to this. We'll have to get wed . . . an' quick.'

Terror replaced the shock on his face as he considered the options. What would be worse, facing the wrath of Edward Mundy or tying himself to someone he didn't love for the rest of his life?

Deciding that he needed time to think, he forced a smile to his face. 'Happen yer right, gel. Sorry fer the way I reacted. It was just a bit of a shock when yer told me, that's all. But here's what we'll do. You get yerself away home now an' try an' act as if nothin's wrong. Then after work tomorrer, I'll be round to see yer dad, eh?'

She smiled tremulously through her tears. 'Do you really mean it, Lennie?'

'Course I do. Now go on, get yerself away afore he realises yer not there.' All the time he was talking he was backing away from her. She was longing to throw herself into his arms and tell him how very much she loved him, but realising that he needed time to come to terms with what she had told him, she nodded and reluctantly watched him turn about. In no time at all he had disappeared into the stormy night and she was left to make her way home alone. But still, at least he had said he would stand by her, and this time tomorrow the worst would be over and they would be planning their future together. The thought put a smile on her face and a spring in her step as she hurried home through the darkness.

Chapter Two

By the time Maria arrived back at the cottage the sleety rain had stopped and a thick frost was forming. Martha had been predicting snow for days, and now as Maria shivered her way along the deserted lane she had no doubt that soon her mother would be proved to be right.

She was almost home when a fox suddenly shot from the bushes and ran across the lane in front of her, so close that she might have reached out and touched him. Maria's heart leaped into her mouth and she had to pause to compose herself before hurrying on. It was the first time in her whole life that she had ever been out so late on her own, and it was not an experience she was enjoying. Thinking about it now, she thought how unlikely it was that she should find herself in this position, for her father was very strict and allowed her no freedom at all. But then he had no hold over her whilst she was working, and it was in her short lunch-breaks that the love affair between herself and Lennie had blossomed.

She flushed with pleasure in the darkness as she thought back to the first time he had entered the shop where she worked and the way his eyes had lit up at the sight of her. He was the first young man who had ever flattered her, and within days of their meeting she had fallen for him, hook, line and sinker.

She allowed her mind to drift back to every single moment they had spent together, and soon the dark trees lining the lane and the cries of the night animals were forgotten.

'How do yer do? My name's Lennie Glover. Can't say as I've seen you in here before.'

Maria blushed prettily, casting a cautious glance across her shoulder to make sure that Mrs Everitt, the shopkeeper, was still in the back room having her lunch.

'I haven't been working here long,' she admitted shyly. 'My name is Maria. Maria Mundy.'

''Ere – your dad ain't Minister Mundy, is he?' Lennie asked.

When Maria nodded, he threw back his head and laughed, setting his thick dark hair dancing in a halo around his handsome face. 'Well, stone the crows. I'd never have thought he'd be capable o' producin' a looker like you. No wonder he's kept yer hidden fer so long.'

Maria's blush darkened as he eyed her approvingly up and down.

'Ever let you out of a night, does he?'

Maria's head wagged from side to side under his scrutiny and when he leaned over the counter towards her she thought her heart would leap out of her chest. Just then, Mrs Everitt appeared from the door behind the counter and glared at him disapprovingly.

'So what can we be doin' fer you then, Lennie Glover?' she asked icily.

'Personally, not a thing,' he retaliated. 'But I've a list o' things 'ere as me mother's in need of, if yer'd be so kind.'

'Maria, go into the back room and have your lunch. I'll see to this,' Mrs Everitt ordered, and bowing her head, Maria scuttled meekly away.

When she returned to the shop fifteen minutes later, Lennie was gone and Mrs Everitt was waiting for her with a face like a sour lemon.

'That . . . young man who came in a while back,' she said sternly. 'I don't want you havin' nothin' to do with him. Do yer hear me? He's a bad 'un. In fact, the whole family is. His mother is nothin' short of a— Well, let's just say that she'll never be a lady. I know yer father would have a fit if he knew you'd even spoken to Lennie Glover, so be warned, my girl.'

'Yes, Mrs Everitt.'

'Now get to and stack those shelves over there – and neatly, mind. I take a pride in my shop. It's only a shame as I can't choose who walks through the door. I've no doubt the Glovers have never so much as set foot in your father's chapel. But then not everyone can be so godfearing as he is. You're a lucky girl to have such a fine father.'

Maria wondered if Mrs Everitt would still have been of the same opinion if she knew what a vicious man her father could be at home, but wisely she held her tongue and hurried away to do as she was told.

Over the next few days, Lennie appeared at the shop every lunchtime – always when he was sure that Mrs Everitt was out of the way – and slowly, Maria felt herself falling in love with him. One day he asked, 'Look, couldn't yer tell the old biddy yer have an errand to run fer yer mam in yer lunch-break? The old dear needn't be any the wiser an' we could take a stroll over the fields where no one could see us.'

Maria chewed on her lip as she considered his request. She had never done anything dishonest before, but then the thought of some time alone with Lennie was very tempting.

'All right,' she said eventually. 'I'll meet you at the end of Plough Hill Road tomorrow at one o'clock. But I'll only be able to be away half an hour at the very most.'

The smile he gave her set her pulses racing, and for the rest of the day, and night too for that matter, she could barely concentrate on anything.

The next morning at breakfast her mother raised her eyebrows as she noticed that Maria was dressed in her Sunday-best blouse and skirt.

'I spilled something down my work clothes in the shop yesterday,' Maria muttered by way of an explanation. She hated lying to her mother, but then how could she turn up to meet Lennie in her drab grey work dress?

The way his face broke into an approving smile when she met him made the lie worthwhile. As they began to stroll along Plough Hill Road he noticed the way her eyes darted fearfully from side to side and he asked, 'Would yer rather we struck off across the fields?'

When she nodded numbly he took her small hand in his large one and guided her through a gap in the hedge. They found a tree and he gallantly laid down his coat for her to sit on under a leafless oak tree.

From then on she met him at least twice a week and soon she became adept at coming up with excuses to get away from the shop without making Mrs Everitt suspicious. She found herself living for those days and soon knew without a shadow of a doubt that she could not bear to lose him. It was on one such day in late October that the heavens opened as they strolled along and the rain came down in torrents.

'Quick – let's shelter in here.' Taking her hand, Lennie dragged her towards a disused cattle shed on the outskirts of a field.

Once inside they laughed as they took off their saturated coats and shook the rain from them. And it was there that Lennie kissed her properly for the very first time as lightning lit up the sky and thunder rolled above them.

When his hand first roamed across her small firm breasts, Maria tensed and gazed at him from troubled eyes, but he was gentle and soon he had awakened feelings in her that she had never known she had.

'It'll be all right,' he whispered. 'It can't be wrong if we love each other, can it? An' I do love yer, Maria.'

His warm hand was working its way up her skirt leaving a trail of fire in its wake. Her mother and father had taught her that it was wrong to be alone with a boy before you were married, but as Lennie had said, they did love each other, so that surely made it all right.

When he unbuttoned her blouse and his hot lips closed around her erect nipple she was sure that she would die of pleasure, but then commonsense had taken over and she had somehow managed to stop him from going any further, much to his disgust. But then as she had told him, they had all the time in the world, and she knew that she was his girl forever then. Why else would he have tried to make love to her?

She was so lost in thought that it was almost a shock when the cottage where she lived loomed up out of the darkness in front of her, pulling her thoughts sharply back to the present.

Tiptoeing round to the back door, she breathed a sigh of relief when the doorknob turned easily in her freezing hand. Slipping soundlessly into the kitchen, she shut the door softly behind her and paused to listen. There was only silence – so she swiftly pulled off her damp clothes and tossed them over the large wooden clothes-horse that stood in front of the banked-down fire. Then, quiet as a mouse, she crept up the stairs in her petticoat and sidled into her bedroom. Emma was still fast asleep and in the moonlight that winked though a crack in the curtain she looked like a little angel. Maria crept in beside her, revelling in the warmth of her sister's tiny body, then she tossed and turned the night away as she thought of the day ahead.

It was hard to concentrate at work the following day, and to make matters worse, Mrs Everitt was in a terrible mood.

'Maria, watch what yer doin'!' she ranted. 'Yer were just about to fill the sugar barrel up wi' salt.'

'Sorry, Mrs Everitt,' Maria apologised, as the small portly woman glared at her with her hands on her hips.

Patting the tight grey bun that balanced precariously on the back of her head, the woman tutted her disapproval. 'I don't know what's got into yer today,' she complained. 'Yer give Mrs Wilkes the wrong change not an hour since, an' yer know how she of all me customers watches every penny.'

'Sorry, Mrs Everitt.'

'Will yer please stop sayin' sorry an' concentrate on yer work, girl! Are yer losin' yer marbles or what? You'll be a candidate fer Hatter's Hall at this rate.'

Maria shuddered at the thought. Hatter's Hall was a mental asylum on the outskirts of Ansley Common. It was a dark forbidding place, shunned by the locals, particularly at night when the howls of the poor souls who had been committed there echoed eerily around the tall brick walls that surrounded it.

As a child, Maria's father would threaten her with

Hatter's Hall if she was naughty. 'I'll take you and leave you there if you don't learn to behave,' he would bellow, and even now the very mention of the place could strike terror into Maria's heart.

Luckily, the shop door opened just then and Mrs Everitt turned her attention to her customer, all sweetness and light.

'Ah, Mrs James. An' what can I be gettin' yer, dear?'

Maria scuttled away to compose herself and for the rest of the day tried to keep out of the older woman's way.

By the time the shop closed her nerves were at breaking point. She had hoped that Lennie might call in at lunchtime, but she had seen neither hide nor hair of him all day. Still, she consoled herself, no doubt he was telling his mother and making plans before he called on her father that night.

When Edward Mundy did finally make an appearance that evening, he too was in a filthy mood, made worse by the fact that the meal was dry because he was late for it. The children were silent as they eventually gathered around the table for Grace, then their mother gallantly fought to scrape the dried-up hare pie from the dish as he glared at it in disdain.

'Couldn't we have some bread and dripping instead?' Henry dared to ask as he eyed the shrivelled food with dismay.

'You Godless ungrateful boy,' his father shouted. 'There are many sitting with nothing in their bellies tonight so just be grateful for what you have and let me hear no more.'

The whole family made a valiant attempt to eat the meal in front of them but it stuck in their throats and Martha had to keep rising from the table to fill the water jug.

At last the meal was over and Maria rose to help her mother clear the pots into the sink whilst Edward threw himself into the fireside chair.

23

'May I ask what detained you?' Martha asked tentatively.

Edward sniffed. 'I was called to Hatter's Hall to say a few words over an infant that died there.'

'How awful – the poor little mite.' Martha's kind heart was saddened at the news but Edward almost bit her head off.

'Awful my foot! The child was a flyblow, born to one of the unmarried mothers there. It didn't deserve to live. It was a child of sin. It will be buried in unhallowed ground within the confines of the Hall grounds. The only shame is that the mother didn't die too.'

The colour drained from Maria's face and she had to hold onto the edge of the deep stone sink to keep from fainting with terror. This evening was definitely *not* going to be easy. Thank God that Lennie had promised to stand by her or it might have been *her* incarcerated in that dreadful place. Rumour had it that many of the inmates at the Hall were unmarried mothers – locked away there and forgotten for all time by families who could not bear the shame of what their daughters had done.

Glancing at the tin clock on the mantelpiece, she offered up a silent prayer. *Please come soon, Lennie, and get this over with*. Turning back to the sink she then began to scrub salt into the bottom of the pots as if her very life depended on it.

When her father began his Bible-reading at eight o'clock with still no sign of Lennie, it took every ounce of willpower Maria had to look as if she were listening to what he was saying.

Her ears strained for the sound of Lennie's footsteps approaching the door and she breathed a sigh of relief when her father eventually closed the Bible and yawned.

'Away to your beds,' he commanded, and his children immediately rose from their seats to do as they were told.

Maria took Emma upstairs, and after tucking the child into bed she crossed to the window and twitched the curtain aside, fearfully gazing up the lane for a sight of Lennie. Seeing it was deserted, her spirits plummeted still further. What could have delayed him? Worse still was the fact that it was Saturday evening, which meant she would have no chance to see him now until Monday.

Somehow, she knew that he wouldn't be coming tonight, so after slowly undressing she slipped into bed beside Emma. Fretfully she stared up at the cracks in the ceiling until sleep eventually claimed her as the first cold fingers of dawn snatched at the sky.

Chapter Three

'Is Isabelle not joining us for breakfast again?' Charles Montgomery barked as his eyes raked the dining room.

His wife visibly quaked before forcing a smile and telling him, 'No, dear. Isabelle is feeling unwell, so I told her maid to prepare a tray for her.'

Charles raised his eyebrows as he strode over to the highly polished mahogany sideboard and proceeded to help himself to a generous serving of kidneys, sausages and bacon from the silver salvers that stood upon it. He carried his plate back to the table and scarcely had time to seat himself when the maid rushed forward with a silver teapot in her hand.

'Tea, sir?'

When he inclined his head, she swiftly poured some of the steaming liquid into a delicate china cup and saucer. She then lifted the cut-glass milk jug but he waved her impatiently away as he addressed his wife again, saying,

'And what is wrong with the spoiled little madam this time?'

His wife, Helena, dabbed delicately at her lips with a white linen napkin before replying timidly, 'I fear she has come down with a cold, dear.'

'Huh!' he snorted, clearly not believing a word she said but he kept his thoughts to himself, for now at least. It would not do to give the servants anything to gossip about. He speared a sausage and began eating.

Helena meantime found that her appetite had fled and looked glumly down at her plate as her husband ate his breakfast. They seemed to have done nothing but argue about Isabelle ever since she had been expelled from the finishing school she had been attending in France two months before. Helena knew that her husband had every right to be angry with their daughter, but even so she always tried to make excuses for the girl's rash behaviour, which was stretching their already fragile relationship to breaking point. Isabelle was now eighteen years old, a year younger than her brother, Joshua. They were so alike in looks that they had often been mistaken for twins. Both had the same dark hair and green eyes that they had inherited from their father. But there, any similarity between them ended, for they were completely different in nature. Joshua was a kind-hearted, hardworking young man, keen to help his father in his many businesses, whereas Isabelle was somewhat selfish and wilful.

Helena was painfully aware that this was mainly her fault. Never the strongest of women, she had almost died giving birth to Isabelle and the doctor had stipulated that there should be no more children. Until that time, if asked, Helena would have said that her marriage was perfect – but soon after Isabelle's birth, Charles had moved into another room and from that day on Helena had spoiled her tiny daughter shamelessly. Now she was reaping the rewards and had no idea what to do about it.

Glancing at her husband now from the corner of her eye, she suppressed a sigh. Charles was still a very handsome man although his dark hair was now streaked with grey at the temples and above his ears. Strangely, this did nothing to detract from his looks. In fact, it made him look even more sophisticated. Helena had long harboured suspicions that he had a mistress tucked away somewhere, hence the occasional night when he failed to come home to Willow Park. But what could she do about it? And so she had put all her efforts into her children. There was little else for her to do in the house although it was quite huge. They had a very efficient housekeeper and enough staff to keep it running smoothly. All she had to do was plan the menus each week, and now that the children were older, time hung heavily on her hands.

She had become so lost in thought that she started slightly when her husband repeated, 'Did you hear me, Helena? I said that I may not be home this evening, so don't wait up for me.'

'Oh? Why is that, dear?'

A look of annoyance passed fleetingly across his face but he answered politely enough. 'I am travelling to my new factory in Leicester, so I shall probably stay in a hotel for the night.' As he spoke he pushed his chair back from the table and rose, offering her his hand. She took it without a word, and after he had escorted her to the drawing room he made a little bow and departed without another word.

Crossing to the window, Helena stood looking out at the front of the house, where one of the grooms was standing at the foot of the front steps holding the door of the carriage open for his master.

She watched as it moved away down the drive, then sighed as she sank heavily down onto one of the brocade-covered chairs.

In a way she was quite relieved that Charles was not coming home that evening. A good talk with Isabelle was long overdue and she would have more opportunity to do it with her husband out of the way. In fact, she decided, there was no time like the present, so standing again, she smoothed her skirts and swept from the room in a rustle of silk.

On the landing outside Isabelle's door she paused, then tapped gently. It was opened instantly by Polly, Isabelle's maid, who informed her, 'Miss Isabelle ain't feelin' so good, ma'am. She's still abed an' she refused to eat her breakfast again.'

'Very well, Polly.' Helena smiled at the girl. 'Why don't you go and have a cup of tea with Cook? I'll see to Miss Isabelle.'

'Yes, ma'am.' The girl bobbed her knee, then lifting her black serge skirt she scuttled away along the landing, glad of an excuse for a break.

Once she was sure that the maid was gone, Helena entered the room and closed the door behind her. She could see Isabelle's shape huddled beneath the bedcovers, so crossing to the velvet drapes that hung at the high windows, she swished them open.

'Oh, Mama, *must* you?' Isabelle groaned as the light made her blink.

'Yes, I must,' Helena replied firmly as she moved back across the room. 'I think you and I are in need of a little talk, don't you?'

As Isabelle's tousled head emerged from the sheets she stared at her mother cautiously.

'What do you mean?'

'Oh come, Isabelle! I am not a complete fool, you know,' Helena scolded. 'I have received a letter from the school, and in it Mademoiselle Bourgeois tells me of a certain young man that you had been creeping out of the premises to meet. Is this true?'

Isabelle had the grace to flush as she sat up and folded her arms, and stared stubbornly towards the window.

'What if it is?' she replied sulkily. 'I am not a child, Mama. I am eighteen years old.' She threw herself back against the lace-trimmed cushions as her mother frowned.

'I know you may think that you are grown up now, but you are still very young,' Helena said softly. She could never stay angry with her headstrong daughter for long. Even now, with her thick dark hair tangled and a scowl on her face, she still managed to be beautiful – and sometimes Helena wondered how she had ever managed to produce someone so perfect – in looks, at least.

'I suppose Papa has sent you to talk to me,' Isabelle griped. 'And don't think I don't know what he's hoping for. He wants me to marry Philip Harrington, doesn't he, and he's *boring*!'

Helena swallowed before saying tentatively, 'But Philip is one of the most eligible bachelors in the whole of the county, Isabelle. And he's very good-looking.'

'Huh! What you mean is, his family are very *rich*!' Isabelle said pettishly. 'Papa would marry me off to Old Nick himself if he had enough money.'

'That isn't true,' Helena answered sharply, but deep down she knew that there was more than an element of truth in what her daughter said. Charles had thrown Isabelle and Philip together at every opportunity ever since they were children, and the Harringtons had dropped enough hints to sink a warship about the compatibility of the two young people. They had even planned a summer ball and had openly said how delighted they would be if the young couple were to announce their engagement at the event. Helena had secretly hoped for a union between them too. Philip was a sensible young man with his feet firmly on the ground, whereas much as she adored her daughter she was forced to admit that Isabelle was a little wayward. But now, if her worst fears were confirmed, Helena knew that any chance of that happening was remote.

Rising to her full height she braced herself to ask, 'Have you had your monthly course, Isabelle?'

'Mama! How could you ask such an intimate thing?' Isabelle cried, but Helena saw the fear in the young woman's eyes and her heart plummeted.

'I can ask because I am your mother,' she said in an uncharacteristically sharp voice. But before she could say another word, Isabelle suddenly clapped her hand across her mouth, then, throwing her legs over the edge of the bed in a most unladylike manner, she ran to the basin on the marble-topped washstand and was violently sick into it.

When she eventually stood up and took a shuddering breath, she looked at her mother and saw tears streaming down the woman's cheeks.

'I knew it!' Helena began to pace up and down the room, her skirts billowing about her. She was clearly very agitated and for once Isabelle said nothing but watched her guardedly.

Eventually Helena stopped in front of her and asked, 'Are you ready to talk to me now? This is not something that will go away.'

Isabelle's head drooped as she nodded miserably and muttered eventually in a small voice, 'I met Pierre one afternoon when I and some of the other girls were out walking with our tutor and Mademoiselle Bourgeois in the park.' Her lips formed into a smile as she recalled the occasion. 'He was *so* handsome, Mama, and when he spoke to me I swear I felt my heart flutter.'

Helena almost felt sorry for her. Once Charles had had the same effect on her – but that seemed in a different lifetime now.

'Whilst our tutor was buying us cold drinks from a street vendor, Pierre spoke to me,' she went on with a dreamy look in her eye. 'And before I knew it, I had agreed to sneak out that evening and meet him.' She quickly looked away from the disapproval on her mother's face and rushed on: 'It was quite easy to get away, and the other girls covered for me. But I wasn't the only one that did it.' She said this as if it would somehow make a difference, but Helena remained tight-lipped, so Isabelle went on: 'We continued to meet each other for quite a few weeks, but then one evening I was caught slipping back into the school. The rest you know, I was expelled and now I shall never see him again.' Her eyes filled with tears as her lips trembled, but Helena was finding it difficult at that moment to have any sympathy for her. How could her daughter have been so naïve and stupid?

'And who is this Pierre and where does he live?' she asked.

Isabelle lowered her voice as she mumbled, 'I don't know where he lives but I know his father was a farrier.'

'A *farrier*!' Helena was horrified. Even if they could trace this Pierre, which she doubted, there was no way in the world Charles would ever allow his daughter to marry the son of a working-class man – so what was she to do now?

She chewed pensively on her lip for a time before saying, 'There is only one way I can see out of this. You will have to marry Philip, and as soon as possible. Then when the child is born we will tell everyone that you delivered it early.'

'I will not!' Isabelle's eyes blazed with defiance. 'I could never marry Philip, Mama. I told you – he's so *boring*!'

'He may well be, but can you see another solution to your problem?' Helena snapped. 'I have no doubt that even if we managed to find this Pierre, he would run a thousand miles once he heard about your condition. Heaven only knows what your father is going to say when he finds out about it.'

Isabelle gulped, then after a few moments had passed, she whispered, 'Could I not go away somewhere, have the baby and give it up for adoption, Mama? Then Father need never find out about it.'

'Go where?' Helena stared off into space as she tried to think of a way out of this, but her mind was a blank. Crossing to the window, she gazed absently out over the spacious lawns. Two of the gardeners were busily planting bulbs but Helena was so preoccupied that she didn't even see them. 'I need a little time to think,' she said quietly, and then turning, she rustled from the room.

Polly had come back up and was waiting patiently on the landing outside. Helena told her, 'You may go in and help Miss Isabelle to get dressed now, Polly.'

'Yes, ma'am.' The girl dropped a curtsey and Helena wearily made her way to her own room. Normally at this time of the morning she would sit downstairs and work on some embroidery, but right now she had no heart for it.

Once Polly had finished helping her to dress and had left to attend to her other duties, Isabelle sat at her dressing-table and stared into the mirror as her mind tripped back in time. She could remember every second of the time she and Pierre had spent together, and even though she now found herself in this grave predicament she could not regret a moment of it. He had been so handsome and charming, quite unlike anyone she had ever met before. His face flashed in front of her eyes and her heart ached. She had had many mild flirtations before and enjoyed the way young men followed her about like adoring puppy dogs. She was beautiful and she knew it and loved to trifle with their affections – but she had been so heavily chaperoned at home that she had never gone beyond flirting and couldn't have, even had she wished to. But something about Pierre appealed to her instantly, and when she saw him heading towards her she gave him her prettiest smile and batted her long eyelashes becomingly.

'You will come to meet me 'ere tonight?' he had whispered in broken English as he had strolled past her, and keeping a close eye on Mademoiselle Bourgeois she had nodded as colour flamed in her cheeks and her companions giggled beneath their parasols. And so their affair had begun, and in no time at all Isabelle could not get enough of him.

The other girls had thought it highly romantic and covered for her when she slipped away to meet him, eagerly awaiting her return when she would tell them of Pierre's passionate kisses and the whispered words of love he would pour into her ear. But soon stolen kisses were not enough and she thought back now to the first time she had given herself to him.

It had been a warm balmy evening and when he led her into the shelter of the trees in the park she had gone willingly.

Almost before she knew it, he had laid her on the soft grass, and his kisses had become more urgent. She had known that what they were doing was wrong and yet she felt powerless to stop it. In fact, she had been as eager as he was, as feelings she had never known before enveloped her. And then he had slipped her dress from her shoulders, and the combination of the soft breeze and his strong fingers caressing her bare breasts had driven her into a frenzy of desire and she had arched her back towards him as she kissed him hungrily. In no time at all their clothes had been strewn about on the grass around them, and for the first time she had lain in a man's arms completely naked and revelled in the feel of his muscular body hard against hers.

'Are you sure you want this, *mon amour*?' he had gasped eventually as he rolled on top of her, and she had nodded as her hands played across his taut buttocks. There could be no going back now. She knew that from that moment on, she would be his for all time, just as it was meant to be. And then she knew a moment of intense pain as he pushed into her, before pure pleasure took its place.

Her thoughts returned to the present and tears traced down her cheeks as her hand played across her stomach. If only she hadn't been found out . . . if only she hadn't fallen for a child. But it was too late for 'if onlys' now, and she dreaded what would happen when her father learned of her condition.

It was almost a week later when Charles learned the truth – and it was quite by chance. He had come down with a heavy cold, and fearing that it was the lead-up to the terrible influenza that was decimating the town, Helena pleaded with him to stay at home for that day at least. She knew how ill he must be feeling when he agreed with very little argument. She had his manservant serve him breakfast in bed but by ten o'clock Charles was bored and decided to get up, put on his dressing-gown and go down to his study.

It was as he was passing Isabelle's bedroom door that he heard something that sounded like someone being violently sick. He tapped at the door and without waiting thrust it open, only to find his daughter leaning across the washstand.

'What is this? Are you still no better?'

Isabelle stared at him fearfully – and suddenly he knew; his feverish cheeks reddened still further as his hands curled into fists.

Isabelle promptly burst into tears and he had his answer. 'Does your mother know about this?' He took a menacing step towards her and Isabelle nodded quickly. Then without another word he turned on his heel and stormed from the room, leaving the door to swing closed behind him.

He found Helena in the drawing room as he had known he would. She was sitting in the windowseat with her embroidery frame on her lap, but her hands were idle and she was staring from the window.

'I have just come from our daughter's room.' His voice was so cold that it made her shiver, and as she looked into his face she saw that he knew.

'How long have you known?' he growled.

'Since just last week.' There seemed no point in lying. Charles was not a stupid man.

'My God, we shall be ruined if word of this gets out.' When he began to pace up and down the room like a caged animal, Helena felt a moment of bitterness. How like Charles it was to worry more about their reputation than the condition their daughter was in.

'Who else knows?' he asked eventually.

'No one,' his wife answered him. Then, 'Oh Charles, I have been beside myself with worry. What are we to *do*? I suggested that we should announce her engagement to Philip and marry them off as soon as possible, but Isabelle flatly refuses to even hear of it.'

'Oh, *does* she now.' He snorted with disgust. 'I would have thought in the condition she is in, she would be glad of any man who was prepared to make an honest woman of her.'

When Helena began to cry his tone softened. Deep down, he still nurtured fond feelings towards his wife even though they had not lain together in the marital bed for many years.

'You must leave this with me,' he told her, and with that he turned abruptly and left the room.

Late that evening, as Helena lay propped up against the pillows in her bed reading *Jane Eyre*, there was a tap at the door and Charles entered the room. He looked remarkably handsome in his tails and his smart waistcoat, and Helena blinked with surprise.

'I have come up with a solution to Isabelle's problem,' he announced.

She stared at him hopefully. 'Oh *really*, Charles? What is it?'

His tongue flicked out to moisten his dry lips. He knew that his wife would not approve of what he was about to suggest, but after spending the whole day racking his brains it was the only idea he had managed to come up with.

'We shall send Isabelle away until after her confinement, then once it is over we shall get someone to take the child.'

'And where shall we send her?'

Avoiding her eyes he sat down on a small gilded chair that Helena had had shipped across from France.

'I thought the safest place for her would be . . . in Hatter's Hall.'

'*What!*' Helena's face was horrified. 'But you *couldn't* do that to her, Charles! The poor girl would suffer terribly if you incarcerated her there. It is a lunatic asylum!'

'Not all of it,' he denied. 'And I should know – I am the main benefactor. You would be surprised how many of our neighbours have placed their daughters there for exactly the same reason – and they pay well for the privilege, let me tell you. There is a separate wing that is quite luxurious and she would be safe there away from prying eyes.'

Helena shook her head dazedly. 'She would never agree to it in a thousand years.'

'I'm afraid in this matter she won't have a choice.' He stood and glowered at his wife. 'For once our dear daughter is going to have to do exactly as she is told. It's for her own sake. Think of it, woman. What man will ever want her if word gets out that she is having a bastard? She will be destined to become an old maid.'

'B-but the child will still be our grandchild,' Helena said falteringly.

Charles rolled his eyes in frustration. 'You must get that idea out of your head immediately,' he scolded. 'The child will be taken away the minute it is born. I shall see to it all, so you may as well get used to the idea. I will have no flyblow laying claim to what I and my father before me have worked years to establish.'

Seeing that Helena was close to tears, he then left the room, closing the door quietly behind him. He had said what he had intended to say; now he would leave her to come to terms with the idea.

Just as Helena had feared, Isabelle screamed in protest at her father's suggestion. 'I won't go!' she raged, folding her slender arms across her chest. 'How could you even *think* of locking me away with a load of lunatics? The idea is preposterous!'

'What is even more preposterous is the idea of you thinking that you can bring a bastard brat into this house,' her father retaliated. He was sitting at his desk in his study and staring at her steadily, but she turned about and slammed out of the room with her blue silken skirts swirling before he had the chance to say as much as another word.

As she exploded from the room, Isabelle almost collided with her brother Josh, who had just come in after a gallop across the countryside.

'*Whoa* there!' He grinned as he caught her elbows and drew her to a halt but she shook him off, her mouth set in grim lines.

'Oh, just leave me alone, Joshua,' she hissed and raced away as he scratched his head in bewilderment. He stood and watched her flounce away up the stairs for a moment then shrugging he continued on towards the kitchen to persuade the cook to part with a slice of her excellent fruitcake. He knew to steer clear of his little sister when she was in one of her moods.

Alone again in his study, Charles rose from his desk and crossing to the tasselled bell-pull that hung at the side of the fireplace, he yanked on it viciously. Almost immediately there was a tap at the door and his manservant Jacobs appeared. Jacobs was a small portly man with thinning hair and faded blue eyes. He had served his master faithfully since Charles had been scarcely out of short trousers, and now he bowed before saying, 'Yes, sir?'

'Jacobs, I have a small errand I wish you to do for me.' When he had finished explaining to the man what he wanted, he added, 'And could you tell Miss Isabelle's maid that I wish to see her before you go?' When Jacobs left the room, Charles went to stare down into the flames that were roaring up the chimney. He did not look forward to what he was planning, but there seemed no other option open to him. There was another tap on the door and this time Polly appeared.

'Ah, Polly.' Charles gave her a rare smile. 'I've seen how

hard you have worked since Miss Isabelle came home from school, and I think you have earned a night off.'

Polly's mouth fell into a gape but she shut it hastily as the master went on, 'Why don't you go home and see your family this evening after you have prepared Miss Isabelle for bed? You may spend the night with them, but be sure to be back here bright and early in the morning.'

'Why . . . thank yer, sir.' Polly could hardly believe her luck. She bobbed her knee and scuttled from the room before he could change his mind. The master must be mellowing in his old age. Normally she only got one Sunday afternoon a month off!

Charles then strode around to the stable-block where he had a hasty word with Hoskins, the head groom. Like Jacobs, the man was completely trustworthy. And then he went back to his study. All he could do now was wait.

Dinner was a somewhat strained affair that evening despite Joshua's attempts to start a conversation. Isabelle was obviously still in a sulk over something or another, while his mother seemed to be a bag of nerves. Although the young man did his best to lighten the atmosphere, even his father only spoke when spoken to, so eventually he gave up.

Following dinner, Charles went off to his study, Helena retired early pleading a headache, and Isabelle went off sulkily to her room. Joshua shrugged and left them all to it.

Chapter Four

That evening, as the grandfather clock in the hall chimed eleven, Charles rose from his desk and straightening his cravat, he strode towards the door. Just as he had instructed, Jacobs was there waiting for him in the hallway.

'Did you get it?' Charles asked tersely and the man held up a small corked bottle.

Charles nodded. 'Excellent, and is Hoskins at the front with the carriage?'

'Yes, sir. Ready and waiting.'

'Good, then follow me, and be quiet about it.'

Side by side the two men climbed the sweeping staircase and once on the galleried landing Charles took a large white handkerchief from his pocket and shook it out, muttering, 'Give me the chloroform.'

The servant did as he was told, and holding the handkerchief at arm's length, Charles liberally tipped some of the contents of the bottle onto it.

'Now wait here until I call you,' he ordered when they reached the door to Isabelle's room, and Jacobs shrank back into the shadows.

Quiet as a mouse, Charles inched the door open and peered inside. Isabelle was asleep with one arm flung above her head and her luxuriant hair spread in a fan across the pillow. The room was in darkness save for the glow from the fire, but that was sufficient to guide him to the bed. He knew a moment of deep sorrow as he stared down at his daughter. She was truly beautiful, and had she not got herself into this mess he had no doubt she could have had her choice of husband. But then he consoled himself, all was not lost. If he could just keep her hidden until the child was born, no one need ever be any the wiser – and in the not too distant future she could resume her life.

Bracing himself, he leaned forward and quickly pressed the chloroform-soaked handkerchief against Isabelle's nose. Almost instantly her eyes flew open but he increased the pressure, efficiently holding her down with his other hand. She panicked and her hands began to flail wildly in the air, one of them catching him a sharp cuff on the cheek. Charles gritted his teeth and continued to hold her down . . . within seconds her efforts to escape became weaker and her eyes fluttered shut as her hands dropped limply to her sides. When Charles was quite sure that she was completely unconscious he released his hold on her and straightened. Then crossing to the door he opened it and beckoned Jacobs inside.

'Help me wrap her in this blanket,' he hissed, stripping one from the bed. 'And then we must get her down to the coach.'

Grim-faced, Jacobs did as he was told without question. He knew better after all his years of service than to question his master. Isabelle was as slim as a reed but because she was a dead weight both men were panting by the time they had got her to the bottom of the steep staircase. It had started to snow as they hefted her out onto the steps and they both shuddered as they manhandled her towards the carriage where Hoskins had the door open ready. When Isabelle was lying comatose on the seat, Charles said breathlessly, 'Take us to Hatter's Hall, Hoskins.'

'Yes, sir.' Hoskins touched his cap as Charles climbed in beside Isabelle and soon the carriage was bowling down the long drive.

Some minutes passed, and then they were drawing up at the gates of Hatter's Hall. A night watchman hurried from the shelter of a small wooden hut to swing the big gates open. He too touched his cap when he saw who was inside the carriage and then Hoskins whipped up the horses again. At the huge wooden doors to the asylum, two burly men were waiting with a stretcher. Once they had lifted Isabelle onto it they hurried inside and began to carry her along a number of twisting corridors until they came to a staircase that led up to the first floor. A severe-looking woman in a starched white cap and a long grey serge dress with a lace collar was waiting for them there and Charles instantly enquired, 'Is all in readiness, Mrs Bradshaw?'

'Oh yes, Mr Montgomery,' the Matron assured him. 'I myself shall be seeing to Miss Isabelle's needs personally until someone trustworthy can be employed to look after her.'

Charles glanced at his daughter, who thankfully was still out cold. 'It is imperative that no one knows she is here, so you will have to be most careful whom you employ,' he warned.

The woman clasped her hands together and simpered, 'Of course, sir.' It was Charles Montgomery's donations that mainly kept the asylum running and she had no intention of upsetting him. Their footsteps echoed on the cold tiles as they trooped along, with Mrs Bradshaw hurrying ahead to lead the way – but eventually she paused and took a key from a bunch suspended from a chain about her waist and unlocked a door.

'In here,' she directed the two men who were carrying the stretcher.

Charles followed them into a room that was warm and comfortable. It was by no means as luxurious as Isabelle's bedroom back at Willow Park, but he was pleased to see that it was more than adequate.

Whilst the two men lifted Isabelle's inert figure onto a large four-poster bed that stood against one wall, Mrs Bradshaw opened another door. 'This is her private sitting room,' she said. 'And she will have her own dressing room here,' she assured him, opening a third door. 'Hot water will be carried up here from the kitchen so she should be perfectly comfortable. There is a separate room for a lady's maid.'

His lips compressed, Charles nodded then turned and went back into the bedroom to examine it properly. A large marble fireplace had a fire roaring in the grate, and a comfy chair was placed against the high bay window. The curtains were closed now, but he imagined there would be a good view during the daytime. A bookcase contained a fair selection of books, and there was also a matching suite of dressing-table, wardrobe and chest of drawers in mahogany. Bright Persian carpets were thrown down on the floorboards and all in all Charles was satisfied that his daughter's comforts would be seen to for as long as was necessary.

As the Matron opened the door to usher out the porters, a wail from one of the inmates floated along the corridor, and Charles started in shock. Mrs Bradshaw hastily closed the door.

'One of our patients having a bad night,' she said, and he could not suppress a shudder. It was then that Isabelle groaned softly, and as they looked towards the bed, her eyes opened blearily.

'Wh-where am I?' Panic appeared in her eyes as she found herself in strange surroundings.

'It's all right, my dear,' Charles soothed as he hurried to the bed and gripped her hand reassuringly. 'You are some-where safe until after the ba— Until the confinement is over.'

'What?' Isabelle struggled up onto her elbow, and as she looked about her she began to cry. When her eyes fell on the stern face of Mrs Bradshaw she cried even harder.

'Where is this place? I don't like it here,' she wailed. 'Please take me home, Papa.'

He extricated his fingers from hers. 'I am afraid that is out of the question,' he told her as he backed towards the door, feeling guilty and anxious to escape. 'Now you just be good. Mrs Bradshaw will take excellent care of you and I shall have your things packed up and sent along to you tomorrow.'

'No!' She would have got out of bed and gone to him but her head still felt woozy. 'Please don't leave me here, Papa. *Please.'*

The Matron opened the door and urged, 'I should go now, sir. There is no good in delaying.'

He gave a cursory nod before stepping out into the corridor with Isabelle's screams ringing in his ears.

'Papa! Papa, come back!'

As the door closed between them he sagged against the wall, hearing Isabelle's screams grow louder.

'No, no! Get away from me, get your hands off me!'

'Now, now, dear,' he heard Mrs Bradshaw say. 'There is no point in getting yourself all upset.'

Charles pushed himself away from the wall and set off along the corridor, unable to bear hearing any more. *But what else could I have done?* he asked himself. If word were to get out that Isabelle was with child, she would never be able to procure a respectable husband and might well end her days as an old maid. No, however unpleasant this was, it was for the best – and now that he had reached the decision he would stand by it. One day, Isabelle would thank him.

Once back in the carriage, Jacobs eyed his master with concern. He was as white as a sheet and sweating profusely despite the bitterly cold weather.

'Are you all right, sir?' he dared to ask.

'Yes,' Charles answered distractedly. His mind was racing ahead now, for in the morning he would have to come up with some explanation for Isabelle's disappearance to Helena.

The carriage moved away, throwing the men about in their seats as it trundled across the pot-holes in the dirt track. Charles stared morosely from the window, and Jacobs wisely fell silent.

Once back at the Manor, Charles immediately went to his study and poured himself a large brandy. He threw it back in one great gulp and quickly had another – then another – coughing as the fiery spirit slid down his throat. And then it came to him. In the morning he would tell Polly to pack Isabelle's things and inform her that her mistress had unexpectedly gone to stay with one of her schoolfriends who was ill. He would tell his wife the same, although he doubted whether she would swallow it. He rubbed his face wearily with his hand. The worst part was done now. He would face Helena's interrogations when the time came. All he wanted now was his bed.

Chapter Five

The weekend seemed to go on forever, but at last it was Monday morning. Maria rose and after hastily washing in the cold water she had left on the wash-stand the night before, she then pulled her work clothes on and hurried down to the kitchen to stoke up the fire and put the kettle on. Her mother was already there stirring a pan of porridge on the old black-leaded range, and she smiled at her as the girl entered the kitchen. Maria still looked peaky and Martha was gravely concerned about her, but continued to pray that her suspicions were wrong.

Maria hurried away to fetch some logs in from the log store and after banking the fire up she filled the kettle from the bucket of well water on the wooden draining board and pushed it into the heart of the flames. Henry was sitting at the table yawning and not looking forward to his shift down the pit one little bit.

'I'll try my hand at catching another couple o' rabbits

in Montgomery's woods after work tonight, Mam,' he promised. 'The last two were right tasty, weren't they?'

'Yes, they were, but just make sure you don't get caught, lad. You know how strict Montgomery is about anyone trespassing on his land.'

Henry waved his hand airily. 'Huh! As if he'd miss a couple o' rabbits,' he scoffed. 'He owns practically 'alf o' Nuneaton and he still isn't satisfied.'

Glancing nervously towards the stairs door for a sight of her husband, Martha lowered her voice. 'That's as maybe, but I still want you to be careful. They reckon that new gamekeeper of his is red hot and not one to show any mercy to anyone he catches.'

'I'll be fine, Mam.' Henry kissed her affectionately on the cheek as she ladled some porridge into his dish, but all conversation halted when they heard Edward's footsteps on the stairs.

He strode into the room and took his seat at the table without a word as his wife hurried to serve him. 'Have you a busy day ahead, dear?' she asked nervously.

His brows drew together in a dark frown. 'All my days are busy. You should know that by now! Idle hands make work for the devil. I shall spend my morning visiting the sick. There seems to be no sign of the epidemic slowing as yet. And then this afternoon it will be lessons as usual.' Each Monday afternoon Edward used their small front parlour to tutor those of the children from the village whose parents could afford the penny fee for the privilege – not that Martha ever saw any of it.

'Of course, dear.' She held her tongue. Personally, she considered that Edward had an easy time of it compared to the other men in the village. There were no long shifts down the pit or hours spent bending over a loom for him, which accounted for his lily-white hands. She glanced at her own, reddened and sore from the many hours she spent doing her own and other people's washing, but she made no comment.

After hastily swallowing his breakfast, Henry rose and taking his snap box from the end of the table he headed for the door.

'Make sure you wrap up warmly,' his mother urged as she glanced towards the window. ''Tis enough to cut you in two out there.'

Henry grinned as he yanked on his great coat, worn now and ill-fitting, then without a word for his father he went out into the snow which was fast turning into a blizzard.

Maria was nearly ready to leave for work too. She forced her feet into the sturdy leather boots her mother had bought for her from the pawnshop in town the year before. They were at least a size too small for her now and regularly gave her blisters, but at least they would keep her feet reasonably dry. She then drew her woollen shawl across her head and crossed it over her chest before tying it at the back as Martha looked on.

'Eeh, I'm afraid that's going to give you little protection in this weather,' her mother fretted. 'As soon as I can I'll visit the rag stall in town and see if they don't have a warm coat for you.'

Maria smiled at her warmly. 'I've not that far to go, Mam, so don't get fretting.' She pecked her on the cheek then hurriedly followed her brother through the back door. Despite her brave words, the bitter cold took her breath away, and head bent she trod through the thick white carpet. Within minutes the snow had found its way over the top of her boots, and her feet and the bottom of her skirt were sodden, but Maria's steps never faltered. The sooner she got to the post office the sooner she would be in the dry, the way she saw it. As she moved along, her thoughts returned to

Lennie and tears stung at the back of her eyes. She had just spent a miserable weekend worrying about why he hadn't kept his promise and come to speak to her father, and the mood she was in now he was due for a tongue-lashing when she did manage to catch up with him. If he didn't have a very good excuse, that was.

By the time the post office came into sight Maria was panting with exertion. It was no easy task wading through the ever-deepening snow and her mood did not improve when she saw that there were no lights on within. Normally Mrs Everitt was pottering about by the time Maria arrived but today the place appeared to be deserted. Pressing her nose against the cold glass, Maria peered inside before rapping sharply on the door. She waited some seconds then knocked again, louder this time but no one came.

'Oh dear, what now?' Maria grumbled to herself. If Mrs Everitt had overlaid, no doubt it would be she who would pay for it. Mrs Everitt was not the sweetest-natured of women at the best of times. Seeing no alternative, the girl now went around the side of the building to the back door that led into small living quarters. The curtains were still drawn but Maria could see a faint glow through them.

She rapped and called, 'Mrs Everitt . . . are you there?'

After a while she heard a shuffling and then the sounds of a bolt being drawn. Next minute the door opened and Mrs Everitt appeared with her thin grey hair hanging loose about her shoulders and still dressed in a long voluminous nightgown.

'Goodness me!' Maria exclaimed. 'You look awful, Mrs Everitt.'

'I feel awful,' the woman croaked. 'I think I'm coming down with this influenza that's going around, so you'll not be needed today, Maria. The shop will remain closed.'

51

'There's no need for that,' Maria said hastily, afraid of losing a day's wages. 'I could keep it open for you.'

The woman shook her head. She had never trusted anyone enough to be in charge of her till, even Maria, who had always appeared to be very trustworthy.

'No, that will not be necessary. I shall send for you when and if I need your assistance again.' The woman then closed the door abruptly, leaving Maria standing there.

'Damn,' she cursed beneath her breath, thankful that her father wasn't there to hear her. It sounded suspiciously as if she had just been dismissed, so now what was she to do? Her father would never allow her to sit at home with idle hands, but jobs were hard to come by. It seemed that things were going from bad to worse – if that were possible. There was nothing for it but to return home and tell her mother what had happened, but first she decided she would pay an impromptu visit to Lennie.

With her mind made up, she turned and headed purposefully for his mother's cottage. On the road she passed a few of the village men who were making their way to the pit to begin their shifts and they all raised their caps to her. The lanes were deserted and she was sure that no one would have ventured out on such a day unless they had to.

When she finally reached Lennie's home she was again confronted with drawn curtains, but now that she had come all this way she had no intention of going away without seeing him, so she rapped on the front door.

'Bugger off!' a woman's voice shouted and Maria pursed her lips. Mrs Glover had obviously been planning a lie-in. She knocked again and heard cursing as someone approached the door. The woman peered out at her bleary-eyed and said, 'Oh my Gawd, it's you again. What do you want this time, eh?'

Maria was more than aware of the rumours that circulated about Dora Glover. It was said that she was never short of male company – or a bob or two, if it came to that – and she wasn't particularly fussy about who the males were either. Single men, married men, young men, old men . . . it made no difference to her so long as they had the means to pay. But Maria wasn't concerned about the woman's reputation at present. She had far more pressing things on her mind.

'I er . . .'

As Maria faltered, the woman went on, 'After our Lennie, are yer? Well, you'll 'ave yer work cut out to find 'im now! I don't know what it were as yer said to 'im but within an hour o' yer visit he'd packed his bags an' scarpered like a cat wi' its tail afire. Gone to sea, so he has, an' I've no idea when – or if – I'll see him again. Now sod off an' leave a body in peace, can't yer!' And with that another door was slammed resoundingly in Maria's face.

She stood there feeling as if the bottom of the world had dropped out. Lennie had gone! He had left her to face her trouble alone. But what would happen to her now? She knew that her mother had already guessed at the plight she was in, but if her father was to find out, there would be blood on the moon.

Tears trickled down her frozen cheeks as she stood there but she was so shocked that for a time she did not even realise that she was weeping. Eventually she turned and slowly made her way home. There was nowhere else for her to go.

'Why, whatever brings you back so soon?' Martha gasped when Maria staggered in some half an hour later.

'Mrs Everitt is ill so she isn't opening the shop today,' Maria said in a small voice.

Martha peeled her shawl from her daughter's shoulders and after shaking the snow from it she threw it across the large wooden clothes-horse that stood in front of the fire. It instantly began to steam along with the other wet clothes that Martha had just washed as the woman pressed Maria down at the scrubbed oak table.

'A good hot brew will do you a power of good,' she commented as she bustled away. Seconds later she returned with a large brown earthenware teapot, and after pouring some into a cup she handed it to her daughter saying, 'Now get that down you, lass.' Wiping her wet hands down the front of her apron she then took a seat opposite and asked, 'And what else is on your mind?'

Maria knew full well what her mother was referring to but after the shock she had just had from Dora Glover she still wasn't ready to confide.

'The thing is . . . Mrs Everitt intimated that I might not be needed again, even when she is better.'

'Oh.' Disappointment clouded Martha's face. 'Then we'll just have to find you some other form of employment, won't we? If you're fit enough to work, that is.'

Again, Maria ignored the insinuation and shrugged, saying miserably, 'Of course I'm fit enough.' As she drained the cup of tea, however, she felt warmth begin to flow through her again.

'Right, then go and get changed out of those wet clothes before you catch your death of cold,' Martha ordered. 'You can help me with all this washing today if you've a mind to. We'll face tomorrow when it comes.'

Without a word Maria rose and went to do as she was told. As Martha watched her go, she bit down on her lip. Oh, her lovely girl – what was to become of her? Turning about, she snatched up another pile of dirty washing and carrying it to the copper boiler that stood in the corner by the scullery she pushed it deep down into the hot soapy water with a pair of long wooden tongs.

'So what is this then?' Edward asked when he came in shortly before lunchtime. 'Why aren't you at your job, girl?' He stamped the snow from his boots as Maria continued to lay the spoons and dishes on the table.

'Mrs Everitt is ill,' Martha answered for her, with a warning glance at her daughter. 'But worse than that, it appears that she may have no further need of Maria even when she is recovered. It comes as no great surprise really. She has never made a secret of the fact that she begrudges having to pay someone to help her, has she?'

'I see.' Edward scowled as he sat down at the table and Martha instantly hurried away to fetch the pot of boiled bacon, barley and potatoes that was bubbling on the range and began to ladle a generous portion into his dish.

'In that case I may have the solution,' he said as he lifted his knife and fork. 'I heard today that they are looking for a new worker up at Hatter's Hall. Someone who will be prepared to live in.'

'Oh, Edward! You *surely* would not consider sending our Maria to work in that place?' Martha exclaimed in horror.

'Why not? It's good honest work and someone has to do it,' he said. 'We cannot afford for her to sit at home idle, woman. And the fact that she is the preacher's daughter will go a long way to securing her the job.'

Martha glanced at Maria but surprisingly the girl didn't seem to be overly concerned at the suggestion. The way Maria saw it, if she had to live in, it would give her a little time to try and resolve the situation in which she found herself. If the worst came to the worst, she could always pay a visit to Mother Cox. The old woman, who lived in an isolated cottage on the outskirts of Ansley Common, was feared by most of the villagers and given a wide berth, but it was a well-known fact that some of her concoctions could rid women of unwanted pregnancies. The way things were going, Maria could see no other way out of her predicament.

'I am not averse to working at the Hall,' she stated now, although her stomach was doing somersaults at the very thought of it. 'And as long as I am allowed to come back and see everyone occasionally, I would be happy to live-in there.'

Edward was pleased at her response. He had expected her to object like her mother. 'In that case there is no time like the present. Jobs are hard to come by so you should take yourself off there and be interviewed before someone else snaps up the job position.'

'But Edward, look at the weather,' Martha said, gesturing towards the window. 'It's fit for neither man nor beast to be out in this. Surely she could go tomorrow?'

'It's all right, Mother,' Maria assured her. 'I shall be perfectly all right if I dress up warmly.'

'But your boots are still sodden.' Martha pointed towards where they were steaming on the hearth.

'Then I shall wrap some rags around my feet before I put them on.'

Ten minutes later, Maria was all bundled up and ready to leave although it was clear that Martha was not happy about it.

'Now be sure to come straight back home,' she fretted as she saw her daughter to the door.

Maria nodded and set off. The walk to Hatter's Hall took her twice as long as it normally would have, for the snow was growing deeper by the minute, but at last she reached the gates, and shielding her eyes, she peered through them.

The old watchman shuffled out from his little wooden hut to ask, 'Who goes there an' what would yer be wantin'?'

Maria gulped deep in her throat before answering. 'I have come to apply for the position that is vacant.'

'Hmm, yer'd best come in then.' The old man unlocked the high gates and once Maria had slipped through them he waved his hand in the direction of the Hall. 'Just foller the road an' yer'll come to it.'

'Thank you.' Maria lifted her drab skirts and plodded on, amazed at how long the drive was. Thankfully it was tree-lined for most of the way so the snow wasn't quite so deep here and she was able to move along more easily. When Hatter's Hall finally came into view she paused to stare at it. She had heard many stories about it but had never actually seen it before, and now that she had she didn't particularly like what she saw. It looked a dark, sinister place. She could see metal bars across the many windows, and here and there a spiral of smoke rose into the winter sky from the chimneys. The house was built of grey stone and all around it grew tall leafless trees, as if they were standing guard over it. Maria took a deep breath and ploughed on. She had not come this far to turn back now.

Once she reached the house, she climbed the steps leading to the enormous double doors and tugged on the bell-pull hanging at the side of them. The snow had muffled all other sounds and the clanging of the bell within the Hall seemed very loud.

There was the grating of heavy bolts being drawn and a young girl in a mob cap opened a door and peered out at her.

'I have come to apply for the position that is vacant,' Maria told her with her head held high.

'Then you'd best go round to the servants' entrance. The housekeeper will see yer then.' The young woman, who looked very pale, waved her hand in the general direction Maria was to take before closing the door firmly in her face without another word.

Maria began to walk around the outside of the house. At the back of it was a large stable-block and a dairy, and eventually she spotted what she hoped was the kitchen door.

This time when she knocked it was answered by a stout rosy-cheeked woman, and when Maria explained what she was there for, the woman ushered her inside immediately, saying, 'Why, you must be froze through, lass. You are brave to venture out on such a day. I'm the cook by the way, Mrs Bunting, but it's Miss Belle you'll be needin' to see – she's the Housekeeper.' Then, turning to a young girl who was scrubbing a mountain of dirty pots in a huge stone sink, she told her, 'Nancy, run an' fetch Miss Belle. She should be in her sittin' room.'

'Yes, Cook.' The girl, who was painfully thin, instantly swiped her hands down the front of her apron and scuttled away as the cook waved Maria towards an enormous scrubbed table that stood in the middle of the room.

'Sit yerself down, she shouldn't be too long,' she told Maria pleasantly enough, then lifting a large knife she went back to peeling a huge pile of vegetables. Maria took the opportunity to look about her. The kitchen was the size of her own home all put together, she was sure. Great gleaming copper pans hung above a large cooking range but other than that there were no homely touches about the place. But then she supposed that was to be expected. She was in an asylum, after all, not a coaching inn.

'Do you happen to know what the job I am applying for entails?' Maria asked after a time.

The cook raised an eyebrow. The lass was nicely spoken, there was no doubt about it. She glanced towards the door before answering in a hushed voice, 'I heard as there's a new resident on the east wing as needs a lady's maid.'

'A *lady's* maid?' Maria was puzzled. 'But I thought this was a lunatic asylum?'

'It is, but there's more to this place than meets the eye.' The cook paused. 'The east wing is reserved for gentry, an' not all of them are loonies if yer get me drift.'

'I'm afraid I don't.'

The cook sighed. 'Well, let's put it this way then. There are certain young ladies that find themselves in . . . shall we say *a certain condition* – an' o' course it wouldn't do fer them to have a child out o' wedlock, so their folks pay fer them to come here till the birthin' is over. I have to prepare special meals fer them, though the rest o' the poor sods have to eat what's given to 'em, an' between you an' me it ain't much better than pigswill. Not that many of 'em know the difference.'

'Oh, I see.' Maria had sat there for some minutes mulling over what the cook had told her when the green-baize door suddenly opened and the young maid reappeared, closely followed by a middle-aged woman with a stern face. The woman was tall and thin, smartly dressed in a full-skirted pale grey bombazine dress that matched the colour of her hair, which she wore in a tight bun on the back of her head – a style that did nothing to enhance her appearance. Maria thought briefly how colourless she was; even her eyes were grey and they were now raking Maria from head to foot.

Nancy returned to washing the pots and the cook kept her head down as the woman spoke. 'I believe you have come to apply for a position?'

'Yes, ma'am.' Maria stood up and gazed back at her solemnly as the woman continued to stare at her.

Could Maria have known it, Miss Belle was actually quite pleased with what she saw. The girl looked clean – well, cleaner than most from these parts – and although she was wet with snow, the woman could see that she was tidy. The last girl she had employed from the village had been infested with headlice, which had led to many of the inmates having to have their heads shaved.

'Have you had any experience of working in places such as this?' she enquired now.

'No, I haven't,' Maria admitted. 'I have been working in the post office in the village.'

'And may I ask your name, girl?'

'My name is Maria Mundy and my father is the preacher at the chapel in Chapel End.'

'I see.' The woman stared at her thoughtfully, then lifting her skirts she instructed her: 'Come through to my sitting room and we will continue this conversation there.'

She moved away and as Maria followed her, the cook gave her an encouraging wink.

Maria soon found herself in a room that appeared to be almost as bleak as the rest of the place, save for a fire in the grate and a comfy chair at the side of it. A bed, which was neatly made, stood in one corner and there was a small table and chair where Miss Belle sat to read and eat her meals. On another wall stood a plain wardrobe and a chest of drawers. There was also a well-stocked bookcase but Maria noted that the floor was bare, and despite the fire in the grate the room felt cold.

'Now then,' Miss Belle said when she had closed the door. 'Let me tell you about the job. First of all, I would have to have your solemn promise that you would never speak to anyone outside these four walls about anything or anyone that you see here. Would you feel able to do that?'

When Maria nodded solemnly she hurried on, 'We have a certain new er . . . resident who is expected to be here for a few months. The lady in question is of good family and therefore she will need the services of a lady's maid to assist her with dressing, bathing, et cetera. Again I must stress that your discretion would have to be without question. Your wage would be eight shillings and sixpence per week and you would get free meals. You would also be issued with a uniform. You would be given each Sunday afternoon off, but other than that you would not be allowed off the premises. How does that sound to you?'

'It sounds perfectly satisfactory,' Maria assured her calmly. She had only been paid five shillings per week at the post office, and had to go home for her meals.

For a moment the woman surveyed her thoughtfully. Then, making a decision, she told her, 'Very well, I am happy to offer you the post. If you are agreeable to the terms, I will ask you to sign the employees' register.'

Maria nodded as the woman marched away to return with a large ledger.

'Put your mark there. A cross will do,' she instructed, dipping a quill into a small inkpot that stood on the table and handing it to Maria.

Maria took it from her, and as she neatly wrote her name the older woman's eyes stretched.

'You can write!' Her voice betrayed her amazement.

'All of my family can write – my father taught us,' Maria answered proudly. 'Now when would you like me to start?'

'Would tomorrow morning at seven o'clock be convenient?'

'Yes, ma'am. It would.' Maria rose from her seat then, leaving Miss Belle slightly nonplussed as she watched her go. She just hoped that the girl would be as confident once she had met her new charge, since Isabelle Montgomery, as Mrs Bradshaw had informed her, was proving to be somewhat of a handful – to put it mildly.

Chapter Six

Charles and Helena Montgomery were at breakfast on Monday morning when there was a tap at the door. Charles frowned with a mixture of irritation and anxiety. Joshua had already left for the ribbon factory and the staff knew better than to disturb him and their mistress whilst they were eating, but he guessed who it would be. No doubt Polly would have returned to find that Isabelle was missing by now.

'See who it is,' he instructed the young maid who was hovering at the end of the table.

'Yes, sir.' She bobbed her knee and hastened away, only to return almost immediately to tell him, 'It's Polly, sir. She says she has to speak to the mistress on a matter of some urgency.'

'Can it not wait?' he snapped.

'It's all right, Charles,' his wife assured him as she rose gracefully from the table. 'I shall soon see what the problem is. Perhaps Isabelle is unwell again.'

She moved past him leaving the scent of rose petals in her wake, but she had barely reached the door when he said anxiously, 'Actually, I believe that Boyd has come to tell you that Isabelle is not in her room.'

'What?' Helena stared at him blankly then with a wave of her hand she dismissed the servant.

'So where is she then?' she asked bluntly once they were alone.

Shame-faced, her husband avoided looking at her. 'Let's just say that since I learned of our daughter's . . . condition, quite by chance some days ago, I have taken steps to ensure that she will not ruin the rest of her life.'

The colour drained out of Helena's face and she leaned heavily on the edge of the table. Surely he could not have carried out his threat to place their child in Hatter's Hall. He could never be so cruel . . . could he? Especially as he knew how strongly she had been against the idea.

'Surely you realised that we had to address the problem?' His voice was loaded with accusation now, and lowering her head she nodded miserably.

'Of course I did. But what have you done with her, Charles?'

'I have placed her somewhere where she will be safe and well cared for until after the birthing.' His eyes dared her to argue with him. 'You must see that I had to do something before her condition became common knowledge.'

Helena could not argue with that. Hadn't she been thinking along the very same lines? But even so, she had to know where her daughter was.

'Is she somewhere local?' she asked in a trembling voice.

Charles stared back at her. 'It should not concern you where she is,' he said stubbornly. 'I have told you she is safe and that is all you need to know. You will see her again when this whole sorry mess is over with. As soon as the child is born I will find someone to foster it and no one need be any the wiser.'

'B-but the baby will be our grandchild,' Helena objected, as she had done before. 'And what will we tell Polly and the rest of the staff? They will find it strange that Isabelle left so quickly.'

'I have already thought of that.' Charles strummed his fingers on the table, a clear sign that he was agitated. 'We shall tell them that a schoolfriend of hers has taken ill and Isabelle has gone back to France to stay with her for a few months. But as for your remark about a grandchild, you must rid yourself of that notion immediately! How could we *possibly* have the child here without setting the tongues wagging? The staff are not completely stupid, you know!'

Composing herself as best she could, Helena took a deep breath. 'And how is Isabelle supposed to manage if she has none of her clothes with her?' she asked in a voice that was as cold as the snow outside.

'You may tell Polly to pack her trunks and have them placed by the front door. I shall get Jacobs to have them delivered to her.'

'Very well.' Her heart was pounding now. If Charles was sending his manservant with Isabelle's things then that must mean she was not that far away. But where? Could he really have carried out his threat? Her mind was working frantically as she considered the other places he might have taken her to. It was all very strange though. Why hadn't Isabelle said goodbye to her – and why would she have left without her clothes and her possessions?

As she headed for the staircase, Helena had to accept the fact that Charles must have removed Isabelle from the house by force. But where could she be, other than at Hatter's Hall?

There was no way that Helena was prepared to wait until after the child's birth to see her daughter again. Somehow she was going to have to find out where Charles had taken her. The way she might do this occurred to her as she climbed the stairs. But first she would instruct Polly to pack Isabelle's possessions as Charles had requested.

As soon as she had spoken to Polly, she hurried back downstairs. Opening the green-baize door at the end of the long hallway, she strode through the kitchen, causing Cook's mouth to drop open as she hastily stood up from the table where she had been enjoying a cup of tea following the breakfast rush. It was a rare thing to see the mistress in the kitchen apart from when she came to discuss the menus each week.

'It's all right, Cook, do carry on,' Helena told her as she let herself out into the snow in the back yard. She then lifted her billowing skirts and daintily picked her way across to the stable-block where Hoskins was busily rubbing down one of the horses.

'Is your Steven about?' she enquired without preamble and Hoskins scratched his head.

'Aye, ma'am, he is that. He's up above wi' his mother.' He pointed to the crude wooden staircase at the end of the stable-block that led up to the living quarters he shared with his family.

'Then would you be kind enough to tell him that I wish to see him immediately?'

'Yes, ma'am. Right away.' Hoskins shot off to do as he was told as Helena stood there tapping her foot impatiently. The horses whinnied and scratched at the straw-covered floors of their stalls, but at that moment Helena was oblivious to them.

Young Steven Hoskins came down the staircase looking

anxious. "Ave I done summat wrong, missus?' he asked, full of concern.

'Oh no, not at all,' Helena assured him with a smile as she took his hand and led him to the other end of the stable-block where they could not be overheard. Steven was eleven years old. A good, hard-working lad already and Helena had a soft spot for him.

'I would like you to do a little errand for me if you would,' she told him.

He nodded instantly. 'O' course I will, missus, if I can.'

'Good boy. Now here's what I want you to do . . .' Helena leaned down to him and after a whispered conversation he nodded.

An hour later, Jacobs loaded the trunks containing Isabelle's possessions into the carriage and climbed inside, and as Hoskins urged the horses on, Helena watched from the drawing-room window as young Steven slipped from the shelter of the stables and leaped up onto the back of the carriage.

A pang of guilt sliced through her. The poor boy. The weather conditions were appalling and she just hoped that he would be able to hang on long enough to report back to her where Isabelle was. If he could manage to do that, she would see that he was well rewarded, but for now all she could do was wait for his return.

Two hours had passed when the maid came to inform her, 'Young Steven is here, ma'am, and he says he needs to see you.'

'Send him in please, Rose.'

The maid looked mildly surprised but went to do as she was told and the boy came into the room holding his cap respectfully as he peered about him in awe. He had never been further than the kitchen before, and the house beyond the green-baize door was even grander than he had imagined.

'So, Steven, did you manage to do what I asked of you?' Helena's nerves were taut and she spoke more harshly than she had intended to. The poor child looked frozen through.

'Yes, missus, I did.' He shuffled from foot to foot for a second then went on, 'I clung onto the back o' the coach fer dear life an' luckily me old man didn't spot me. Then when it stopped at some big gates I realised it was goin' to go through 'em so I jumped off an' hid in the bushes.'

'And where were these gates?' she asked anxiously.

'They were the gates leadin' to Hatter's Hall, missus.'

Helena suppressed a shudder at the thought of her daughter being confined in such a place, and her worst fears were confirmed. How could Charles have done such a wicked thing? But she forced herself to say calmly, 'Are you quite sure, my dear?'

He nodded vigorously. 'Oh aye. An' when the coach went in I legged it back 'ere in case me da spotted me.'

'You have done very well,' she told him, pressing a number of coins into his hand. 'Now there is just one more thing I need you to do for me. I want you to promise me faithfully that you will not speak of this to anyone.'

'Yes, missus.' Steven was staring down at the coins in his hand in wonder. The mistress had given him a whole shilling and already he was wondering how he was going to spend it.

'Very well, off you go then. And thank you, dear.'

He made a slight bow before turning and skipping from the room like a spring lamb.

Once left alone, Helena gave way to her emotions and tears trickled down her cheeks. Her poor girl. She would become as mad as the other afflicted souls who were incarcerated in that dreadful place if she left her there for long. But what could she do about it, and where else could Isabelle go? As she paced restlessly up and down the fine Turkish carpet, her mind sought a solution – and finally it came to her. Without wasting another second, she hurried to her little writing table and began to pen a letter.

Once the letter was sealed, Helena pushed it deep into the pocket of her billowing skirts. On the hall table was a silver tray where Charles placed the mail that he wished to be posted. Normally she would have added hers, but today she had no wish for him to know who she was writing to, so for the second time that day she went to the stable-block again in search of young Steven.

Cook was kneading dough at the table and again her mouth dropped open as the mistress appeared.

'Don't mind me, I have no wish to disturb you,' Helena told her as she wafted past.

'I wonder what's goin' on?' Cook said musingly to no one in particular when Helena had disappeared into the swirling snow, then shrugging she continued with what she was doing. Something was afoot; she could sense it, what with Miss Isabelle disappearing and the mistress in and out of the kitchen. But then no doubt she'd discover what it was all in good time.

Helena found Steven sitting on a haybale in the stables whittling away at a piece of wood. At sight of her he jumped up and she smiled at him kindly before saying, 'I wonder if you would like to earn another shilling to go with the one you already have, Steven?'

His eyes sparkled greedily as he nodded. 'Yes, missus, I would that.'

'Then I have another errand for you, but once again I would prefer it if you told no one about it.'

'I can do that all right, missus.'

Helena glanced towards the door. 'Do you think you could make it to the village? I have a letter that needs to be posted as a matter of urgency. I hear that Mrs Everitt who owns the post office is indisposed but I believe that her niece has arrived to keep the shop open for her until she is better.'

Again Steven nodded, so now she withdrew the letter from her pocket and handed it to him with some money. 'You will find there is more than enough to cover the cost of postage, and you may keep the change.'

'Thanks, missus. I'll go right now.' And whilst I'm there I'll treat meself to a twist of aniseed balls, the lad thought to himself, his mouth already watering at the thought.

Seconds later he had shot away and Helena stood there for a moment watching him until the snow had swallowed him up. She just hoped that he would get there and back safely. She would never forgive herself if anything were to happen to him. There was no need for her to worry about him knowing who the letter was addressed to. Steven was not educated and therefore he could not read. Not that it would have made much difference even if he could.

As she picked her way back across the icy cobblestones to the kitchen door, Helena Montgomery chewed on her lip. Now she must decide how she was going to put the rest of her plan into action. But first she would go and visit Isabelle, whether Charles liked it or not. She was her mother, after all.

Chapter Seven

Maria was exhausted by the time she got home and her mother quickly led her to the fire and helped to pull her sodden boots off.

'So how did it go, pet?' she asked anxiously, half-hoping that Maria had not got the job.

'I am to start tomorrow,' Maria said dully. 'I shall live in but I shall be allowed to visit home every Sunday afternoon.'

'Oh!' Martha began to knead the girl's hands. She looked fit to drop and not at all well. Martha could hardly believe that after tomorrow she would only see her precious child once a week, and the thought of her working in that dreadful place almost broke her heart. Could she have known it, Maria was worried about her too. She hated the way her father treated her mother and often wondered why Martha had stayed with him. He treated her more as a skivvy than a wife, but then the girl knew better than to ask. She supposed her mother must have her reasons.

Now Martha hurried away and returned with a bowl of thin gruel. 'Drink this,' she urged. 'It will take the chill off and then you can tell me what the place is like.'

The whole of the village was curious about Hatter's Hall, although not curious enough to want to venture anywhere near the place.

'I shall not be working in the asylum side of it.' Maria took a sip of the steaming drink before going on, 'I shall be working as a maid to a young lady of quality who is to be there for some months, although I have no idea who she is.'

'Hmm!' Martha said caustically. Obviously the young lady in question had got herself into trouble. There were more than a few youngsters dotted about the village who had been fostered out after being born in Hatter's Hall. As her concerns about her own daughter surfaced, Martha's frown deepened. It would be ironic if Maria had to wait on a young woman who was in the family way, if *she* was in the same condition herself. But Maria had not actually owned up to that, so she could only go on praying that her fears were not justified.

It was then that Edward strode in from the small sitting room at the front of the cottage with his Bible tucked under his arm, and much as her mother had done only moments before, he asked, 'So how did your interview go?'

'I start tomorrow.'

Martha noted the look of satisfaction that played briefly across his face and resentment surged through her. How could he even consider sending Maria to work in such a place? But then she should not have been surprised. Edward had never had any time for the girl, and no doubt it would suit him to have her tucked away in that godforsaken hole.

Seeing his wife's expression, he said meanly, 'Is that not good news then, Mother?'

71

'There are many positions I would rather have seen her in,' Martha retorted. She rarely answered him back or disagreed with him, but today she could not help herself.

'I think she will be admirably suited to working there,' he answered mockingly. 'And her wages will come in more than handy each week. No doubt they will pay more at Hatter's Hall than Mrs Everitt did.'

Martha took a deep breath before she said something she might regret, and sensing a row brewing, Maria said hurriedly, 'I shall be perfectly all right, Mother, really I shall.' *But I wish I could take you and Emma with me*, her heart cried silently.

Her little sister, who had been listening to the exchange, inched up to her with tears sparkling on her long dark lashes. 'You aren't going away, are you, Ria?' she asked shakily.

'Not *very* far away,' Maria assured her. 'And I shall come home to see you every single Sunday afternoon. That will be nice, won't it?'

'But why can't you stay here with us?' Emma was openly crying now at the thought of losing the big sister she adored.

'Because she is old enough to pay her way in the world and she needs to take whatever job she is offered and be thankful for it,' her father rasped harshly.

Just then, a knock sounded on the door and grumbling, he hurried across to open it, which was just as well as it stopped Maria from responding.

The minute Edward opened the door a young, pitifully thin lad who was clad in clothes that were nowhere suitable for the terrible weather conditions outside tumbled into the room, bringing a gust of icy air and a flurry of snow with him.

'What do you want, boy?' Edward asked with not an ounce of sympathy in his voice.

'It's me dad, sir,' the poor child managed to say through chattering teeth. He dragged his greasy cap off and nervously twisted it in his hands. 'Me mam said to ask you to come quick. She thinks he's not long fer this world.'

'Oh, you poor little soul,' Martha said quickly before Edward could respond. 'Of course he will come. Won't you, Edward? But whilst he is getting his coat on you must have a warm drink. You look perished. Come on, come over here and sit by the fire.'

She saw the look of displeasure flicker across her husband's face. No one had turned up for lessons today, no doubt because of the inclement weather, and she knew that he had been hoping to spend a quiet day at home. She had recognised the child instantly. He was one of the Bellamy children from the pit cottages in Chapel End, if she wasn't much mistaken. Her heart ached for him as she hastily poured some of the leftover gruel into a thick pottery mug. He was one of at least seven children and she wondered how his poor mother would manage if she lost her husband. Ted Bellamy was a miner at the local pit – a good, hard-working man – but now it looked as if he was going to be the next victim of the flu epidemic, poor soul. And what would happen to his family then, she wondered. The cottage was tied so there was a terrible possibility that they might all end up in the workhouse in the Bull Ring in Chilvers Coton. She shuddered at the thought but was powerless to do anything about it.

Edward meanwhile was getting into his outdoor clothes and looking none too pleased about it. Eventually he lifted his Bible and told the boy unfeelingly, 'Come along then or there's every chance your father will have died before we even get there.'

The trembling child quickly drained the mug, then

flashing a grateful smile at Martha, he followed Edward out into the snow without another word.

'Poor little mite,' Martha muttered. 'What will become of him if his father dies? Happen it will be the workhouse for that family.'

But then her thoughts returned to her own family's pressing problems and she breathed a sigh of relief. At least now that Edward was out of the way she would have a chance to speak to her daughter alone. Emma had gone to settle on the rug in front of the fire and was playing with her dolly, so now Martha drew up a chair and taking her older daughter's hand, she said softly, 'Are you *really* all right to go and work in that place, pet?'

Maria nodded, and as she looked into her mother's eyes an unspoken message passed between them. 'Yes, Mam, I am. It will give me some breathing space to decide what I'm going to do.'

In that moment, Martha's fears were verified and the breath caught in her throat. 'How far on are you?' she asked bluntly.

Maria lowered her head. 'I reckon a little over two months.' Tears began to trickle down her cheeks then as she mumbled brokenly, 'I'm so sorry I've let you down. But . . . but Lennie said he loved me.'

'Eeh, not young Lennie Glover.' Martha groaned as she rubbed a workworn hand across her forehead. 'Oh lass, didn't I warn you to stay well away from him? Surely you knew he had the gift of the gab? Why, he's bedded half the lasses in the village with his sweet-talking. Have you told him?'

'Yes, I did,' Maria sniffled. 'And he promised he'd come and talk to Father about us getting married – but then he . . . he ran away. His mother says he's gone to sea and there's no telling when he'll be back. But I'm sure he will when he's had time to think about it. He loves me, Mam. He said so!'

'Dear God.' Martha stood up and began to pace up and down the length of the kitchen. Edward would surely kill her if he ever discovered she was with child, or at best, he would disown her. What was she to do if Lennie did not come back for her very soon? As if picking up on the fraught atmosphere, Emma looked up from her play and Martha told her sharply, 'Go and play upstairs in your bedroom, Emma!'

'But it's cold up there,' the child objected.

'Do as you are told *now!*'

Not used to being shouted at by her mother, the little girl skittered away, her footsteps clattering on the bare wooden stairs. Seconds later, the sound of her bedroom door being slammed reverberated through the small cottage.

Martha turned back to her elder daughter. 'Hatter's Hall is the last place I would ever have wished you to work in,' she said in an unsteady voice. 'But happen it's as well you've got the job. At least it will get you out from under your father's feet while we decide what to do.' She could scarcely believe that her Maria could have been so foolish. She had always been such a good, obedient daughter. But then perhaps that was the problem. Edward had always ruled her with a rod of iron, giving her no freedom whatsoever, so Lennie Glover with his sweet-talking tongue would have seemed like a being apart. And how could she be a hypocrite and judge her daughter when . . . She stopped her thoughts from going any further. There was no good to be gained by looking back into the past. She must look to the future now, whatever it might hold.

'Come on, lass,' she said in a stronger voice. 'Let's away and get your bundle packed up. The Good Lord will provide us with a solution.'

Praying that her mother was right, Maria followed her upstairs.

'Now you be sure to come straight home on Sunday,' Martha fussed as she pulled Maria's shawl up over her glorious mass of thick fair hair early the next morning. She was aware that Edward was sitting at the table watching their farewell with a satisfied glint in his eye, and in the whole of their life together she had never been closer to telling him exactly what she thought of him. He seemed to be taking a perverse pleasure in the fact that Maria was going to work in that awful place. And it *was* an awful place. Everyone in the village knew that. There were even those that would have gone to the workhouse before they would set foot in the grounds. But with things as they were . . .

Maria had already said her goodbyes to Henry before he left for his shift down the mine, and now she lifted her small bundle. Then after hugging Emma, who had got up early and was crying softly, she kissed her mother's pale cheek before turning and saying, 'Goodbye, Father.'

'Be sure you bring the whole of your wages home,' he said. 'And no frittering any of it away.'

Seeing the anger spark in her mother's eyes, Maria swiftly opened the door and left. There was no point in delaying.

Thankfully it had stopped snowing sometime during the night but it still lay deep upon the ground and within minutes Maria was breathless as she tramped through it. But for all that, she found pleasure in her surroundings as she moved along. The snow made the soot-covered roofs of the little pit cottages she passed look clean and bright, as if some great unseen hand had whitewashed everything in sight. Soon the cottages were left far behind her as she trudged on, and eventually the high walls surrounding

Hatter's Hall came into sight. Maria paused and pulled her shawl more tightly about her. This would be her home for the foreseeable future. Until Lennie came for her, that was. It was a daunting prospect.

Once again when she reached the gates the old man shuffled from his hut to open them, and when she had passed through them, he quickly closed and relocked them before disappearing back into the warmth of his shelter without a word. As Maria forced herself to move on she had never felt lonelier in her life but she was painfully aware that there could be no going back now.

It took her some minutes to walk the length of the long winding drive, and again the sight of the stark brick walls and dark shuttered windows struck terror into her heart. She had the urge to turn and run back home, but what would happen to her then, when her father discovered that she was to have a child? The way she saw it, she could either stay here or risk being sent to the workhouse – and at that moment, this seemed the better of the two options, though only slightly.

Taking a deep breath, she lifted her head, and this time when she neared the house she turned towards the servants' entrance. The kitchen was a hive of activity as breakfast was being prepared, and the cook scarcely had time to look at her apart from to say, 'Ah, there yer are then. Miss Belle said as we were to expect yer, lass. No doubt she'll be here in a minute. Just sit over there an' get warmed through while yer wait, eh?'

Cook had barely uttered the words when the Housekeeper walked into the room. Her eyes instantly settled on Maria and she smiled stiffly. 'Ah, good. I am pleased to see that you are punctual, girl. Come with me.'

Maria did as she was told and in no time at all was

following the woman through a labyrinth of corridors, her sodden boots echoing on the cold stone tiles. Every now and again the sound of a wail from some poor demented soul floated on the air and Maria gulped deep in her throat. There seemed to be locked doors everywhere she looked and she rightly guessed that this must be the part of the asylum where the lunatics were kept.

Sensing the girl's unease, the Housekeeper looked over her shoulder with a semblance of a smile as she assured her, 'Don't worry. They are all safely locked away. They cannot harm you.'

Eventually they came to a large sweeping staircase, at the top of which was another locked door.

'This is where our more elite guests are kept,' Miss Belle informed her as she unlocked the door from a number of keys that dangled from a chatelaine about her waist.

Maria found herself in much more pleasant surroundings. There was wallpaper on the walls here, and fine carpets were scattered across the highly polished floorboards. A number of paintings in heavy gilt frames hung at regular intervals along the walls. Maria would have liked to stop to admire them but she resisted and followed Miss Belle meekly.

At last the woman stopped in front of a door, and lowering her voice she told her, 'The young lady you will be serving is within. You will address her as Miss Isabelle and ask no questions. Her first name is all that you need to know about her. Is that quite clear?'

'Yes, ma'am.'

The woman nodded and tapped at the door, which was opened almost immediately by the sternest-looking woman Maria had ever seen.

'Ah, Mrs Bradshaw, you will be pleased to know that the

girl who I told you was coming to relieve you has arrived,' Miss Belle said primly. 'This is Maria Mundy.'

Mrs Bradshaw eyed Maria from head to toe before she said in a low voice, 'And good luck to you, Miss Mundy. This one has a temper on her the like of which I've not seen for many a long day. In you come, girl. She's all yours.'

Maria cautiously stepped into the room. She found herself in a bedroom that made her gasp with admiration. A large four-poster bed surrounded by heavy damask drapes stood against one wall, although most of the drapes had been ripped down and were strewn across the floor. There was fine carved furniture polished to a mirrorlike shine, and on the mahogany dressing-table, a number of perfume bottles had been overturned, the combined scents making the air smell sickly-sweet. Beautiful clothes were scattered everywhere and in the deep bay window a chair lay on its side. In all, it looked as if a hurricane had swept through the room – but there was no sign of the occupant.

'Miss Isabelle is through there in her sitting room,' Mrs Bradshaw informed her. 'From now on it will be your job to see to her every need. You will sleep in the adjoining room when Miss Isabelle is settled for the night – but you may not retire until you are quite sure she has no further need of you. Do you understand, girl?'

When Maria nodded solemnly the woman ushered her back out into the corridor.

'First of all we will let you put your things into your room,' she said, nodding towards Maria's meagre bundle. 'And then we will supply you with a uniform. It would not do for you to wait on Miss Isabelle in *those* clothes, young lady. Start to put your things away whilst I go and get it for you.'

As Maria entered her room, she was fuming. What on

earth did the woman mean? She was wearing her Sunday-best dress! But then she forgot all about that as she looked around. Her room was nowhere near as luxuriously furnished as the apartment next door, but all the same, it was more comfortable than any room she had ever slept in before. There were no carpets here, but there were curtains at the window and a single brass bed with what looked like a comfortable feather mattress on it, equipped with two neatly folded woollen blankets and a fluffy feather pillow. It was bitterly cold in there and Maria briefly thought how strange it would be without Emma's little body to cuddle up to at night, but she quickly pushed the thought away. It would not do to start crying now before she had even begun her new job. There was a wooden wash-stand with a china jug and bowl standing on it and a pewter candlestick with a whole candle in it on a small chest of drawers at the side of the bed. The modest-sized window gave a view of the gardens, and there was a hard-backed wooden chair and a small table where she could sit and read.

Mrs Bradshaw pointed to a bell suspended from the wall. 'That connects to Miss Isabelle's room. Should she need you during the night she will ring for you and you will go to her immediately.' She then waved her hand in the direction of an oak tallboy. 'Put your clothes in there and wait for me here.' With that she was gone, closing the door firmly behind her.

By the time she came back Maria had done as she was told and was patiently sitting on the side of the bed.

Mrs Bradshaw laid two dresses across the end of it then added some soft house shoes, stockings, petticoats and a selection of fine woollen underwear to the pile.

'The last maid who wore these was slightly taller than you, but you may alter them to fit in your own time if they are too long. That is, if you can sew?'

'I can,' Maria assured her as the woman looked at her closely. She had to admit, Miss Belle had been right about the girl. She was very articulate and looked as clean as a new pin, even if her clothes were somewhat shabby. Her hair was shining with no headlice apparent, which made a nice change from the last maid they had employed. She had lasted barely a week and Mrs Bradshaw had been relieved to see the back of her.

'Your door will remain unlocked,' she told Maria now. 'I will give you the key to Miss Isabelle's suite, but you must always remember to keep that one locked at all times whenever you enter or leave the room. Your meals will be brought up to you and you will eat in here when you have seen to Miss Isabelle's. Should she by any chance ever manage to get past you, she will not be able to escape as the door at the entrance to this wing is also locked. Are there any questions you would like to ask?'

Maria shook her head and now the woman told her, 'In that case I will give you ten minutes to get changed then I will take you to meet Miss Isabelle.'

That sounds like something to look forward to, Maria thought wryly as she began to strip off her damp clothes.

Just as the older woman had told her, the dress she put on was slightly long and trailed along the floor, but even so Maria felt like a queen in it. It was a pleasant dove-grey colour, nipped in tight at the waist and with a full skirt. There was a tiny lace collar and little pearl buttons all the way up the front, and once it was on, Maria tried to look at herself in the small mirror that hung above the wash-stand. The material was a soft wool blend and she marvelled at the feel of the petticoats beneath it and the fine woollen underwear against her skin. She slid her feet into the supple leather shoes – another luxury she had never experienced before – then she quickly took up her hairbrush and brushed her hair before tying it neatly at the nape of her neck with the only ribbon she possessed.

When Mrs Bradshaw reappeared she stared at her approvingly although she made no comment about her appearance. It would never do to give maids ideas above their station. She simply said, 'Are you ready then, Maria?'

'Yes,' Maria said with what courage she could muster. She suddenly felt very nervous.

'Very well then.' Mrs Bradshaw ushered her out of the room and within seconds was unlocking the door to Isabelle's suite.

There was still no sign of her new mistress and so now Mrs Bradshaw told her, 'The coal will be delivered to the room each morning, and it is your job to make sure that the fires are kept lit. When the maid brings the meals up she will knock at the door to be admitted. You must see to Miss Isabelle's needs before taking your meals in your own room.'

Maria nodded and then jumped as the sound of a crash from the adjoining room made both their heads turn in that direction.

Mrs Bradshaw tutted. 'I shall leave you to introduce yourself then,' she said. She passed Maria a key and without another word, turned and left the room.

Maria stuffed the key down into the deep pocket of her dress, then, drawing herself up to her full height, she cautiously approached the door where the noise had come from. As she inched it open and stepped inside she found herself in a very comfortable sitting room. She stood there for a moment admiring it, at the same time becoming aware of stifled sobs coming from a large wing-backed chair placed to one side of the fireplace.

'Hello.' The word had barely left her lips when a young woman with a shock of wild dark hair leaped out of the chair, her fine linen and lace nightshirt billowing about her.

'And who the hell are *you?*' she screeched as her small hands bunched into fists.

Maria felt sorry for her; she had obviously been crying and her eyes were red and swollen. 'I am your new maid,' she told her quietly. 'My name is Maria.'

The girl's lips drew back from her teeth. 'New maid *indeed!*' she said scornfully. 'I've no doubt you are one of the lunatics that are locked away here. I want Polly, my *own* maid!'

'I'm afraid that isn't possible,' Maria told her as she bent to right a small table that had been overturned. 'But I promise I shall do my best for you, miss. Now is there anything I can get for you?'

'Not unless you can get me out of this godforsaken place,' Isabelle snarled as she began to pace agitatedly up and down.

Ignoring the comment, Maria quietly continued putting the room to rights. There were books flung everywhere and a number of broken ornaments scattered across the carpet. As she lifted the fragments into a wastepaper basket, Isabelle's temper deteriorated even further.

'*Look* at me!' she shouted. 'How *dare* you ignore me!'

'I wasn't ignoring you, miss.' Maria's voice was calm and level. 'I am merely picking up these broken things because I don't wish you to stand on them and cut your foot. Would you like me to help you get dressed?'

'No, I would not! What's the point of getting dressed?' Isabelle said peevishly. 'There will be no one but you to see me. I am being kept a prisoner here!'

'As you wish.' Maria sailed through the door into the next

room and once there she drew a long shuddering breath.
Just as Mrs Bradshaw had warned, it appeared that she was
going to earn every penny of her wages working for that
spoiled little madam!

Chapter Eight

By the time Sunday afternoon arrived, Maria's nerves were as taut as piano wires. Isabelle was still flatly refusing to eat or get dressed, and on many occasions Maria had been forced to duck the things that the other girl threw at her. Throughout all the tantrums, Maria had managed to keep her calm – although at times she had felt like screaming back at the girl. After all, she wasn't the only one in a pickle, was she? But Maria couldn't tell her that, of course, much as she would have liked to.

Her mood was glum when she went to her room to put her boots on. Mrs Bradshaw had given her permission to wear her uniform to go home in, and Maria was looking forward to showing her family how fine it was. But most of all she was longing to see them – all except her father. It had felt like a release, to be away from *him*. She had missed the others more than she could have imagined, and felt as if she hadn't seen them for months, not just a few days. And of course, there was always the chance that Lennie would have seen the error of his ways by now and come back for her. He might even be at the cottage right now.

She came out of her room to find Mrs Bradshaw the Matron waiting for her with her first week's wages.

'Here you are – and I must say you have earned them,' she said in a kindlier voice than Maria had heard her use before. 'Enjoy your afternoon with your family, but be back here for five o'clock sharp. I shall stay with Miss Isabelle until then. And here.' To Maria's great surprise she held out a thick cloth cloak with a hood on it. 'You may borrow this. I noticed that you only have a shawl, and although the snow has stopped it is still bitterly cold out there.'

'Why, thank you,' Maria uttered, taking the cloak with some surprise. Perhaps the woman had a heart, after all.

The Matron unlocked the door at the end of the corridor where Kitty, the skivvy who delivered the meals and the coal to Miss Isabelle's room each day, was waiting to show Maria to the front door. It was just as well, for she would surely have lost her way without some guidance. The place was enormous, and she had no wish to wander into the asylum part of it where the poor unfortunates were kept. Sometimes she had glimpsed them from Miss Isabelle's window as they took their exercise in the gardens with the staff watching them closely. It was hard to distinguish the men from the women, for they all wore shapeless grey shifts that reached to their ankles, and they had all had their hair shorn. It almost broke Maria's heart just to watch them as they shuffled along. They didn't even seem to know where they were, and the same vacant expression was in all their eyes. Sometimes when she lay in bed at night, their screams would echo along the corridor and turn her blood to ice. But today she was determined to enjoy every single second of her freedom, so when her escort eventually bade her goodbye at the servants' entrance, she set off with her head held high along the lengthy drive.

She would give her wages to her mother, she decided, and she could well imagine how pleased Martha would be, knowing that she could feed the family well for the rest of the following week. After the stuffy atmosphere of the rooms she had been confined in, the cold air on her face was welcome and she breathed in deeply, as if she was trying to store it up to last until the next time she was allowed out. Her spirits lifted further as she jangled the coins in her pocket. Thankfully her morning sickness seemed to have passed now but she was still no further forward in knowing what lay ahead. As yet, her stomach was still flat, but what would happen when the child began to show? She supposed that Mrs Bradshaw would throw her out in disgrace – and then where would she go? She already knew that she would not be able to go home, her father would see to that. Still, for now she would try to think of happier things so she pushed it as best she could to the back of her mind and hurried on.

Once she reached the gates, the old watchman let her out with a nod as he sucked on his pipe, and soon after the cottages in Chapel End came into view. The hoarfrost on the roofs made them sparkle, and the girl thought how pretty everywhere looked although she was glad of Mrs Bradshaw's cloak, for the cold was enough to slice a being in two.

At last she reached her home, and the second she opened the kitchen door, Emma, who had been watching for her from the window all day, almost threw herself at her.

'Eeh, Maria, I've missed you,' she cried as she wrapped her skinny arms about her big sister's waist. 'And by, you don't half look posh. Is that a new cloak you're wearing?'

'Well, it isn't really mine,' Maria confessed as she slid it from around her shoulders and hung it on a nail on the back of the door. 'Mrs Bradshaw said I may borrow it. But never mind about that for now. How are you all?'

Martha had her in a fierce hug now, and as their eyes met, she asked, 'How has it been, lass?' The girl certainly looked smart, that was a fact. She could almost have been taken for gentry, looking like that.

'Oh, not too bad.' Maria lied rather than worry her. 'Though the young woman I am waiting on has a terrible temper on her.' She grinned as she thought of Isabelle's many tantrums.

'You are not in any danger from her, are you?' Martha's face was creased with concern now.

'Not so long as I can duck to avoid anything she cares to throw at me,' Maria chuckled, then, 'Where are Father and Henry?'

'Oh, Henry is off on some jaunt or another with his friends and your father is still at chapel. But Henry says he'll be sure to be back to see you before you go,' Martha responded as she filled the kettle and put it on to boil. Emma had drifted away by then, and glad of the chance for them to catch a few minutes alone, the woman said, 'Is there any change, pet? In your condition, I mean.'

'No, but let's not spoil what little time we have worrying about that,' Maria said as she drew her wages from the pocket of her skirt and pushed the money across the table.

Her mother gawped at it for a moment before asking, 'And what's all this?'

'It's my wages, of course.'

'Well, I'm not taking all that off you, that's for sure.' Martha swiftly pushed half of the money back towards her daughter.

'But why not? And what will Father say?'

'Your father doesn't know how much you're earning and you'll no doubt have need of some of this in times ahead,' Martha said gravely.

Seeing the sense in what her mother said, Maria reluctantly dropped the money back into her pocket, although she didn't really think she would need it. When Lennie came back for her he would look after everything, wouldn't he?

Martha bustled away to pour the boiling water over the tealeaves she had measured into the brown teapot, then, taking a seat again, she began cautiously, 'I'm afraid I have some bad news for you, pet, so I may as well get it out of the way now as later.'

Maria's heart began to race as she stared at her mother, who seemed to be trying to choose her words carefully.

'The thing is . . . I went into the village the other day and I bumped into Lennie Glover's mother. In a right old tizzy she was. You see, she'd had word that Lennie had been in a fight at the docks just before he boarded his ship to sail. It seems he got drunk and . . .'

'*And?*'

'And . . . some sailors found him slumped in an alleyway a while later. He'd been stabbed through the heart. One of them travelled here to break the news to Mrs Glover. Lennie is dead. I'm so sorry, Maria.'

'Where have they buried him?' Maria asked in a choked voice.

Her mother shrugged. 'I have no idea, pet. Happen the sailors would have seen to it. But you know . . . Lennie was a bad lad. I always feared something like this would happen to him one day. He had a lot of enemies.'

Maria felt as if the room was shifting around her. Deep down she had been certain that soon, Lennie would realise that he loved her and would come back to make an honest woman of her. But he would never be able to do that now, would he? So what was to become of her? She didn't even know where he had been laid to rest. At that thought, she fell into a kind of faint.

Martha was chafing her hands and her voice seemed to be coming from a long way away . . . but eventually Maria's head cleared and the room swam back into focus. Her mother pressed a mug of water into her shaking hands and Maria gulped at it greedily just as her father appeared through the door.

'Ah, so you're back then.'

He stared at her without warmth, taking in her expensive attire.

'Doesn't she look fine, Edward?' Martha said nervously.

'Vanity is a sin,' he stated coldly. 'And have you handed your wages over to your mother?'

'Yes, she has,' Martha told him before Maria had a chance to answer. 'And right hard she has had to work for it as well.'

'Hard work never hurt anyone,' he rapped and Martha had to bite her tongue. This from the man who had never done a real day's work in his life.

Although Maria had been back home for less than half an hour, she suddenly knew that she must get away to think. Rising, she took Mrs Bradshaw's cloak from the back of the door and slipped it on.

'Ah, but you're never going already, pet?' Martha chewed on her lip in consternation as she bunched her apron in her hands.

'I'm afraid I have to this time,' Maria lied, doing her utmost to keep her voice light. 'But I shall be able to stay longer next week. Tell Henry I'm sorry I missed him, won't you?'

The goodbyes were hastily said and then Maria escaped as quickly as she could. Once outside, she paused. There were still over three hours to go until she was due back at Hatter's Hall, so she headed for the Hayes in Hartshill, hoping to find a quiet corner where she could put her thoughts into some sort of order. It was a good stiff walk that took the best part of half an hour, and when she finally got there she headed for the shelter of the trees and sat down on the frozen ground to stare out at the panoramic view spread before her. This was one of her favourite places, but today it held no pleasure for her even though she could see clear across two whole counties. In the distance, the winding canal sparkled beneath its layer of ice and the barren trees looked as if they had been painted with diamond dust, but she just sat there staring sightlessly ahead. Lennie was dead. She would never see him again and she did not know how she was going to bear it. He had been so young, so handsome, so full of life with plans and dreams – but now none of them would ever come true.

She sat on as the watery sun moved across the sky, numb with grief until eventually she stood up and, shaking out her skirts, set off in the direction of Hatter's Hall. She had no idea if she was going to be late and just then she didn't much care, but she arrived with minutes to spare to find Kitty anxiously looking out for her.

'Eeh, I were right worried yer were goin' to be late an' feel the length o' Mrs Bradshaw's tongue,' the young girl told her as she began to lead Maria back along the seemingly endless corridors. 'She's a right stickler fer time-keepin', is the Matron.'

Maria eyed the girl quizzically before asking, 'Don't *you* ever get any time off, Kitty?' She was so pale that she looked as if she had never stepped out into the fresh air at all.

'Not me, miss,' Kitty answered. 'I ain't never been beyond the gates o' the Hall in me whole life.'

Despite her own misery, Maria was appalled. 'Why ever not?'

'Seems they found me mam layin' outside the gates an' fetched 'er in. Then she died shortly after I were born an' they've kept me in 'ere ever since. I've been workin' since I were eight years old. I don't even know what me mam's name were or where I come from.'

'But that's just awful!' Maria gasped. 'Why don't you tell them you want to leave?'

'An' where would I go if I did?' Kitty grinned at her ruefully and for the first time Maria really looked at her properly. She was small for her age, which Maria judged to be a couple of years younger than herself. She was painfully thin too, but Maria suspected that dressed in different clothes and with her hair loose instead of hidden under a mob cap, she might actually be quite pretty: her eyes were a lovely amber colour and the tiny wisps of hair that had escaped her cap were a deep brunette. Just for a moment the girl had taken her mind off her own problems and now Maria felt ashamed. Poor Kitty. It looked as if the girl would live and die in this wretched place without ever having known any other life at all.

They were climbing the stairs to the wing that housed Miss Isabelle now and Maria made a mental note to speak more kindly to Kitty in future.

'There y'are then, miss,' the maid said when she had unlocked the door. 'I'll be back up shortly wi' your suppers.'

'Thank you, Kitty.' Maria watched her walk away then hurried to her room to get changed into her house shoes and tidy herself up.

*

'Ah, so you're back at last, are you?' Isabelle snapped, the second Maria set foot into her rooms. 'It must be nice to be allowed some freedom instead of being caged up here like some animal at a sideshow!'

'I'm sure it will not be for too much longer, miss,' Maria replied patiently as she began to tidy away the stack of books that the girl had flung about the room in her absence. It was as she was lifting one particular book that the title caught her eye and she could not prevent herself from glancing at the first page.

'Why are you looking at that?' Isabelle asked irritably.

'It's *David Copperfield*, miss. A book I've long wanted to read.'

'Read? You can read?' Isabelle repeated incredulously. She raised an eyebrow. 'Then prove it to me, girl. Read something aloud!'

When Maria sat down and began the first chapter, the young woman's mouth gaped wide open. Not only could this chit read, she could read well.

'I didn't think that servants were literate,' she interrupted.

Maria looked back at her with her head held high. 'Servants are people, miss – flesh and blood, just the same as you, but without the privileges. Perhaps you should remember that!'

For the first time in their acquaintance, Isabelle was rendered speechless. She stared at Maria in amazement.

Then Maria coolly placed the book down and quietly left the room, locking the door securely behind her. Let the spoiled little madam think on that and stew in her own juice for a while, she thought as she wearily made her way to her own room. She was sick and tired of her, and at that moment she didn't even care if she was dismissed. After all, now that she had lost Lennie, what did she have to look forward to?

Chapter Nine

Maria did not venture into Isabelle's room again until Kitty came up with their evening meal. When she carried the tray in, the girl was much more subdued and for once did not instantly spew out a mouthful of abuse. Isabelle could see that Maria had been crying but she made no comment as Maria set the food out on the table.

Normally she would scream that she wasn't hungry, but tonight she meekly took a seat and after lifting her knife and fork, began to eat the meal that the cook had prepared for her. Maria was secretly pleased, although she had no intention of commenting on the fact. Isabelle had hardly eaten enough to keep a sparrow alive since she had been there, and the girl knew that it could not be good for her or the unborn child she was carrying. No one had actually confirmed that Isabelle was with child, but the signs she was displaying were identical to how Maria herself was feeling – and she was no fool.

94

'Will there be anything else, miss?' she asked as she poured some wine into a cut-glass goblet.

'No, thank you. You may go and have your own meal now.'

Disguising her shock, Maria turned away. It was the first time that Isabelle had spoken to her as if she was a human being, let alone said *thank you*, so Maria took it as a major step forward. Once back in her own room, she lifted the lid on her dish. Cook had prepared two plump lamb chops and a selection of vegetables for Isabelle, but Maria's meal consisted of two cold sausages and a dollop of mashed potato. It didn't really bother her. At least the food here was plentiful, if plain, and tonight she wasn't hungry anyway.

Crossing to the window she stared sightlessly through the glass to the darkness beyond, and for the first time she was forced to acknowledge what a truly terrible position she was in. Until now she had held firm to the belief that Lennie would come for her like a knight on a white charger and rescue her from shame, but that could never happen now.

Choking back a sob, she composed herself, and after lifting the candle she went back to Isabelle's room leaving her meal untouched. She was pleased to see that the young woman had at least eaten a portion of her supper tonight and as she loaded the pots back onto the tray, Isabelle said, 'I think I may get dressed tomorrow.'

'As you wish, miss,' Maria answered expressionlessly and she then left the room, placing the trays on the landing table for Kitty to collect. In her present mood it felt as if it was going to be a very long night.

The following morning, Kitty delivered a plateful of bacon, sausages, mushrooms and two fat kidneys for Isabelle's breakfast. There was a dishful of watery porridge for Maria, which she forced herself to eat once she had seen to the needs of her mistress.

When the meal was over, Isabelle told her, 'I think I would like to take a bath today. Could you arrange that for me?'

Within minutes of Maria ringing the bell, Kitty and another of the servants were carrying up cans of steaming water and filling up the large bath-tub. At home they each took turns in a tin bath in front of the fire, so this was luxury indeed to Maria. When the bath was ready for her, Maria helped Isabelle to undress and steadied her as she stepped into it. The young woman sank down beneath the hot water, telling Maria, 'Wash my hair, please.'

Maria obliged, using French soap and jugs of clean hot water. Half an hour later, as Isabelle sat at her dressing-table in a silk negligée, Maria began to gently comb out the tangles in her hair.

'Have you ever dressed anyone's hair before?' Isabelle asked.

Maria shook her head. 'No, miss, but I'm quick to learn if you'll tell me how you'd like it.' She fumbled with the pins as Isabelle gave instructions and sometime later she stood back to study her efforts. Not bad for a first time, even if I do say so myself, she thought to herself. Isabelle's hair was beautiful, long and thick with a tendency to curl. Maria had swept part of it up onto the top of her head and now, as it dried in the heat from the fire, it looked very becoming falling in tiny ringlets down her back. Isabelle turned her head this way and that in the mirror, then rose without comment and went to her wardrobe where she began to withdraw a number of silk gowns that had Maria's eyes popping.

'I think I shall wear this one,' she said eventually, throwing a blue gown trimmed with lace across the foot of the bed. 'Help me into my stays and my petticoats now, would you?'

Once dressed, the girl was totally transformed, and Maria could not help but stare at her admiringly. Isabelle was truly beautiful, a fact of which she was all too well aware.

'Oh well, that got rid of a little time,' Isabelle said peevishly. 'Now we just have the rest of another long day to get through.'

Maria made no comment as she went about gathering the damp towels together for Kitty to take down to the laundry.

Once the bath was emptied – a laborious process – and the rooms were tidied, Maria suggested, 'Would you like me to read to you, miss?'

'I suppose so. There is nothing else for us to do,' Isabelle said sulkily.

Maria suppressed a sigh. Since the evening before, Isabelle had been slightly less irritable, but now it looked as if she was going to revert to her normal spoiled self.

'Which book would you like me to read?'

Isabelle had begun to pace again and now she waved her hand impatiently. 'Oh any, I suppose. I am not really interested anyway.'

Maria began to peruse the beautiful leather-bound books on the shelf and it was then that Isabelle suddenly paused to ask, 'Do you know why I have been locked away here, Maria?'

Maria answered carefully. 'Well, I haven't been told, miss, but I think I have a good idea.'

Isabelle was stroking her stomach thoughtfully. 'I am going to have a child,' she confided. 'And I just pray daily that I might lose it. You are of the working class – do you not know of a way I may achieve this?'

'I'm afraid I don't, miss.' Maria stared at her steadily as Isabelle stamped her dainty silk-shod foot.

'Oh, *damn and blast*,' she cursed as she built herself up to yet another tantrum. 'Why did this have to go and happen to *me*? And why did Papa see fit to lock me away in this hell-hole! Surely he could have found a better place for me to go until this bastard is out of me. I hope the monster dies at birth for all the grief it has caused me!'

Maria was so shocked that she was rendered temporarily speechless. Isabelle meanwhile was tapping her foot at the injustice of it all. It had never occurred to her that the position she was in was partly her fault.

'My parents want me to marry Philip Harrington. Have you heard of him?' she demanded.

Maria nodded. Everyone in Ansley and Hartshill had heard of the Harringtons. Much like the Montgomerys, they were a very influential family.

'Do you not like Philip then?' she asked innocently. She had seen him a few times in the family carriage or on his stallion and thought what a handsome young man he was. She had certainly never heard a bad word said about him, or his father for that matter, who was commonly known to be a fair man. But the mother was cut from a different cloth entirely: rumour had it that she was a shrew who led her poor husband a merry dance.

'It's not that I don't like him exactly. He is certainly good-looking, and when his parents die he will be very wealthy indeed. It's just that after knowing my Pierre he is so utterly *boring*. Like a little puppy dog, if you know what I mean.'

'Would it be such a bad thing to be married to a man who is kind?' Maria said practically. 'What is it about him that you find boring?' She could only assume that Pierre must be the father of Isabelle's unborn child.

Isabelle tossed her head. 'Just about everything!' She spread her hands expressively. 'He works every single day in one or another of his father's factories because he says he wants to know everything about them before he inherits. Can you believe that? It's so ridiculous when he can well afford to just put a manager in.'

Maria secretly thought it was admirable of Philip to want to feel that he was earning his living, but she wisely held her tongue. Also, as much as she disliked her father for the majority of the time, and although he was merely a poor preacher, he was actually a very learned man and had insisted that his children should be well educated, for which she was truly grateful. Maria had always been like a sponge when it came to learning, and she was sure that she was more knowledgeable than her mistress, had it been put to the test. Isabelle's head seemed to be full of nothing more than the latest fashions and getting her own way, whereas Maria was keen to know about world events as much as was possible. But then they had been brought up so very differently. It was doubtful that Isabelle would ever have experienced what it was like to be hungry, as Maria herself had been at times, or to know how it felt to have no decent shoes to wear.

Isabelle idly flicked the lid of her jewellery box now and withdrew a sparkling ring with a green stone in it surrounded by diamonds set in gold. 'Have you ever seen an emerald before?' she asked as she placed it on her finger and held her hand out so that Maria might admire it. The stones snatched at the light, throwing rainbow prisms across the walls, and Maria thought she had never seen anything quite so splendid. In truth, the only piece of jewellery she had ever seen was her mother's plain gold wedding band, but she had read about various gemstones in books.

'No, I haven't,' she admitted. 'It's quite beautiful.'

Isabelle withdrew another ring; this time with a red stone

in it. 'This is a ruby,' she informed Maria. 'And they are worth a fortune.' Her eyes became crafty then as she said cajolingly, 'If you could get me out of this place I would give them to you. Think of it – you would be rich.'

Maria stared at her. 'But that would be nigh on impossible,' she answered honestly. 'The door at the end of the landing is securely locked at all times. Even I cannot get out.' It seemed that Isabelle would stop at nothing to escape her prison; she had already tried pleading and threatening, and now she had resorted to bribery.

'Oh!' Fury twisted Isabelle's pretty face into a mask of hatred as she picked her hairbrush up and aimed it at Maria. 'You are no better than the rest of them,' she screamed. 'Pretending to be my friend but all the time you are as intent on keeping me locked up here as they are!'

She was just about to launch the hairbrush when Maria leaped forward and caught her wrist in a vice-like grip as something inside her snapped and her blue eyes flashed fire. She had endured all Isabelle's tantrums, the tears and the accusations, the rantings and the ravings, but now she had had enough.

'I have *never* professed to be your friend,' she ground out. 'I am merely employed as your maid. But that does *not* give you licence to treat me as you wish. Do you *hear* me?' Her face was as red as Isabelle's now as all her fears and frustrations surfaced. 'I have served you as best I could,' she rushed on. 'But I'll tell you now, I will not allow you to throw another single thing at me! You are so spoiled you are utterly unbelievable. What makes you think that you are the only person in the world who is in trouble, eh? Because let me tell you, my fine madam, you are *not*!'

Isabelle's mouth gaped open. All her life she had been pandered to and given everything she demanded. No one had *ever* spoken to her as this girl was doing now. But what could she have meant when she said she was not the only one in trouble? And then suddenly it came to her in a blinding flash as she shook her wrist free.

'*You* are with child too, aren't you?' she choked.

Maria's shoulders suddenly sagged and in that moment Isabelle knew that she had guessed correctly. That would explain Maria's red swollen eyes and her quietness.

'Yes, I am.' Maria knew that it would be useless to lie. Hers was not a condition that could be hidden indefinitely.

Isabelle regarded her steadily but eventually Maria's fighting spirit returned and she told her, 'You can tell Mrs Bradshaw if you wish – I have no doubt you will. I shall be dismissed, of course, but I dare say I shall survive.'

'I shall be telling her nothing,' Isabelle retorted. 'The truth will come out eventually anyway, but until then I should like to keep you with me.'

'You would?' Maria was astounded. She had thought Isabelle hated her but perhaps she had been wrong.

'You intrigue me,' Isabelle said with a shrug. 'I have never known a servant girl like you. Should you be properly dressed, I have no doubt you could be mistaken for gentry. In fact, sometimes you put me to shame.' She grinned ruefully then before confiding, 'I know that I have been spoiled shamelessly, which is probably why I am in this condition now. But *you* . . . you are so very rational, Maria. I would have thought you would have had more sense.'

'We are *all* fools when it comes to love.' Maria's eyes welled with tears as she explained, 'I have had a very strict upbringing and so when I met a lad from the village who showed me some affection, I was swept off my feet. He told me that he loved me and I believed him. I thought that with him I would lead a different sort of life. Then one evening he . . . Well, let's just say that things went a little too far and I soon realised that I was with child. I went to see him to tell him that he was going to be a father but then he ran away to sea. He would have come back though,' she said quickly, 'but then when I went home on Sunday my mother informed me that he had been involved in a brawl at the docks and was stabbed. He is dead,' her voice grew fragile, 'and once my father discovers I am with child he will disown me.' Her eyes filled with tears.

'How awful,' Isabelle exclaimed, forgetting her own troubles for the time being. 'So what will you do now?'

Maria sighed and wiped her eyes. 'I shall have to find another job and somewhere to stay, and then I shall try to work until the baby is born.'

Isabelle felt ashamed. At least her parents were prepared to stand by her, even if they had had her locked away until the confinement was over.

'How far along are you?' she asked now.

'A little over two months.'

'And so am I,' Isabelle answered quickly and the two of them lapsed into silence as they each pondered on their dilemma.

It was Isabelle who broke the silence when she said, 'I think the best thing we could do is keep silent for now. You are so slim it is likely the child will not even be evident for some time. Once it is . . . well, we will cross that bridge when we come to it.'

For the first time, Maria found herself liking Isabelle. Beneath her airs and graces and her hoity-toity ways, she was only a girl like herself, after all.

'If you are quite sure,' she said hesitantly. She had no wish to get Isabelle into trouble.

'I am quite sure. Now come, read some more of *David*

Copperfield to me. We must devise some ways of passing the
time or we shall both end up as mad as some of the lunatics
in here.'

In that instant, a friendship was forged, one that gave
each of them comfort. Their relationship had changed
dramatically, and for the better.

For the rest of that week, Isabelle was far calmer. Each
morning she allowed Maria to help her dress and she even
had a kind word or two for Kitty when she delivered their
food and the logs for the fires to the rooms each day.

Kitty had obviously taken a shine to Maria. After all, she
was the first person to ever go out of her way to talk to her
and she began to linger for as long as she dared whenever
she had an excuse to visit their suite of rooms.

It was one morning when she had carried Maria's
breakfast into her room that she commented, 'It don't seem
fair to me that Miss Isabelle dines off the fat o' the land while
you an' me 'ave to make do wi' lumpy porridge.'

'It's always been that way, Kitty. One rule for the rich and
another for the poor.' Maria grinned as Kitty chewed on her
lip, obviously wanting to say something more but not sure
if she should.

'But what if you weren't really poor?'

Maria sat down at the table to eat her breakfast. The
waistband of her long skirt felt a little tighter than usual but
she was trying not to think of it.

'Whatever do you mean, Kitty?'

'You *are* Maria Mundy, ain't you? The daughter o' the
local preacher?'

'You know I am. What of it?'

Kitty licked her lips before whispering, 'Well, I over'eard
Cook an' Miss Belle talkin' in the kitchen t'other day, an'

Cook were sayin' that Miss Isabelle is Master Montgomery's daughter from Willow Park. An' she also said—'

'*Kitty!* Whatever are you doing loitering about up here? Cook is waiting downstairs for you. Away to your duties at once, girl!'

Kitty almost jumped out of her skin as she glanced around to see Mrs Bradshaw standing in the open doorway of Maria's room.

'Yes, ma'am.' She scuttled away like a cat with its tail on fire and once she had gone Mrs Bradshaw shook her head before saying, 'Oh, that dratted girl. She can be such a trial. But never mind her for now. How is Miss Isabelle? Things certainly seem to have been a little quieter up here for the last few days. And I also notice that you have managed to persuade the young lady to get dressed.'

Maria nodded as she lifted a spoonful of the fast-cooling porridge to her mouth. 'Yes, she has been calmer and she has even allowed me to read a little to her,' she agreed.

The Matron surveyed her thoughtfully, wondering if any of the rumours that were flying around about Maria were true. She had thought from the first second she saw her that this girl was a cut above the rest in the village, and as the days had progressed she had been proven right. The girl's skin was clear, not pock-marked or roughened by outdoor work, and her eyes were bright and intelligent. Her back was straight and she carried herself well, a sign of a reasonable diet no doubt, and her hands, the older woman noted, were soft and white, free of the usual calluses.

Maria, meanwhile, was studying her. She had never really taken much notice of the woman before, but now as she looked more closely at her she imagined that Mrs Bradshaw must have been a very handsome woman in her younger days. Her hair, although greying now, was still sleek and her teeth were excellent, even and white. When she walked she held herself regally and Maria briefly wondered where Mr Bradshaw might be and why the woman had chosen to become Matron in such a place as Hatter's Hall. But then she supposed it was really no business of hers at the end of the day. As she was fast discovering: in this place, everyone had their own story to tell.

Chapter Ten

Joshua placed his knife and fork down, then looked across at his mother and father, who had breakfasted in complete silence.

Since his sister's hasty departure more than a week ago, a pall seemed to have settled over the house. His parents did not appear to have exchanged more than a dozen civil words, and then only when it was absolutely necessary.

'Have you heard from Isabelle about how her friend is yet, Mother?' he asked now, hoping to start a conversation. In truth he did not believe a word of the story his father had fed him. He knew that Isabelle would never have simply taken flight without taking him into her confidence. Something was wrong, he just knew it.

Before Helena could reply, something akin to a growl issued from Charles Montgomery's throat. Pushing his chair back, he stood and strode out of the room with a face as dark as a thundercloud.

Helena's eyes fluttered nervously after him before coming again to focus on her son. 'No, dear, I have received no word from her as yet but I am sure we shall do so in due course.'

'I see.' Joshua frowned. Isabelle was a spoiled little minx. She had always been the bane of his life and yet for all that he had a great affection for his little sister. It was he who had taught her to ride her first pony, spending hours leading her on a guiding rope around the level field adjoining the stable-block, alternately encouraging, or scolding her when she did not do as she was told, which tended to be often. It was he who had taught her to take her first steps in the nursery and he who would sit each night and read fairy stories to her until she fell asleep when she was a child. At one stage she had followed him about like a shadow until he had been close to screaming at her to leave him alone. And yet now that she was gone, it was as if the sunshine had gone out of the house, and without her cheerful chatter about inconsequential subjects that held absolutely no appeal to him, he found that he missed her.

Joshua had always been the total opposite of his sister in nature. He took a great interest in his father's many businesses, especially the ribbon-weaving ones, aware that one day he would inherit them, and he was well liked by all Charles's work staff, for he was not afraid to get his hands dirty and wished to learn everything from the bottom up. Although they did not always see eye to eye, he had a grudging admiration for his father; Charles Montgomery had not been born into the gentry, but was merely an ambitious man who had achieved his current status through sheer hard graft and determination. Now there was scarcely a man, woman or child in the whole of the county or even beyond who had not heard of the name Montgomery – and

Joshua had always striven to be a son of whom Charles might be proud. He felt he owed him that at least.

Now as he glanced again at his mother he saw that she was twisting her fine lawn handkerchief between her fingers, a habit she always adopted when she was nervous; it was as if she had forgotten his presence. Joshua saw from the exquisite French ormolu clock that stood on the mantelpiece that he must leave soon or he would be late at the new ribbon factory his father had recently acquired in Abbey Street in Nuneaton. Old George, the foreman there, was going to give him another lesson on working the looms today. The women who worked them made it look so easy, but Joshua had already discovered that there was great skill to becoming a good weaver.

'Mother.' His voice brought her thoughts back to the present and she smiled at him falteringly. 'Are you quite sure that there is nothing wrong? You have not been yourself at all since Isabelle's departure.'

Her lips worked soundlessly for a time as if she was wrestling with something she wished to tell him, then clearly making a decision she lowered her voice and said, 'There *is* something I need to speak to you about, Joshua. Will you come to me in the drawing room and have coffee with me after dinner this evening when your father has retired to his study for his port and his cigar?'

'Of course I will.' He rose and bent to kiss her cheek, and it struck Helena how handsome he was and what a young gentleman he had become without her even noticing it. Her son was tall and lean, and his hair was a deep brown, with hints of copper running through it that turned to gold in the summer. His eyes, like Isabelle's, were green and they glittered if he was angry, which Joshua often was, for like his father he did not suffer fools gladly. And yet he could also be very kind and patient, traits she liked to think he had inherited from her. His silk patterned waistcoat was immaculate, as were the shirt and cravat that he wore beneath it, and his legs were clad in fine tweed breeches that disappeared into high leather boots. However, Helena knew that this would be due to his manservant, for Joshua had never been a slave to fashion and by the end of the day would no doubt probably be covered in lint from the looms.

She watched him leave with a feeling of regret. She had always planned to have a houseful of children and it had broken her heart after Isabelle's birth when the doctor had sternly told her that any more children could well be the death of her. Her life had changed from that day on, for Charles had taken the doctor's warning to heart. They had been very much in love back then, and Charles had said he would never be able to live with himself if he should lose her in childbirth. And so he had left her bed never to return, and for a while the loneliness had been hard to bear. But then, she consoled herself, she did have two healthy children and so she had poured all her love into them. Now look at the result. Isabelle would soon be a mother herself and Helena would be a grandmother, but she would never even get to hold her first grandchild in her arms. Sighing heavily, she hurried away to check the post just as she had every day since Isabelle's departure, even though she knew that it was far too soon to expect a reply to the letter she had written.

It was Saturday evening and once again Maria was looking forward to seeing her family on the following afternoon. Isabelle's mood had remained calm, although she was still prone to severe bouts of depression, when she would sit and sob. Maria could sympathise with this. There were times when she herself would have loved nothing more than to weep at the injustice of it all. But of course, she knew that it would have been pointless. As she had told Kitty, there was one rule for the rich and one for the poor, and she was just going to have to get on with it.

Kitty had taken away the remains of the evening meal and now Isabelle was sitting with her feet on a small pouffe in front of a roaring fire sipping hot chocolate. Suddenly there was a commotion on the landing outside and the girls stared at each other in dismay.

'Stand aside this instant, woman, or by all that is holy I swear I shall knock you out of the way!'

Recognising her mother's voice, Isabelle banged her chocolate down on the side table so hard that the delicate china cup overturned and the chocolate began to form a pool on the fine carpet.

'*Mama!*' She was out of her chair and across the room in a flash as the door opened inwards, and then Maria saw her fling herself into a woman's outstretched arms as she started to sob.

'Shush, darling. I am here now,' the woman soothed as she stroked the stray curls back from Isabelle's forehead. They stood like this for some time as Maria silently looked on, and then the woman turned to Mrs Bradshaw, who was appearing mightily distressed, and told her: 'Leave us, Matron. I shall ring for you when I am ready to leave.'

'But madam, this is most improper. Your husband expressly instructed us that no one – *no one* – should be allowed to visit Miss Isabelle.'

Mrs Bradshaw's face was so suffused with colour and distress that Maria feared that she was about to burst a blood vessel.

'Your husband is the main b-benefactor of this establishment,' Mrs Bradshaw stammered, 'and should we incur his wrath—'

'Oh, just be quiet and go away!' Helena responded furiously. 'I am not just *any* visitor, I am this poor young girl's *mother*! Now leave us, and believe me, should my husband ever get to hear of this visit, I shall see to it that you never get another penny from our family – or elsewhere!'

'Yes, ma'am.' Mrs Bradshaw bobbed her head and hastily backed out of the room. When she was gone, Helena shook off the hood of her warm cloak and peered closely at her daughter.

Maria meanwhile peered closely at *her*. She had only ever seen Mrs Montgomery briefly as she passed through the village in her carriage on her way into the town, but now she could see how alike she and her daughter were.

'How are you, darling?' the woman asked now.

Isabelle broke into a torrent of weeping. 'Oh, Mama, please don't leave me here any longer,' she implored.

Helena shook her hands up and down gently. 'Now listen closely,' she began, and then as she became aware of Maria she stopped talking abruptly.

'It's all right,' Isabelle assured her. 'You may speak normally in front of Maria. She is my maid and perfectly trustworthy.'

'Oh.' Helena looked mildly concerned but knowing that it would not be wise to linger any longer here than was necessary, she went on, 'I am going to get you out of here, darling.'

'Really?' Isabelle wiped her eyes and took a long, shuddering breath. 'But when? And how?'

'I have written to your Uncle Freddie in Tasmania and told him to expect you. Sadly I can dally no longer waiting for his reply. Of course he will have no idea when you will be arriving, but I know that he will not turn you away!'

'Tasmania!' Isabelle looked dumbfounded.

'Yes. Joshua will accompany you and remain with you until after the child is born. I have already spoken to him about it, and although he hates to let his father down he has agreed to go. Now all I have to do is find a suitable lady's maid to accompany you and a servant to see to Joshua's needs, cleaning his cabin and attending to his laundry and so on. I am afraid it is a rather long journey, but at least you will be safe there once you arrive, and it would be better than having to stay here. I had thought of asking Polly to go with you, but I am afraid it would cause too much gossip amongst the staff.'

'Maria could come with me,' Isabelle said calmly as Maria gawped at her speechlessly. 'And there is another girl here, Kitty, who I fancy would jump at the chance of getting away from this place.'

'Really? And are both of these girls trustworthy?' Helena glanced at Maria apologetically as she asked the question.

'Yes, they are,' Isabelle answered firmly.

'In that case I can go ahead with booking your passages on the ship if they are agreeable to the idea.'

'But won't Felicity mind Joshua going with us? And how long will it take?' Isabelle questioned without waiting for a response from Maria.

Her mother rose and began to pace the floor as she answered. 'Joshua will tell Felicity that he is going abroad on business but not until the day before you leave. We have already discussed it. And I should be able to ensure that you sail by the end of next week. Now this is how we are going to get you out of here; you must have all your things packed for Tuesday evening. Can you do that, my dear?'

She addressed Maria now and when the girl, who was wondering who Felicity was and still reeling from shock, nodded, Helena turned to Isabelle again and went on, 'Your father is in Manchester on business for a couple of nights next week, so if we can get you away on the day he leaves, it will be the perfect opportunity and you will be long gone before he returns.'

'But Mrs Bradshaw will never let you take us out of here.' Isabelle's eyes were wide with fear.

'You just leave Mrs Bradshaw to me!' Helena said forcefully, then pulling the hood of her cloak up she said regretfully, 'I must go now. It would not do for your father to come home and find me missing. Just be brave, my love, and you will be away from here before you know it. And do not mention a word of this until I come for you. It is imperative that Mrs Bradshaw does not find out what we are planning.'

Crossing to the bell, she yanked on it – and the instant Mrs Bradshaw appeared, she left with a last smile for her daughter.

Once the two girls were alone again, Maria looked at Isabelle, aghast. 'I cannot possibly come with you,' she told her.

'Why ever not?' Isabelle challenged as she flounced about, her skirts twirling.

'You know full well why not,' Maria sighed. 'I am with child too, or had you forgotten?'

'No, I had not forgotten, and that is all the more reason why you *should* come. Don't you see? This is the answer to all your prayers. If you come with me, we will be far away before your child is even properly showing. Once we arrive in Tasmania we can tell everyone that you are a widow and no one will know the turth. And it goes without saying that Kitty will jump at the chance of escaping this place.'

Maria stared thoughtfully into the flames that were roaring up the chimney. Isabelle was quite right, of course. But it was such a big step to take – and what about her mother? How would she cope without her support and her wages? And yet she knew deep down that Martha would see this as a resolution to her problem. At least if she was well out of the way her mother would not have to face the shame of having an illegitimate grandchild, and Maria would escape her father's wrath. She had a sneaky feeling that he would like to see her on the other side of the world. For some reason he had never shown her any affection.

'Do you really think Kitty would agree to come with us?' she asked now. Hurrying across to the bell that connected to the kitchen, Isabelle rang it.

'I'm almost sure of it, but there is only one way for us to find out and that is for us to ask her – and there is no time like the present,' Isabelle declared. 'I shall tell her that we need some more logs bringing up for the fire as an excuse to get her up here, and that will give you a chance to speak to her. But do you think we can trust her to hold her tongue? If she should speak to Miss Belle or Mrs Bradshaw, we are done for.'

'I do not think Kitty would betray us,' Maria answered, and they then waited for the sound of the key in the lock at the end of the long corridor.

Kitty appeared some minutes later with a flushed face and her mob cap all askew. Maria was waiting for her on the landing and she wasted no time in putting the idea to the girl.

'Kitty, how would you feel about getting out of this place?'

Kitty stared at her with wide eyes. 'Eeh, miss, whatever are yer talkin' about?'

'As you are probably aware, Miss Isabelle's mother has just paid her an impromptu visit and she is trying to arrange for her to go to stay with her uncle in Tasmania.'

'*Tasmania?*' Kitty gulped as her hand flew to her throat. She had had little or no education but even she knew that this was a long way away. 'But ain't that on t'other side o' the world?'

'Yes, it is, and you and I have the chance to go with Miss Isabelle and her brother.'

'But how would we get there?'

'On a ship, of course. Mrs Montgomery is going to book the passages very soon. Think of it, Kitty! It could be the start of a whole new life for you.'

Kitty still looked uncertain. She had always longed to see the world beyond the walls of Hatter's Hall, but now the chance was being offered to her on a plate the thought of leaving was daunting.

'When would we be going?' she asked now as Maria took her hand and gently rubbed it. It was shaking like a leaf in the wind.

'We would be gone from here by the end of next week. Oh, do *please* consider it, Kitty, and until you have decided, promise me that you will mention this to no one.'

'I promise,' Kitty answered immediately.

'Very well. Now go down and fetch up some more logs, would you, otherwise Mrs Bradshaw will wonder why we rang for you. And remember . . . not a word!'

Kitty scuttled away, her small face creased in wonder at the opportunity that was being offered to her but still not quite able to take it in.

It was the following morning after she had set out the breakfast trays that Kitty drew Maria out into the corridor.

'I've decided,' she told her, wiping her hands nervously down the front of her long calico apron. 'I's a comin' wi' you . . . that's if yer still want me to, that is.'

'Oh, Kitty, I'm so pleased.' Maria hugged her, bringing a flush of pleasure to the girl's cheeks. She had never known affection before. 'Now what you must do is pack your things and be ready to go when Mrs Montgomery comes for us. She will be here by Tuesday at the latest.'

'Huh, that won't take long,' Kitty said caustically. 'I only 'ave what I'm stood up in an' one other change o' clothes.'

Maria gave her a final hug before hurrying away to tell Isabelle the good news. Now it just remained to inform her mother of her plans – a daunting prospect and not something she was looking forward to.

Chapter Eleven

Bunching her skirts into her hands, Maria picked her way across the slushy puddles. There had been a thaw during the night although it was still bitterly cold, and everywhere looked wet and miserable just as she felt. Her precious wages were tucked deep into the pocket of her dress, and this week Maria was determined that her mother should have every penny of them. It was the last that Maria would be able to give her, for the foreseeable future at least, and although she had grown used to the idea of the adventure she was about to embark on, she still dreaded the thought of leaving her family behind.

The walk to the cottage seemed to take twice as long as it normally did, for the ground underfoot was slippery and treacherous, but at last it came into sight, a thin plume of smoke rising from its chimney.

'Hello, pet.' Martha was sitting with a pile of mending when Maria entered the kitchen but she immediately

117

stopped what she doing and hurried across to kiss her daughter firmly on the cheek. Emma was clinging to her big sister's skirts by now, her face upturned and beaming, and Maria felt a stab of regret. She would miss them all so much.

'Hello, Ria.' Henry had been stacking the fallen logs he had carried from the nearby wood at the side of the hearth, but he too straightened up to greet her. A quick glance around assured Maria that her father was not there and she was relieved. It would not hurt her to leave without saying goodbye to him.

Soon she was seated at the side of the fire with a steaming mug of tea in her hand and a scone to go with it. The four of them chatted quietly, simply glad to be together again, and when Maria had finished her tea, she asked timidly, 'Could we go into the front parlour, Mother? I have something I need to talk to you about.'

Looking vaguely surprised, Martha nodded. It was cold in there as there was no fire lit and she knew that Maria would not want to linger in it for long.

As Maria entered what her mother had always referred to as her 'best room' her eyes flicked about. Here, Martha kept her best pieces, few as they were. There was a large aspidistra plant balanced in a big pot on a wooden stand, and dainty crocheted arm-covers that her mother had spent long hours making on the two mismatched overstuffed armchairs. A small number of chipped plaster ornaments that her mother had won on a stall one year at the Coventry Pot Fair stood on a table, and a gaily coloured peg rug had pride of place in front of the fireplace. It was pitifully little to show for all the years of hard work the woman had spent bringing up her family, but she expected no more.

'I have something to tell you,' Maria told her when the door was closed. There was no point in beating about the bush. 'I . . . I have been given the opportunity to travel to Tasmania to act as Miss Isabelle's maid – and – and I have accepted it.'

Martha's face paled as her hand flew to her mouth and she dropped heavily onto the nearest chair.

'We will be going to stay with Miss Isabelle's uncle until her confinement is over . . . and mine,' Maria ended lamely. Seeing her mother's stricken expression she placed an arm about her shoulders. 'Don't you see? It's better this way,' she said gently. 'I cannot hide my condition for much longer and this could be a whole new start for me.'

'I . . . I don't want you to go,' Martha sobbed, bereft at the thought of losing this child who meant so much to her.

'I don't want to go either,' Maria said with a catch in her voice. 'But what will happen once Father learns about the baby? He will turn me out onto the streets or put me in the workhouse – and we all know that once I go in there, I may never come out.'

'Will you ever come back?' Martha eventually asked in a small voice. She knew that Maria was speaking the truth, and although she felt as if her heart was being torn out of her, she couldn't bear to think of her daughter suffering either of those fates.

'I don't know yet,' Maria sighed, then suddenly remembering the money in her pocket, she quickly withdrew it and pressed it into her mother's hand.

She had expected Martha to continue to object; to tell her that she was not allowed to go, but surprisingly the woman conceded: 'It is better this way, as you say. You will have a brand new start there. But how will you manage when the child comes?'

'Miss Isabelle is fully aware of my condition and she has assured me that she will help me. But no one must know that we are going. Mrs Montgomery is coming to fetch us some time on Tuesday whilst her husband is away on business in Manchester. It was Isabelle's father who placed her in Hatter's Hall, you see, and should he find out he would not allow her to go.'

So the rumours that had been flying about the village were true then, Martha thought. People were whispering that the Montgomery girl had gone and got herself into trouble. But who would ever have thought that her daughter would be acting as lady's maid to the likes of the Montgomerys? They were the closest thing to gentry in the whole of the county, and not people to be trifled with – as many of the locals had found to their cost. Charles Montgomery owned over half of all the businesses in the town, and many a man had been given his marching orders for going against his wishes.

She rose and hugged her daughter, and they went back to the others and for the rest of the afternoon they treasured each moment, knowing that they might well be the last they would ever spend together. All too soon the afternoon began to draw in and Maria knew that it was time to go. She hugged and kissed Emma till the child squirmed in her arms. Henry had gone out some time before so now it only remained to say her goodbyes to her mother.

There were tears in their eyes and Maria was shaking as they clung together at the door but then Martha nudged her gently away. 'Go on, pet,' she urged. 'And try to write to me when you are settled.' Already she could guess at the gossip that would do the rounds when a letter all the way from Tasmania and addressed to her arrived at the post office.

Maria staggered away on feet that felt like lead, blinded by tears and glad of the warm cape that Mrs Bradshaw had once again kindly allowed her to wear. At least the hood would shield her upset from prying eyes.

Once she had left the little straggle of cottages behind, she paused to wipe her streaming cheeks and blow her nose before walking on. There was no going back now.

By the time Tuesday morning dawned both Kitty and Isabelle were all of a dither, but Maria was remarkably calm. She had prayed for a solution to her problem and this was the one the Good Lord had sent her. Isabelle's trunks were packed, along with an overnight valise containing essentials that would tide her over until they reached the ship. Kitty's few paltry things were all ready to go too, and Maria's were tied into a neat bundle hidden beneath her bed. If Mrs Bradshaw should enter their rooms before Mrs Montgomery arrived, Maria had ensured that she would see nothing that could give rise to suspicion.

The day passed ominously slowly with Isabelle constantly at the window peering off down the drive. Neither she nor Maria had been able to eat a single thing, and by two o'clock in the afternoon Isabelle was pacing frantically.

She had dressed in her warmest gown, a full crinoline over numerous petticoats made of the finest wool that money could buy, and Maria had also selected a thick silk-lined cloak for her to wear over it.

'Oh, I'm sure something has gone wrong!' Isabelle wailed, wringing her hands in frustration. 'Mama should surely have been here by now!'

Maria had already heard the same words at least a dozen times during the course of the day and now she had given up trying to reassure her. It was then that the sound of horses' hooves could be heard approaching on the drive outside and Isabelle dashed to the window again, her face ecstatic. 'She's here at last!' Her joyous shout echoed around the room and now Maria raced across to join her and peer over her shoulder. A fine coach and four perfectly matched black horses had drawn up outside the entrance, but although the girls craned their necks they could not see anyone get out. Holding their breath, they waited – and sure enough, minutes later they heard the click of the key in the lock of the landing door and raised voices.

'This is really *most* irregular!' Mrs Bradshaw screeched. And then the door was opened and Isabelle rushed into her mother's arms.

'Have you packed your things?' Helena asked, her face grim.

Isabelle nodded and snatched up her cloak as Mrs Bradshaw's face turned an alarming shade of purple.

'I . . . I *really* cannot allow you to take Miss Isabelle, madam,' she blustered. 'Your husband left her here in my safekeeping, with the express instruction that she was not even to be allowed out into the gardens.'

'Yes, well, there has been a change of plan,' Helena said coolly. 'And now I am taking my daughter back into *my* safekeeping. But don't be concerned, Matron. I shall make absolutely sure that Charles knows this was none of your doing, and you will not be out of pocket, I assure you. And now, I wish to see Miss er . . . Kitty, I believe her name is.'

'Kitty has no other name,' Mrs Bradshaw said repressively. 'Her mother was a pauper found outside the gates just over sixteen years ago. She was heavily pregnant at the time and we gave her shelter, but she died shortly afterwards giving birth. Kitty was the result and I have cared for the girl ever since. But why would you wish to see *her*?'

Helena could just imagine the sort of 'care' the poor girl must have received. She had probably been worked almost to death, and beaten if she so much as put one foot wrong.

'Because I intend to take her, and also Miss Mundy, out of here too,' Helena informed the Matron imperiously.

'I could ring for her,' Maria suggested, knowing that Kitty would be on the alert. Helena nodded then turned back to Mrs Bradshaw, who was clutching at her heart.

'B-but this is *preposterous*,' she stuttered. Kitty was one of her hardest workers. She had never asked for anything – nor been given anything, if it came to that – except for food and shelter.

Seconds later, light footsteps sounded in the corridor and Kitty appeared, clutching a small bundle, her cheeks flushed and excited. She shuffled from foot to foot, still not quite believing that a new life was about to begin.

A man followed her into the room now and Helena told him, 'Hoskins, kindly take these trunks and the young ladies down to the carriage for me.'

'Yes, ma'am.' He hoisted the first of Miss Isabelle's trunks up onto his shoulder as if it weighed no more than a feather then left the room with Maria and Kitty trailing after him, keeping a fearful eye on Mrs Bradshaw who looked as if she was about to explode with rage. As Kitty went to pass her, Mrs Bradshaw made a lunge for her arm but racing across to the woman, Helena smacked it away.

'Let the child go,' she ordered, her eyes flashing blue fire. 'You have no right to keep her here if she wishes to leave. She is not a prisoner or a lunatic.'

Mrs Bradshaw looked on helplessly as Kitty scuttled away.

'You *wicked*, ungrateful girl,' she hurled at her receding figure. 'Is this all the thanks I am to get after all the years I have nurtured you?'

Helena snorted. If Kitty had been 'nurtured', she dreaded to think what state the unfortunates who were locked away here were in. The poor little soul looked as if one good puff of wind would blow her away. And the girl was so pale she resembled a corpse! She stood there glowering at Mrs Bradshaw until Hoskins had carried all the luggage down, then sweeping towards the door in a rustle of silk she said to the Matron, 'Good day to you. My husband will be in touch shortly to settle whatever we owe you.' And with that she followed Hoskins without another word, leaving Mrs Bradshaw in a state of shock and bristling with indignation.

Helena found the girls waiting in the carriage for her, Isabelle on one side and Maria and Kitty on the other. Kitty's face was streaked with tears and she was crying bitterly, as she nestled deeper into Maria's arms

'Do you not wish to come, my dear?' Helena asked her kindly. 'And do you not have a shawl? You are shivering.'

Kitty sniffed in a most unladylike manner as she wiped the tears from the end of her nose with the back of her hand.

'I ain't got a shawl, missus,' she said. 'An' I ain't cryin' 'cos I don't wanna go. I'm cryin' 'cos I do, if yer get what I mean?'

'I think I do,' Helena said softly before leaning from the window as she shouted, 'Drive on, Hoskins.'

The carriage began to lurch slightly as it pulled away and Kitty clung on to Maria for dear life, terrified that something might still happen to prevent her leaving. But soon the old watchman had let them through the gates and as Kitty stared from the window, her eyes grew almost as large as saucers. Her whole life had taken place within the confines of Hatter's Hall and the world was far bigger than she could ever have imagined. The fields seemed to go on forever and she gazed in amazement at the cottages they passed. Everything was new and exciting, and yet she felt fearful too; very small and insignificant. What would become of her now if things should go wrong? Her whole life had been bound by strict routine but now there could be no going back, and she realised in that moment that her life as she had known it was about to change forever. Her eyes stretched wider as they passed the parish church and she gasped in awe at the stained-glass windows sparkling in the frosty air. She felt like a blind person whose sight has been miraculously restored to them, and in her heart she knew that she had made the right decision.

'So what will happen now, Mama?' Isabelle looked so relieved that her mother could not help but smile.

'You will travel by train to Liverpool and board the ship on Thursday evening; it will sail at noon on Friday. I have managed to secure all your passages. Isabelle, you will have a double cabin that you will share with Miss Mundy. Joshua will have a single cabin and Kitty, as a general maid, will be in the single women's quarters.'

'W-will I ever be able to come back to England?' Kitty dared to ask and Helena immediately reassured her.

'When Miss Isabelle eventually returns home you may accompany her if you wish – and the same applies to Miss Mundy.'

'Where is Joshua?' Isabelle asked now, suddenly noticing his absence.

'He will be waiting for you at the station in Liverpool. I have booked you all into a hotel for tomorrow night, do not fear. Everything is arranged. You will even have time to do a little shopping for appropriate clothes.' She glanced at Kitty as she spoke. The poor little mite would certainly need something more substantial than the threadbare rags she was wearing now before they set sail, and she had supplied Joshua with adequate funds to ensure that she got them.

Kitty was reeling from everything she had been told. A

boat. A train. And full steam ahead for a pauper girl who had never even left the confines of Hatter's Hall! It was a lot to take in.

'Which ship shall we be sailing on, Mama?' Isabelle asked now, as if sailing to the other side of the world was an everyday occurrence.

'You will be on the *Northern Lights* sailing to Melbourne, Australia,' Helena responded. 'But I should warn you it is not luxury accommodation. The better cabins had all been taken. It was the best I could do at such short notice, but I'm sure you will manage.'

The carriage was rattling down Nursery Hill now, the horses' tails flying out behind them and their breath hanging on the air like fine lace. Maria glanced silently from the window as the familiar landmarks flashed past, aware that she might never see them again, and she ached for a final sight of her mother as the enormity of the journey she was about to embark on came home to her. They passed through Chapel End and down Tuttle Hill then through Abbey Green, and soon the carriage drew to a halt outside the railway station. Maria had seen the outside of the station often when she came to the market in Nuneaton town centre, but she had never set foot inside before and had no idea what to expect.

It was then that Isabelle glanced at Maria before telling her mother, 'Mama, I feel it is only right that you should know before we leave that Maria is carrying a child too.'

'I see.' Shock registered on Helena's face for the briefest time before the woman responded, 'Well, there is nothing we can do about it now, but I will write to your uncle again and explain so that he understands the situation.'

Helena's heart raced as she tried to digest this latest piece of news. The girls were both so young and she had been relying on Maria to care for her daughter – but how would she be able to do that if she was to have a child too?

Hoskins jumped down from the carriage and after finding a porter he instructed him to have all Miss Isabelle's luggage placed into the guard's van at the back of the train for safekeeping. He then helped the ladies down, dreading what the master would say when he learned of his part in their escape. But then he could hardly have refused his mistress's orders, could he? Helena ushered them all through the ticket office and onto the platform.

'I'm afraid your train does not depart until a little later,' she apologised. 'But I think you will be safe here in the Ladies' Waiting Room, away from prying eyes. And there is a cosy fire in here, too. I have booked a sleeping compartment for Isabelle but unfortunately it was the last one available so you two will have to travel in a third-class compartment.'

'That's quite all right,' Maria assured her. 'We shall be fine, won't we, Kitty?'

The girl nodded, her tearful eyes looking far too big for her small, pinched face.

'Right then. I suggest we go and find ourselves a nice warm cup of tea.' Helena led them along the platform to a small tea room and soon they had a large pot of tea in front of them and some slices of rich fruitcake.

'Do tuck in,' she advised. 'You may not be able to get food on the train in third class, and this may well be all you have until you get into Liverpool Lime Street early tomorrow morning.'

The cake did look delicious but both Maria and Kitty were so nervous that neither of them could eat a thing. Eventually Helena shook out a clean white handkerchief and wrapped the cake in it for them, urging Maria to put it in her pocket. 'Just in case you get peckish later on,' she explained.

The afternoon wore slowly on, but at last Helena led them out of the warmth of the Ladies' Waiting Room onto the platform again. An icy wind was whipping along it and the girls shuddered. But thankfully a train rumbled into sight, belching smoke, and Kitty sank into Maria's side again, frightened half out of her wits. It looked like some sort of iron monster racing towards them and she had no idea how she was going to force herself to climb aboard it. But with Maria's support and encouragement, she managed it. Soon they were standing in a small passageway as Isabelle leaned out of the window and clung to her mother with tears pouring down her cheeks.

'You are going to be in such dreadful trouble with Papa,' she sobbed.

Helena smiled bravely although she felt as if her heart was being wrenched out of her chest. 'Don't you get worrying about that, my love. By the time he even realises you have left Hatter's Hall you will have set sail and there will be nothing he can do about it. Just take care of yourself and write to me as soon as you can, to let me know that you are safe.'

A guard was walking along the length of the train now, slamming doors, and the two women kissed each other hurriedly as he blew a shrill whistle and waved his green flag.

'Goodbye, darling, and good luck.' Helena stood back as the train chugged into life, the tears she could no longer hold back streaming from her eyes, and then with a blast of smoke from the engine it was pulling away and the three girls hung out of the window as best they could and waved until Helena was swallowed up by the fast-darkening afternoon. A guard approached them, and after looking at the tickets that Helena had pressed into Isabelle's hand, he first led Maria and Kitty to their third-class compartment before taking Isabelle along to the sleepers' section of the train. The two girls sat down on hard wooden bench seats in a compartment that was full of men and women all dressed in their working clothes, then Kitty held on to Maria for dear life as the first leg of their journey began. They were on their way.

Chapter Twelve

They alighted from the train early the next morning. Isabelle looked refreshed, but in third class the hard seats and the overpowering smell of unwashed bodies had ensured that Maria and Kitty had only been able to doze for a few moments at a time. Now their eyes were red and gritty from lack of sleep and they looked totally exhausted. Even so, within minutes of stepping from the train their eyes were stretched wide.

Liverpool Lime Street station was nothing at all like the small Trent Valley railway station in their home town. It was positively enormous! Vast glass and iron roofs loomed above them, where smoke from the trains rose to form ethereal twisting shapes. Finely dressed men and women hurried past them – ladies in coloured crinolines and fine bonnets, resembling multi-coloured butterflies, on the arms of top-hatted gentlemen. Seats were arranged the whole length of the platform along one wall, and after instructing a porter to fetch her luggage, Isabelle urged them to sit down and wait with her until Joshua arrived. In her pretty silk skirts she blended in well, but Kitty and Maria felt distinctly out of place although luckily no one appeared to be giving them so much as a second look. Sometime in the early hours of the morning, the two girls had shared the fruitcake Helena had wrapped for them but now their stomachs were growling ominously and they just longed to lie down.

The luggage was delivered in due course and then Isabelle began to pace distractedly up and down.

'Where *is* that brother of mine?' she groaned.

And then suddenly a young gentleman walking in their direction caught her eye and with a whoop of joy she raced towards him and flung her arms around his neck.

'So here you are at last,' Kitty and Maria heard her say, and then tucking her arm into his she marched him towards her companions, who rose to greet him.

'Joshua, this is Kitty. She will be our general maid during the voyage.'

'Pleased to meet you, Kitty.' Joshua took her hand, causing Kitty to blush to the very roots of her hair as he bowed over it.

'And this is Maria, who is my lady's maid.'

Joshua now turned to Maria, and as their eyes met and locked, the most curious thing happened, for suddenly everything around them faded into the background and there was only each other.

'Maria,' he said courteously. She was easily the most beautiful girl he had ever seen and for one of the rare occasions in his life Joshua was speechless.

Maria meanwhile was thinking what a handsome young man he was. His eyes were the colour of green leaves and kindly, and his smile seemed able to light up the drab surroundings of the station. He was holding her hand and his touch was burning her, whilst a thousand butterflies had begun to flutter in her stomach. No man had ever affected her this way before, not even Lennie, and suddenly she was feeling very shy.

'Come along, you two. We shall miss breakfast at the hotel if you dawdle for much longer.'

Isabelle's voice pulled them both sharply back to the present and Joshua suddenly dropped Maria's hand as if it had scalded him.

'Right then. Let's get the porter to bring this lot outside and find us a cab, shall we?'

Avoiding Maria's eyes he allowed Isabelle to take his arm and with Kitty, Maria and the porter following with all their luggage on a long trolley, he led them from the station.

The girls' eyes were out on stalks as they entered the busy streets of Liverpool. Horse-drawn cabs and crowds of people jostling each other were everywhere they looked, and they were sure that they had never seen so many people all in one place before. If it came to that, they had not even realised there *were* so many people in the world. It was all so very different from the little market town they had left behind.

'We're staying at the Angel Hotel tonight,' Joshua informed them. 'And I think you will find it very comfortable. I'm sure you must all be tired after the train journey, so I suggest when we arrive there, you can order some breakfast and then go and rest for a while. Then later on, if you feel up to it, I can take you all shopping to purchase suitable clothes for the voyage. Mother has supplied me with the funds for this purpose, and no one is to be left out.'

He held up his hand and a horse-drawn cab pulled up at the side of them almost immediately. The porter unloaded the trunks and helped the cabbie to secure them with ropes, and Joshua tipped him generously. He then helped his sister inside. Kitty hastily followed, as did Maria, who avoided his touch. She was still in a tizzy after their meeting. The cab was something of a disappointment, as there was stale straw on the floor and the windows were draughty, but the passengers barely noticed as they peered out at the teeming streets with interest. The horses clip-clopped along the cobblestones, weaving this way and that through the traffic until eventually they drew to a halt in front of a very smart-looking hotel.

Joshua disappeared inside to fetch yet another porter to deal with the luggage, and whilst he was gone Kitty leaned against Maria and whispered fretfully, 'Eeh, I can never go into a place like that dressed this way. They'll chuck me out on me arse!' Suddenly remembering Miss Isabelle who was sitting opposite, she clapped her hand across her mouth but Isabelle chuckled.

'I can promise you they won't if you are with me,' she assured her imperiously.

Minutes later, Joshua returned and whilst the luggage was unloaded he paid the driver who tipped his cap courteously.

'Eeh by gum!' The luxurious foyer had Kitty dumb-founded. She had never seen anything like it in her entire life, nor ever thought to; neither had Maria, if it came to that.

They stood there admiring the glittering chandeliers and the thick carpets on the floor whilst Joshua went to the desk to collect their keys. A hotel porter took them up a splendid staircase that led to a galleried landing.

'We're all on the first floor,' Joshua told the girls. 'And I took the liberty of ordering a late breakfast to be sent to your rooms. I hope that is all right? I thought you might be more comfortable that way rather than going down to the dining room.'

The two girls nodded, too tongue-tied to speak, and when the porter unlocked the door to Isabelle's room, they had a quick peek at the panoramic view of the city from her window.

'We shall all meet down in the foyer at one o'clock after we have had a rest,' Isabelle told them. She beamed. 'And then we shall go shopping.'

The two girls nodded in unison as Joshua strode with them further along the corridor. 'I thought you two might be happier sharing,' he said gently. 'So I booked you a twin room.'

'Oo er!' Kitty gulped as she stared at the two neatly made beds and the silken counterpanes. ''Tis fit fer the good Queen herself.'

'I'm glad you approve,' Joshua said with a friendly smile. Then with a little bow he left them, to go with the porter to his own room. Suddenly forgetting how tired she was, Kitty raced around touching and stroking everything in sight.

'Ain't Mr Joshua just the 'andsomest chap you ever saw?' she breathed dreamily. 'An' so kind an' all! Yer'd never believe he were a gent, would yer?' Then with her eyes sparkling mischievously she added, 'An' I reckon he's right taken wi' you even if he does have a lady friend back home! Felicity, her name is if I remember rightly. I heard Mrs Bradshaw talkin' about him once in the kitchen at Hatter's Hall. But did yer see the way he looked at yer when yer were introduced?'

'Don't be so silly, Kitty,' Maria said more sharply than she had meant to.

Kitty's face dropped a mile and, instantly contrite, Maria caught her hand. 'Sorry,' she apologised. 'I think I'm more tired than I realised. But you mustn't say things like that. Mr Joshua and I are poles apart. He would never look kindly on a servant, and if what you heard is correct he probably has a fiancée already.'

She was feeling utterly confused. Only the day before, she had been grieving for Lennie, and now here she was feeling drawn to Isabelle's brother who was a gentleman. It was quite ridiculous.

Never one to bear a grudge, Kitty clambered up onto one of the beds and let out a sigh. 'I reckon these are feather mattresses.' But she had time to say no more, for at that moment there was a tap at the door and a maid appeared pushing a trolley.

'Your breakfast, madams.' She looked down her nose at their shabby apparel. 'Do please ring if there is anything else you require,' she said haughtily then she flounced from the room wondering what the world was coming to, to allow two such people to stay in a place like this. The Angel was one of the best establishments in the whole of Liverpool, so what the hell were those two common street girls, who probably congregated on the corners each evening, doing there? Sticking her nose in the air she hurried about her business.

Kitty meanwhile had hopped off the bed and lifted the lid of a silver salver to find a sturdy breakfast staring her in the face, and enough for at least four people into the bargain.

'Cor, would yer just come an' look at this,' she gasped in awe as her mouth watered. It was a world away from the lumpy porridge she was used to back at the Hall. 'There's sausages, bacon, mushrooms, eggs, kidneys an' all manner of treats here, Maria. I reckon I must have died an' gone to heaven!'

Maria chuckled as she lifted a plate and began to help herself to some of the food. It certainly did look delicious and she was determined to do it justice. There was little left on the trolley by the time they had both finished, and with their bellies full and in a slightly happier frame of mind, they climbed onto their beds to take a short rest and within minutes were both fast asleep.

Just before one o'clock as arranged, Maria and Kitty made their way down to the foyer to meet Isabelle and Joshua. They had washed and tidied themselves as best they could but in their drab clothes they still stuck out like sore thumbs and attracted more than a few curious stares as they found some seats in a corner and tried to look inconspicuous. Thankfully Isabelle and Joshua joined them within minutes and Maria was amazed at the change in her mistress. Now that she was away from Hatter's Hall she was all smiles, with no sign of the volatile young woman she had been forced to wait on.

'Ah, here you both are.' Her cheeks dimpled as she beamed at them. 'Let's go shopping then. There is not a minute to waste.' Turning to her brother, she said, 'Would you ask the page to whistle up a cab for us, Josh?'

'Of course.'

In no time at all they were heading for the city centre and Maria was shocked at how big it was. There were surely more shops in one street here than there were in the whole of Nuneaton.

Once Joshua had paid the driver, he went off to smoke a cigar in a nearby establishment, and to read *The Times*, while his sister steered the two young women towards a large emporium.

Kitty stared disbelievingly at the beautiful gowns displayed in its window.

'I think we shall see to you two first,' Isabelle declared. 'You will need some warm clothes for the journey, and of course a good thick cloak each. And also some lighter apparel for when we get there. Josh says Tasmania can get as hot as an oven in the summer. He still has the clothes he wore last time.'

Within an hour, both girls were the proud new owners of two good quality gowns and a warm cloak each.

Kitty was beside herself with excitement by then and could hardly wait to get back to the hotel to try them on. For her, Isabelle had selected two gowns in a pearl grey, that would suit the general maid of a lady. They may have been a similar colour to Maria's uniform at Hatter's Hall, but there the similarity ended. The cut and finish were far more luxurious. Her cloak was a darker grey with a hood and a fine wool lining, and Isabelle had also insisted that she should have some sensible lace-up boots, the first that Kitty had ever owned, as well as some warm undergarments and nightclothes. The items were all packed into enormous boxes, which Isabelle arranged to be delivered to the Angel Hotel later in the day. Maria's gowns were slightly more elaborate as befitted a lady's maid, in a pretty shade of blue with full skirts and tiny pearl buttons all up the front, and neat velvet collars. Her cloak was a richer shade of blue that enhanced the colour of her eyes, and like Kitty, Maria was delighted with the purchases. Neither of the girls had ever been in such a fine shop before and they followed their mistress about in a state of wonder.

Isabelle bought surprisingly little for herself, apart from a new bonnet that she declared she really could not resist. She already had trunks full of clothes back at the hotel, but Maria did whisper at one stage that it might be a good idea to buy a couple of gowns in a larger size? Isabelle's eyes darkened momentarily, but then seeing the sense in what Maria said, she reluctantly obliged, hating the thought of how she might look by the time she was forced to wear them. They then shopped for some lengths of a lighter material which Maria informed her mistress she could make into dresses for herself and Kitty. Of course, by the time they reached Australia, she would be needing looser gowns herself.

When eventually they had all they needed they sent for Joshua, who settled the substantial bill. The afternoon was darkening and he suggested, 'Perhaps we should go back to the hotel now and have a meal? Then we can all get a good night's sleep before we board the ship tomorrow.'

Maria kept her head down and left Isabelle to answer. For some reason she felt tongue-tied in his presence and yet she found herself continually glancing towards him from the corner of her eye. He had shown such patience during the course of the afternoon that she was amazed. Not many men would have been as helpful and understanding as he had, and yet he had made no single word of complaint. He really did seem like a genuinely kind young man.

By the time they arrived back at the hotel their purchases had been delivered to their rooms, and Kitty wasted no time in getting into her new clothes, twirling in front of the cheval mirror and whooping with delight at the sight of herself.

'Eeh, I feel like a toff!' she chuckled.

Maria smiled indulgently. There was something very naïve and innocent about the girl that made her feel protective towards her.

'And you look wonderful too,' she assured Kitty. 'But now you should get changed back into your old things again and keep those clean for tomorrow. Our meal is being brought to the room soon and you don't want to spill anything down it.'

When Kitty's eyes suddenly welled with tears, Maria was alarmed. 'Whatever is the matter?' she asked.

Kitty sniffed before replying, 'It's just everythin', Maria. I mean, stayin' in a place like this an' all me new clothes . . .

But most of all it's you. Yer see, nobody's ever been kind to me afore an' it's takin' some gettin' used to. I keep expectin' Mrs Bradshaw to appear an' whisk me off back to Hatter's Hall again, or to wake up to find all this has been just a lovely dream.'

Maria hugged the girl compassionately. She had thought her own life had been hard, but compared to Kitty's, it had been idyllic. At least she had had a mother who loved her. Kitty had never had anyone.

'Everything is going to be just fine for you from now on,' she said comfortingly. 'Now come on, let's get you changed before our dinner comes. I'm starving, aren't you?'

Much later, as they lay in the comfortable featherbeds before drifting off to sleep, Maria heard Kitty sigh with contentment. The long train journey and the shopping trip had caught up with them now, but Maria lay awake long after Kitty's gentle snores were echoing about the room. This would be her last night on English soil. This time tomorrow they would be aboard the ship, waiting for it to sail to foreign lands.

She thought of her family and a pang of loneliness, sharp as a knife, sliced through her. Then she thought of the child that was growing within her and tears pricked at her eyes. Suddenly she was able to see with crystal clarity what she had felt for Lennie for what it really was. A silly infatuation. To him she had been just another conquest, and much as it hurt to admit it, she knew now that he would never have come back for her. She had allowed herself to be seduced by his handsome face and his sweet-talking tongue, but the worst of it was she had no one to blame but herself. After all, she had encouraged his advances – before they had got out of hand, that was. And now she would be branded forever as a loose woman once the child was born, unless she went along with Miss Isabelle's suggestion and told everyone that she was a young widow. Even then, if she were able to do it, she could lie to everyone else – but *she* would know the truth.

Berating herself for a fool, she finally fell asleep with tears on her cheeks and the image of Master Josh's handsome face swimming behind her eyes.

First thing next morning, two small valises, which Joshua had thoughtfully provided, were delivered to their room. Kitty and Maria hastily packed them with their belongings. They were served with breakfast and then they waited in a fever of excitement and trepidation for the summons from their mistress.

When it came, Kitty left the room and swept down the stairs with her head held high for the first time in her young life. In her smart new gown and cloak, and her good quality buttoned boots, she felt equal to anyone – and Maria could not help but smile as she watched her. The night before, Kitty had had a proper bath, also for the first time in her life, and Maria had washed her hair for her and brushed it until it gleamed. Now she looked like a different person and was acting like one too.

Joshua was waiting for them in the foyer to inform them that Isabelle was already in a cab outside. Colour flamed into Maria's cheeks at the sight of him and she wondered how she was going to bear almost four months aboard ship in such close proximity.

She followed him sedately out to the cab where Isabelle was already seated, her face decorated with a severe frown. Maria could sense that now that their departure was imminent, the young woman suddenly wasn't so sure that she wanted to go. But then what other option was open to either of them? Surely anywhere was better than being confined in Hatter's Hall for months to come. Isabelle had made no secret of the fact that she already hated her unborn child, and Maria was secretly relieved that it would be fostered out to someone who wanted it and would take good care of it.

Soon the cab was darting through the streets, weaving in and out of the traffic at an alarming rate. Every now and again, Maria closed her eyes and clung to the edge of her seat, certain that they were going to collide with something, but at last they reached the docks without incident.

Whilst Joshua got a burly seaman to unload their luggage, the three women stared about them: the whole place was a hive of activity. Ahead of them towered the *Northern Lights* and Maria gulped nervously. On the way Isabelle had told her that the ship would be carrying over four hundred people, and although it – no, one had to call a vessel *she* – although she was huge, the girl wondered how they would all fit onto her. A gangplank stretched from the ship down to the dock, and sailors ran up and down it, carrying a variety of things onto the deck. Piles of luggage were scattered everywhere as well as barrels and huge tubs that appeared to be full of salted meat. There was even livestock being led aboard. Matelots of all nationalities thronged about them – black men, Chinese men, Arabic men – and Kitty grasped Maria's hand nervously. There were also women in low-cut tops with painted faces brazenly strolling amongst them, and deeply embarrassed, the girls averted their eyes.

'We shall need to see the Medical Officer before we are allowed to board,' Joshua told them as he guided them through the teeming crowds. Maria shuddered as she saw a rat that was easily as big as a cat scamper amongst the cabin trunks, but she wisely did not comment on it. Kitty was nervous enough as it was. They found the Medical Officer in what could only be described as a shed, and although he barely looked at Joshua and Isabelle, he poked and prodded Maria and Kitty and listened to their chests, causing them to flush with humiliation. Eventually he gave them permission to board, and as they struggled past the queue of passengers who were waiting to see him, Kitty said indignantly, 'What were all that about?' She was not used to being manhandled in that intimate way by a strange male.

'They have to ensure that everyone travelling is reasonably healthy, otherwise a serious illness could be carried aboard, and in such confined spaces it would sweep through the ship like wildfire,' Joshua explained patiently, overhearing her complaint.

At last they reached the end of the gangway, which was swarming with people going aboard now, and Kitty's stomach churned as she caught her first ever glimpse of the sea. Black and stormy, it was slapping viciously against the side of the dock, and all manner of debris was floating on it. It was nothing at all like the serene blue waters and golden sandy beaches she had glimpsed in the books that some of the richer inmates at Hatter's Hall occasionally left behind . . . but she had no time to ponder on it for Joshua was urging them upwards now, and Kitty clutched at the ropes at the sides of the gangplank for dear life.

After what seemed like an eternity they reached the deck and crossed to the rails to catch their breath. It looked a very long way down to the docks now and Kitty's nervousness increased. Passengers standing by them were hanging over the rails shouting to people below who waved frantically back. Some of them were much more poorly dressed than they were and Kitty guessed that these must be the people who were going to Australia hoping to make their fortune. But the moment had passed for second thoughts. Joshua was keen to see everyone to their cabins and he hailed a steward.

The man, who appeared to be almost as far around as he was high, checked the tickets that Joshua handed over, then with a little bow in Isabelle's direction he asked them to follow him. 'You and the young lady are cabin passengers, sir,' he told Joshua. 'They are along this way.'

They followed him down a steep wooden staircase and along a narrow corridor until eventually he stopped in front of a door and motioned Isabelle, with Maria close on her heels, inside.

'Goodness me, it is very tiny. How are we supposed to manage in here?' Isabelle groaned. Right next door to their cabin was a small water closet and this too had her wrinkling her nose in distaste. Another door from Isabelle's room led into the maid's quarters and this proved to be tinier still with nothing but a small cot bed attached to the wall and room for one trunk on the floor at the very most.

Next, the steward led Joshua to a single cabin just along the corridor and then, turning to Kitty, who was visibly trembling by now, he told her, 'You'll be down in steerage, m'dear, with the single females.'

He led her on to another set of steep wooden stairs and pointed down them. 'This 'ere is the companionway,' he informed her. 'An' down there is the single women's quarters.' He then turned and walked off, leaving Kitty to find her own way.

It looked very dark down there but knowing she had no choice, Kitty slowly and carefully began to descend. When she eventually entered the women's quarters she gazed about in shocked disbelief. There were two rows of bunks along either wall and already women of various shapes and sizes were lounging about on them. The floor was cluttered with their luggage and already the smell of stale sweat and unwashed bodies hung on the air. All down the centre of the room was a table with benches either side of it which were all firmly nailed to the floor, but other than that the place was bare. Not even a port-hole that might admit a little fresh air. But then Kitty supposed they must be well below sea-level down here.

As she stood there hesitantly a huge woman with her hair scraped back into a severe bun came marching towards her.

'Name?' she barked, glancing at a list she held.

'It's Kitty, miss.' Kitty's heart was pounding and she was sure she had never been so terrified in her life. But then this woman could strike terror into the hardest of hearts.

'Kitty who?'

'J-just Kitty, miss.'

'Hmph! Ah, here we are then! Come with me.' She drew a line through Kitty's name. 'I am Miss Henshaw, the Matron in these quarters, and for the duration of the voyage you will be answerable to me. I shall expect you to keep your own bunk tidy, and there is to be no fraternising with the sailors. You will not be allowed out of this room after ten o'clock at night for any reason, and it will be the worse for you if you disobey me. Is that clear?'

'Yes, ma'am,' Kitty muttered, disliking the woman more with every passing minute.

'Good, then seeing as you are so small, you shall have one of the upper bunks. This one here will do.' She had led Kitty almost to the end of the long room and now, after pointing up to one of the bunks, she turned and hurried away, leaving Kitty alone. The girl threw her valise up ahead of her then clambered up onto the hard straw-filled mattress, suddenly dreading the voyage ahead. This was certainly a far cry from the luxurious hotel she had stayed in the night before, but then she supposed beggars couldn't be choosers, as Mrs Bradshaw had always told her. She was just going to have to make the best of it.

Chapter Thirteen

The following morning, Maria was woken by the sound of a bell clanging up on deck. She started awake then winced at the crick in her neck. The striped ticking mattress on the bed was so hard that she felt as if she had slept on the floor, and the cot was so narrow that she had not even been able to turn over. Sitting up cautiously, she stretched – then swinging her feet out of bed she wrapped her old shawl about her shoulders and tapped on the adjoining door.

'Come in.'

She entered to find Isabelle propped up in a bed that was only slightly more comfortable than her own with her arms folded tightly about her chest. She was in a bad humour. 'This cabin is *abominable*,' she snapped pettishly. 'Surely Mama could have found us something better than this. We shall never survive for four months in here, and it's so *cold*!'

Maria smiled at her encouragingly. 'Why don't we get you dressed then, miss? You can take a turn about the deck then and go to the dining cabin for breakfast. That will warm you up.'

'I dare say it will be better than sitting here,' Isabelle moaned as she climbed out of her bunk.

She washed hastily in the cold water that Maria poured into the bowl for her then after helping her to dress, Maria pinned her hair up.

'There, that's better, isn't it?' Maria said as if placating a child as she fetched Isabelle's warm cloak.

'Slightly, I suppose,' Isabelle admitted grudgingly. 'But you get dressed too now Maria and go for your meal. I believe there is a different dining area for servants. You can tidy my clothes up when you have eaten.'

Once Isabelle had gone, Maria quickly did as she was told and soon she too was up on the deck, amazed at all the activity going on around her. High above her, the ship's sails flapped and cracked in the wind, and after asking directions she hastily made her way to the servants' dining cabin. A woman in a voluminous white apron was standing at a table ladling out bowls of porridge and sloshing stewed tea into cracked mugs, and as Maria looked around she was relieved to see Kitty sitting alone with her head bowed looking very sorry for herself. After quickly fetching her breakfast, which looked as unappetising as anything she had ever eaten, she joined Kitty.

A look of relief washed across the girl's face. 'Oh, Maria. I'm *so* pleased to see you,' she gabbled. 'It's horrible down in the women's quarters and the Matron is *so* sour-faced, I reckon she could even give Mrs Bradshaw a run for her money!'

Maria grinned. 'Well, I'm sure you'll be fine just so long as you do as you're told.' She grimaced then as she took a mouthful of porridge which was just as disgusting as it looked.

Kitty brightened. She always felt better when she was with Maria. "T'ain't as posh as the breakfast we had yesterday, is it?' she said. 'But what's your cabin like?'

'Tiny,' Maria answered. 'And Miss Isabelle isn't best pleased with hers either but I dare say we'll manage.'

When the girls had finished eating they moved back out onto the deck, glad of the warm capes that Miss Isabelle had bought them, and leaned on the rails. The seamen were working feverishly now to prepare for sailing in less than two hours' time, and they had to be careful to keep out of their way. The gangplank had been pulled up now and Maria felt a pang of apprehension. It was as if the last link to the world she had known had been severed – and who knew what the future would hold?

At noon a pilot took control of the ship to guide it out of the estuary, and as the enormous craft pulled away from the dock, Kitty clung to Maria fearfully. She had cleaned Master Joshua's cabin and was now in the process of doing the same to Miss Isabelle's, but suddenly both girls had the urge to see their last sight of dry land.

'Let's go up on deck!' Kitty said daringly and with a smile Maria agreed and they grabbed their cloaks and headed along the corridor.

Once on deck they were shocked at the number of people there. Children were racing about, oblivious of the cold, and emigrants hung across the railings determined to watch their homeland until it was out of sight. Smartly dressed ladies in crinolines paraded up and down on the arms of dapper gentlemen who were hanging onto their hats for fear of the bitter wind snatching them away. The ship had begun to rise and fall now and Kitty gripped the rail as a wave of nausea swept through her. Others were already leaning over the railings depositing their breakfasts into the sea, and the sight of them made Kitty feel even worse if that was possible, although she clung on bravely.

It was as they were standing there that Maria became aware of someone right next to her and when she glanced around, she saw Joshua.

'I thought I would come and see how you both are,' he said pleasantly. 'Isabelle is listening to a band in the main salon.'

The salon, she had been informed, was to be used for many activities that the passengers would invent during the course of the voyage, but Maria preferred to be out in the fresh air – for now, at least.

'I am very well, sir, thank you,' she responded primly. 'Although I fear Kitty is not so.'

A hurried glance at Kitty's white face confirmed what she had said and Josh instantly asked, 'Would you like to go and lie down, Kitty?'

'Oh no, sir, thanks very much but happen I'm best where I am,' she managed to answer. With every second that passed, the docks were receding into the distance. Seagulls squawked and wheeled overhead and Maria felt painfully aware of Joshua's closeness.

Glancing up at the sails now, he told her, 'The pilot will leave us when we reach the lighthouse and then we will have to wait for the wind to fill the sails.'

On the other side of him a young couple with their four little children clutching at their mother's skirts were openly crying and Maria felt sorry for them. Like her, they were no doubt wondering if they would ever come home again. As if reading her thoughts, Joshua lightly rested his hand on hers and she felt fire burn up her arm.

'I think you will like Tasmania,' he told her, hoping to

take her mind off the receding coastline. 'It is sunny almost all of the time there. Not at all like England, and the wildlife there is quite extraordinary. They have parrots where we are used to sparrows. Do you know anything about Australia, Maria?'

He was so kind that she felt herself begin to relax a little and even managed a faltering smile. 'Not much, sir, only what I have read in books that I managed to get from the free reading rooms,' she replied.

'Ah, then I think you will be pleasantly surprised. Tasmania is well known for its sheep farms, and our uncle has one of the largest there. I visited once with my parents a few years ago, and I must admit I loved it so much I scarcely wanted to come home.' He chuckled at the memory but the conversation was halted when Kitty suddenly leaned across the railings to be violently sick.

'Oh dear,' Maria said in dismay as she placed her arm about the poor girl's heaving shoulders. Kitty had turned an alarming shade of green. Joshua hurried away, only to return minutes later with a glass of water. The girl accepted it gratefully and gulped at it, but unfortunately this only seemed to make matters worse and within seconds she was being sick again, as were many more of the passengers by now.

'Perhaps you should leave me to look after her, sir,' Maria suggested, deeply embarrassed that he should have to witness his maid being so ill. But Joshua was having none of it.

'I most certainly will not,' he answered firmly. Then: 'Come along, Kitty. I shall escort you down to the steerage. Perhaps a lie-down for a short while will make you feel better.'

He hustled her away with her small hand clapped across her mouth, and at the door to the single ladies' quarters

Miss Henshaw stopped him with a stern expression on her face.

'I'm sorry, sir, but gentlemen are not allowed beyond this point.' She stood resolutely blocking the door and Joshua had to stifle a grin. Anyone would have thought she was guarding the crown jewels.

'Then could you see that this young lady is taken care of,' he managed to say, keeping a straight face. 'I'm afraid she is feeling rather unwell.'

'Of course, sir.' So are half of the other passengers, the woman thought to herself. But they don't get their masters escorting them to their beds. It really was most inappropriate! She then grasped poor Kitty's elbow with her mouth set in a grim line and whisked her through the door, leaving Joshua standing there like a spare part.

He shook his head and chuckled softly as he turned and took the steep staircase two at a time, but once back on deck the smile vanished as he saw that Maria had gone.

Later that afternoon, when the boat reached the lighthouse, the pilot took his leave. As he clambered down a ladder into the small boat that would take him back to shore a cheer went up amongst the steerage passengers who were well enough to be out on deck. They were truly at sea now, and all they had to do now was to wait for the wind to fill the sails. It came within the hour, making the sails snap like gunshots, and the vessel began to bounce across the waves at an alarming rate, making the people who were already unwell feel even worse.

Isabelle was one of the casualties, and as Maria mopped her damp forehead with a cloth she groaned and clutched her stomach.

'Oh dear,' she whimpered as she leaned over the bucket

Maria had placed at the side of her bunk bed. 'I fear I am going to die, Maria.'

'No, you're not, miss,' Maria told her gently, grateful that she wasn't suffering from sea sickness too. 'One of the sailors on deck told me that once we get further out to sea it will be calmer and then you will start to feel better.'

In actual fact the sky had darkened before the waves subsided, and by then Maria was exhausted. She had slipped down to the women's quarter's to see how Kitty was faring, only to be turned away at the door by Miss Henshaw.

'Kitty will be fine,' she told her. 'I am quite used to caring for passengers with weak stomachs.'

'But I thought if I could just see—'

'No, I am afraid that is quite out of the question,' Miss Henshaw told her, holding her hand up to stop the girl's flow of words. 'Now I suggest you get back to your mistress. I am assuming you *are* a lady's maid?'

Feeling quite intimidated by the woman, Maria nodded numbly.

'Then off you go. I am sure Kitty will be well enough to resume her duties by the morning.'

Realising that there was no more to be said, Maria slowly climbed the steep wooden staircase and wandered over to the railings. Above her, the sky was full of stars that made the black waters sparkle, and despite the cold, Maria was sure she had never seen anything quite so pretty.

'It's a wonderful sight, isn't it?'

Startled, she whirled around to see Joshua standing behind her and instantly she was flummoxed.

'Er . . . yes, yes it is,' she stuttered, wondering why he always had this effect on her. 'It is quite breathtaking.'

They remained silent for a time as they watched the sea slapping against the side of the ship. The deck was almost deserted and Maria was very conscious of his closeness.

'Are you feeling all right, Maria?' he asked solicitously after a time and she nodded.

'Oh yes, I'm fine, thank you, sir.'

'We are going to be on board for a long time. Could you not call me Josh? Sir is so formal.'

'I . . . I don't think that would be right, sir,' she answered, feeling totally out of her depth. Joshua was a gentleman whilst she was merely a servant. And a pregnant one at that! She wondered what he would think when he learned of her condition. Very soon now her bump would be obvious, and suddenly she did not want to wait for the look of condemnation that would cross his face when he found out. She would far sooner get it out of the way now, and so taking a deep breath, she began, 'Sir – there is something I think you should know.'

He turned to look at her and the moon turned his green eyes to a glorious emerald.

She licked her lips, which were suddenly dry. 'The thing is . . . well, there is no easy way to say this, so I shall just come out with it. I – I am with child. Miss Isabelle knows and insisted I should still come with her anyway, but I promise that this will not interfere with my care of her.'

'I already know of this,' he answered quietly. 'Isabelle told me whilst we were at dinner before the ship sailed.'

Her eyes grew round. 'And . . . and you do not condemn me? I am unmarried and—'

'Maria, you do not have to explain anything to me,' he assured her kindly. 'Perhaps one day you will trust me enough to relate the circumstances that led to this condition, but until then it is not for me to judge.'

In truth, he had been shocked when his sister told him. Somehow he had thought Maria was a cut above the other girls of her station. But who was he to judge? He stared away across the ocean then, and could she have known it, he was thinking how unfair life was. And how guilty he felt – for had he not had an illegitimate child too?

His mind spun back in time to the comely housemaid who had taken his virginity. He had been home from boarding school on holiday when their affair began and he had been unable to take his eyes off her shapely curves and her sweet dimpled face. Edith had made no secret of the fact that she found him attractive, and somehow they had ended up in the hay barn one day and it had gone from there. Even now when he closed his eyes he could remember how soft and yielding her body had felt beneath his inexperienced hands. How could he have known that Edith had bedded half of his parents' male staff too? Whenever he came home from school after that, for months they would sneak off together and inevitably one day she informed him that he was going to be a father. He could clearly remember the elation that had swept through him and he had expressed his undying love as only a lovesick youth could. 'We shall be married and I shall look after you forever,' he had promised her. Unfortunately his father did not agree with his proposal when he finally told him, and Charles Montgomery had shaken him as a dog might shake a rat.

'You young idiot!' he had ranted. 'All young men should sow their wild oats and I do not condemn you for that. Better to lose your virginity to a maid than a whore. But you *do not* marry a servant! Your mother and I have brought you up for better things. It has long been an understanding between her family and ours that one day you and young Felicity Pettifer will become betrothed.'

'But what will become of Edith if I do not marry her?'

Josh had asked falteringly. 'And Felicity and I have never been anything other than friends.'

'We shall pay her off,' his father had informed him coldly. 'She will go back to her family and that will be an end to it. And you, young man, will return to school immediately – and when the time is right, you will ask Felicity's father for her hand in marriage, and you and Felicity will announce your engagement.'

And so Josh had gone back to school, with a heavy heart. It was some months later that he had heard the cook and one of the maids gossiping in the kitchen and learned that Edith had given birth to a son who had only lived for three days. Heartbroken, he had made a vow there and then that he would never make such a mistake again. Instead, when he left school he had become involved in his father's businesses and to his surprise had found that he enjoyed being busy. But then recently his mother and father had begun to parade Felicity in front of him at every opportunity and he had realised that they felt he was ready for marriage. Well, let them think it. *He* would decide when he was ready to take a bride and he would not choose Felicity Pettifer. She was a nice enough girl, admittedly, but he didn't feel drawn to her in the slightest and he suspected that she felt the same about him too. All she could talk about was the latest fashion and embroidery and who was betrothed to whom!

Josh supposed this was why he had not objected when his mother had asked him to escort Isabelle to Tasmania. He would enjoy spending time on his uncle's sheep ranch and it would get him away from their match-making – for a time at least. What he had not counted on was meeting someone like Maria. She was unlike any girl he had ever met before. Beautiful, intelligent, kind and caring. Not that anything could ever come of it, of course. He was not about to make the same mistake twice, but surely that should not stop him from enjoying her company?

She had been standing silently at his side, but now pulling his thoughts sharply back to the present, he asked, 'Would you like to find a more sheltered spot? The wind from the sea is rather cold. We could sit over there.' He pointed to a bench that was screwed down to the deck away from the railings.

'I think I should be getting back to see how Miss Isabelle is, sir.' Maria stepped away from him, still reeling from the knowledge that he knew about her condition. And then without another word she turned and fled, and he stayed and watched her go until she was out of sight.

The next day they sailed into bad weather and people took to their bunks in droves as the ship pitched and turned, first this way and then the other. The stench of vomit hung on the air in Isabelle's cabin, and when Kitty finally managed to get there it was to find a bucket of soiled nightclothes waiting for her.

'I'm so sorry,' Maria apologised as she pointed to them. 'But I need help. I have had to change Miss Isabelle's night-gown twice during the night and again early this morning.'

Glancing towards her mistress, who was the colour of bleached linen, Kitty raised a weak smile. She still felt very fragile herself but Miss Henshaw was not one to let anyone lounge about unless they were so ill they could not stand.

'Don't go worryin' about it,' she said sturdily. 'The sailors have cleared a corner on the lower deck where we can do the laundry. They've even strung some lines up fer us. But I can't promise how clean the clothes will be, as we're to wash 'em in seawater that they're drawin' up in buckets. No doubt they'll be stiff as boards by the time they've dried.'

'Well, at least they won't smell,' Maria replied as she handed the heavy bucket to Kitty. 'But you just be careful if you're going on deck. I wonder if you shouldn't wait until the ship is a little steadier.'

'I'll be fine,' Kitty assured her. 'To be honest I think I'd sooner be outside. There are so many people ill, the whole ship reeks.' Lifting the bucket she disappeared then as Maria turned her attentions back to Isabelle. She had been up for most of the night with her, but seeing that she had now dropped into an uneasy doze, Maria decided to take advantage of the fact and try to snatch a rest herself . . .

Josh entered the cabin a short time later to find Maria fast asleep in the small chair at the side of Isabelle's bunk. Even with her clothes crumpled and her hair escaping its pins she still managed to look beautiful. Not wishing to disturb them, he crept away with a frown on his face. There was something about that girl that drew him to her like a magnet – but he really must stop being so silly. His mother and father would be appalled if they were to discover he was attracted to a servant girl again, and Maria had enough problems to deal with already without him adding to them.

Up on deck he found Kitty and some other girls scrubbing out clothes in a variety of large buckets. He inclined his head as he passed her and she paused for a moment to nod in return and watch him go by. He were a handsome bloke, that Mr Josh, an' no mistake, she thought to herself, then she went back to her task.

By evening time, the ship had sailed into calmer waters and people began to emerge from their cabins looking pale and wobbly. Someone was doing Bible readings in the salon and many headed there, glad of a distraction, whilst the children raced about the deck playing Catch Me If You Can, pleased to be free of their confined quarters for a time.

Isabelle had managed to keep some soup down and was feeling a little better, so she told Maria, 'Why don't you go and get some fresh air? You've been cooped up in here all day with me and you must be exhausted.'

'I think I will if you're sure you don't mind, miss.' Maria grabbed her cloak and headed for the lower deck where the servants and emigrants were allowed to exercise. The upper deck was for the use of the cabin passengers, so she hoped that she would avoid seeing Joshua.

Once alone, Isabelle stared dismally at the small port-hole and for the first time the full gravity of her situation came home to her as her hand dropped to rest on the tiny mound that was Pierre's child growing inside her. How had it come to this? she wondered. This tiny cramped cabin was not what she was used to and she suddenly missed her mother and longed for her luxurious bedroom back at home. During her affair with Pierre she had given no thought to the fact that their lovemaking might have consequences. She had been far too infatuated with him to care – and now she would give birth to his child on the other side of the world and he would never even know that he was a father. The girl was wise enough to realise that the chances of ever seeing him again were slim. Her parents would see to that – and when she returned home, they would no doubt be in a hurry to marry her off to the first suitable young man, probably Philip. But how could she ever love anyone now, after knowing Pierre? And worse still, she must first face giving birth; the mere thought of it filled her with dread. She had heard horror stories of women dying during childbirth. What if that was to happen to her? Even if she did survive, would she ever be the same again? Isabelle was very vain and the thought of losing her figure was horrifying. Lowering her head into her hands, she cried bitter tears of self-pity.

Up on deck, a group of sailors were lounging against one of the masts in their free time drinking rum, and as Maria passed they whistled and cried after her. She walked on with her nose in the air and one of them shouted, 'Eeh, look at little Miss Hoity Toity. Thinks she's too good fer the likes of us, she does, lads.'

Maria paused to stare at him coldly. He was a huge man with hands like hams and a ruddy complexion that spoke of the many hours he spent outdoors. At some time his nose had been broken and now it spread across his face, giving him a fearsome look. His long hair was black as coal and tied back with a bow at the nape of his neck.

He winked at her cheekily, and casting a withering look in his direction, Maria lifted her skirts and hurried on. What with Miss Isabelle and Kitty being poorly and one thing and another, it looked set to be a very long voyage indeed – and it had scarcely even begun yet.

Chapter Fourteen

By mid-February, Kitty and Isabelle had grown their sea legs and were looking much better. In fact, Kitty was positively blooming. The plain hollow-cheeked girl who had left Hatter's Hall now had a glow to her skin, and her mousy-coloured hair was streaked with golden highlights that glinted in the sun. She worked from morning until night each day tending to Master Josh and Miss Isabelle's needs without a word of complaint, for they were always kind to her, which was something she had never experienced in her former home. But it was Maria to whom she was closest. Maria had become the big sister she had always dreamed of having, and Isabelle often teased Maria that if she had asked Kitty to walk the plank for her, she would have. Nothing was ever too much trouble for the girl, and she went about her work with a smile, humming happily to herself.

By now, both Isabelle's and Maria's waists were expanding at a rapid rate, a fact that Isabelle lamented; much of their time was taken up altering their gowns and letting out their waistbands. Surprisingly, Isabelle was a remarkably neat seamstress and under her guidance Maria became almost as good. If the weather was balmy, Isabelle would stroll along the decks during the afternoons, shaded from the sun by her parasol. As she was often heard to say, it would never do to become brown like a gypsy. Ladies should have pale skin. Maria thought this might be quite difficult to maintain if Tasmania was as hot as she had heard it was, but she wisely held her tongue. Maria rarely saw Joshua now. Apart from when he visited Isabelle in her cabin, he tended to keep to the upper deck.

On one particularly mild day as Isabelle and Maria were taking the air, they had to step aside to let a little herd of children pass by. The children were rolling hoops across the deck and Maria smiled as she was reminded of Emma.

'My sister loved playing with her hoop in the lane,' she remarked and Isabelle glanced at her, detecting the note of regret in her voice.

'Do you miss your family?' she asked.

Maria nodded as tears stung at the back of her eyes. 'Yes, I do,' she said chokily. 'Do you miss your parents?'

Isabelle had never really said much about it before but now she admitted, 'I suppose I do sometimes. Especially my mama. But then by this time next year I shall be home again so it is not as if I am never going to see her again, is it?'

'No, I suppose not.' Maria was stopped from saying any more when a shout went up.

'*Man overboard!*'

Looking back, they saw the huddle of children they had just passed grouped at the rail crying pitifully. She raced back towards them and a little boy clutched at her hand as he sobbed, 'Please, miss. It's our Nellie. She fell through here!'

Hanging over the railings, she looked back at the churning sea just in time to see a small hand reaching above the waves.

A number of sailors had joined her now and pointing in the direction where she had just seen the child she told them, 'Over there, look. Can you see her waving?'

One of the sailors kicked his boots off and scrambled up onto the railing preparing to dive in, but before he had the chance, one of his comrades caught the back of his trousers and hauled him back.

'It's no use, Jed,' he told him sorrowfully in a thick Irish accent. 'Look, the sea has swallowed the little lass up, so it has. There is nothin' to be done, man!'

Maria looked back again but there was nothing to be seen but the churning of the waves in the ship's wake. The little girl had disappeared.

'You must stop the boat,' she told them as the children huddled about her with terrified tears on their cheeks.

The sailor shook his head. ''T'would do no good, miss. By the time the ship stopped she could be miles back. We could never find her, God rest her soul.'

A number of people were racing towards them now and one, a woman with a shawl drawn tightly about her, grabbed hold of the little boy.

'Billy, where's our Nellie?' she demanded. 'I told yer yer must keep her safe.'

He pointed a trembling finger. 'She tripped just here, Mam, an' afore I could get to her she'd slipped through the railin's an' into the sea. But 't'weren't my fault, honest it weren't.'

The woman's hand flew to her mouth as the colour drained out of her face like water from a dam.

'So what can we do?' She was looking at the sailors now

with desperation in her eyes but they each shook their head.

'Sorry, missus, but she's gone.'

The woman began to wail then, a terrible sound that echoed across the now silent deck, and taking Isabelle's arm, Maria quickly led her away, badly shaken.

'How terrible,' Isabelle muttered. 'It was as if the sea just sucked her under, wasn't it?' It was the first death they had witnessed since coming aboard. Little could they know that it was to be the first of many.

Later that day, there was a memorial service for the little girl. The decks were crowded as the solemn-faced Captain read from the Bible. He prided himself on running a tight ship, and although it was rare to make a crossing without at least one death, when it was that of a child it seemed to be so much worse.

Joshua joined Maria and Isabelle for the service, grieving at the tragic waste. 'A little girl with her whole life before her,' he sighed with feeling.

The two young women nodded in agreement as the crowd began to disperse. Back at the cabin, they found Kitty scrubbing the floor as if her life depended on it.

'I shan't be long,' she told them cheerfully as she slopped yet more water onto the floor and attacked it with a scrubbing brush.

Isabelle tutted with annoyance; the first sign that the better moods were rapidly coming to an end. Taking her bonnet off, she flung it onto the bed and pouted as she raised her hand to her hair.

'It's as stiff as a board,' she complained. 'Why can't they catch the rainwater for us to use for washing?'

'Because every drop of fresh water is needed for drinking,'

Josh pointed out patiently. 'They are already having to flavour the barrels of water they brought aboard with lime and we still have a way to go yet.'

'Well, I'm not used to having to manage in such a fashion,' Isabelle declared, as she stamped her pretty foot on the floor.

Seeing the beginnings of a tantrum, Maria caught Kitty's eye. 'I'm sure that is good enough for now,' she told the girl with a kind smile. 'Why don't you take the washing I've put out ready for you up on deck and get it done whilst the weather is favourable? I heard the Captain say that he felt we were heading into bad weather.'

'Yes'm.' Kitty threw the brush back into the bucket and rose awkwardly, rubbing her wet hands down the front of her apron. Then, snatching up the bundle of laundry under one arm, she hefted the bucket, bobbed her knee and disappeared out into the corridor, which was beginning to smell quite badly now because of the water closets positioned there.

'I too shall leave you two ladies to rest now,' Joshua told them as he backed out of the cabin door. 'Will you be dining in your room tonight or in the dining room?'

'I haven't decided yet.' Isabelle tossed her head and, recognising the signs, Joshua made a hasty exit, feeling sorry for Maria.

As it turned out, hardly anyone ate dinner that evening, for as the afternoon lengthened they sailed into stormy waters just as the Captain had prophesied. The ship began to rock alarmingly, sending most folk scuttling away to lie in their bunks. Isabelle was terrified and lay wide-eyed clutching the sides of her bunk as the ship seemed to rise into the air then drop like a stone.

'We're all going to die,' she groaned dramatically as Maria tried to comfort her.

'No, we are not,' she soothed although she too felt sick and ill. 'Just try to sleep and hopefully by the time you wake we will be through the worst of it.'

'How do you know that? You *simpleton*!' Isabelle shrieked, but for now Maria chose to ignore her.

The ship rode the storm until the early hours of the morning and many people began to feel as Isabelle did, sure that the vessel was going to break up and deposit them all into the churning sea as it creaked and groaned and rocked alarmingly. The seawater and strong winds whistled down the corridors, and everything in the cabins that wasn't nailed down rolled about the floors, adding to the terror of the passengers. On deck they could hear the sailors shouting to each other as they tried to batten down the hatches and battle with the enormous sails. But thankfully, just as everyone was certain they were all doomed the waters became calmer and by morning the sea was like a millpond again.

Isabelle had fallen into an exhausted sleep by then and Maria shakily made her way to the deck to grab a breath of fresh air. The first person she saw was Joshua leaning against the rails. She quickly turned to slip away, but before she had a chance to do so he spotted her and called, 'Come and stand over here for a while, Maria. You look a bit wobbly.'

'I feel a bit wobbly,' she said, joining him reluctantly. Some of the masts had been damaged during the storm, and she watched fascinated as the seamen clambered up and down them as sure-footed as monkeys as they tried to repair them.

'It was a pretty bad ride back there for a while, wasn't it? How is Isabelle bearing up?'

'Oh, you know . . .'

He glanced at her. 'That means she's been a prize bitch all night, no doubt.' He chuckled before confiding, 'I'm afraid she has been rather spoiled.'

Maria shrugged. 'We were both afraid,' she said, not wishing to cause trouble.

'Well, if she starts with one of her tantrums you just give as good as you get,' Josh advised.

'Don't worry. I can handle Miss Isabelle,' she replied calmly. 'After all, that is what I am being paid for.'

Her comment made them suddenly aware of the differences between the two of them, and Maria moved away now, eager to escape. Sometimes when she was with Joshua she found herself talking to him on a level and that would never do. She must remember that she was merely a servant.

His expression darkened as he watched her carefully pick her way across the deck again. There was something about her that he found strangely intriguing and it was not just her striking good looks, although he was forced to admit to himself that he did find her attractive. It was the way she spoke; the way she held herself; the way she walked. Sometimes, if he had not known better he could have taken her for more of a lady than his sister, and she was sweeter-natured too, although, he grinned ruefully, that did not take much doing. Isabelle could be a complete harridan when she chose to be. He returned his gaze to the ocean when Maria disappeared from sight, feeling slightly cheated, then gave himself a mental shake. He really must stop being so silly. It was probably being so far from home and having so little to do, but even so instead of the wide expanse of water it was her face that remained in front of his eyes.

It was then that he became aware of a noise coming from behind one of the life boats. As he looked towards it, he saw one of the women steerage passengers cavorting with a sailor. Her skirt was up around her waist and the sailor's trousers were down around his ankles as he thrust into her.

It wasn't the first time that Joshua had witnessed a coupling between one of the women from below decks and a sailor, and he doubted it would be the last on such a long journey. It was a known fact that the sailors were usually desperate for a woman after a period at sea, and if the women were willing, as some of them were, for a share of the man's rum or extra food, then the Captain tended to turn a blind eye. Joshua was keen to do the same, so ignoring the guttural sounds that were issuing from the couple as their lovemaking reached its climax, he lowered his head and hurried away, kicking aside a large rat as he went. The bad weather had disturbed them and brought them up on deck, and Joshua shuddered as his foot connected with the soft body. If the rumours were true, he could well find himself eating the very same creature before they reached Australia, should the salted meat run short; the thought of it turned his stomach.

Maria arrived back in the cabin to find Isabelle in a towering rage.

'Where the hell have you been?' she demanded the second Maria stepped through the door. 'I wish to go out on deck and you were not here to help me get dressed. That is what my mother is paying you for, in case you had forgotten.'

Here we go again, Maria thought as she began to lay out Isabelle's clothes on the narrow bed. She then poured water into the china bowl and discreetly turned her back whilst Isabelle flung her nightgown off and began to wash.

'I'm sick of having to wash in cold water,' she griped pettishly. 'And not particularly clean water at that.'

It was then that a tap sounded on the door and seconds later Kitty appeared, her cheeks rosy and her eyes bright.

'I've come to start the cleanin', miss,' she said cheerfully, but when Isabelle rounded on her furiously with a towel pressed over her breasts, the girl shrank back against the door.

'How *dare* you come in here before you are invited?' Isabelle bellowed. 'Can't you see that I am not even half-dressed yet, you dimwit!'

With a muffled sob, Kitty fumbled with the door handle then almost fell back out into the corridor in her haste to escape.

'Was there really any need for that?' Maria asked levelly. She was fully aware of her position, and Kitty's too if it came to that, but even so she could see no excuse for speaking to the girl in such a manner.

'You just hold your tongue,' Isabelle warned as she turned so that Maria could help her into her undergarments.

Maria bit her lip as she began to lace her mistress into her stays. She had learned back in Hatter's Hall that it was no use trying to reason with Isabelle whilst she was in this mood.

'Pull them *tighter*,' Isabelle insisted as she stared into the only mirror that the small cabin possessed. She was increasingly concerned with the way her figure was thickening by the day and painfully aware that there was not a thing she could do about it. Damn and blast the bastard that was growing inside her! And blast Pierre too for getting her into this mess in the first place. Never for a second did she allow herself to accept that she was partly responsible for the condition she found herself in, nor admit that she had pursued him just as shamelessly as he had her.

Once the corset was adjusted to her liking, which Maria considered was far too tight, she then helped her into the many layers of petticoats.

'I shall wear the blue crinoline today,' Isabelle informed her, waving her hand towards it. Once again, Maria obediently fetched it although she thought the gown was far too elaborate for day wear. Better to just do as she was told, she decided, and let Isabelle go and walk her temper off on deck.

Finally she dressed the young woman's hair as best she could, piling it onto the top of her head and teasing it into ringlets.

Isabelle slid her feet into pretty satin shoes and then examined herself critically in the mirror before saying ungratefully, 'I dare say that will have to do. Fetch me my parasol.'

Maria knew that the parasol would probably blow inside out within minutes but she dutifully did as she was told, bringing a warm cape too and reminding her, 'You'll need this, miss. If you find it too cold out on deck you could perhaps go to the salon. I believe they have a fiddler playing there to entertain the children.'

Sitting in a room full of screaming brats was not her idea of entertainment and Isabelle was about to make some scathing response but then, obviously thinking better of it, she draped the cape about her shoulders. When she finally sailed out of the cabin, Maria breathed a sigh of relief and set about tidying the clothes that the girl had flung all over the place. That was another crisis averted, for now at least.

For the rest of that month, things went from bad to worse as Isabelle's moods deteriorated even further, but Maria held her tongue and went about her duties uncomplainingly. There was little else she could do. By then she was spending half of the days sitting in the cabin letting out the seams on Isabelle's gowns and her own whilst Isabelle took advantage of whatever entertainment was available in the salon. She had finally decided that even that was preferable to being cooped up below deck. Thankfully Maria was a very reasonable seamstress now, which was just as well for Isabelle refused to so much as pick up a needle any more.

All she seemed to do – when the weather was warm enough, that was – was parade about the poop deck like a caged animal.

The poop deck was used by the upper-class passengers and Maria had never been allowed up there, not that she wanted to. She was quite happy to exercise on the lower deck where the servants of the gentry were beginning to form friendships.

She would watch the sailor high up in the crow's-nest whilst others swabbed the decks or scuttled about like ants securing sails and seeing to the smooth running of the ship. If she ever thought of home, she would try to push those thoughts to the back of her mind and look ahead, although as yet she had not dared to think what might happen when they arrived in Tasmania and her own child was born.

By now, the ship had slowed to such an extent that Maria sometimes wondered if it had stopped altogether.

'They are having to go slowly because of icebergs,' Joshua informed them one afternoon when he visited their cabin.

'Icebergs!' Isabelle was appalled. 'But what if we should collide with one of them?'

Joshua patted her hand. 'There is little chance of that,' he reassured her. 'They are keeping a close watch from the crow's-nest and the ship has slowed so that it has time to steer away, should they spot one.' Then glancing towards Maria, who had a book spread across her lap, he asked, 'What are you reading?'

'It's *Scenes of Clerical Life*, by George Eliot,' she answered.

'And where did you learn to read?'

'My father taught us all,' she answered. 'And I used to spend most of my spare time in the free reading rooms.'

'Which other writers do you enjoy?' Joshua enquired.

'Well, I especially like the Brontë sisters.'

'Ah, so does my mother. You have that in common.'

'Oh, can't you two talk about something more interesting than damn books?' Isabelle complained, tired of the conversation.

'But books aren't boring,' Maria objected. 'In fact, until I embarked on this voyage I had never set foot outside my home town. Well, apart from to go to the Goose Fair in Coventry once with Mother and Father. And yet despite that, books have given me a good insight into what it is like in faraway lands.'

'Huh!' Isabelle frowned. 'Well, give me a good shopping trip or a new gown in place of a book any day.'

Joshua and Maria exchanged an amused glance and in that instant their relationship changed subtly.

'Look, why don't you both come up to the salon?' he suggested now. 'I hear the band is going to play this afternoon and it may whittle away a little time for you.'

Maria bowed her head. 'I couldn't really,' she said quickly. 'Servants are not allowed on the upper deck.'

'And who is to know you are a servant if you are with us?' Joshua challenged her.

When Maria glanced down at her plain dress, he instantly understood. The dress was actually the finest that Maria had ever owned, but it still set her apart from the upper-class ladies in their fine crinolines.

In a rare good humour at the thought of a pleasant diversion, Isabelle clapped her hands together. 'Why, you could borrow one of my dresses,' she said excitedly. 'It would be nice for me to dress you up for a change.' She eyed Maria critically as if she was seeing her for the very first time. 'We are about the same size and height. Now let's see, which one would you like to wear?'

As Maria began to strongly object, Joshua made a hasty departure. He knew only too well what his sister was like when she got an idea into her head, and had no wish to be present whilst she titivated Maria up.

'I'll meet you both on the poop deck in half an hour,' he informed them before rushing from the room, but Isabelle didn't hear him; she was too busy rummaging through the trunks in search of something suitable for Maria to wear. Clothes began to fly in all directions as Maria continued to object, but eventually she drew out a pale green crinoline and held it up beneath Maria's chin.

'I think this colour would look wonderful on you,' she declared, already undoing the row of buttons that ran all the way from the waist to the high neckline of Maria's dress.

Deeply embarrassed, Maria stood still as Isabelle stripped the dress from her. 'And of course you shall have to have some extra petticoats.'

Isabelle was enjoying herself now and Maria did not have the heart to stop her. Once she was dressed, Isabelle then took the pins from the neat bun at the back of Maria's head and shook her hair loose before attacking it with a hairbrush.

'Your hair is very thick,' she complained as she tried to secure it in a more becoming style on the top of the young woman's head. It seemed to take forever but at last she stood back and sighed with satisfaction.

'Goodness me.' She beamed with satisfaction. 'I swear you look more of a lady than I do,' she declared as she led Maria to a mirror. When Maria looked shyly into it she gasped in amazement and colour instantly flooded her cheeks.

The dress was cut low and Maria, who had always worn dresses that covered her from neck to ankle, felt almost indecent at the small cleavage that peeped back at her. Her hair was in much the same style as the one that Isabelle favoured, high on top with fair silky ringlets arranged around the crown of her head, tied up with a cluster of green silk ribbons that matched the colour of the dress.

'Now, we must do something about your boots.'

Maria wriggled her toes in her soft leather boots, wondering what on earth was wrong with them but Isabelle was already rooting through the cabin trunks again.

'Ah, here we are. I'm afraid I have no green ones, but these should do nicely.' Waving a pair of satin silver shoes in the air she advanced on Maria who obligingly held her foot out. It was soon apparent that Isabelle's feet were slightly larger than hers, but Isabelle insisted that the slippers were just perfect. 'After all, no one is going to be staring at your feet with you looking like this, are they?' she giggled.

But Maria was still apprehensive. 'What if the Captain sees me?' she fretted.

Isabelle waved her hand nonchalantly. 'What if he does? He would never realise that you are my maid. And anyway, it is highly unlikely that he will be about at this time of the day. He will be too busy avoiding icebergs. Now come along or the band will have finished playing before we even get there.'

And so for the first time in her life, Maria followed Isabelle from the cabin feeling like a real lady.

Chapter Fifteen

The band consisted of a motley crew of people, mainly from the steerage section, playing popular airs on a variety of instruments ranging from flutes to violins. Even so, the sound they created was pleasing, and when Maria and Isabelle entered the salon their feet were tapping along to the music in no time at all. Joshua was clearly impressed with Maria's appearance although he was too much of a gentleman to embarrass her by saying so. When she shrugged the heavy cloak that Isabelle had loaned her from her shoulders, Joshua was aware of more than a few admiring glances directed her way. Maria was a charming girl, and very good company, and he found himself looking forward to the short times they spent together.

Young men, glad of any diversion to interrupt the tedium of the voyage, began to step forward to ask the two young women to dance in the space that had been cleared in the middle of the room. Isabelle went willingly but Maria quietly refused each one, preferring to sit with Joshua. She felt more than a little out of place and was not keen to suddenly be the centre of attention although she found it was nice to be able to talk to Joshua.

'I think you'll like Uncle Freddie,' he told her as they watched Isabelle whirl past in the arms of a young gentleman. 'The countryside surrounding his ranch is quite beautiful and the sun always seems to be shining there.'

Maria listened, enthralled by the pictures he was conjuring up.

'Uncle Freddie was always the rebel of the family,' Joshua confided. 'He hated working in the factories and mills back home, even though they would be partly his one day. He was always more of the outdoor type, if you know what I mean.' He chuckled. 'I can remember Grandfather being absolutely appalled when Uncle Freddie declared his intention of emigrating, but he won him round eventually and Grandfather even gave him part of his inheritance early to give him a start there. Between you and me, I think Grandfather expected him to fall flat on his face and be home in no time at all with his tail between his legs, but Uncle Freddie shocked him and made a go of it.' He sighed before saying thoughtfully, 'Life is a funny thing, isn't it? I mean, there was Uncle Freddie with what most people would give their right arms for. He was brought up in the lap of luxury and didn't even have to work if he didn't wish to, but it wasn't what he wanted.'

Maria found it incredible that anyone would want to leave that kind of existence behind, but then she supposed everyone wanted different things from life.

'Were you close to your father?' Josh asked then, seeing the sad expression on her face. 'He's a preacher, isn't he?'

'Yes, he is,' Maria answered quietly. 'And no, I have never

had a close relationship with him. Perhaps it's because I was a girl. Most men want their firstborn to be a son, don't they? But I was very close to my mother.' Her eyes welled with tears now as a wave of homesickness seized her. 'To be honest I could never understand why she stayed with him,' she surprised herself by saying. She had never admitted that to anyone before. 'He is a very harsh man and treats her as little more than a skivvy.' She was like a flower opening up in the sunshine as she spoke of her family and he found it hard to drag his eyes away from her face. She then went on to tell him of her relationship with Lennie.

'I suppose the attraction was that he was so different to my father,' she confessed. 'But looking back now I realise what a fool I was.' Her hand unconsciously stroked the small mound of her stomach and she sighed. 'He used me – and even then I was prepared to forgive him. But now our child will be born out of wedlock and it's all my fault.'

Josh chewed on his lips for a time as he sought for words to comfort her. 'I'm sure you will find a solution to your problems in Tasmania,' he said. 'But should you not wish to stay, Mama will be more than happy to pay your fare back home once Isabelle's child is born.'

Her face softened and she smiled, but she had no chance to respond, for just then Isabelle flitted back to the table looking like the cat that had got the cream. She was used to being admired and today's little diversion had gone a long way towards restoring her confidence.

'Oh goodness, I swear I am quite exhausted,' she giggled, fanning her face with her hand for all the world as if she were at some grand ball.

'Perhaps you should rest for a while. You do have to think of the child,' Josh suggested tactfully.

Isabelle's expression darkened. 'Oh yes, always the

child!' she hissed. 'But what about *me?* It is all its fault that I am here in the first place! I wish I could just get rid of the horrid thing!'

Josh stared at her coldly, his expression as cutting as the wind that was hammering at the salon doors.

'Perhaps you should have thought of that, dear sister, before you began your little liaison with Pierre. And perhaps you should also consider yourself fortunate that Mama has seen fit to offer you a way out of your dilemma, against Father's wishes. Many parents would have disowned you and thrown you out on the streets for dishonouring the family name. Furthermore, Maria here is in exactly the same position as you, and I don't see *her* feeling sorry for herself. All her concerns are for her unborn child.'

'Huh! But she is merely a servant,' Isabelle spat unkindly. 'And everyone knows that her sort breed like rabbits.'

Maria was deeply hurt, but seeing that this was fast developing into a row, she said hastily, 'Why don't you sit down, miss? I could fetch you a drink.'

'I don't *want* a drink!' The young woman's dainty hands clenched into fists as colour rose in her cheeks.

'How dare you be so rude,' Josh said roundly. 'We are all entitled to respect, no matter where we come from. And may I add that from what I have seen, Maria here is more of a lady, miss, than you will ever be! At this precise moment in time I am ashamed to call you my sister and sorry that I ever agreed to accompany you on this journey in the first place.'

'Oh yes, *you* defend *her*.' Isabelle was unused to being spoken to in this way by her brother and was bubbling with rage. 'And of course it is obvious why! Don't think I haven't seen the way you look at her.'

'*Enough!*' Josh roared as he leaped to his feet, causing people to turn and stare at them. 'You are making a spectacle of yourself, madam. Now kindly get your cape and I will accompany you back to your cabin.'

'I don't want to go back to the cabin,' Isabelle said like a petulant child. 'I want to stay here and enjoy myself – not be locked away like some boring old spinster.'

'Then stay.' He turned then and offering his arm to Maria, who was cringing with embarrassment, he told her, 'Come along.'

She picked up her cloak without argument and with her head bent, quickly followed him out onto the deck where the bitter wind snatched at their clothes and took their breath away.

'I wish to apologise for my sister's atrocious behaviour,' Joshua told her as he took her elbow and steered her towards the cabin quarters.

'I'm sure she was just distraught.' Maria excused Isabelle although her words had made her smart with shame and humiliation. Suddenly she was wishing with all her heart that she had never agreed to embark on this voyage. But there was no going back now and she knew that she would just have to make the best of it.

They were halfway across the deck when Maria became aware of someone watching them – but when she glanced around whoever it was hastily stepped back into the shadows. She supposed it was just some sailor who had enjoyed more than his fair share of rum and she pushed it from her mind.

They made the rest of the short journey in silence, and at the door to their cabin, Josh bowed before taking his leave with a grim expression on his face. It would be a long time before he could forgive his sister for the despicable outburst he had just been forced to witness.

Kitty was there scrubbing down everything in sight, and

one look at Maria's pale face told her that something was wrong. When Maria took her cloak off and flung it onto the bed, Kitty's mouth gaped open as she saw her in all her finery.

'Why, Maria,' she gasped. 'Yer look right lovely. Are they Miss Isabelle's clothes yer wearin'?'

'Yes, they are, and I'd be most grateful if you would help me to get out of them,' Maria answered as she swiped a tear from her cheek.

Ten minutes later she was back in her own clothes; she had removed the ribbons from her hair and tied it back into the neat bun she normally wore. Thankfully, Kitty had not pressed her for any explanations, and Maria was grateful for that at least. She still had the rest of the journey to get through and knew that she must try and hold herself together. She put Isabelle's clothes away, and then when Kitty departed she sat on the bed and waited for her mistress's return with some trepidation.

The afternoon had darkened by the time Isabelle put in an appearance. She had obviously been drinking some of the rum that Maria had noticed was being passed around the salon, and her eyes were feverishly bright.

'Help me get undressed,' she slurred as she staggered towards the bed.

Maria laid her book aside. It looked like there was a difficult evening ahead and it was still quite early. In fact, they hadn't even eaten yet, but looking at the state Isabelle was in, there was no way she was going to make it to the dining room. Flopping onto the side of the bed Isabelle sat there like a limp rag doll as Maria struggled to undress her.

Eventually she managed to get her mistress into her nightgown, and as she then turned to pull back the bed-clothes, Isabelle suddenly leaned forward and was violently sick all over the cabin floor.

The smell was nauseating, but instead of apologising, Isabelle merely flopped onto the bed, croaking, 'And clean that mesh up, it shtinks!'

Disgusted, Maria gritted her teeth and headed to the deck where the mops and buckets were stored. On returning to the cabin, she was relieved to find that Isabelle was out cold, which was just as well because the way she was feeling right at that minute, she would have been in grave danger of giving her a tongue-lashing. Eventually the mess was cleaned up, but there was nothing she could do about the lingering smell – although she wafted the door to and fro in a desperate effort to clear it. Maria decided to go and get her meal in the dining salon and bring something back for her mistress on a tray.

After shrugging herself into her warm cape she headed for the deck where a solitary sailor was sprinkling salt to try and make the planks less slippery for anyone who cared to venture onto them. She ate a solitary unappetising meal of salted pork and vegetables that had been cooked almost to a pulp, then after loading a tray for Isabelle, she stepped back out onto the deck and began to pick her way gingerly back towards the steps that led down to the cabins. It was very dark now and the lower deck was deserted with no sound but the pounding of the waves against the side of the ship and the wind whipping the sails. A thick mist had descended, and as she moved on, a number of barrels containing the precious drinking water loomed out of the darkness. She was almost past them when another dark shape stepped out in front of her and she almost dropped the tray with shock as it blocked her path.

'Would you kindly move out of my way? You startled me,' she said crossly. As her eyes adjusted to the darkness, her heart skipped a beat and she tried to tell herself that she was seeing things. But then the man spoke and she knew that he was all too real.

'Lennie!' she gasped – and yet Lennie was dead – wasn't he? In a nightmare vision, he was leering at her, and as he bent closer, his foul breath, reeking of rum, made her want to retch.

'B-but I thought you were dead,' she said in a voice that trembled.

'Thash what yer were supposed to think,' he slurred. 'An' all the others what I owed money to. But here I am, large as life. Seems we were meant to be together, after all.'

Holding her head high, she focused her eyes on his nose, which she saw was broken now. Revulsion ran through her. How could she ever have thought she was in love with this man? 'I suggest you move right now,' she said, her voice belying the fear that was growing in the pit of her stomach.

'Elsh what, me beauty?' His eyes were mocking her. 'I've been watchin' you fer a while an' a right pretty little thing you are an' all. I never really realised it before. Why not be nice to your Lennie, eh? You've no call to act so 'igh an' mighty. Not wi' my flyblow growin' in yer belly.'

Rage and humiliation flooded through her, replacing the fear, but there was little she could do but try to side-step him without dropping the tray, although her hand itched to smack his face.

'How dare you talk to me like that!' Her eyes flashed fire. 'I strongly suggest you let me go on my way this very minute otherwise I shall make sure that the Captain hears of your despicable behaviour.' She was still reeling from shock but he merely chuckled, a low raspy sound that made the hairs on the back of her neck stand to attention.

'An' do yer really reckon that he'd take the word of a little trollop like you against one of his own men? Now come here. Yer know yer want it just like yer did that night in the churchyard.'

The tray clattered to the deck then as he lunged at her. Maria opened her mouth to scream but she was too late; he already had one hand clamped across it whilst the other grabbed her around the waist and began to drag her into the shadows cast by the enormous barrels. She began to kick and fight, but Lennie was a powerful man and her strength was no match for his.

He flung her to the deck and the breath was instantly knocked out of her. She felt the cold air on her legs as he began to haul her skirt and petticoats up and heard the sound of buttons popping as he tore at the bodice of her dress. His work-roughened hands pinched and clawed cruelly at her tender skin and pain seared through her.

'No – please!' Her voice came out as a whisper as she continued to struggle, and now she felt his calloused hand on the soft skin of her inner thigh and terror shot through her. She managed to free one of her hands and seconds later had the satisfaction of feeling him wince as her fingernails raked down the hardened skin of his cheek. But it did nothing to deter him; in fact, it seemed to have quite the opposite effect.

'Eeh, I like a gal wi' a birro fight in her,' he chuckled as his hand slipped inside her pantaloons and found her most private place. Then his mouth fastened on her pert nipple and pain exploded as he bit on it.

Tears were coursing down her cheeks now, and opening her mouth again she emitted another scream but this time it echoed across the decks as his heavy weight fell on her. And then suddenly she felt him being lifted off her and she heard a scuffle taking place as someone whacked him firmly on the chin and he dropped to the deck like a dead weight.

'Maria? Oh my dear, are you all right?' Suddenly she was

held in Josh's arm and sobbing as he tried to pull her skirt down with the other.

'He . . . he tried to . . .'

'I know.' His voice was soothing. 'But it's all over now and believe me, after I've told the Captain what he tried to do, it will be a long time before he attempts that again. There are plenty of women on board who are willing to pleasure the sailors, without him needing to pick on one who is not. Now, let's get you back to the cabin. Do you think you can stand? Look, let me help you up then you can lean on me.'

He lifted her, which was just as well for her legs had turned to jelly, then taking her weight he tenderly wrapped her cloak about her to hide her near naked-breasts and led her towards the stairs.

Once inside the cabin he glanced towards the comatose, snoring figure of his sister with contempt before helping Maria into the chair. After pouring her a glass of water he pressed it into her shaking hands and she gulped at it gratefully as his arms came around her again. She leaned against him as if it was the most natural thing in the world to do and sighed as she felt him softly kiss her forehead. It was a feather-light kiss but it made the blood in her veins pump wildly and she wished that the moment might never end. And then he suddenly released her and she instantly felt bereft, as if she had lost something beautiful and precious.

'Th-thank you,' she muttered eventually when she had managed to calm herself a little. 'If you had not come along when you did, he would have . . . would have . . .'

'Don't think about that now,' Josh urged as he gently stroked a stray curl from her brow. 'I did come along, and that is the main thing. But now I must get someone to help you. You are in no state to be on your own just yet. And then

I shall go and see to that drunken oaf on deck. I'll fetch Kitty to stay with you, shall I?' And without waiting for an answer he headed for the cabin door.

He was back within minutes with a very concerned Kitty close on his heels. The girl had grown to love Maria unreservedly and was horrified to hear what had almost happened to her.

'Eeh, Maria,' she choked as she dropped to her knees and placed her head in her lap. 'I can scarce believe what Master Josh has just told me. But don't worry, yer safe now. I'll look after yer.'

Satisfied that Maria was in good hands, Josh turned and left, informing her, 'Don't leave her alone tonight please, Kitty.'

'No sir, yer can be sure I won't. But would yer just call down to the single women's quarters an' tell Miss Henshaw where I am, else I'll be fer it.' Scrambling to her feet, Kitty gently took the cloak from Maria's trembling shoulders then rushed to the wash basin to get a cloth to bathe the bite-marks on her breasts.

'He ain't no better than an animal,' she said angrily as Maria flinched. Bruises were already appearing on her breasts and Kitty had no doubt they would be black and blue by morning. She then sighed as she looked at Maria's torn dress. It had been such a lovely dress too, but then knowing what a dab hand Maria was with a needle, she'd no doubt be able to fix it when she had the inclination to, poor sod.

Up on deck Joshua was staring down at the figure of Lennie, who was still out for the count.

'Stick him in the hold until morning,' Captain Dickens roared at two sailors who were standing beside him. 'I will not tolerate such behaviour aboard my ship. Tomorrow morning he will be tied up to the mast and given twelve lashes. We'll see if he is so keen to try and take advantage of my passengers after that.' He then bowed to Josh, and strode away.

Just as promised, Lennie was dragged from the hold at the crack of dawn and his shirt was stripped from him as he glared malevolently at the Captain, who stood with his arms behind his back, grim-faced. His wrists were then tied high above his head and he shivered in the icy morning air.

The whole crew had been ordered on deck to witness the punishment and they stood silently as Captain Dickens nodded towards a sailor standing behind the disgraced man. The man was holding an evil-looking six-foot-long leather whip; with a flick of his wrist, it whistled through the air.

'Proceed, Able Seaman Mohammed. It will be twelve lashes.'

'Aye aye, Cap'n,' the sailor replied.

Lennie cast one more glare towards the Captain from red eyes, but then as the whip cracked and connected with his bare back he howled in agony. A wound opened up and blood began to trickle down his back. *I'll have me day wi' that bitch*, he swore to himself. *Aye, I will – if it's the last thing I ever do!* By the time the Able Seaman had administered six lashes, Lennie was jerking like a marionette on a string but the Captain was not about to show mercy. Following the tenth lash, Lennie suddenly went limp and it was obvious to all present that he had passed out as he dangled at the end of the ropes that bound him. One young seaman, who was on his first voyage, dropped to the deck like a stone in a dead faint but everyone ignored him. And then it was over and another sailor rushed forward to throw a bucket of cold water over Lennie's back, making the deck swim red with his blood.

'Now cut him down,' the Captain instructed sternly. 'And let this be a lesson to all of you.' He then turned and walked away to the poop deck, leaving his crew in no doubt whatsoever of what was in store for them, should they ever disobey him.

Chapter Sixteen

When Josh entered the ladies' cabin the next morning he found poor Kitty almost run off her feet. She had spent the entire night running between Isabelle, who had continued to be ill all night, and Maria, who lay in her tiny compartment looking as white as a ghost. She was obviously now in deep shock.

'You look tired, Kitty,' Josh commented sympathetically but she merely smiled.

'Oh, I's all right, sir,' she responded as Isabelle pulled herself up onto her pillows. 'But neither o' these pair has had a very good night, an' that's a fact.'

'Oh, be quiet, girl, and fetch me a glass of water,' Isabelle said irritably. She had a splitting headache and was dehydrated.

'I hardly think there is any need to talk to the poor girl like that when she has spent the whole night caring for you,' Josh told her sharply.

'I shall speak to her any way I choose. She is only a servant.' Isabelle then glanced towards Maria before asking, 'And what is wrong with *her*? I thought it was her job to care for me, not Kitty's.'

'Maria had a rather unpleasant encounter with a seaman when she was on the way back to the cabin with your meal last night. But don't worry. The matter has been dealt with and the sailor has been punished.'

Pushing her thick curtain of hair over her shoulder, Isabelle raised an eyebrow. 'What do you mean – an encounter? Are you trying to tell me she was raped . . . *again*!'

'No, no, not at all, but it may have come to that if I had not heard her scream.' Josh went in to Maria, who was lying very still staring sightlessly at the ceiling of the cabin. Gently taking her hand he asked, 'How are you feeling today, my dear?'

It took a while for her to register that anyone was speaking to her but then the grip on his hand tightened momentarily and when she looked at him he saw recognition there.

'Thank Gawd fer that,' Kitty said in her own inimitable way. 'I thought she'd gone off her rocker fer a while there.'

'I-I'm fine,' Maria said faintly. 'But I really should be up and dressed. What time is it?'

'Don't worry about that for now,' Josh soothed. 'I think you should have a day of complete rest now. You can cope, can't you, Kitty?'

'Not 'alf.' Kitty would have walked over hot coals for Maria, and even though she was tired to the bone she had no intention of deserting her.

'In that case I shall have your meals delivered from the dining salon for you all,' Josh told her. 'And should you need me during the day, Kitty, ask the steward to fetch me.'

'Right you are, sir.' Kitty bobbed her knee, her eyes

dreamy. He was right handsome, was Mr Josh, and kind too, into the bargain. But then Isabelle was loudly demanding something again and she had no more time for daydreams as she scuttled off to see to her mistress.

Maria moaned as memories of the night before crowded back into her mind. She could still feel Lennie's rough hands kneading her tender breasts, and remember how terrified she had been as he had tried to force himself upon her. If not for Master Josh intervening he would have succeeded – and she would be forever grateful to him for that. Had Lennie no concern for the child – *his* child – that he knew she was carrying! And then she vaguely remembered the feel of soft lips on her forehead and muttered endearments when Josh had got her back to the cabin, and colour stained her tear-streaked cheeks. But of course, she scolded herself, he was only being kind. Anyone would have done the same in his position. Even so, the feel of the kiss lingered and she gave herself a mental shake. What was she thinking of? Joshua was a gentleman and she was a servant. There could never be anything between them – ever. His family would never allow it. But now that Lennie was here, what was he capable of? She was still reeling from the shock of discovering that he was still alive after believing him to be dead. Throwing her legs over the side of the narrow bunk, she feverishly began to put her clothes on, much to Kitty's horror.

'But Maria, Mr Josh said you was to rest today,' she protested. 'You's had a nasty shock.'

'I am perfectly all right now,' Maria answered stubbornly as she slid a petticoat over her head. Her breasts were criss-crossed with black and purple bruises but she tried to ignore the pain as she struggled into her chemise. 'Now you get off back to your quarters and get some rest. You look fit to drop, bless you. And thank you for taking such good care of me.'

Kitty looked doubtful. 'Well, all right then. But only if yer sure you can manage.'

'I'm quite sure.' In truth, Maria was still feeling very shaky but she was made of stern stuff and she knew her place. She had been paid to care for Isabelle and that was exactly what she intended to do. Much better that, than lie in bed weaving silly daydreams. She said goodbye to Kitty, then with a determined sigh she turned to Isabelle to ask, 'Now what can I do for you?'

Two weeks later, the first case of measles was diagnosed by the ship's doctor and in no time at all, people were dropping like flies.

'A poor little lass down in steerage died wi' it this mornin',' Kitty informed them one day with tears in her eyes. 'An' they reckon the ship's sickbay is full to overflowin'.'

'Oh, how awful.' Isabelle shuddered. 'I do hope we don't get it. Can't they quarantine them or something?'

Kitty glared at her. 'How's they supposed to do that on a bloody ship?' she answered cheekily, sickened by Isabelle's heartless attitude. 'They ain't got enough people to nurse the sick so I reckon I'm goin' to volunteer.'

'And I'll help too,' Maria piped up.

'You most certainly will *not!*' Isabelle shrieked. 'If you expose yourself to it, you could bring it back here and pass it on to me.'

'Then I won't come back here. I'll stay in steerage with the patients.' Maria was sick and tired of Isabelle's spoiled ways by now, and with every day that passed it was getting harder to control her temper, especially as she was now terrified of stepping out of the cabin in case she bumped into Lennie again.

'But then who will look after me? How am I supposed to

manage without someone to help me dress and do my hair?'

It was then that something snapped inside Maria. Leaning towards her, she informed her coldly, 'Do you know what, Isabelle? I really don't care! You are nothing but a spoiled, vain brat and you should be ashamed of yourself. People are dying and all you can think of is how you look.'

Josh had just entered the cabin and his mouth gaped as he witnessed Maria and Isabelle rowing.

'So what's going on here then?'

Maria lowered her eyes, embarrassed that she had let her feelings get the better of her.

'It were my fault,' Kitty piped up and went on to tell him about the measles epidemic. 'The problem is, there's too many people down wi' it fer the ship's doctor to cope wi', so me an' Maria were saying we ought to help wi' the nursin' but Miss Isabelle ain't keen on having no one to look after her, sir,' she ended breathlessly.

'I see.' Joshua was looking very handsome in a dark frockcoat, under which he wore a heavily embroidered waistcoat and a silk cravat. His trousers were tucked into knee-length shining leather boots and he looked every inch the gentleman, so he shocked them all when he said, 'I think your offer is most commendable, Kitty, and yours too, Maria.' He paused then to frown at his sister. 'And as for *you*, miss, well, it wouldn't hurt for you to pitch in and help too. People are dying; in fact, I just heard there is to be a burial later today!'

'What?' Isabelle was horrified. 'But surely there are enough servants to attend to their own kind!'

'Illness does not recognise where it strikes,' Josh informed her flatly. 'And should it spread to the cabin passengers, I assume *you* will expect someone to care for you.'

'Of course I should.' Isabelle tossed her pretty head. 'The

ship's doctor should give priority to the cabin passengers. We are paying more, after all.'

Josh sighed, then turning his attention back to Maria and Kitty, he told them, 'You go and see what you can do to help and I will join you shortly.'

'*You!*' Hardly able to believe what she was hearing, Isabelle stared at him incredulously. 'Josh, I forbid you to expose yourself to this! And Maria cannot go yet, I need her to help me to dress. I don't know where anything is.'

'Then I suggest you look for it.' Josh gave her a last contemptuous glance before ushering the two young women out into the corridor and closing the door behind them. The smell from the water closets situated there was overpowering now and they were all keen to get up on deck into the fresh air. There they found two grim-faced sailors wrapping two bodies into canvas shrouds ready for burial.

'Oh dear,' Kitty groaned. 'Looks like there's been another death besides the little lass that passed away earlier.'

The conditions they found down in the steerage part of the ship were abominable, and the smell was even worse than the ones issuing from the water closets. The sick lay on straw mattresses all along the length of one wall as people who looked little better than the patients rushed to and fro trying their best to tend to them – not that there was much they could do apart from bathe the feverish foreheads and offer kind words.

'My God!' Josh looked shocked as he stared around him. But then after shrugging off his fine jacket he yanked his sleeves up and with a determined expression he approached the ship's doctor, asking, 'What can we do to help, sir?'

The doctor, a harassed little chap with thinning grey hair and a droopy moustache glanced up from the person he was tending. He initially looked surprised but then he shrugged helplessly.

'As long as you realise the danger you are exposing yourselves to I'll not refuse help,' he said quietly. 'Just tend to whoever looks in the most need.'

And so for the next few hours, that is exactly what they all did.

As the afternoon darkened they all began to tire but still they went from one person to another, dripping water into parched mouths or soothing those who were delirious and burning with fever.

It was the doctor who finally told them, 'I think you should all take a break now. There is no point in making yourselves ill. Go up to the dining salon and get something to eat, but be sure to wash thoroughly first.'

'Yes, sir.' Josh rounded up Kitty and Maria and led them away. Back up on deck, they were just in time to see the burials. Two sailors stood on either side of a plank resting on the rail on which was balanced the weighed-down canvas shroud containing a body. Across the body was stretched the Union Jack flag. The ship's captain led the prayers and then the minister recited the words of the funeral service and finally ended, 'We now commit the body of Mary Jane White to the sea. May God have mercy on her soul.'

The two sailors then tipped the plank and they all watched horrified as the small bundle plopped into the sea to instantly disappear from view beneath the waves. Only yesterday Maria had watched that poor child playing with her friends on the deck. It was sobering to think that the little mite would never get the chance to experience a new life in Australia. As they stifled their sobs, they washed in the huge barrel of seawater that a sailor had been instructed to place there for the purpose.

The food they were served was very unappetising – some sort of watery stew with chunks of vegetables and slices of salted beef floating in it – and none of them ate much. But even if they had been faced with a feast fit for a king, the sights they had seen that day had robbed them of their appetite.

'Ah well, at least it filled an 'ole,' Kitty remarked, ever the optimist once she had eaten. 'I reckon I feel ready to go back down below now.'

'I shall just go and check on Isabelle and then I am going back too,' Maria told them as she rose from her seat. She was feeling very weary but knew that she couldn't rest when there were so many poor souls still needing help.

Josh's eyes were full of admiration as he watched her leave the dining salon. She had worked tirelessly all day without a word of complaint and he could not help but think what a remarkable young woman she was. She had been very subdued since the night of the attack and very nervy – but then he supposed that was to be expected. She seemed to jump at her own shadow and was forever looking over her shoulder.

Maria found Isabelle in a flaming temper, with a face as dark as a thundercloud.

'Oh, so you decided to come back at last, did you?' she said sarcastically. 'Have you any idea at all how tedious it has been for me today? No one to talk to; no one to read to me; no one to help me dress. And I dare not even go out on deck for fear of meeting someone who is contaminated with this filthy illness.'

'How awful for you,' Maria said with fake sympathy, her hands on her hips. She had hoped to find Isabelle in a more reasonable frame of mind, but she might as well have hoped for snow in summer. 'Cramped up in here all alone whilst people are *dying* all around you.'

Isabelle sniffed. 'Well, now that you are back you can read to me for a while.'

'I'm afraid I can't,' Maria told her firmly. 'I only came to see that you were all right, and now I am going back to the people who are sick. I think they need me much more than you do at present.' Maria then turned and left the cabin without another word, thinking what a thoroughly selfish young woman Isabelle was.

Back down in the bowels of the ship, the doctor was still doing his best to help those worst affected, but it seemed that his was a thankless task. Maria saw him wipe a tear from his eye as he pulled a thin blanket across the face of yet another victim who had succumbed to the illness. Seamen appeared at regular intervals to collect the bodies of the departed and carry them up on deck where they were prepared for a sea burial, and Kitty and Maria felt as if they had been caught in the grip of a nightmare.

The epidemic lasted for a further four weeks before it started to abate, and during that time it claimed five more lives. By then they had sailed into warmer seas. The children were being encouraged to go back on deck into the fresh air, and they shouted with delight as they stared down into the crystal-clear waters.

'Look! What's that over there?' A little boy tugged excitedly at Maria's skirts as he pointed towards the back of the ship and Maria smiled as she told him, 'I think it's a whale but I don't know what sort. You'd have to ask one of the sailors.'

It was nice to see the children smiling again, but there was still work to be done, so gently untangling his fingers Maria made her way back below.

The heat was stifling and those who had survived the

illness were still very fragile and weak, so there was no let-up for Josh, Maria or Kitty as yet.

'I really don't know what I would have done without you all,' the doctor told them when they joined him after a few snatched hours' sleep. He then peered across the top of the glasses that were perched on the end of his nose to ask Kitty, 'Are you feeling all right, my dear? You look very flushed.'

Maria peered at her too then, and was distraught to see the tell-tale red blotches beneath her skin. 'Let me look behind your ears.' And without waiting for permission she tugged Kitty's ear to one side and gasped with dismay to see the cluster of angry spots there. She then felt her forehead and groaned softly.

'I'm afraid you have caught it too, Kitty,' she told the girl, placing a comforting arm about her shoulders. 'Come along, we must get you into bed.'

Within twenty-four hours, Kitty was burning up with fever and Maria and Josh took it in turns to be with her constantly, praying that she would pull through. Kitty had worked tirelessly for weeks, and now in her weakened state they were gravely concerned about her, as was the doctor. She had become delirious, and did not even seem to know them although they spoke to her and murmured endearments.

'I have no medication left to give her,' the doctor said sadly. 'And even if I had, I fear it is in God's hands now. When the fever breaks, she could go either way.'

Maria was so weary she could scarcely keep her eyes open, but even when Josh urged her to go and take a rest she refused.

'No, I shan't leave her,' she vowed, surprised at how much she had come to care for Kitty. 'It was me who suggested to your mother that Kitty should accompany us so I feel responsible for her. If she had stayed at Hatter's Hall she would still be safe.'

Josh sighed sadly before admitting, 'You are probably right, Maria. But I think I can safely say that if asked, Kitty would not have had it any other way. She adores you, anyone can see that. What sort of life would she have had incarcerated there, I ask you? The poor girl had never seen beyond the walls of the place so you must not blame yourself.'

But Maria did, and as she sat there gripping Kitty's burning hand her mind wandered back to the girl she had met at Hatter's Hall. It was amazing to think that little Kitty had come so far. And now this! There seemed to be barely an inch of her that wasn't covered in bright red spots, and as her head thrashed from side to side on the coarse pillow her eyes rolled.

When the doctor next came to check her he shook his head, his face grave.

'Surely there is something we can do?' Maria said beseechingly and yet she knew deep down that there wasn't. The doctor knew it too and he merely squeezed her shoulder before moving on to his next patient.

It was almost midnight when Kitty reached the climax of her illness. Maria had fallen into an uneasy doze on the floor at the side of her but something – and she never knew quite what – made her eyes suddenly spring open to find Kitty staring at her with recognition.

'Oh, sweetheart, thank God!' Tears trickled down Maria's cheeks as she stroked Kitty's hand, which was slightly cooler now although she still looked dreadful. She had never been a robust girl but now she looked positively skeletal. But then

Maria told herself, it was nothing that a little fattening up could not cure, if only Kitty was spared.

'You scared me half to death there,' she told her gently as she dribbled a little water past her parched lips. 'I thought I was going to lose you for a while.'

'You'll not get rid o' me that easily,' Kitty responded hoarsely. 'You're the first person that's ever been kind to me an' I ain't plannin' on leavin' yer just yet.'

And then Maria held her in her arms and they cried together.

The doctor was delighted when he returned in the early hours of the morning.

'Well, bless my soul. You've got some fight in you, little lady. I don't mind telling you I thought you were a goner when I checked on you a few hours ago.' However, he wasn't so pleased with Maria. She looked totally worn out and there were dark shadows beneath her glorious blue eyes.

'I'm going to put my foot down with you next, young lady,' he told her sternly. 'Kitty here is on the mend now so you must go and get some sleep otherwise you will be ill too, and then you'll be no good to neither man nor beast. I'll get one of the other women to keep their eye on Kitty now till morning.'

Seeing the sense in what he said, Maria slowly rose. Every limb felt sore, and the back-ache that had plagued her all afternoon seemed to be worse than ever. She had a griping stomach-ache too, which she assumed had been caused by the many hours she had spent sitting on the hard wooden floor in one position. Perhaps a turn about the deck might blow a few cobwebs away before she retired?

She kissed Kitty's clammy forehead, promising to be back first thing in the morning, and headed for the door. However, before she could get there, she suddenly felt something warm and sticky on her inner thighs and glancing down she was horrified to see a dark stain spreading across the front of her limp skirt.

She turned to stare at the doctor from frightened eyes and opened her mouth to speak . . . and that was the last thing she remembered before a terrible pain tore through her and she dropped into a deep darkness.

Chapter Seventeen

'Oh, my dear, dear girl.'

The voice seemed to be coming from a long way away, and Maria felt as if she was battling through a fog as she tried to open her eyes. Someone was stroking her hand tenderly, but when she tried to see who it was, she groaned. She felt as if someone had torn her insides out.

'Josh? Where am I? And what happened?' It was he holding her hand, and for a moment he was unable to answer her as he blinked back tears of relief.

'You are in your cabin,' he told her softly, and when she managed to glance around she saw that he was telling the truth.

'But Kitty – I left her – is she all right? I was going to rest and that's the last thing I remember. I must get back to her.' She struggled to rise but realised that she was as weak as a kitten as she dropped back heavily onto her pillows.

'That was three days ago,' Josh told her now. 'And Kitty

is recovering well. It's you that has given us a scare this time. I'm afraid . . .' He gulped deep in his throat before forcing himself to go on. 'I'm afraid you lost the baby, Maria. And for a time we thought we were going to lose you too.'

Isabelle appeared next to him then. But she was not the quarrelsome girl Maria had grown accustomed to, for her face was full of concern.

'Oh, thank God you've come through it,' she gasped, dropping down beside Josh and stroking Maria's hand. 'I was so awful to you, and I couldn't have borne it if we'd lost you before I had a chance to tell you how sorry I am.'

Maria lay trying to digest what they had told her. Surely they were mistaken? But as her hand fell to stroke the small mound of her stomach she knew that it was true. Her stomach was flat now. A tear squeezed from the corner of her eye and raced down her cheek. The child had been forced on her and she had never truly wanted it. It would have been a constant reminder of her foolishness, and of Lennie, whom she now hated, but even so it was sad that it had not lived.

'What was it?' she asked dully, and Isabelle and Joshua exchanged a troubled glance.

'It was a little boy.' Josh saw no reason to lie to her. He reached forward to wipe her tears away, his own falling at the same time. 'I'm afraid that you have overdone it over the last weeks and the doctor thinks that this is what may have brought on the birth before its time. I'm so sorry, Maria.'

Isabelle took control then, telling him, 'That's enough for now, Josh. Run up to the dining salon and get Maria something light to eat. We must build up her strength again, and whilst we do, I shall look after her.'

Josh whistled silently in surprise. This was a side of his sister that he had never seen before, and he quite liked it.

Whilst he was gone, Isabelle washed Maria's hands and

face in cool water and brushed her hair then settled her against the pillows, saying, 'I will not allow you to set foot out of bed for at least three days, and then it will be only to sit quietly on the deck until you are fully recovered – so no arguments, miss, do you hear me?'

Despite the sorry condition she was in, Maria had to stifle a grin. This was certainly a case of the servant becoming the master if ever she had known one.

Josh was back in no time carrying a tray with a bowl of thin, greasy-looking gruel on it and a cup of milk, fresh that morning from one of the cows in the hold.

'I'm afraid it doesn't look very appetising,' he apologised. 'But I'd like you to try a spoonful at least. We need to make you strong again.'

Maria tried to oblige and when her carers were content that she had something inside her they discreetly left her to rest and come to terms with what had happened.

By the end of April, Maria was fully recovered and was once more caring for Isabelle, although their relationship had changed considerably. Isabelle had continued to be much more placid as her pregnancy progressed. In fact, they had become quite close.

Instead of insisting that her hair was teased into intricate styles each morning, Isabelle now wore it loose with nothing other than a bright ribbon to tie it back from her face and it suited her. She was now almost six months' pregnant, with the bloom of pregnancy about her, and although her figure was now out of control and she was beginning to waddle, she no longer seemed to mind. She had taken to confiding in Maria when they were alone, and one day she opened her heart as she began to speak of Pierre.

'He was so handsome,' she confided with a dreamy look

in her eyes. 'But I have to admit that I did not want this child.' Her hand caressed her stomach. 'It came as something of a shock to me when I discovered that I was to have a baby, but I have accepted it now. After all, as you once told me, it is not the child's fault, is it?' Maria shook her head as she paused in the act of folding one of Isabelle's gowns.

'I wonder what Pierre would have said if he had known he was to be a father,' Isabelle mused.

'We will probably never know the answer to that question now,' Maria answered sensibly, then, 'Do you think he might have married you?'

Isabelle shook her head. 'I doubt my parents would have allowed that. He was the son of a farrier and they had high hopes of me making a good marriage.' She sighed before making her way up onto the deck to take the air, leaving Maria alone with her thoughts.

Sometimes Maria would look at Isabelle and be consumed by sadness as she thought of the child she had lost, but she never commented on the fact. She had spotted Lennie a couple of times on deck and he had glared at her, but he had never approached her, even though she was aware that he must know she had lost their child – and she was glad of that at least. She never wished to speak to him again. At least now, once Isabelle's confinement was over, she would be able to return home. The thought of having to live under her father's strict regime again brought her no joy, but she looked forward to seeing the rest of her family, especially her longsuffering mother whom she missed more than she could say.

The voyage had been considerably delayed because of the bad weather they had encountered but now there was an air of excitement on board, for the Captain had informed them only the day before that land should be sighted any day now. Up in the crow's-nest a sailor with a telescope watched hopefully and they all waited for his shout with anticipation. It had been a long and tedious and sometimes tragic voyage, and everyone was looking forward to setting foot on dry land again.

It was early in the morning of 1 May 1857 when the cry came from the crow's-nest: 'LAND AHOY!' And they all rushed up to the decks to peer expectantly across the vast expanses of ocean. But as yet, there was nothing to be seen by the naked eye.

It was almost dark when the eager passengers caught their first glimpse of Hobson's Bay outside the city of Melbourne, and it was somewhat of a disappointment, to say the least. At first the coastline was little more than a hazy blur in the far distance, but then as the ship drew closer they saw a huge wooden jetty poking out across a sandy beach into the sea. Beyond were hills covered in trees with sparse foliage upon them and Joshua explained, 'It is winter here. Were we at home they would be bare by now.'

The grass looked scrubby and the trees looked dusty and tired. Houses were dotted here and there, if they could be classed as houses; for they were little more than timber cabins. Even so, Maria could scarcely wait to disembark and put some distance between Lennie and herself. Then she hoped she would never have to set eyes on him again. She had learned a hard lesson.

During the afternoon, Maria had packed their trunks helped by an excited Kitty, who couldn't seem to stop chattering. During the voyage Joshua had shown her books full of pictures of the strange animals that lived in Australia and Tasmania, and now she was keen to see them in the flesh.

'I can't wait to see a kangaroo,' she told Maria excitedly.

'Josh says their babies are called Joeys an' the mothers carry them about in a pouch on their belly.'

'I think I might just know how they feel,' Isabelle commented wryly and they all laughed, relieved that the long voyage was almost at an end. Soon the sailors began to draw down the sails and the ship slowed, still some way out to sea. Two guns and two rockets were fired when the ship finally dropped anchor.

'They are fired to ask for a pilot to come out to guide us in,' Josh explained. 'The coral reefs around Australia are notoriously dangerous but I doubt they will send anyone out to fetch us in until morning. It's beginning to get dark now.'

The three girls looked somewhat disappointed, especially when Josh was proved to be right, but then, they reasoned, what was just one more night when they had already been at sea for so long? In actual fact it was quite pleasant to be in shallower waters with the waves gently lapping at the sides of the boat, and when they leaned over the rails they could see shoals of jewel-like fish swimming about the reefs far below the surface. The evening that followed took on a party atmosphere and everyone was in fine high spirits, although at some point the Captain asked them to say a prayer with him for the poor souls who had died during the voyage. After a hearty, 'Amen!' the merriment continued. The children raced about the decks, their faces tanned and happy again, excited at the first glimpse of the land that was to become their new home.

'Oh, I'm so excited and so looking forward to seeing Uncle Freddie! I shall never be able to sleep tonight,' Isabelle declared when she and Maria finally retired to their cabin. But her head had barely touched the pillow before she was snoring softly.

Maria lay awake, reliving certain parts of the journey. She often thought back to the time when she had woken to the sound of Josh's voice following her miscarriage, and it never failed to make her heart flutter. He had sounded so tender, as if he had really felt something for her, just as he had on the night when Lennie had almost raped her. But she knew she must be mistaken, for since then he had been careful never to be alone with her, and she in turn had kept her distance from him. Oh, he was always friendly and polite admittedly, but that special feeling she had felt when he had held her hand and muttered endearments had never been repeated. She blinked away the tears that were welling in her eyes at the memory.

Maria was a sensible girl who had long ago accepted that there could never be anything between her and Josh, but now she was forced to admit her feelings, if only to herself. She loved him with all her heart and it was not the immature sort of love she had once felt for Lennie. It was all-consuming, to the point that she now knew that if she could not have Josh, she would never have anyone. She was destined to spend her life as an old maid. It was a sobering thought and she eventually fell asleep with tears still wet on her cheeks.

The following morning, a pilot joined the ship to take the *Northern Lights* closer into Hobson's Bay and then long rowing boats arrived to transport the passengers to shore. The cabin passengers were allowed off the ship first, much to the disgust of the steerage passengers who stood back watching sullenly. It felt strange to be on firm land again and Kitty clapped her hands with joy although deep down she was a little disappointed. She had expected towering buildings and busy towns, but this place seemed very quiet.

A seaman eventually delivered their trunks to them and the women waited while Josh asked directions to the nearest hotel. Sadly, they now faced yet another 150-mile trip on another boat to get to Tasmania and he had decided that they would rest first and tackle that journey the following day.

Maria glanced back at the ship just once and her stomach lurched when she saw Lennie up on the deck, watching her closely. She had rarely ventured up on deck since the night of her attack, but sometimes she had glimpsed him – and each time he had stared at her malevolently. Kitty had heard some sailors talking the week following his flogging, saying that he was still lying flat on his stomach because the weals on his back were not healing and had become infected. Maria had taken no pleasure from the knowledge. Indeed, it had filled her with dread because she had realised then that Lennie would never forgive her for what had happened even though it was he himself who had brought it about. But she hastily turned her attention back to her travelling companions, thankful that there was a good distance between them.

Isabelle was still quiet and pleasant, and Kitty and Maria both prayed that it would continue. In truth she had been like a different person since Maria had lost her baby. Oh, Maria still tended to her needs admittedly, but the old Isabelle was gone and in her place was a much more compassionate and considerate girl. Now she was happy to wear whatever Maria laid out for her each day, and with her glorious hair loose about her shoulders or tied back with a simple ribbon, she appeared younger and somehow more vulnerable.

Josh came back to them with a rueful smile on his face. 'I'm afraid I have been told that there is only one hotel here, if it could be classed as such. But I dare say it will be comfortable enough and tomorrow we can return and take a boat to Port Arthur in Tasmania. That kind gentleman I approached is arranging transport right now for us.'

Behind them, all was hustle and bustle as the rest of the passengers were transported ashore. Burly seamen were toting trunks and leading livestock from down in the hold. The poor beasts had spent most of the trip in total darkness; many of them had not survived the journey and those that had, blinked in the bright light looking frail and weak. Now they had to face being dragged through the water with ropes around their necks, until they could feel the sand beneath them.

'Eeh, the poor things,' Kitty said.

'Oh, they'll soon pick up again here,' Josh assured her with a kindly pat to her hand. 'The grazing land around here is perfect for cattle and sheep.' He did not have time to say any more, for then an open cart pulled by two horses drew up beside them.

'Are you the gen'leman wanting a lift to the inn?' the ruddy-faced driver asked in a curious accent that neither Maria nor Kitty had ever heard before.

'We are, sir.' Josh smiled.

The man pointed to the bench seats in the back of the cart, eyeing Isabelle curiously. 'Then you climb up alongside o' me,' he said, 'an' help the ladies into the back while I fasten on all your luggage.'

Josh grinned, thinking how different this conveyance was to the fashionable carriage they were used to back at home, but he did as he was told without a murmur and eventually they were trundling along the rough dusty track.

Kitty sat between Maria and Isabelle giggling as they were thrown from side to side and thoroughly enjoying the adventure whilst they clung to the sides of the cart for dear life. The horses slowly pulled the cart up a steep hill with the driver urging them on all the time, and at the top they found that the view was quite breathtaking. Ahead of them, fields full of sheep stretched into the distance for as far as the eye could see, whilst behind them the ocean was a sparkling azure blue. They passed humble habitations dotted here and there on the hillside and they took in their surroundings as the cart rumbled on. Eventually they came to a small township and the cart stopped in front of a large wooden building.

'This is it then,' the driver informed them, hopping lithely down from his seat. 'Ma Preston runs the inn. She does the best steak pie you'll ever taste, an I'll return to take you's all back to port tomorrow.'

Josh thanked him and gave him a generous tip, then with his help began to hump all the trunks and valises to the door, which was opened by a middle-aged lady who spoke in the same strange accent as the driver who had transported them there.

'Is it rooms you're wanting?' she asked with no preamble.

Josh nodded and bowed, 'Yes, please, madam. Two singles and a double if you have them available.'

'I reckon I can manage that.' She could tell folk of quality when she saw them and quickly ushered them inside. 'And how long will you be staying?' she asked as a man, possibly her husband, appeared over her shoulder.

'Just until we can get the ship to Port Arthur tomorrow. Our uncle lives in Tasmania,' Josh explained.

She nodded, telling the man, 'Frank, get this luggage up to the rooms if you please while I make these good people a nice pot of coffee. I've no doubt you will all be thirsty. And I have some hot biscuits straight from the oven that will keep you going until dinnertime if you'd care for some.'

Frank, a short man in a cap and plain breeches and shirt, jumped to do as he was told and Josh grinned to himself. If this was Mr Preston, there was no mistaking who was the boss in this household.

Maria and Kitty meanwhile were staring about in astonishment. Every single thing seemed to be made of wood. The walls, the floors, the ceilings; even the furniture appeared to be all hand-carved, but it was homely all the same and spotlessly clean – or at least as clean as the dusty road outside would allow it to be.

'Come this way,' Ma Preston urged them as Frank grabbed the first of the enormous trunks and began to haul it up a staircase that was little more than a glorified ladder.

They obediently followed her down a hallway and entered a large kitchen, again consisting mainly of wood.

'Sit yourselves down,' Ma Preston instructed, gesturing towards a rough plank table in the middle of the room, and while her back was turned, Josh gave Maria an amused wink. This was obviously a woman who was used to getting her own way, although for all that, she seemed pleasant enough.

Soon they were drinking fragrant coffee, liberally laced with sugar and milk, and eating home-made wheat biscuits fresh from the oven. A large range took up most of one wall and the room was stifling, making Isabelle's cheeks glow.

'Thank you, that was most welcome,' Josh said after a while. 'But now if you don't mind, I think my sister would welcome a lie-down before dinner. She tends to tire easily.'

'Hmm, I dare say she does.' Ma Preston made a point of staring at the third finger of Isabelle's left hand before her eyes dropped to her protruding stomach. But she made no comment. They were paying guests, after all, and what the young madam had been up to was no business of hers at the end of the day, although she wouldn't mind betting the girl wasn't wed.

Frank, who was obviously as far under the thumb as it was possible to be, had just entered the room after shifting all the luggage up to the rooms and now she barked at him, 'Kindly show these good folk up to their rooms, please, Frank. Mrs er . . . the young lady wishes to have a lay-down afore dinner.'

He nodded obligingly and they all rose and trooped after him, Josh bowing politely before he took his leave of Ma Preston.

When her husband entered the kitchen again some minutes later, the woman grinned at him. 'That young lady won't be long before she drops her load,' she whispered conspiratorially. 'An' I'll bet you any money it's a bastard she's carryin'. Why else would her brother be bringin' her all this way in that condition, I ask yer?'

Her long-suffering husband shrugged. 'Well, Mother, 't'ain't none of our business, is it, just so long as they pay their bill an' don't make any mischief for us.'

She sniffed but she supposed he was right and went about her chores. Ma Preston prided herself on having the cleanest house in town, and winter or not, the damn dust floating through the open window was settling all across the furniture again like nobody's business.

Upstairs, Maria was helping Isabelle out of her gown so that she could rest before their meal.

'Thank you, dear,' Isabelle told her meekly as she swung her legs up onto the bed. Again Maria was struck by the change in her mistress – not that she was complaining, far from it. In the weeks since Maria had lost her baby, Isabelle had changed almost beyond recognition and the changes

211

were all to the good. It was hard to believe that this was the same wilful, selfish young lady who had boarded the ship in Liverpool. The foot-stamping and tantrums seemed to be things of the past now. Instead, she would sit contentedly for hours quietly stroking the mound that was her unborn child and Maria wondered now if she had had a change of heart about it. Maria could scarcely remember the last time Isabelle had called it a bastard or raged about the condition she found herself in.

Now Isabelle sighed happily as she settled back onto the soft pillows in their crisp white covers. 'I do believe this is a feather mattress,' she said. After the stiff straw mattresses on board ship, she felt as if she had died and gone to heaven.

Maria smiled indulgently as she slid the clean woollen blanket that was neatly folded across the bottom of the bed over Isabelle's ungainly shape.

'Good, I'm glad you are comfortable. Now you try to rest while I just go and check on Kitty, then I might come back and have a nap myself.' Another, narrower bed stood across from Isabelle's and at the moment it was looking very tempting. She was much better now following her miscarriage, although she still tended to tire easily and she had not regained all the weight she had lost, despite Kitty's and Josh's best efforts to persuade her to eat. The food on board, particularly during the latter part of their voyage, had not been very appetising, but she was sure that now she was on dry land again she would soon make a full recovery. She folded Isabelle's gown across the back of the chair and tiptoed away to see Kitty, who was in the next room, leaving Isabelle to rest.

Kitty was grinning like a Cheshire cat as she pointed towards the window with a look of wonder on her face. 'Eeh, yer'd never think they were comin' up to their winter, would yer? It's so warm, ain't it? An' when do yer reckon we'll get to see one o' them kangaroos?'

'I shouldn't think it will be too long,' Maria told her with a smile. 'Have you everything you need?'

'Ooh, not 'alf,' Kitty chuckled. 'An' to think I'm havin' me dinner cooked fer me an' bein' waited on, eh?'

'Well, don't get too used to it,' Maria warned with a wry grin. 'Once we get to Isabelle's uncle's I've no doubt we'll both have to pull our weight again.'

Kitty was standing at the window now, staring down into the street and suddenly she gasped as she spotted a brightly coloured bird settle on the branch of a nearby tree.

'Why, would yer just look at that!' she breathed in awe. 'I don't think I've ever seen anythin' so pretty!'

Maria hurried to join her and had to agree. 'I think it might be a parrot,' she remarked.

'I knew this were goin' to turn into an adventure, I just *knew* it,' Kitty said dreamily, and with a grin Maria left her to it and went to rest.

Chapter Eighteen

The next morning following a hearty breakfast Mr Preston arranged for the same open-backed trap that had delivered them to his home to take them all to the port, and so at last the party of four began the final leg of their sea journey on the *Dolphin*. None of them was too keen to leave terra firma again, but feeling refreshed after a good night's sleep and knowing that this voyage would be nowhere near as long as the first, they all endured it cheerfully.

'Oh my, would you just look at that.' Kitty clapped her hands with delight as the boat approached Port Arthur. Lush green hills covered in an array of colourful plants and flowers towered above them and Kitty was sure she had never seen anything quite so pretty. The boat they had travelled on was smaller than the *Northern Lights* and the crossing from Hobson's Bay to Port Arthur had been calm and pleasant.

Once the boat was anchored, they were rowed ashore and their luggage was unloaded onto the jetty by a ruddy-faced seaman. Josh gave him a handsome tip that sent the sailor scuttling off to find transport for them. Meanwhile other sailors continued to unload great barrels of rum and flour, livestock and any number of goods from the ship's hold. Isabelle was looking enchanting in a loose satin dress of sapphire blue that she had purchased from the emporium in Liverpool, and she was receiving more than a few admiring glances, despite her condition. However, she seemed oblivious to them as she stared dreamily up into the hills. She wore a fringed shawl about her shoulders in a lighter shade of blue and her magnificent hair was tied back with a matching ribbon. Kitty and Maria had also gone to great lengths to look their best to meet Josh and Isabelle's uncle and were neatly turned out in their finest, although they were plainly dressed compared to their mistress.

'Ah, here we are,' Josh said after a while as an open-backed carriage pulled by two tired-looking horses trotted towards them. 'It won't be long now, ladies, and you'll get to meet the rebel of Mama's family.'

Maria would have liked to ask him what he meant, but knowing that it was not her place she remained silent as Josh helped them all up onto the seats. The luggage was strapped to the back, and then after being given directions, the driver climbed into the seat and they set off slowly up the steep hill leaving the pretty little port with its cerulean blue seas behind them.

On the way Josh pointed out different plants and flowers, and Kitty listened enthralled.

'That is a cactus plant over there – look. It thrives here because of the warm dry climate.'

Kitty studied the prickly green leaves and the vivid pink trumpet-like flowers.

'And that there is funnel, and over there are wild orchids.

Those on that side are wax flowers, very common here, as are those Blue Gum and Golden Wattle trees.'

He then went on to tell them that until quite recently, Tasmania had been known as Van Diemen's Land, and they listened intently.

It seemed to take forever for them to reach the top of the hill and Maria began to worry about the poor horses but at last they made it and the countryside was spread before them in all its glory. It was like something Maria had read about in fairytales. Green and lush and so beautiful it almost took her breath away. Wild rhododendrons grew in profusion on either side of the rough dirt track, thick with blooms, and the scent of flowers hung heavy on the air. There were vast areas of woodland and streams that sparkled in the sunlight.

'Uncle Freddie's ranch is about four miles away,' Josh informed them as the horse picked up speed. 'And I'm sure you'll like it.'

They all fell silent then as they admired the passing countryside and there was nothing to be heard but the buzz of insects and the sound of the horses' hooves. They passed a waterfall cascading down into a pool so clear that they could see right to the bottom of it and Maria would have loved nothing better than to take her clothes off and scramble into it – not that it would have been a very ladylike thing to do, of course, but the thought made her smile all the same.

Another two miles further on, the horses suddenly slowed and Kitty's eyes stretched wide with pleasure at her first sight of a kangaroo as it hopped across the lane in front of them.

'Would you just look at that little Joey in her pouch,' she screeched excitedly. 'Ain't it clever? Why, it's a shame we humans can't have a little sack o' skin on our bellies fer the same purpose. It would beat havin' to carry the babies about all day, wouldn't it?'

Josh beamed at her pleasure. Kitty had really come out of her shell since leaving England and in no way resembled the shy, downtrodden girl they had taken from Hatter's Hall. Her hair was now streaked with gold from the sun and she had regained a little weight following her illness, which suited her. But it was her eyes where he saw the greatest change. They had lost their haunted look and now sparkled with delight.

Poor child, he found himself thinking, for even now what future could she have? She was an orphaned bastard brought up in a mental asylum – and who would want her when they discovered that? But then the Colonies were a place for new beginnings, where different rules applied. She might thrive here. He turned his attention to Isabelle, who was sitting quietly with her parasol shielding her from the sun. She had spoken scarcely two words the whole morning, and even though he felt the change in his sister was for the better, it was taking some getting used to.

And then finally he allowed himself to peep at Maria. She still had dark shadows under her eyes and her clothes hung loosely on her now, but he hoped that this would change once they reached his uncle's ranch and she could get some decent food inside her.

They continued in silence, each of them enjoying the picturesque landscape, and then at last as they reached the top of yet another rise Josh pointed down into a valley.

'There is Uncle Freddie's ranch.'

All eyes turned in the direction of his pointing finger and Maria's face lit up brighter than the sun that was shining down on them.

The homestead, which looked enormous even from a

distance, was nestled deep down in a valley surrounded by lush green fields where fat sheep were contentedly grazing. Maria was sure that there must have been hundreds of them. The house was a long, one-storey building surrounded by a white picket fence, and like the rest of the buildings they had passed it was made entirely of wood. People were rushing around like ants and even from this distance Maria could see that the majority of them were black. They were no doubt the local indigenous people employed by Uncle Freddie to help run the sheep-farming business.

As the carriage began its descent into the valley, Maria peered out, intent on not missing anything. It took quite a while to coax the horses down the steep incline, even when all the passengers jumped down to walk until they were back on level ground, and she soon realised that the ranch was much further away than it had appeared to be. But then this whole place was enormous, as she was fast learning.

Eventually the horses drew to a halt in front of a long verandah that wrapped right the way around the wooden structure. A wooden swing, which would offer shelter from the sun, stood to one side of the door, and Maria saw that all the doors and windows that were visible were open and draped in fine mosquito nets.

As Josh approached the house, tired and sweaty from the long journey, a small female figure dressed in an emerald-green crinoline suddenly pushed aside the mosquito net on the main entrance and darted onto the verandah with a broad smile on her face.

'Esperanza!' Josh hurried forward to hug the woman and they spoke for a while in a language that Maria did not understand. The woman was clearly not English, but she was without doubt one of the most beautiful women that she had ever set eyes on. Her skin was olive-coloured and flawless, and her hair, which cascaded down her back, was coal black and curly. Her eyes were dark too, and as Maria watched her she suddenly turned her attention to the women in the party and smiled a radiant smile that revealed small white teeth.

'Ah, Isabelle,' she said now as she came forward with her arms outstretched, merely glancing at Maria and Kitty. 'Your uncle is working on the land. He did not expect you until later.' She waved her hand vaguely in the direction of the fields behind her that seemed to be full of sheep and then urged, 'But come. You must be tired and thirsty. I shall have Binda prepare you some refreshments.'

She helped Isabelle down from the carriage and as Maria fell into step with Josh behind them, she whispered, 'Who is she?'

Josh grinned. 'Well, if you remember, I told you that Uncle Freddie was the rebel of the family. Esperanza is his mistress.'

Maria's eyes almost popped out of her head. 'What? You mean they . . . they live together and they're not married!'

'That's about the long and short of it,' he chuckled. 'Although it isn't for the want of Uncle asking her. He'd marry Esperanza tomorrow if she'd have him, but she seems to be quite happy as she is and they're totally devoted to each other. They've been together for years and have two children, whom I'm sure you will meet in due course.'

'Oh.' Maria gulped, for she couldn't think of anything more to say. She was well aware that back home it was accepted that the gentry had mistresses, but they didn't live together openly with them; the women were usually set up in some small establishment where the men discreetly visited them. Obviously things were very different in Tasmania – and who was she to question them, after just losing a child out of wedlock?

By now they were entering the ranch-house and Maria looked about with interest as Kitty stayed close to her side, apparently overawed at her surroundings. Just like the outside of the building the inner walls were made entirely of wood, but the furnishings might have come straight from the rooms of a palace; and Maria couldn't help but be impressed. Velvet-upholstered settees on spindly gilt legs were set here and there with tiny occasional tables at the side of them, and a large marble Adam-style fireplace that would have graced a stately home stood against one wall, not that Maria thought it would be needed very often. Fine Turkish rugs were strewn across the highly polished floorboards and oil paintings aplenty adorned the walls. Maria assumed this must be the sitting room as she and Kitty followed Esperanza and Isabelle into the room beyond. In here, a fine mahogany table took centre stage, surrounded by a dozen matching chairs with cabriole legs and embroidered seat-covers. A matching sideboard stood nearby, over which hung an enormous mirror. For a moment, Maria was speechless.

It was then that a small round woman bustled into the room and Esperanza said, 'Ah, Binda. Our guests have arrived. Would you prepare them some tea, please? English-style of course.' She grinned at the visitors, then, saying, 'I know how fond you people are of your tea, so Freddie has had some shipped out for you, enough to last for a few months at least. We prefer coffee here, but then each to his own.' Then more discreetly she addressed Maria and Kitty, suggesting, 'Perhaps you would like to go through to the kitchen with Binda and take your refreshments there?'

Josh looked uncomfortable but Maria was happy to go with Kitty and soon they found themselves in a very splendid kitchen. A large range stood against one wall, and copper pans, which gleamed in the sunshine that poured in through the open back door, were suspended from a thick beam above it.

The black woman smiled at them and gestured towards the large oak table in the centre of the room. 'You sit down, yes?' she said pleasantly and although Maria and Kitty would have loved to have a wander around, they did as they were told.

It was whilst they were sitting there that two very lovely, well dressed children charged into the room, stopping dead in their tracks to stare curiously at the visitors.

Binda instantly spoke to them in a language that neither Maria nor Kitty could understand, and the boy, who looked to be about nine or ten years old, stepped forward and solemnly extended his hand.

'How do you do,' he said formally. 'I am Alfonso and this is my sister Rosa.'

With their thick black hair and deep brown eyes, Maria instantly guessed that these must be Esperanza's children, and she thought that they were both exquisite. The little girl, who hung back shyly behind her brother, looked to be about six or seven and Maria smiled at them. A lump formed in her throat as she thought of her own little sister back at home.

'I am very pleased to meet you,' she told them. 'My name is Maria and this is Kitty.'

'We knew you were coming,' Alfonso told her importantly. 'Papa told us, and Aunt Isabelle and Uncle Josh are here too, aren't they? But you are not going to be staying here. Mama has had the guesthouse made ready for you.' His face dropped a little then as he confided, 'Mama has told us that we must not come troubling you and making a nuisance of ourselves.'

'Oh, I'm sure you could never be nuisances,' Maria assured him gravely with a smile in her eyes. 'And as far as I am concerned, you are welcome to come and see us whenever you choose.'

'That would be very nice, thank you. But of course we are with our tutor for much of the day doing our lessons. Mr Brady lives in a small dwelling not far from the guesthouse so I am sure you will meet him at some stage. Papa says education is very important. Can you read and write?'

'Yes, I can,' Maria told him and he looked mildly surprised as he glanced towards Binda who was busily laying a tea tray while the kettle boiled on the range.

'Most of our servants cannot write,' Alfonso confided, then addressing Kitty he asked, 'Can you?'

Kitty blushed. 'Just a little bit. Maria here has been teachin' me on the journey.'

'Ah, then that is good.' Alfonso flashed a smile and Kitty's heart melted. She had a feeling that she would get along with these two just fine, even though the little girl appeared to be much shyer than her brother.

They then spent another half-hour pleasantly drinking tea and eating freshly baked griddle scones until Joshua appeared in the doorway.

After the children had greeted him he told Maria, 'It seems that you and Isabelle are to stay in the guesthouse along with Robbie McPhee, Uncle's right-hand man. He'll make sure that all the heavy jobs are tended to during your stay. You and Kitty are free to take care of Isabelle. Are you happy with that arrangement?'

'Perfectly,' Maria assured him, secretly relieved that she would not have to be too close to him. She knew that it would be unwise in the circumstances.

They said goodbye to the children, who were reluctant to let them go, and in no time at all they were in the carriage again heading for the guesthouse.

'Is it very far?' Maria enquired as the vehicle slowly rolled along the rough track.

'About a mile or so, I should say, but don't worry. Robbie will be there and if you should need us he can be back here for help in no time.'

Maria sat back to enjoy the scenery and soon enough a small guesthouse came into view. It was nowhere near as big as the ranch-house, but charming all the same. Again the main structure was made of wood and it had a verandah at the front. To one side was another building that Maria guessed must be the stables, and beyond that were a number of large outbuildings surrounded by trees. Shelter for the sheep in inclement weather, perhaps?

Isabelle was looking tired and drawn by now, and had not uttered so much as a single word since leaving her uncle's home, so Maria was relieved that they had finally arrived so that she might rest.

Josh helped them all down and together they went into the smaller dwelling, which proved to be surprisingly spacious inside.

'Nearer to Isabelle's time, Binda will be coming to stay with you so that she's on-hand to deliver the baby,' he informed Maria as he began to carry their luggage inside.

When Maria raised an eyebrow he grinned. 'Don't look so worried. I think Binda has delivered more babies than we've had hot dinners, Alfonso and Rosa included. Isabelle will be in very safe hands and should she need a doctor, Robbie will ride into town to get one.'

'Binda is a very unusual name,' Maria commented, and he nodded.

'It means "deep water",' he explained. Maria thought it was enchanting.

He placed a trunk at the side of the door as Maria looked about at what was to be her home for the next few months. The house was comfortable and cosy. A large settee was placed in front of a wooden fireplace, and animal skins were spread across the floor. The next room was a very serviceable dining room with an oak table and six solid oak chairs placed around it, and the room further on proved to be a very adequate kitchen with everything they would need.

A long corridor led to three bedrooms and a bathroom with a large enamel bath. At one end of the house was a water closet that stood slightly apart from the main building, which Maria was silently pleased about.

'Eeh, it's really grand,' Kitty sighed delightedly as she skipped back along the corridor to look at the bedrooms again. After the cramped conditions she had endured in the steerage quarters aboard ship, the brass bed appeared positively enormous. There were pretty curtains fluttering at the window and the whole place was spotlessly clean.

Josh looked pleased by her reaction, but hastily assured her, 'If there's anything else you need, you only have to ask. Esperanza will have it sent straight over to you along with your food supplies, which will be delivered daily together with fresh milk and so on. But now perhaps we'd better get Isabelle to lie down.' He glanced worriedly at his sister, who was as white as a sheet. Maria instantly took Isabelle's elbow and steered her towards the best bedroom. The girl went without complaint, too weary to even comment.

As Josh watched them go, his eyebrows drew together in a frown. Isabelle didn't seem to be herself at all and looked quite unwell. But then he supposed it was to be expected. She was with child, after all, and the long sea voyage from Liverpool had taken its toll on all of them. But now that they were here and with good fresh air and good food inside her, no doubt she would soon be her normal irritating self. Hoping he was right, he went to join Kitty who was joyfully exploring the kitchen.

Chapter Nineteen

It was later that evening when Maria and Kitty first met Robbie McPhee. He breezed into the kitchen with a big smile on his face and Maria knew instantly that they were going to get along. Robbie was a great giant of a man with hands like hams and a bushy beard. His hair, which was on the long side, had a tendency to curl and was bright red, and he had a freckled suntanned face from the many hours he spent outside.

When he spoke it was with a broad Scottish accent as he settled himself at the kitchen table and said, 'So is there anything to eat going? If I'm goin' to be stayin' here with you lassies, I shall expect you to feed me. A grown man needs his tucker!'

Kitty giggled as she rushed away to fetch bread and cheese from the cold shelf, and as Rob watched her go he thought what a canny little lass she was. Her giggle was quite infectious.

Once Kitty had disappeared, he turned his attention to Maria to ask, 'So do you have everything you need?'

He was thinking what a pretty girl she was although the shapeless dress she was wearing did nothing to enhance her appearance. But then Freddie had told him to expect two pregnant women, so Maria was probably one of them. Robbie had already guessed without being told that Freddie's niece must be the other one, and a right little tartar she was by all accounts. He hadn't actually met her yet and Robbie had always been one who liked to form his own opinion of a person.

Now Maria smiled at him as she wiped her hands down the front of her apron and answered, 'Yes, thank you, we seem to be well supplied with everything. In fact, I'm sure we shall be very comfortable here once we settle in. But was I right in assuming that you would be staying here with us?'

'Not exactly.' Robbie smiled at Kitty as she came back into the room and she blushed becomingly. 'I shall actually be staying in my own place, which is just around the back there.' He gestured towards the open window. 'I'm in the process of buildin' my own cabin, as it happens.'

'Really?'

He nodded. 'Aye, I am that, but I still have a long way to go. There's only three rooms habitable at present but I get by just fine.'

'And does your wife live there too?' Maria asked innocently, and when his face darkened she instantly wished that she had kept quiet.

Ignoring the question, he began to carve some slices from the loaf that Kitty had placed on the table while Maria busied herself making him some coffee to go with it. The atmosphere had become tense and she wondered what she could have said that was so wrong. She had only asked him about his wife, assuming that he was bound to have one.

When the coffee was made she poured it into a jug and carried it to the table along with sugar and milk so that Robbie could help himself. Kitty skittered off to fetch him a mug and Maria was amused to see that the girl seemed to be very taken with him. From the corner of her eye Maria glanced at him, trying to assess how old he might be, but it was hard to judge with his heavy beard and his weather-worn skin. He could be anywhere from his early twenties to forty, from what she could see of him – not that it was any of her business, she told herself hastily.

Robbie finished the rest of his meal in silence then rising from the table he told them, 'I'll be away to fetch the logs in for you now. You need to keep the range stoked up for cooking. I'll also see to the cleaning out of the closet each day and do any heavy work that needs doing, but during the day hours I shall be away working around the ranch. I'll also need to teach you both how to handle a gun and ride.'

'Whatever would we need a gun for?' Maria asked, horrified, and he smiled again now.

'Just in case you get any visits during the day from any stray bears,' he told her calmly. 'But don't look so scared, it isna a regular occurrence. And you need to be on the look-out for spiders too. Most of them are harmless, but some of them can pack a rare old bite. The male Funnel Web is the worst – he'll rear up at you and attack if he thinks he's being cornered. He tends to like warm moist conditions, so take care when you visit the dunny, eh? The little devil likes to hide beneath the seat.'

Kitty visibly paled as her hand went to her throat but Robbie hadn't finished. 'Be on the look-out fer snakes too, especially of an evening when everywhere is quieter. The three to watch out for are the Taipan, the Brown Snake and the Tiger Snake.'

Seeing how distressed Kitty was getting, Maria quickly changed the subject when she asked, 'And why do we need to know how to ride?' She had never been astride a horse in her whole life and had absolutely no inclination to do so.

'Just in case you should need help here in the day whilst I'm out on the ranch,' he explained affably. 'There's a stables out back with my own and another horse in it. Gentle as a lamb, old Bessie is, so you might enjoy learning to ride her. Handy if you want to go into town too. Hobart is the nearest settlement, and it's where we go to get any provisions that we can't grow ourselves. Esperanza shops for clothes there and all, and some of the ranch hands go there of a night for a pint or two. Being able to ride will make you feel less isolated.'

'I dare say it would,' Maria agreed, although she still wasn't at ease with the idea.

'Right, well, there's no need to rush things.' Robbie headed for the door. 'I dare say you'll all be wanting to turn in, after your journey. You must be bushed so I'll get the logs in and then I'll leave you in peace to bunk down.'

The minute he had left the room, Kitty looked around fearfully as if a spider or a snake might appear at any second. 'I like the sound o' the kangaroos an' the wallabies but I ain't so keen on the idea o' the snakes an' spiders,' she muttered.

'Well, I dare say Robbie was only warning us, but I doubt we'll even see one,' Maria answered stoutly, praying that she was right. She didn't much like the sound of them herself, but Kitty was quite spooked enough so she wisely didn't say so.

Maria stifled a yawn as she flicked the mosquito net aside on Isabelle's bed and peeped in at her. It had been a long,

long day and now she was ready for bed herself – but first she wanted to check that there was nothing that her mistress needed.

'Are you all right?' she asked softly as she lifted the candle she was holding high.

The light spilled onto Isabelle's face and she smiled sleepily. She had been in bed ever since they had arrived, but then Maria supposed this wasn't a bad thing. The journey had been long and tiresome, and Isabelle was heavily pregnant now. She had roused just once to eat the meal that Maria had carried into her earlier on but now she shook her head.

'I'm fine, thank you. Go and get some rest.'

'Are you sure that there's nothing you need?'

'No, nothing. Goodnight, Maria.' Isabelle then turned over and was fast asleep again before the other girl had even had time to answer her.

After carefully dropping the net into place Maria quietly made her way to her own room further along the corridor. The night was warm and balmy and the curtains in the corridor fluttered gently in the breeze. Outside she could hear the night creatures in the forest and she shuddered as she thought of the snakes and the spiders Robbie had warned them about. Through one of the windows she could see the glow of an oil lamp and she guessed that this must be coming from the cabin that Robbie was in the process of constructing. It was nice to think that a man was close by, should they need him. She moved slowly into her room where she slumped exhaustedly on to her bed and slept like a baby till early the next morning.

The sound of Yellowtails and Cockatoos in the surrounding trees brought Maria springing awake, and as she yawned and stretched she saw with dismay that she must have over-slept. Brilliant sunlight was pouring through a gap in the curtains and sounds were issuing from the kitchen which could only mean that either Kitty or Isabelle was already up and about. She lifted the mosquito net hastily aside and after slipping her feet into her house shoes she put on her dress-ing-gown and headed along the passage. When she burst into the kitchen to find Robbie sitting at the kitchen table with Kitty, her hand rose self-consciously to her hair which was tangled about her shoulders.

Nodding a greeting at Robbie she asked Kitty, 'Why didn't you wake me? What time is it? And have you been in to see if Miss Isabelle wants anything?'

'Hold yer horses,' Kitty chuckled. 'I can only answer one question at a time, yer know.' Her eyes were sparkling and she looked happy and almost pretty. Her cheeky personality, which had been thoroughly repressed in the asylum, was beginning to shine through and her bright smile was infectious. Robbie obviously thought so too, if the way his eyes were following her about was anything to go by.

'Right then, in answer to yer first question: I didn't wake yer 'cos I have everythin' under control in here an' I thought yer looked done in last night an' that a little lie-in would do yer the power o' good. The time is . . .' she glanced at the clock on the wall and after studying it closely and narrowing her eyes, she said cautiously, 'half past eight.' Maria had been teaching her on the voyage to tell the time as well as to read and write. 'Not so very late, yer see. An' yes, I have been in to Miss Isabelle an' she's right at this minute enjoyin' her porridge an' a cup o' tea in bed. So I ain't completely useless, am I?'

'I never for a second meant to imply that you were,' Maria muttered, feeling somewhat foolish, then without another word she scuttled off to her room to wash and dress.

On her way back to the kitchen she called into Isabelle's room to find her propped up against her pillows, staring blankly towards the window. Her breakfast had barely been touched. 'So how are you feeling today then?' Maria asked cheerfully. 'Better, I hope, now that you have rested.'

'What? Oh yes . . . thank you, Maria. I am quite well but I think I should like to stay here for a while if it's all the same with you.'

Maria straightened the colourful eiderdown. 'But I thought you said that Esperanza had invited you over to the ranch this morning?'

'Did I?' Isabelle shrugged carelessly. 'Well, I dare say I could always go over this afternoon if I feel like it, but for now I am quite comfortable where I am.'

'Very well.' Maria pointed to a small bell on the bedside table. 'I shall go and help Kitty with the cleaning now, but if you need anything, just ring.'

No answer was forthcoming so after a moment she left the room, closing the door quietly behind her.

Robbie was gone when she next entered the kitchen, and Kitty told her, 'Robbie has gone to work but he said he'd pop back mid-morning to see if there was anything we needed and to bring fresh supplies.' She sighed happily as she gazed about the tidy kitchen. 'It's lovely here, ain't it? Like another world. All fresh air and wide open spaces.'

'And all snakes and spiders too,' Maria said without thinking, and then could have bitten her tongue out as she saw Kitty's face fall.

'Sorry,' she mumbled. 'I think I must have got out of bed the wrong side this morning. But what was Robbie doing here?'

'Well, he stuck his head round the door to see if there were owt we needed before he left, an' seein' as I'd made far too much breakfast, I gave him some. He enjoyed it an' all an' said I were a right fair little cook.' She giggled then. 'An' he also said as how tonight he's gonna give us our first lesson on how to handle a gun,' Kitty rattled on.

Maria wasn't too keen on that idea at all but this time she wisely held her tongue and concentrated on her food as Kitty flitted about humming merrily to herself.

An hour later when the kitchen was once again swept and clean as a new pin, she went back to check on Isabelle, but the girl was still in the same position as she had left her in, wide awake and simply staring off into space.

'So what would you like to wear today?' Maria asked, crossing to the large pine wardrobe that took up almost all of one wall. She had only unpacked one of Miss Isabelle's trunks up to now, but there were a number of day dresses available for her to choose from.

'Oh . . . any,' Isabelle said vaguely and Maria was so surprised that she gawped at her. Isabelle had always been so choosy about what she wanted to wear but lately it had begun to seem as if she didn't care. But then, Maria told herself, she must be so uncomfortable now that perhaps she didn't really feel right in anything.

'What about this one then? It won't be too heavy if it gets warm.' She took out a full-skirted cotton gown covered in tiny yellow rosebuds and held it out for Isabelle's inspection.

The girl barely looked at it. 'I dare say that will do,' she shrugged.

Maria laid it along the bottom of the bed before rummaging through another of the trunks for suitable petticoats to wear beneath it. Eventually she had everything she needed neatly laid out and she then asked, 'Would you like me to fill the bath for you? You must feel very dusty and dirty after the journey yesterday. I could wash your hair for you as well if you liked?'

'Oh, just put me some water in a basin. A wash will do,' Isabelle told her as she struggled to the edge of the bed.

Half an hour later she was dressed. Maria had done what she could with her hair but it was full of dust and looked lank and lifeless despite her best efforts. Perhaps she would be able to persuade Isabelle to bathe later that evening. Isabelle wandered away then, leaving Maria to the rest of the unpacking, and after finding the swing on the porch she settled there and stayed there for most of the day.

'Miss Isabelle is in a strange mood, ain't she?' Kitty whispered as she and Maria were preparing dinner together. Robbie had been as true as his word and had arrived mid-morning with fresh vegetables, bread, butter, milk fresh from the cows that morning and some of the weirdest-looking steaks that Kitty had ever seen.

'Is this beef?' Kitty had asked suspiciously as she stabbed her finger at them and he had laughed and tapped the side of his nose as if it was some big secret.

'Not exactly, but I'll guarantee they'll melt in your mouth if you cook them right, lass. Just sprinkle them with a little pepper and smear them with lard, then pop them in the oven till they're tender. You'll like them, trust me.'

Strangely enough, Kitty did trust him although they had only just met and she flashed him a warm smile as he left the kitchen to go back to his chores.

'He were sayin' this mornin' that Miss Isabelle's uncle has over *three thousand* sheep on this ranch,' she told Maria. 'An' behind his ranch is a bunkhouse where all the ranch-hands stay – 'ceptin' Robbie, o' course – an' as he told us last night, he's buildin' his own place just over yonder.' She sighed wistfully then as she began to peel some carrots on the scrubbed table. 'Can yer just imagine how wonderful it would be to have yer very own place? I used to dream about that when I were back at Hatter's Hall. Havin' me own place what no one could ever take away from me an' bein' able to earn enough money never to have to rely on nobody.' She looked embarrassed then and hastily lowered her eyes as pity swept through Maria. As she had thought many times before, while she hadn't had the happiest home life – her father had always seen to that – compared to this poor lass, she had been lucky. She had known the love of her mother and her brother and sister, whereas poor Kitty had never had anyone.

Thoughts of her family brought hot tears stinging to the back of Maria's eyes. Now that she had lost the child she had been carrying, there would be nothing to stop her returning home once Miss Isabelle's confinement was over – and she intended to do just that. But what would Kitty choose to do? Already she seemed to be embracing this new way of life, but Maria was feeling out of her depth. The huge wide open spaces would take some getting used to, as would all the different races of people she had encountered, not to mention the strange animals and trees. Even the flowers were different here. She felt very isolated and vulnerable, but then she supposed Kitty would feel differently, of course, never having known freedom before.

Chapter Twenty

Over the next couple of weeks the girls' lives fell into a routine, and before they knew it they were into June. They would rise each morning and after seeing to Isabelle's needs, Kitty and Maria would then tackle the household chores, including the washing and ironing. None of them had ventured very far from the homestead as yet, although Maria had persuaded Isabelle to visit her uncle's ranch on a couple of occasions and each time she had accompanied her.

It was during the second visit that Maria met Isabelle's uncle for the first time, and she thought what a truly nice man he was – although she would never have guessed he was the owner of such a huge ranch had she not been introduced. Freddie dressed much as his ranch-hands did, and was proud of the fact that there was no job he could not do, which was probably why he was so highly regarded amongst his staff. Every day he would work side by side with them, and he seemed to be truly contented with his lot and welcomed Maria warmly.

There was only one slightly uncomfortable moment when Esperanza first introduced them, and that was when his eyes lingered momentarily on Maria's stomach. She realised that Isabelle's mother would have written to advise him that she too was with child, and as she still favoured the baggy dresses she had worn on board ship, she guessed that he had no idea that she had lost her baby during the voyage. She decided not to enlighten him of the fact right then. Time would tell its own story when no child was forthcoming, and for now all her concerns were for Isabelle. The girl had become very withdrawn and reclusive, and sometimes it was difficult to persuade her to even get out of bed. On the increasingly rare times when Maria did manage it, Isabelle would head for the swing on the porch and there she would stay for the rest of the day, at times even taking her meals there. When she did talk, it was usually about Pierre and it pained Maria to realise how much she must have loved him.

Josh visited quite often, and the sight of him galloping towards the small homestead on one of his uncle's steeds would set Maria's heart thumping. But she always ensured that they were never alone, and as soon as she had settled him with Isabelle, she would hurry away to fetch him a cold drink and then make herself scarce for the rest of his stay.

During the balmy evenings, Robbie was teaching Kitty and Maria to ride and handle a gun; Maria was finding it extremely difficult to acquire either of these skills. It was one thing to try and aim at a tree, but she wondered if she would ever have the courage to actually pull the trigger if a live creature was lumbering towards her. Her riding skills were little better, although Kitty seemed to have taken to it all like a duck to water. Already she could canter on her own whilst Maria could still only manage to trot around the barn at the end of a long rope guided by Robbie.

'You'll get the hang of it eventually, lass,' he would tell her patiently. 'It just takes some a bit longer than others.'

But Maria wasn't so sure that she would, nor even that she wanted to, for that matter. She had noticed that Robbie and Kitty had grown closer, and sometimes the fact troubled her. Robbie was undoubtedly a nice man, but very guarded when it came to his personal life and she wondered if Kitty might end up getting hurt – not that she could do anything about it. Kitty was now seventeen years old and her own person, but Maria still fretted about her.

She found Robbie sitting at the kitchen table one evening when she entered the room after settling Isabelle for the night, and he smiled at her as Kitty refilled his mug with coffee.

Kitty had taken to cooking a little extra so that he had a meal to come back to after work each day and he was now a regular visitor to the kitchen.

As Maria joined them at the table he told her, 'I was just asking Kitty if she fancied going in to Hobart with me on Sat'day evening. There's a barn dance there and I thought she might enjoy it. You're very welcome to come too, o' course, if you've a mind to, but I dare say you won't be wantin' to leave Miss Isabelle. I could always get Binda to come and keep an eye out for her, if you fancied it?'

'Thanks, but I don't think I will,' Maria answered. There was no need to ask if Kitty wanted to go, however, for she was positively beaming from ear to ear.

'I thought we could go in the trap,' Robbie went on. 'I've no doubt Kitty'll want to get her fancy clogs on and she can't really ride astride dressed in all her finery.'

'I shall have to try an' find sommat suitable to wear,' Kitty fretted now, suddenly realising that her wardrobe was somewhat restricted. The plain woollen dresses that Miss Isabelle had bought her were the finest she had ever owned, but would they be suitable for a dance? She very much doubted it, but Maria saved the day when she told her, 'Don't get worrying about that. I'm sure that Miss Isabelle will have something she will be happy to loan you, and although you're slimmer than she is we should be able to make it fit with a stitch here and there.'

'Do yer really think she would?' Kitty asked, clasping her hands in excitement.

Maria nodded but then the mood was broken when Robbie scraped his chair back across the wooden floor and told her, 'Well, if you still want to come and have a wee look at my humble abode we'd better be on our way. I don't mind admitting I'm jiggered, and I wouldn't want to fall asleep on you. It's been a long day. Some of the sheep escaped and I had to ride miles to find the little devils before I could herd them all back home.'

Kitty snatched up her shawl, then turning to Maria she asked worriedly, 'Yer don't mind, do yer? I shan't be gone long, I promise.'

'Of course I don't mind,' Maria assured her. 'I'm not your keeper, Kitty. You are free to come and go as you please.'

But then as she watched the girl accompany Robbie across the yard her worries returned. She would hate to see Kitty have her heart broken – but what could she do about it?

As they approached Robbie's dwelling, the breath caught in Kitty's throat for she was sure she had never seen anything so beautiful in her whole life. So far there were only three rooms completed – a kitchen, which as yet was still not properly furnished, a bedroom and a sitting room that had wonderful views across the valley. The sun was setting, turning everything to pale gold, and Kitty stared about her in awe.

'Why, I never realised yer'd have such a view from here,' she told him. 'I thought yer'd be surrounded by trees an' it would be dark.'

He shook his head as he went to place the kettle on a small stove in a far corner. 'That's why I deliberately chose to build it this side of the copse,' he answered as he struck a match. 'I didnae want it to be gloomy and I've a fancy it'll be fine sitting here of an evening when it's all finished – when I get round to getting meself a couple of chairs, that is!'

'It is a bit bare at the moment,' Kitty commented as she glanced around, then she began to wander about the room, telling him, 'What yer need is a couple o' comfy fireside chairs here, an' a nice big rug in between that yer can rest yer feet on. You'd be cosy, but still see the view from the winder then. An' over here . . .' She moved to the centre of the room and spread her arms, 'is a nice big table an' chairs where yer can eat or sit an' read if you'd a mind to. Then over there by the sink yer need a number o' shelves fer yer pots an' pans, and on that wall there a nice big dresser where yer could display all yer best china. An' per'aps some pictures on the walls an' pretty curtains hangin' at the winders.'

Getting quite carried away, she then strode into the bedroom without being asked and wrinkled her nose as she saw the chaos there. Dirty clothes were scattered about the floor, and apart from the bed, which was unmade, the room was quite empty. She began to gather the clothes up as she told him across her shoulder, 'This room needs a woman's touch an' all. Why, it's a fine brass bed, but it needs a nice patchwork quilt and some flowery curtains at the winder. A wardrobe an' some drawers wouldn't go amiss either.

Yer'd have somewhere to keep this lot then. Talkin' o' which, I'm goin' to take them an' wash them through fer yer. An' yer needn't argue,' she told him sternly as he opened his mouth to protest. ''T'ain't no trouble at all. I have some of our washin' to do tomorrow anyway. Now, let's go an' have a look at this sittin' room, eh?'

Robbie stifled a grin as she deposited his dirty laundry on the floor and marched purposefully past him into the last room where, once again, she was delighted with what she saw. Like all the houses she had seen since arriving in Tasmania, all the rooms were on one level and this one, like the kitchen, had a panoramic view across the valley although as yet it was completely empty.

'Now this could be the formal parlour,' she told him as her imagination ran riot. 'Fer when yer have visitors or fer usin' at Christmas an' special occasions. All the best houses have parlours, yer know.'

Suddenly seeing the way his lips were twitching, Kitty lowered her head, deeply embarrassed. 'Sorry,' she muttered. 'I didn't mean to sound like I were interferin'. I dare say yer do all right fer a bloke livin' on his own.'

'Don't apologise,' Robbie answered. 'You are right – this place does lack a woman's touch. I'll be the first to admit I'm no' so good at choosin' the right bits an' pieces for the place.'

'I could help yer if yer wanted me to,' Kitty whispered hopefully.

'As it so happens, there's a chappie not so far away who is a dab hand at making tables and chairs,' Robbie said thoughtfully. 'I dare say I could call in and see him and get him to make a start on them. And then there's a fine shop in Hobart that sells all the fancy stuff, including material if you'd a mind to come an' show me what's needed.'

'I'd love to,' Kitty answered joyfully.

241

'Then that's what we'll do.' Robbie smiled at her. 'How about we go one day next week? Could you spare the time?'

'Easily. I can whip through me chores in the mornin' an' we could go in the afternoon.'

'Excellent. Thank you, lass. I know you'll be a grand help.'

Kitty nodded and bustled away to the next room, hoping he wouldn't hear her heart which was beating like a drum, while he stroked his beard and watched her go.

By the time Saturday evening came around Kitty was in a state of high excitement. Isabelle had kindly loaned her a beautiful crinoline dress in a pale blue marbled silk and Maria had altered the waist to fit her. Now with her hair piled high on top of her head and teased into curls, the orphan girl was barely recognisable.

'Aw, Maria, I feel like the Princess Royal at one o' them Buckingham Palace parties,' she breathed. 'I just love how you've done me hair. Thank yer so much. It's a shame about the shoes though.' She lifted her skirts to scowl at her high buttoned boots. Unfortunately, her feet were at least two sizes bigger than Miss Isabelle's, and no amount of shoving or squeezing had allowed her to get any of her dainty slippers on, so she would just have to wear her own, far more sensible boots.

'Never mind,' Maria said as she tweaked out Kitty's skirts. 'It's not as if anyone is going to see your shoes anyway, is it? I just hope Robbie makes an effort now, with you looking like that.'

At that precise moment they heard him enter the kitchen and Kitty drew herself up to her full height. 'Lawks!' she squeaked. 'This is worse than goin' to see Miss Belle for a tongue-lashin'.'

When she and Maria entered the kitchen, it was hard to say who was the most shocked. Robbie looked astounded when he caught sight of Kitty, and she was speechless when she saw him.

There was no sign of the bushy red beard the girls had grown accustomed to, for he was clean shaven now. His hair had been neatly trimmed, and was slicked down close to his head with macassar oil. He was dressed magnificently in a smart fitted jacket, a clean white shirt with a black bow tie and – most impressive of all – a red and black kilt in what must be the McPhee clan tartan, complete with ornate sporran. He looked every inch a true Highland warrior.

'Och, lass, you look really grand,' Robbie said eventually, breaking the stunned silence.

'S-so do you,' Kitty managed to stutter. He looked so handsome and seemed to have shed years; revealing that he was nowhere near as old as they had taken him for – probably only in his late twenties at the very most.

'Here,' Maria said, snatching up Kitty's shawl from the chair. 'You might need this on the way home. It can still get chilly later on. Now be off with you and I hope you both have a wonderful time. But do take care. The tracks are so bad around here I shan't rest until you are both safely back.'

'You've no need to worry on that score,' Robbie said proudly as he held his arm out for Kitty to take. 'I know every pot-hole from here to Hobart so she's in safe hands. Goodnight, Maria.'

As they left the kitchen arm-in-arm, a pang of envy sliced through Maria. Here she was, seeing Kitty off as if she was a parent when in actual fact there were only a couple of years at most between them. How she would have loved to be accompanying them with— She stopped her thoughts from going any further as she realised she had been thinking of

Josh. It was different for Kitty and Robbie since they were both from the same class, but she and Josh were poles apart in society, and she knew she really must try to stop thinking about him . . . but it was so hard.

Moving to the door, she watched as Robbie helped Kitty up into the trap. The girl really did look beautiful and was positively glowing with happiness. Then she waved until they were out of sight before turning and heading off to see if Isabelle needed anything.

The next morning, Kitty was full of the night's events and chattered on incessantly as she and Maria washed the breakfast pots together.

'Robbie is quite a good dancer,' she told Maria for at least the third time in as many minutes. 'An' by the end o' the night I weren't so bad either. Well, at least I weren't steppin' on his toes any more.' She sighed happily as she recalled how it had felt to be swept around the dance floor in his strong arms.

'And I hope he behaved in a gentlemanly manner,' Maria said primly.

Kitty was instantly on the defensive. 'Why, o' course he did,' she declared indignantly. 'An' when we got back he saw me right into the kitchen before he went to stable the horse.'

The conversation was suddenly interrupted by the bell that was left on Isabelle's bedside table. It was such a rare occurrence for her to ring it that Maria immediately dried her hands on her apron and rushed to see what was wanted as Kitty watched her go, with a concerned look on her face.

Maria found Isabelle sitting on the edge of her bed. 'Is anything wrong?' she asked anxiously. 'Are you feeling unwell?'

244

When Isabelle raised her head, Maria was shocked to see how ill she looked. There were dark circles beneath her eyes and her once lustrous hair hung limply about her shoulders.

'No, I'm not ill,' she said as she grasped Maria's hand and clung onto it. 'But I just had the strangest dream . . . at least, I think it was a dream and I need to tell you about it. You see, I dreamed that I had had the baby. It was a little girl and I called her Faith. Don't you think that's a beautiful name, Maria?'

When Maria nodded, the other girl licked her lips before going on, 'The thing is, I've realised that I don't want her to stay here in this godforsaken place. I want her to go home to England.'

'But the whole point of us coming here was so that no one would know you had had a child,' Maria said tactfully. 'What would your parents say if you were to return with her?'

Isabelle suddenly appeared more her old self as she tossed her head. 'I don't care. But I want you to promise me that she will go home. Will you do that for me, Maria?'

A cold hand was gripping Maria's heart now as she said soothingly, 'Why don't you just wait until after the child is born and then make your decision? You are not thinking straight at the moment.'

Isabelle eyed her oddly before loosening her hand and saying tiredly, 'I think I would like some tea now, please.'

Maria hovered uncertainly for a second then headed back to the kitchen where she relayed the strange conversation to Kitty.

'Dreams can be like that sometimes,' the girl said. 'Ain't you never had one that were so real it stayed with you after yer woke up? I certainly have. But then if you're concerned about her I could ride over to the ranch an' get Binda to come an' take a look at her.'

'I think that might be a good idea,' Maria answered, unable to shift the feeling of dread that had settled around her like a cloak. 'But wouldn't it be better if you walked there? You've always had Robbie with you when you've ridden before.'

'Huh! I could ride Bessie blindfolded by now,' Kitty scoffed as she took her apron off and smoothed her hair. 'You get Miss Isabelle's tea on the go an' I'll be back afore yer know it.' And with that she headed for the stable-block at the rear of the homestead to saddle up the gentle old nag.

Chapter Twenty-one

'The young missy has been visited by the spirits,' Binda told Maria solemnly after examining Isabelle.

'And what exactly is *that* supposed to mean?' Maria burst out. Anxiety made her sound harsh.

The old woman's chins wobbled as she shook her head gravely. 'The missy is weak and not meant for this world. The spirits have come to warn her.'

Maria's hands clenched into fists as she struggled to control her feelings. She had never heard such a load of ridiculous superstition in her entire life. 'I think I would like a *proper* doctor to visit her,' she told the Aboriginal woman. 'Could you ask her uncle to get one of his ranch-hands to ride into Hobart to arrange it, please?'

The words had barely left her lips when a horse pulled up outside and a rider leaped lightly from the saddle. Seconds later Josh strode into the kitchen and asked, 'What's wrong? I was out on the ranch when one of the men rode out to us to say that Kitty had been to fetch Binda. Is it Isabelle?'

Maria nodded. 'Yes. She doesn't seem herself, although there isn't anything medically wrong with her that I can see. She had a bad dream so I got Kitty to fetch Binda to check her over, just to be on the safe side, but she's just been talking nonsense, saying that Isabelle isn't long for this world. I want a proper doctor to come and see her.'

'I see.' Josh tapped his riding crop against the side of his leg. 'In that case, I shall go for the doctor myself. But first I shall go in to see Isabelle if you don't mind.'

'Of course.' Maria inclined her head in the direction of the passageway and Josh immediately strode away.

Binda stared at Maria sadly. 'You have become close to the young missy, yes?'

'Yes, I suppose I have,' Maria sighed.

Binda gently stroked her arm. 'It is time I moved my things here,' she told her as she turned for the door. 'The birthing will take place soon and you will not wish to be alone with her.'

'But it is still some weeks until the baby is due,' Maria pointed out.

'Babies will come when they are ready,' Binda answered, and with that she left to collect her things from the ranch without another word.

True to her promise, Binda arrived later that day with a little bundle of clothes. By then the doctor had already been and declared that nothing was amiss.

'But where will you sleep?' Maria flustered. 'There are only three bedrooms and we have one each, although I suppose Kitty and I could always move in together.'

'I shall be quite comfortable on the settle by the fire, missy,' Binda assured her.

Maria was horrified. 'But you'll be so uncomfortable,' she protested.

'No. Back in my village I slept on the floor on a rush mat,' Binda said. 'But now that I am here, why don't you and the other missy visit the spring?'

'The spring?' Maria was curious.

Binda gestured past Robbie's homestead through the trees. 'Take the path through the forest at the side of Robbie's place and you will come to a clearing,' she told her. 'There you will find a rock pool. It is fed by a spring from underground and is good to swim in.'

Maria had never been swimming in her entire life but was too embarrassed to say so. Neither had Kitty if it came to that but she looked intrigued. When Maria appeared hesitant, Binda told her, 'I will keep my eye on the young mistress.'

'Come on, Maria,' Kitty encouraged. It was still light so she hoped there would be little chance of encountering a spider or a snake.

'I suppose we could at least take a stroll and have a peep at it,' Maria said. In truth she was beginning to feel a little confined. 'But I'm not promising that I shall go in, unless it's just for a splodge at the edge,' she warned.

The girls set off and within minutes they had found the track that Binda had told them about. The trees were thick here and formed a canopy above them as Kitty took the lead, slapping the ground ahead of her with a stick just in case there were any snakes lurking about. They seemed to walk for a long way, with Maria becoming more apprehensive by the minute, but then suddenly they reached the clearing that Binda had spoken of and they both stopped as one and gasped with pleasure. Ahead of them was a rockface with sparkling clear water cascading down it into a pool. It must be the same one they had passed on the journey from Hobson's Bay.

'Well, would yer just look at that,' Kitty breathed in awe. 'Did yer ever in yer whole life see anythin' so pretty?'

Wild orchids grew in profusion all around the edges of the pool, reminding Maria of a picture she had once seen in a magazine.

'I don't know about you but I'm goin' in fer a splash,' Kitty told her as she sat down and began to unlace her boots.

'But you can't!' Maria protested, horrified. 'Your clothes will be wet through.'

'No, they won't 'cos I'm gonna strip off an' go in in me underpinnings,' Kitty informed her.

'But what if someone should come and see you?'

'Oh yes, an' who is that likely to be then?' Kitty scoffed.

Maria watched helplessly as Kitty undressed, flinging her clothes about in gay abandon until she was standing there in just her pantaloons and her bodice. Then with a whoop of delight, Kitty ran towards the water and, throwing caution to the winds, she leaped in. To Maria's horror she instantly disappeared beneath the surface but as Maria raced towards her she surfaced coughing and spluttering as she trod water.

'Crikey, I didn't reckon on it bein' that deep,' Kitty laughed. 'Why don't yer come on in? It's lovely an' warm in here. Yer really don't know what yer missin'.'

Maria chewed on her lip and dithered. It did look very enticing, she had to admit, and then as Kitty began to splash about she gave in to temptation and started to disrobe. Within minutes she was in the water too, and the girls were laughing and playing about like two children. It was good to let your hair down and feel the cleansing coolness on your skin, Maria thought, and she kicked her legs and waved her arms as she had seen Henry do in the blue lagoon back at home when they were children. It was the first time she had allowed herself to have any fun for months, and she felt thoroughly clean and exhilarated. It was only when the shadows around the pool began to lengthen that the girls reluctantly climbed out and wrung the water from their hair.

'We're going to get our dresses wet if we put them on over these wet underclothes,' Maria pointed out, ever the practical one.

'So we'll take the wet things off an' carry 'em,' Kitty said. ''T'ain't as if there's anyone here to see us, is it?' And they proceeded to do just that.

They were almost halfway back when Kitty suddenly paused to ask, 'Did yer hear somethin' just then?' Narrowing her eyes she peered nervously into the trees behind them. 'It sounded like someone followin' us.'

'I didn't hear anything,' Maria answered, but even so they quickened their footsteps and were relieved when Robbie's cabin came into view. He was sitting outside smoking his pipe, so Maria realised that if there had been someone behind them, it couldn't have been him.

'Ah, so we've discovered the pool, have we?' he asked with a grin.

As the girls nodded he thought how attractive Kitty looked with her hair hanging damply about her face. She was a canny little lass there was no doubt about it, and if things had been different he would have set his cap at her. But as things stood he would be doing her an injustice to even contemplate it. All they could ever be was friends, so bearing that in mind he told her, 'The gaffer's given me a few hours off tomorrow afternoon. Do yer fancy ridin' into

Hobart with me to look for some furniture? I'd be right glad of a female eye, so I would.'

Kitty's heart fluttered as she nodded but then she thumbed across her shoulder and her eyes became fearful as she told him, 'I thought I heard someone followin' us through the woods back there.'

''T'would only have been a beastie,' he reassured her. 'They start to wander about at dusk.'

'Oh.' Kitty looked relieved and, suddenly feeling in the way, Maria moved on. She was convinced now that Kitty had feelings for Robbie but she wondered if he returned them. He had always shown them both nothing but kindness admittedly and he had taken Kitty to the dance in Hobart, but as far as she was aware he had never exhibited any romantic inclination towards the girl. She hoped that Kitty wasn't heading for heartbreak – but then she scolded herself: who was she to try and interfere? The first time she had fallen in love, or thought she had, it had led to an unwanted pregnancy. And the second time . . . She gulped as she thought of Josh. Giving herself a mental shake, she quickened her steps. Josh could be at the house at this very minute visiting Isabelle, and it wouldn't do for him to find her daydreaming like a lovesick schoolgirl.

'Ah, Maria, there you are,' he called, only minutes later, as he walked towards her through the trees. He had obviously decided to come and meet them and his voice was heavy with concern. 'I popped over to see Isabelle and when Binda told me that you and Kitty had gone to the pool, I was worried. It's very easy to get lost in these trees, when it's dark. Are you both all right?'

'We're fine,' she said. 'Kitty is back there planning a trip into Hobart tomorrow with Robbie. But what did you think of Isabelle?'

His head wagged from side to side as he fell into step with her. 'She seems very . . .' he struggled to find the right word.

Maria suggested tentatively, 'Strange?'

'Well, yes. I would have to say she did,' he sighed. 'Not at all like herself. Sort of vacant and far away. I think she even forgot I was in the room at times.'

'She's been like that for a while,' Maria told him. 'And Binda seems to think that the baby could come at any time, which is quite worrying as she still has a few weeks to go.'

'Hmm.' He glanced at her, noting the way her damp hair was springing into curls and the flush on her cheeks. 'Then I should be on the alert if that's the case. I've never known Binda to be wrong and she's delivered hundreds of babies over the years but I don't think we need to send for the doctor again just yet. Binda is very capable.'

They had reached the verandah now and the light from the oil lamps in the kitchen was spilling through the door. Josh's horse was tethered there and was gently pawing the ground. Josh told her, 'I suppose I'd better be off then. No doubt you have things you need to do before you retire for the night. But do get word to me if anything should happen with my sister, would you?'

'Of course,' she promised him politely, wishing that he had allowed her to summon the doctor. 'Goodnight, Josh.'

He leaped lithely into the saddle and she stood there and watched him gallop away until the ever-darkening night had swallowed him up.

Late the following afternoon, Kitty returned from Hobart with Robbie.

'Oh, you'll never believe some o' the bargains we've had.' She threw her shawl across a chair and clasped her hands as she beamed at Maria and Binda. 'Robbie took me to an auction house an' we found a beautiful sofa that will look a treat in his living room. An' I got some material too to make him some curtains and cushion covers. Well, I'm not that good at sewing really but yer will help me, Maria, won't yer?'

When Maria nodded she rushed on, 'We got more pots an' pans, new bedding, an' some lovely rugs that will look wonderful on the floorboards. Then on the way back, we called in at a joiner friend o' Robbie's who's made him a sturdy table an' chairs where he can sit to eat.'

Her eyes were like stars and once again, Maria felt a ripple of unease. Anyone hearing her might have thought that Kitty had been choosing things for her own home, but Maria did not have the heart to say anything and spoil the girl's mood. Eventually, as she realised that she was gabbling on, Kitty flushed guiltily. 'Sorry,' she said. 'But we've had such a lovely day I got carried away. Now what needs doin'?'

'Not a thing,' Maria said lightly. 'Binda and I have everything in hand. There's some stew on the stove, enough for you and Robbie if you haven't eaten yet.'

'Cor, ta.' Kitty rubbed her stomach, suddenly realising how hungry she was. 'Then in that case I'll take the pan over to Robbie's if yer don't mind an' we can warm it up an' eat it there. I can help him to unpack his new stuff an' all then. Yer know what men are like – he won't have a clue where to put anything. That's if you've no objections?' she added anxiously.

'Of course not.' Maria forced a smile to her face as Kitty snatched up the pan and disappeared the way she had just come. Glancing up, she found Binda watching her closely.

'You are worried about the little missy, no?'

Maria sighed and nodded. There was no point in denying

it. Binda seemed to have the ability to see right into her very soul.

'Robbie is a good man,' she told Maria. 'She will come to no harm with him.'

'But I think Kitty has feelings for him,' Maria confided, 'and as yet Robbie doesn't appear to be returning them.'

'He cannot marry her, if that is what you are hoping for.'

'Why? Is he already married?' Maria had feared something like this but it was soon evident that Binda was going to say no more and they lapsed into silence as Maria's mind worked overtime.

It was during the early hours of the morning that Maria awoke, certain that she had heard something moving about on the verandah. She slipped her dressing-gown on then tiptoed along the passageway, her bare feet making no sound on the floorboards.

Binda was fast asleep on the settle and Maria let herself out onto the verandah, having taken her small hand-gun from the kitchen cupboard on the way. Her hands were shaking and she prayed that she would have no cause to use it, but she cocked it ready all the same.

She had gone no more than a few tentative steps when a shadow suddenly loomed up in front of her out of the darkness and she aimed the gun, holding it with both hands.

'Whoa there, don't go firin' that, lassie.' When Robbie's familiar voice came to her she almost cried with relief as she sagged against the wall.

'What are you doing prowling about?' she shakily managed to ask as Robbie came to stand at her side.

'I thought I heard something.' He was peering into the deep night and now that her eyes had adjusted to the gloom, she saw that he was holding his rifle.

255

'What do you think it was?' She was almost afraid to ask but he shrugged, although she sensed that he still wasn't happy.

'I can't be sure,' he answered. 'It could have been a bear but it sounded like a man's footsteps to me. But don't be afraid. Whatever or whoever it was, they've gone now.'

'How can you be so sure?'

He grinned. 'Ain't nothin' gets past me,' he told her. 'I know the sounds of all the night creatures an' I can even tell you how close they are.'

Maria suddenly thought of the noise Kitty had heard earlier that evening as they were returning from the pool.

'Do you think that it might be the same person who was following me and Kitty earlier on?' she asked tremulously. She had felt very safe and secure in the knowledge that Robbie was close by, but suddenly she felt very vulnerable again.

'You don't even know for sure that anyone *was* following you,' he pointed out sensibly. 'But you go on back to bed now. I shall hang about for a bit before I turn in and you'll all be quite safe, I promise you.'

'All right. Goodnight, Robbie.' Maria turned and entered the cabin again, but for the first time she slept with her gun close at hand on her bedside table.

Chapter Twenty-two

Maria was the first to rise the next morning and was surprised to see through the window that Robbie was in almost exactly the same place she had left him in the night before.

Slipping out of the door to join him she whispered, 'Haven't you been to bed yet?'

'Of course I have, but lookie here.' He pointed down to the ground with the barrel of his rifle. It had rained during the night and the dust surrounding the cabin had turned into a quagmire in which a man's footprints were clearly visible. At least, Maria assumed they were a man's. They were very large for a woman's.

'Who do you think it was?' she asked with a tremor in her voice.

'I don't know, but I reckon I'll ride over to the ranch and tell the boss that I'm not turning in today. I think I'll hang about here just in case the feller decides to come back.' Then seeing the fear in her eyes he added, 'It was probably just some chancer come looking for something to steal that he could sell on. Even out here we get them, more's the pity. The number of sheep we have go missing is alarming. Chances are that now they know I'm on to them, we'll not see them again so stop worrying. You're safe as houses.'

'That's all right then,' she answered wryly. 'Isabelle seems to be a bag of nerves, and I really don't think she needs any upsets. But I'd better go in and get breakfast started now. Will you be joining us? I've some bacon and eggs I was planning on cooking.'

'In that case, how could I refuse?' Robbie winked at her and feeling slightly better Maria went back inside to call in on Isabelle before getting dressed.

Once breakfast was over, Binda again examined Isabelle and decided that she would go back to the ranch to pay Esperanza and the children a visit. It was obvious that she missed them, and as Isabelle was quiet and seemingly in no distress Maria had no objections to her going. As it was, there was little to do about the cabin that day so after helping Maria wash up the pots Kitty asked, 'Would yer mind very much if I went over to Robbie's to carry on wi' the cleanin' there? It's startin' to look grand now wi' all the new bits an' pieces he's bought.'

As Isabelle was dozing again, and Maria assumed that there would be little chance of the intruder returning in broad daylight, she thought that it might be quite nice to have a little time to herself. So she gave her consent willingly, and after scrubbing the floor, she pushed the kettle into the heart of the fire to boil again, deciding to make a nice pot of tea and put her feet up for a while. She might even begin one of the books Esperanza had kindly sent over for her.

She carefully measured the tealeaves into the heavy

brown teapot, grateful that Uncle Freddie made sure they had a plentiful supply. Maria didn't like coffee, especially the way the people here drank it – strong and black with no sugar.

She was in the process of pouring out a mugful when she heard the back door open, and thinking that it was Kitty returned for something she had forgotten, she turned with a smile on her face. It died instantly and her stomach seemed to sink into her shoes as she found herself looking at Lennie.

'Wh-what are you doing here? And how did you know where to find me?' she choked out.

He looked wild and unkempt as he eyed her hungrily. Strangely, since she had left the ship, he had been able to think of no one else. No other woman had ever spurned him before, and suddenly he had realised what he had lost, which was why he had jumped ship to follow her.

''T'weren't hard in this neck o' the woods,' he told her with a sickly grin. Then, 'Is there any o' that tea goin' spare? I'm fair parched.'

Maria was over her initial shock now and her eyes blazed fearlessly as she stormed, 'Was it *you* hanging about here last night?'

'What if it was? Ain't yer pleased to see me?'

As he advanced on her, she could smell him – rank with sweat. She quickly put the table between them, telling him, 'I should go now while you can, if I were you. If Robbie catches you here it will be the worse for you.'

He grinned. 'Now that's hardly the way to talk to yer intended, is it? An' you carryin' my babby an' all. I've followed you all this way, even after you got me a flogging.'

'But I'm *not* carrying your child any more,' she spat. 'I lost the baby when I was ill aboard ship. I thought you knew that. And I'm *certainly* not your intended!'

He looked momentarily stunned – then he eyed her shape-less dress and she realised that he was trying to determine if she was telling the truth.

And then he shrugged. 'Aw well, if that's the case we'll have to make another, won't we?' He looked about at the cosy cabin. 'Seems to me yer've fallen on yer feet here, an' I'm sure the gaffer would have no objections to yer beloved joinin' the team. It would certainly beat workin' me guts out on the ship.'

'Huh!' Maria tossed her head in defiance before telling him clearly, 'There's no chance of us *ever* getting back together now, Lennie. I thought I loved you once but you walked out and left me when I was at my lowest, with no thought of what would happen to me should my father find out I was with child. You didn't care about me or what would happen to your unborn child then, did you!'

'Ah, but that were then an' this is now,' he said cajolingly as he began to sidle around the table. It was then that Maria lifted the heavy pressed-glass milk jug, sending the contents sloshing all across the table and the floor as she warned him, 'You come one step closer to me, and I shall hit you with this – I swear it!'

Lennie chuckled. It seemed that Maria was not the timid little miss he had taken her for and suddenly he wanted her more than ever. As he drew closer, the smell of him made Maria's eyes water and it was all she could do to stop herself from gagging. Then suddenly he threw aside the chair that stood between them and it clattered across the floor. As he pounced on her, Maria brought the jug swishing down but it merely bounced ineffectively off his arm as he bore her to the floor.

'Come on now, give us a kiss, yer know yer want to,' he gasped as she struggled beneath him. It was like a repeat of the night in the churchyard and the attack on the ship. She opened her mouth to scream, but his dirty hand had clamped across it and now she did gag as he ripped at her clothes. Helpless tears poured from her eyes as she bucked beneath his weight. The buttons on her blouse popped off and rolled across the floor as he tore at the thin material. And then suddenly a piercing scream rent the air, and Maria turned to see Isabelle standing in the doorway clutching at her stomach. She was screaming loudly enough to waken the dead, but still Lennie grappled with Maria until suddenly he was hauled off her and she rolled away to curl into a sobbing ball.

'Why, you dirty little bastard. What did yer think yer were about?' Robbie roared as his fist slammed into Lennie's face.

Kitty had dropped to her knees beside Isabelle now, and as she held her protectively Lennie spat out a tooth and shouted, 'She's me woman. Let me be, yer barmy bastard!' Blood was pouring from his nose and mouth from the blow and he was trying to hit out at Robbie but the bigger man had him firmly by the scruff of the neck and Lennie's feet were dangling inches from the floor.

'That's the same bloke that attacked Maria while we were aboard the *Northern Lights*,' Kitty informed Robbie.

'Is it now?' he bellowed. 'Then in that case we'd better deliver him back to the Port Arthur authorities, hadn't we? They don't take kindly to deserters, an' no doubt he'll feel the length o' the whip again. He won't be so keen to attack helpless women when he's had another couple o' dozen lashes once they return him to the ship.'

'No!' Even after what he had tried to do to her, Maria could not bear the thought of him being flogged again. She still had nightmares about the way his body had jerked like

261

a puppet's as the lashes rained down on his bare back, and the way his blood had puddled on the deck. 'Just let him go,' she whimpered, but Robbie was resolute.

'I'll deliver him back to the port an' then it's up to them what they do with the lowlife,' he growled. 'What kind of man would try to do such a thing to a woman?'

Their attention was diverted then as Isabelle, who had stopped screaming, suddenly gasped loudly. They looked across at her and saw that she was standing in a puddle of water. The girl had gone deathly pale.

'Jesus, her waters have broke,' Kitty mumbled. She had witnessed childbirth many times back in Hatter's Hall and realised instantly what had happened.

Maria staggered drunkenly to her feet, clutching the front of her torn blouse together, as Robbie manhandled Lennie out of the room. 'You can cool yer heels in the barn till the young mistress has been seen to,' he told him grimly. Then turning back to Maria he said, 'Soon as I've got this chap tied up I shall be ridin' across to the ranch to fetch Binda back. Can you two manage meanwhile?'

'Yes, we can,' Kitty assured him as she took Isabelle's elbow and began to lead her gently back to her room. 'But hurry, Robbie, please.'

Robbie nodded as he pushed Lennie ahead of him. Now that she was alone again Maria sank onto the nearest chair and began to tremble uncontrollably before forcing herself to go and get changed so she could sit with Isabelle and Kitty.

It was almost an hour later when Robbie's horse slewed to a stop in front of the verandah. Binda was sitting behind him and she slithered to the ground quite gracefully for someone of her considerable size.

'Hot water and towels, many of them,' she told Maria as

she raced towards Isabelle's room, wiping the rain from her face as she went. It was lashing down outside and beating a tattoo on the wooden roof.

'Go, let me look at her,' she told Kitty firmly as she entered Isabelle's room and the girl went quietly. Somehow she sensed that it would not be wise to argue with Binda.

'How is she?' Maria asked faintly as Kitty came into the kitchen. She had needed to sit down for a while.

'It's hard to say – she's very quiet. But how are *you* now?' Kitty saw that Maria was almost as pale as the mistress, but then that was hardly surprising after what had happened. She was just thankful that she had heard Isabelle's screams or God knew what might have happened.

'I'm all right,' Maria answered shakily. 'But I find it almost impossible to believe that Lennie followed us all the way here from Melbourne. He thought that I was still carrying his baby and even though I explained that I had miscarried aboard ship, I'm not sure that he believed me.'

'Well, don't you go worryin' no more about him. Robbie's got him trussed up like a turkey cock in the barn an' there's no way he'll get out till Robbie wants him to.' Kitty's small hands balled into fists of anger. She loved Maria like a sister, and at least she was safe now. Robbie was going to deliver Lennie back to the port, and with the authorities taking over, she had an idea that he would not find it so easy to escape again.

The two young women sat quietly for what seemed an eternity, the tension eating into them until eventually Binda appeared looking concerned.

'There is no sign of the birth pains,' she commented. 'That is bad, very bad. If they do not start soon, the missy will have dry birth.'

Maria and Kitty glanced at each other and then Kitty suggested, 'Would yer like me to get Robbie to ride into Hobart for the doctor?'

Binda shook her head. 'Not yet. There is still time and anyway, it is doubtful that anyone could get through with this rain. The paths will be muddy. But she is asking for you.' She nodded towards Maria. 'Go and sit with her, and fetch me if the pains start.'

Maria did as she was told. On entering Isabelle's room, she found the girl staring towards the door for a sight of her. 'Maria.' She held her hand out and Maria instantly grasped it in her own as she sat down in the chair at the side of the bed. 'I'm so glad you came. I need to talk to you.'

'Why don't you save your strength?' Maria suggested. She was still badly shaken up, and despite knowing that Lennie was securely tied up, she could still feel his presence, as if the stink of him was still upon her, despite changing her clothes and washing herself. *How could I ever have thought that I loved him?* she asked herself, but her thoughts were brought sharply back to the present when Isabelle increased the pressure on her hand.

'Maria, *please*. There are things that I must say.' Sweat was standing out in glittering beads on her forehead and yet she was deathly pale and her hand was clammy.

'Very well then, what is it?'

'I . . . I want you to promise me something,' Isabelle said. 'I want you to promise me that when the child is born, you will take her home to Mama in England. Josh will accompany you.'

'But I thought that your uncle was going to find a home for the child when it is born?' Maria said, confused. 'We agreed that we would wait until after the birth before you made your decision.'

Isabelle smiled weakly. 'Ah, but things have changed now.' She stroked her swollen abdomen. '*I* have changed since I felt this little being moving inside me. I realise now that she deserves the best chance that we can give her, and Mama will ensure that she gets that, if you can only get her home.'

Maria chewed on her lip as her brows puckered.

'But if you feel so strongly about this, why don't you take her home yourself? And what about your father?' Maria rushed on. 'What will he do if you turn up back at home with a child that has been born out of wedlock? He would never countenance it.'

'He will,' Isabelle assured her. 'Once Mama has met the child she will persuade him to accept her.'

'You seem so sure that the child will be a girl.'

Isabelle nodded. 'She will be, but will you promise me this one thing, Maria?'

Seeing no alternative without upsetting her, Maria nodded. After all, once the birth was over, Isabelle might have yet another change of heart or decide to take the child back herself.

'Very well,' she said reluctantly. 'I promise. But stop fretting now and concentrate on the birth ahead.'

Above them, the rain was drumming relentlessly down on the roof. Maria had never experienced anything like it. The rain seemed to come down in a solid sheet, drenching everything in seconds and turning the roads into muddy rivers. As Binda had already pointed out, the roads into Hobart might already be impassable; there would be no way of getting a doctor to Isabelle should there prove to be complications. All they could do now was pray that the birth went smoothly.

It was then that they heard the door into the passage

open and then someone tapped on Isabelle's door. It was Josh, soaked through and tormented with worry.

Maria's heart jerked as he moved quickly towards the bed. 'How are you, my darling?' he asked his sister tenderly. 'Have the pains started yet, my dear?'

She smiled wearily up at him. 'No, not yet. I am quite comfortable.'

Seizing her chance, Maria slipped away, leaving the brother and sister to speak in private.

'Anythin' happenin' yet?' Kitty enquired, the second she set foot back in the kitchen. She was answered by the look on Maria's face.

Binda was at the table grinding up leaves and all manner of strange-looking plants and roots with a mortar and pestle.

'It will hurry the birth along,' she informed Maria when she felt the girl watching her. Maria was becoming accustomed to Binda's strange customs now and nodded absently.

Minutes later, Esperanza also appeared and Maria wondered how she still managed to look so beautiful when she was soaked to the skin. She was wearing a dark green cord velvet riding dress that dragged wetly across the floor, and her hat was flattened to her head, but she merely tore it off and tossed it aside as she asked, 'Isabelle's baby – it is coming, yes?'

Binda pursed her lips as she stared back at her mistress, 'She should be well on the way now, but as yet there is no sign.'

'But surely this is normal with a first birthing?' Esperanza raised a fine brow questioningly as Binda shook her head.

'The birth waters have broken. There should be signs of the birth pains by now. But I am mixing her something that will help her along. We must do what we can but the spirits will decide.' She then strained the juice from the mixture into a cup and padded off towards Isabelle's room, while a silence settled on the room, beneath the drumming of the rain on the roof.

Chapter Twenty-three

The storms intensified over the next twenty-four hours and soon the road to the ranch was impassable. And still Isabelle lay with no sign of her contractions starting.

Robbie took food into the barn at regular intervals for Lennie and led him outside to do his toilet on the rope that bound him to one of the wide beams. Each time, Robbie's appearance was met by a stream of abuse, but the Scotsman simply ignored it.

'Why can't that fuckin' bitch bring me food?' Lennie stormed. 'It's her fault I'm here in the first place. She's nothin' but a whore.'

Robbie would just stare at him coldly before fastening him to the beam again, but despite his brave words, Lennie did not try to fight him. One brush with Robbie was quite enough; his strength was no match for the red-haired giant.

'Shouldn't we allow him to come into the homestead?'

Maria questioned nervously at one stage as she gazed towards the streaming windows.

'He's fine where he is,' Robbie snapped. 'It's dry in there, and he has blankets and food. He's lucky I haven't tied him up outside in the storm after what he tried to do to you.'

Maria was still jittery and almost jumping at her own shadow, so she nodded feebly. She was also desperately worried about Isabelle, so when on the second night Binda stood up and made a decision, she was relieved.

'It is time to help nature along,' the woman told them solemnly.

'What are yer goin' to do?' Kitty asked.

Binda merely stared at her before ordering, 'Take hot water and towels to the missy's room.' She rolled up her sleeves, washed her hands thoroughly then disappeared off into Isabelle's room as Kitty rushed to do as she was told.

Joshua was sitting at the side of her bed holding Isabelle's hand and Binda told him, 'This is woman's work now. Go and wait in the kitchen.' Esperanza had returned to her own home the evening before, but Josh had stayed on, napping in the chair in his sister's room.

Bending to plant a gentle kiss on her forehead, he nodded then rose and left the room.

When Maria carried the water into the room, Binda said immediately, 'We need to raise the missy's knees.'

'Very well.' Maria whispered to Isabelle, 'Binda is going to try and hurry things along now, dear.'

Isabelle smiled weakly. Then Binda bent over her and began to knead her stomach.

Isabelle screamed out in pain, but worse was to come.

'I am going to try and feel the baby's head,' Binda told them as she peered between Isabelle's legs – at which the screams intensified. At last Binda stood back with sweat on her brow. 'That should do it,' she stated – and she was right, for within half an hour the contractions started.

Isabelle's baby was born late in the afternoon of the following day as the light was fading. Maria had not left her side and was nearly dropping with exhaustion, but even so when she caught sight of the newborn she cried out with delight.

'Oh, Isabelle, you were right. It's a dear little girl,' she told her as she bent to kiss her feverish forehead, then to Binda, 'Is the child all right?'

A tiny wail was echoing around the room now as Binda cut the cord and handed the bloody little bundle to Maria.

'She seems to be. Very small though – she will need careful tending.'

She was bending to Isabelle again now and the smile died on Maria's face as she noted her expression.

'What's wrong?' she asked with a sinking feeling in the pit of her stomach.

'Missy is bleeding badly.' Binda tutted. 'We must deliver the afterbirth and try to stem it, otherwise . . .'

'Otherwise what?'

Binda did not answer as she waved Maria away, telling her, 'Take the child and bathe her. There is nothing more you can do here now. Just tell Kitty I shall need more towels.'

Maria rushed away with the precious bundle wrapped in a linen sheet she had had all ready.

Josh cried openly at the first sight of his niece and watched in amazement as Maria gently washed her in a tin bowl in the kitchen. Maria then dressed her and wrapped her in a shawl before handing her to him, touched at the look of awe on his face.

'She looks more like you than Isabelle with her fair hair,' he smiled as he cradled the child against his broad chest. She stared up at him and his heart was lost, while Maria looked on with a lump in her throat.

'I believe the colour of a baby's hair and eyes are prone to change as they grow,' she told him softly as he stared down at the tiny miracle in his arms.

Meanwhile, Kitty was dashing back and forth fetching towels and yet more hot water.

Robbie came in soon after, shaking the rain from him like a dog, and he too was instantly bowled over by the new arrival.

'Och, will ye look at the wee bairn,' he cooed. 'Isn't she just the prettiest little thing you ever did set eyes on?'

Kitty smiled at him affectionately before scuttling off to help Binda again.

Time passed slowly. Everyone was tense, and Josh commented, 'They're rather a long time in there, aren't they? Is Isabelle all right?' The words had barely left his mouth when Binda appeared, looking infinitely weary.

'Take the child through to her mother,' she said. 'She wishes to see her.'

'But she's all right, isn't she?' pleaded Josh. 'Surely the worst is over now?'

'I cannot stop the missy's bleeding,' Binda informed him. 'I have done what I can, Master Joshua, but the rest is up to the spirits now.' She then sat down on the settle at the side of the fire, her chin drooped onto her chest and she slipped instantly into an exhausted sleep.

Josh headed for the door with the child in his arms and a look of dread on his face.

Isabelle had been washed, and as he entered the room she turned her head towards him. He was shocked at the sight of her. Her eyes seemed to have sunk deep into their sockets and on her face was a look of suffering. She was ghastly pale but she managed a smile and looked expectantly towards the precious bundle he was carrying.

'F-Faith,' she murmured as she struggled to lift her hands. She was obviously very weak and Josh's heart broke as he laid the baby gently in her arms.

Isabelle sighed with delight as she kissed her daughter's downy hair. 'She is beautiful, isn't she?'

Josh nodded. 'Yes, just like her mother. Now you must get strong again so that you can watch her grow. If you still wish to keep her, that is.'

Isabelle looked at him strangely for a moment before saying, 'Maria must remember her promise. I want Faith to go home to Mama.'

Josh could only begin to imagine the scandal that this would cause; his sister turning up with an illegitimate baby. But now that he had seen her and held her, he could understand why Isabelle did not wish to part with the child.

'Why don't you just concentrate on getting well and then we can discuss everything?' he suggested tactfully.

Again Isabelle looked at him strangely but then her attention returned to her daughter and as she lay there with her hair fanned out on the pillow and a smile of pure joy on her face, Josh thought that she looked like an angel.

'Take her now – I must sleep,' Isabelle said some moments later. 'And Josh, remember – I wish her to be called Faith.'

Josh was feeling more emotional by the second; it was almost as if Isabelle was saying goodbye. He made a conscious effort to clear such thoughts from his mind. The birth was over now; surely she would soon start to recover?

With Faith back in his arms he gazed down at his sister, whose eyes had already fluttered shut, and then softly he crept from the room.

Kitty had concocted some sort of feeding utensil with a teat and filled it with warm goat's milk, and from the second she placed it in Faith's tiny mouth she fastened onto it and began to suck greedily.

'Well, she may only be a little mite but she knows how to feed,' Kitty chuckled as she rocked the baby to and fro. The rest of them apart from Binda were seated at the table eating the salt pork and beans that Kitty had cooked for them, although none of them had much of an appetite.

Josh joined them after a while, but he too merely pushed the food about his plate. A sense of foreboding had invaded him and he couldn't seem to shift it.

'It would have been nice if we could have got word to my uncle and Esperanza about the birth,' he commented eventually, and they all nodded in agreement. Now that the weather conditions had worsened yet again, they were now virtually cut off until the roads improved.

'I'll take some grub out to Lennie,' Robbie said after a while and Kitty immediately hurried away to fill a plate with food for him whilst Robbie shrugged his huge frame into his outdoor clothes.

Maria sat back and watched the interaction between the two of them and suddenly felt sad. It was quite obvious that Kitty loved him, and Robbie's eyes seemed to soften whenever he looked at the girl – and yet he had still not shown any sign of wishing to be more than a friend. Now that the baby had been born their days at the ranch were numbered and they would be returning to England, but she wondered how Kitty would cope with leaving Robbie behind. She had blossomed in the time they had spent here, and now there was barely a sign of the timid girl who had left Hatter's Hall. It was all very sad. She could only hope that Isabelle's mother would find a position for Kitty at

Willow Park when they returned to England – otherwise what was the girl to do? What was she herself to do, for that matter? Her job at the post office was long gone, so once they returned she too would have to look for a new position. She shrugged the sombre thoughts aside as she thought of Isabelle lying so ill. For now she would just concentrate all her efforts on trying to make the girl well and worry about her own future when the time came.

Binda roused from her doze shortly after. The light was gone by then and Kitty was flitting about like a busy little bird lighting the oil lamps.

Without a word the woman hurried away to check on her patient but she had been gone for no more than a few seconds when she shouted, 'Maria, Kitty!'

In their haste to get to her the two girls almost collided in the doorway then they were racing down the corridor.

They both stopped abruptly as they saw Isabelle lying in a pool of blood. She had haemorrhaged.

'More towels!' Binda shouted and Kitty shot away to fetch them as Maria hurried into the room.

Binda swished the blankets aside and instantly began to press yet more towels between Isabelle's legs in a desperate attempt to stem the flow of blood, but all too soon it was clear that her efforts were in vain.

Maria clasped Isabelle's hand tightly and willed the blood to stop, and it was as she was silently praying that Isabelle's eyes fluttered open.

'Y-you have been so good to me,' she murmured and her voice was so faint that Maria had to lean towards her to hear her.

'Don't talk,' Maria urged tearfully. 'Just save your energy.'

Isabelle smiled weakly – and then her eyes closed.

After another twenty minutes Binda threw a clean

blanket across the girl before telling Maria, 'Go and fetch her brother. He may wish to sit with her before she goes to the other side.'

'No!' Maria sobbed. 'She can't die, Binda. She is so young. There must be something more you can do?'

Binda shook her head resignedly. 'The spirits have decided – it is her time.'

Isabelle passed away in the early hours of the following morning, with Josh and Maria at either side of her.

Her ending was so peaceful that she looked as if she was merely asleep, and as Josh wept, Maria held him to her chest and uttered words of comfort. They were just two people grieving the loss of a loved one. And it came as a shock to Maria to realise that she had come to love Isabelle.

'She had her whole life in front of her,' Josh raged. 'It's all just so unfair.'

'I know.' Maria stroked his hair back from his damp face. 'But now we must do what we can for baby Faith. It was what Isabelle wanted.'

'But my father will never accept her if we take her home,' he wavered.

'I understand that. But could you really leave her here to be brought up by strangers now that you have seen her and held her?'

He thought for a moment. 'No, I don't suppose I could,' he admitted brokenly. 'It's bad enough losing Isabelle but to lose Faith too would be beyond endurance.'

'Then we shall take her home and face whatever comes.'

They stood with arms entwined looking down on the beautiful girl on the bed.

Shortly afterwards Binda entered the room and after laying two shiny pennies on Isabelle's closed eyelids, she ushered the others from the room, telling them, 'I must prepare her for her last journey now.'

They found Kitty crying in Robbie's arms and once again it struck Maria how right the couple looked together.

'Poor love,' Kitty choked. 'It ain't fair, is it?'

'There are many things that aren't fair in this life,' Robbie said, and then they all looked towards the child who was sleeping soundly in the little crib that Esperanza had sent over from the ranch some time before. 'But just look at the legacy yon Isabelle has left behind. While you have that bonnie wee bairn, Isabelle will never be far away. She'll live on in her little girl.'

Realising the wisdom of his words, they all nodded in agreement.

Chapter Twenty-four

During the next two days the rain continued to pour down, and Maria and Kitty began to wonder if it was ever going to stop.

Binda spent much of that time locked away in Isabelle's room, chanting.

'She is asking the spirits to accept her and guide her safely over to the other side,' Robbie informed them. And then on the third morning Binda left the room to tell Robbie, 'She is ready now for burial.'

He took up his coat. 'I'll go and make a coffin up from the wood that's stored in the barn.'

Maria was horrified. 'But we can't bury her without a proper Christian service.'

Robbie frowned. 'An' how are we supposed to arrange that when we're cut off from everyone? The nearest church is in Hobart an' there's no way we could get her there.' Noting Maria's distress, he explained to her more gently, 'We need to do it now, as quick as we can. The body is beginnin' to . . . well!'

He had no need to say any more. Maria had noticed that the corpse had begun to smell. At least they could all be present at the burial, which was something at least.

Robbie entered the barn to the usual string of abuse from Lennie but he simply ignored him as he strode towards the woodpile to select some suitable timber.

'What the bleedin' 'ell is goin' on?' Lennie demanded. 'An' 'ow much longer are yer plannin' on keepin' me 'ere?'

'Not a second longer than I have to, you weasel,' Robbie growled. 'And now shut your ugly mouth. I've a coffin to make.'

'Why? Who's died?'

'Miss Isabelle, if you must know!'

Lennie peered at him. 'An' what about the babe? Did that die an' all?'

'No she didn't,' Robbie informed him shortly. 'As soon as this weather clears I shall be getting you back to hand you over, then when the baby's strong enough she'll be going home. And now, whisht, for God's sake, man. I've more important things to do than listen to you whining.'

Lennie sank back down onto his bed of straw. His wrists were red raw from the ropes that bound him but the pain vanished as he suddenly saw a way of getting his revenge on the woman who, he felt, had wronged him so badly. A plan began to form in his mind. So the stuck-up bitch's flyblow was going home to England, was it? It was perfect for what he intended to do, and all of a sudden, facing the wrath of the port authorities didn't seem quite so bad.

Later that day, after being lovingly wrapped in a blanket and placed in the crude wooden coffin that Robbie had made for her, Isabelle was laid to rest in the shade of some huge gum trees not too far away from the small homestead. It had taken Robbie and Josh hours to dig the grave, for it kept filling with water – but there was nothing they could do about that. They returned to the homestead tired and drenched – but there was no point in changing their clothes until the burial had taken place. They carried the coffin to Isabelle's final resting-place with the women trailing miserably behind them whilst the newborn slept the sleep of the innocent in her crib at the side of a roaring fire.

Within seconds of being outside the women were as wet as the men as the rain lashed at their faces and their skirts trailed soddenly behind them. They found themselves ankle-deep in mud but the sorry procession must continue on its way. They all knew that there was no alternative.

The coffin looked in danger of floating as it was lowered into the grave, but at last it was done and Maria muttered, 'Shouldn't we say something? Perhaps say a prayer?'

Josh cleared his throat as the tears on his cheeks mingled with the rain before saying brokenly, 'Our Heavenly Father, we ask that You take the soul of our dearly departed Isabelle into Your care. May she rest in eternal peace. Amen.'

It wasn't much but they all felt that it was better than nothing. They were slipping in the mud now and at serious risk of sliding into the open hole with Isabelle, so Josh told them, 'Get back to the homestead now. Robbie and I will finish up here.'

Robbie had told him that he could do the job by himself, but Josh felt that it was the last service he could ever do for his sister and was adamant that he wanted to help.

The three women turned miserably away. It was done now. Each of them had said their final goodbye.

*

Three days later, the rain finally slowed then stopped, and the sun came out. In no time at all steam was rising from the sodden ground. The following day, the ground was firm enough for Robbie to manage to ride to the ranch to inform his uncle and Esperanza of Isabelle's death. The couple accompanied him back.

'What a beautiful child,' Frederick commented sadly as he stared down at the baby. 'We must think of finding her a home now.'

'We could keep her,' Esperanza told him. 'She eez your flesh and blood, after all, Freddie.'

But before Frederick could answer, Josh cut in, 'Faith will be coming back to England with us.'

Frederick frowned. 'But surely the whole point of you all coming here was to avoid anyone knowing about the child? Your father will not be best pleased if you take her back now.' He knew that his brother-in-law Charles Montgomery could be very inflexible.

'We'll worry about that when the time comes,' Josh informed him. 'Maria and I promised Isabelle that we would take Faith home to Mama and that is what I intend to do.'

His uncle did not argue. A deathbed promise was a sacred matter, and it seemed that Josh had made his mind up.

Meantime Robbie entered the room to tell them, 'I'm going to take the young Jack-me-lad we have locked up in the barn to the coast now. I'll be back when I've handed him over.'

When Frederick looked baffled, Josh proceeded to tell him what had happened and his uncle could barely take it all in. He had been deeply shocked by the news of Isabelle's death; if anything had happened to Esperanza or one of their own babies in childbirth, he would have been devastated.

As it was, he felt desolate. What on earth would his sister have to say? Poor, poor Helena.

Meanwhile Esperanza had lifted the infant from her crib and was rocking her as she cooed down at the babe. 'It eez sad that we cannot keep her, Freddie,' she pouted. 'She would have made a good playmate for the one of our own that we shall have in a few more months' time.'

Frederick stared back at her in amazement. 'But why didn't you tell me before?'

'You have been so busy. But it is good – no?'

'It is *very* good,' he assured her, and for the first time since they had lost Isabelle they all found themselves smiling. It was wonderful to hear some good news after all the sadness.

Lennie was amazingly biddable when Robbie led him from the barn. Maria was in the yard pegging washing to the line and just for a second their eyes locked as Robbie helped Lennie to mount his horse. It was no easy task with his hands still securely tied, but as he stared at her a cruel smile played about his lips. This affected her far more than a mouthful of abuse might have done, and it made her wonder what he had up his sleeve this time. The man was truly evil. Quickly diverting her eyes, she tried to stay the trembling that had started in her hands and seemed to be spreading throughout her entire body. And then Kitty was beside her with her arm protectively about her shoulders as she waved goodbye to Robbie and saw him on his way.

Once the horses had disappeared beyond the gum trees, Kitty led Maria back towards the kitchen, telling her, 'There y'are, see? He's gone fer good now, an' good riddance to bad rubbish – that's what I say. You'll never have to set eyes on him again, so try an' put what happened from yer mind now. We'll have us both a nice cup o' tea, shall we? There ain't nothin' spoilin'.'

Maria allowed Kitty to lead her inside, but she couldn't rid herself of the bad feeling that had settled around her like morning mist as she saw again in her mind's eye the spiteful smile on Lennie's face. But then once back in the safety of the kitchen she felt instantly better when she saw Josh fast asleep in the comfy chair with little Faith curled up contentedly on his chest. It was apparent that he already adored his little niece, but then that came as no surprise. The tiny infant had them all wrapped around her little finger, and Maria could only hope that once the child's grandmother set eyes on her, she would fall in love with her too. How could she resist her? There could be no happy ending for Isabelle, but Maria was determined to do her utmost for little Faith – whilst she had the care of her, at least. It was she who now bathed, fed and changed the child's bindings, and Faith slept in her crib at the side of Maria's bed each night. She realised with a little jolt that it would be hard to part with her when the time came, but for now she must concentrate on getting her strong enough for the long voyage to England.

'How did she do in the night?' Kitty asked as she lifted the kettle onto the range to boil.

'She didn't take as much milk as I would have liked her to,' Maria admitted. 'But then Binda said that this may be due to the fact that she was slightly premature. It's going to take her a while to catch up and start to gain weight.'

'Hmm.' Kitty spooned some tealeaves into the teapot. She too was secretly concerned about the fact that Faith did not seem to be thriving, although knowing how much Maria loved the babe she would never have voiced them. And secretly she was relieved that their departure was not imminent, for now whenever she thought of leaving Robbie she was filled with dread and panic. She knew without a doubt that in him she had found her soulmate and yet despite her broad hints to that effect he had never treated her as anything other than a friend, although from time to time she would glance up to find him watching her. It was all very confusing and she prayed that he might realise how she felt about him before it was too late.

It was as she was carrying the tea to the table that Josh roused and smiled at Maria sleepily over the infant's head.

'Goodness me, I think this little one must be having a bad influence on me,' he grinned as he laid her in her crib and tucked her up. 'I should be out chopping wood. Why didn't you wake me?'

'You looked so peaceful that I didn't like to, and there's no rush,' Maria told him.

'Has Robbie left yet?' Josh asked now as he spooned sugar into his mug.

Her face became straight as she batted a fly away. Now that the weather was warming up, the flies were becoming a nuisance although they were nowhere near as bad as the mosquitoes.

'Yes, he's gone but he'll be back as soon as possible so you can go on home to the ranch-house now if you wish. Kitty and I shall be quite all right here on our own now that Lennie has gone.'

'I wouldn't dream of it,' Josh retorted. 'You'll be glad of an extra pair of hands now that you have Faith to run around after.'

Since Isabelle's death they had become easy in each other's company again and now, just as Kitty was wondering how she would cope without Robbie, Maria was wondering what it would be like to be parted from Josh once they were back in England and she had handed Faith over to her grandmother. No doubt he would marry the girl his parents had selected for him, and they would never see each other again. It was a sobering thought.

'Now that everythin' is back to rights in here, I think I'll go over and hang them curtains Robbie's got fer his front room – if there's nothin' else that yer need doing, o' course,' Kitty said that night after she had washed and dried the dinner pots. 'It'll be nice fer him to come back to find 'em up.'

Maria was feeding Faith in the fireside chair and she nodded, saying, 'Of course, take as long as you like.'

Josh was reading the newspaper on the settle and he too looked up and smiled, saying, 'Yes, you get off, Kitty. I'll see to anything else that needs doing.'

Kitty took off her apron and folded it over the back of a chair before running her hands down the sides of her skirt and patting her hair. Then, after dropping a quick kiss on Faith's head, she bustled away with a broad smile on her face.

'You know, I think Kitty has grown very fond of Robbie,' Josh said thoughtfully as he watched the girl cross the yard from the window.

'I'm sure she has and Robbie seems to be fond of her too, but so far he hasn't expressed his feelings.' Maria tenderly lifted the child across her shoulder to wind her. 'And it's such a shame. I mean – what will become of Kitty when she returns to England? If she can't find a position somewhere, she could well end up in the workhouse. I was hoping for a happy-ever-after ending for her at least.'

She flushed then as Josh raised an eyebrow. 'And you, Maria. What will *you* do?'

'Actually,' she gulped deep in her throat before saying cautiously, 'well . . . I was rather hoping that your mother might need a nursemaid for Faith when we return. After all, the baby does know me now. I am the one who has cared for her since she was born. The idea only occurred to me earlier today, and I was meaning to talk to you about it.'

'I see.' He moved to the fireplace and leaned on the mantel as he gazed down onto the logs. 'As you say, you are the one who has nurtured her since birth – and a fine job you are making of it too, if I may say so. However, although I think your idea is an excellent one, I anticipate trouble on our return. You see, I fear my father will not countenance having the child in the house. He is a good man but he lives by very strict principles and when all is said and done, Faith is a . . .'

As his voice trailed away, colour rushed into Maria's cheeks and she cuddled the infant to her. 'She is an innocent baby,' she said hotly. 'And after all, even though she was born the wrong side of the blanket she is still your father's flesh and blood! Your parents will be gravely upset when they discover that they have lost their daughter, but at least they have a granddaughter now. Surely that will be some consolation to them?'

'I believe Mother will see it that way . . . but Father?' Joshua sighed. 'The whole point of sending Isabelle here to have the child was to avoid the scandal and the shame, but I do intend to respect Isabelle's wish that Faith is returned to England – and then I think we shall just have to wait and see what transpires.'

'I will never allow her to be farmed out to strangers,' Maria said vehemently, 'even if I have to care for her myself. Although I must admit I am not at all sure how I should manage it.'

Seeing the defiant set of her chin, Josh suddenly grinned. Crossing to her, he gently ran his finger down Faith's soft cheek. Full and contented, the child was already fast asleep again on Maria's shoulder, but then that was no surprise. Unlike her mother she seemed to have a very placid temperament and rarely cried at all. Even so, because she was so tiny she took her milk little and often, which put a great strain on Maria, who was looking tired, Josh noted. He just wished that she would let him or Kitty help a little more with the babe but Maria was fiercely protective of her and insisted on doing everything herself.

'Let us not argue,' he said softly now. 'You forget that I love her too, and whilst we have her, Isabelle will never truly be gone.'

Feeling more than a little guilty, Maria hastily lowered her eyes. It was so easy to forget that she was no more than an employee, and that to all intents and purposes Joshua was her better. But she knew that it would be foolish to give him even an inkling of how she felt about him.

He meantime was mulling her suggestion over in his mind and an idea had occurred to him that might solve all their problems. What if he was to set Maria and Faith up in a little house somewhere? As Maria had quite rightly pointed out, the baby was as close to her as to anyone in the absence of her mother, and then he would have an excuse to visit whenever he chose. He dismissed the idea almost instantly, realising that Maria would never agree to being a kept woman. And she deserved more than that anyway. Maria might be from the lower classes but she had a lot of pride. It was common knowledge that many of the gentry kept mistresses, his own father included. Josh had been aware for some time of Mrs Elliot happily tucked away in a house in Abbey Green, although he had never been tactless enough to mention the fact, of course. No, Maria definitely deserved more than that.

Wishing to lighten the atmosphere, he lifted the

log-scuttle, telling her, 'I'll just go and fetch some more logs in before it gets really dark, shall I? I'll put the chickens into their hen-coops whilst I'm at it as well. Robbie informed me that we lost another two last night.'

'But that is my job,' Maria reminded him as she rose to place Faith back in her crib. Now that she had a clean binding and a full stomach she would probably sleep for a while.

'No, no. You see to Her Ladyship there. It won't take me more than a few minutes and then we can sit out on the verandah for a while. It looks set to be a fine night.' He went off and Maria stood for a while gazing down on the baby. She was dressed in baby clothes that Esperanza had sent over for her and it was easy to see that they were the best that money could buy. Should her grandparents choose to keep her, Faith would no doubt become accustomed to fine things – but what if they decided to farm her out? Despite her brave talk Maria was painfully aware that she would be in no position to stop them. But then that was still a long way away. Faith was still far too tiny to begin the journey back to England: Binda had warned that because she had been born early it might be some time before she was strong enough to survive it. Sighing, she took up the soiled binding and put it to soak in a bucket of cold water.

When her chores were finished, she joined Josh on the verandah. It was a beautiful starlit night and as she took the seat at the side of him, her mood lightened. The moon was a great golden orb in the sky and the sounds of the night creatures in the forest hung on the air as shoots of green grass peeped through the earth surrounding the homestead where only days before there had been nothing but a sea of mud. The light from the oil lamp inside spilled through the window onto the decking, and as she settled into her chair

Josh handed her a glass of home-made ale before lighting a cigar.

'It's a beautiful night,' he commented, and Maria agreed. She sipped at her drink, not at all sure that she really liked it. Her father had always forbidden alcohol in the house and she grinned as she wondered what he would say if he could see her now. Her thoughts then turned to her mother and a little wave of homesickness swept over her.

'Are you looking forward to going home?' Josh asked as if he had been able to read her thoughts.

'I'm not sure about that, but I am looking forward to seeing my mother and my brother and sister,' she told him.

'I note that you didn't include your father?'

She said honestly, 'I suppose that is because my father and I have never really got on.' She had never admitted that to anyone before, but Josh was so easy to talk to. 'He is very strict,' she went on, 'and sometimes I think that he treats my mother more as a skivvy than a wife.'

'My father is quite strict too,' Josh owned. 'But thankfully Mother is usually able to bring him round, so I suppose Isabelle and I were fortunate.'

As she peeped at him from the corner of her eye, Maria suddenly wished that they could just sit there as they were forever.

'I was thinking,' he said after a while, 'that a night out might do you good. You work so hard looking after Faith and I'm sure Kitty would love to have her all to herself for a few hours. There is a concert on in Hobart on Saturday evening and I thought that it might be pleasant if we went.'

Maria's heart fluttered at the thought of it. She had never been to a concert before but then practicality took over and she wondered what she would wear to such an event. The clothes that she had arrived in were hardly suitable for what

Josh was suggesting. Also, it seemed too early to go out and enjoy herself when they were all still in mourning for Isabelle.

Seeing her hesitation he said quietly, 'You are thinking it is too soon after losing Isabelle, aren't you?' When she nodded his head drooped and he said, 'I miss her too, you know, but I think this is what she would have wanted. You came to mean a great deal to her, Maria, and she would not want you to be sad.'

'Thank you for asking. It sounds wonderful but I'm afraid my wardrobe is rather restricted and I wouldn't have anything suitable to wear,' she said shyly.

'Ah, I have already thought of that.' He grinned impishly. 'I happened to mention to Esperanza that I thought a treat would do you good and she has already said that she would be more than happy to lend you an outfit. I should think you are about the same size so it shouldn't be a problem. But I also need to tell you that before she died, Isabelle told me that, should anything happen to her, she wished you to have all her clothes and to pass any on to Kitty you did not want. I realise you might not want to wear them yet, and Esperanza will be only too happy to loan you something of hers.'

'Oh.' Maria was lost for words and although her first instinct was to refuse she was sorely tempted to accept the offer.

Still sensing her hesitation, Josh said quickly, 'Please say that you'll accept. I'd really like to go, and you would be doing me a favour if you accept because I won't go alone.'

'In that case, if you're quite sure, how can I refuse?' she responded with a smile. What could be the harm in it? she reasoned. They were only going as friends. And then a little bubble of excitement began to form in her stomach.

*

Over in Robbie's cabin, Kitty stood back to admire the curtains she had just hung at the window. Then, glancing about the room, she smiled with satisfaction. Over the last weeks she had transformed the bare wooden rooms into a home of which anyone could be proud. At least, she knew that *she* would. Copper pans that she had polished until she could see her face in them now hung along the front of the inglenook fireplace, and the shelves that she had persuaded Robbie to put up in the kitchen area now held an assortment of pots. Gay rugs, purchased from Hobart, lay scattered about the floor and everything looked clean and fresh.

A similar transformation had taken place in his bedroom and now the sturdy brass bed was covered with a cheerful patchwork quilt, beneath which were crisp white sheets and pillows filled with duck feathers. She had persuaded him to buy a second-hand wash-stand on one of their shopping trips and it now housed a china jug and bowl that took pride of place at the side of his bed. Straightening a crease in the quilt, she then quietly shut the door and once again stood surveying her handiwork. In another auction they had found two mismatched easy chairs which had been positioned at either side of the fireplace. Kitty had dusted and polished them to within an inch of their lives, and she could just imagine herself and Robbie sitting in them on a cold winter night with a log fire roaring up the chimney as she did her darning and he read his newspaper. The wind and rain might be lashing at the windows but inside they would be warm and snug, and he would look over at her and smile.

Shaking her head to clear it of the dream, she extinguished the oil lamp and sadly made her way back to the other cabin. Dreams didn't come true for girls like her. She had learned that a long, long time ago.

Chapter Twenty-five

Robbie arrived back shortly before the evening meal the following day and the instant she heard his horse, Kitty dashed out to meet him.

'Did yer manage to hand Lennie over to the authorities?' she asked anxiously.

Robbie leaped lightly down from his saddle and fondled the horse's ears. 'I did that, lass, and I don't mind betting he'll not be coming back this way again,' he said. 'The master had him locked in jail along with the rats, and I doubt he'll see daylight again till the next ship sets sail from Melbourne. Serves him right, that's what I say. He's no better than a rat himself.'

He began to lead the horse towards his stabling in the barn, smiling with amusement as Kitty happily skipped along at the side of him. She could always make him smile and he wished— He stopped his thoughts from going any further. There could never be any future for him and Kitty – but if only things could have been different.

Inside the homestead, Maria was again feeding the baby as Faith's loving uncle watched. Maria was marvellous with her, Josh thought, and one day he knew that she would make a wonderful mother. And a wonderful wife, if it came to that. His thoughts suddenly conjured up an image of Felicity Pettifer and he shuddered involuntarily. Thankfully this trip had put paid to any notion his parents had had about them becoming betrothed – for a time, at least – but he knew they would start nagging him about it when he returned home. Felicity was as pretty as a picture and nice enough in her own way, but having known her all his life he found it hard to consider her as anything other than a friend. Furthermore, after witnessing Maria's courage in facing up to everything that had occurred during the last few months since their departure from England, he could not help but compare the two. Maria had endured every trial with dignity and compassion, but somehow he could not imagine Felicity being able to do the same. Much like Isabelle, she had been waited on hand and foot and been pampered and spoiled since the day she had drawn breath.

Sighing heavily, the young man left the room to go and have a word with Robbie. There was no point in making comparisons. His father would never countenance him marrying anyone like Maria, as Joshua had learned to his cost after his brief affair with Edith.

That evening, when they had finished supper, Kitty informed them, 'I'm goin' to take this leftover meat to Robbie fer his supper. It's a shame to let it go to waste an' he's got an appetite on him like Rob Roy's horse. I've no doubt he'll polish this little lot off in seconds.'

Maria chuckled as Kitty draped a clean linen cloth over the dish and went out into the soft evening air. The girl had gone some way, focusing on the light spilling from the window of Robbie's cabin when suddenly a dark shape slithered across the path in front of her and she screamed and dropped the dish she was carrying.

Almost instantly Robbie's door was flung open and he covered the distance between them in a remarkably short time for a man of his size.

Kitty was speechless with fear as she pointed a wavering finger towards the ground. When Robbie glimpsed the snake sliding away he laughed and clasped her to him. 'My dearest wee girl, you've no need to fear,' he soothed as he recognised the greenish-grey colouring in the light of the moon. ''Tis only a White Lipped, and they've never been known to kill anyone with their bite. He's more scared of you than you are of him, hinny.'

But still Kitty continued to shake, so swinging her into his arms as if she weighed no more than a feather he strode towards the cabin as Kitty buried her head in his chest. Once inside he kicked the door shut behind him, concerned to see that Kitty was as pale as a ghost. She clung to him when he would have placed her down and he revelled in the feel of her small body so close to his.

'I-I was bringin' yer s-some supper,' she said, her teeth chattering. 'B-but I dropped it.'

'Well, it's no the end o' the world, lass. I'll not starve for missing out on a bit of tucker. But come on now, calm down. You'll make yourself ill at this rate.'

Very slowly her sobs subsided to dull hiccuping whimpers and he set her gently down on the floor, saying,

'I'll make us a brew, shall I? Then I'll see you back across.'

They were still standing very close together . . . and then somehow her arms were around his neck, and drawing his head down to hers, she kissed him tenderly on the lips. Just for a second his own were unyielding, but then he suddenly grasped her tightly and kissed her back with an urgency that left her breathless. She could smell the raw male scent of him, taste his tongue and she felt as if she were drowning in a deep pool of pleasure. She knew more than ever in that moment that this was where she was meant to be, and as his hands worked their way down her back to her buttocks she gave herself up to him wholeheartedly. His kisses grew more passionate, and when he suddenly released her and took her hand and led her towards the bedroom, she went without resistance. Once inside, he gently laid her on the bed and his great hands fumbled clumsily with the buttons on her coarse cotton blouse. She quietly finished undoing them herself, her eyes fixed on his as he shed his clothes. She had not seen a naked man before, but she was not afraid; in fact, she thought she had never seen anyone look quite so magnificent.

In no time at all they were both naked, and when he joined her and began to fondle and tease her small breasts and nipples with his tongue she sighed with pleasure and arched her back towards him. Eventually he shifted his weight onto her and when he entered her she gave one small moan of pain before giving herself up to pure ecstasy. When it was over she lay contented in his arms as their hearts steadied to a more normal rhythm and she told him softly, 'I love you, Robbie.'

It was then that he tensed, and rising quickly from the bed he began to pull his clothes on as he stared at her in horror, noting the trace of blood on the patchwork quilt.

'You shouldn't be saying that,' he murmured as he buttoned up his shirt. 'And I'm heart sorry for taking advantage of you like that. It shouldn't have happened.'

'But . . . I wanted it to happen!' Confused, she drew herself up onto one elbow as she stared at him. What they had just shared had been the most beautiful experience of her whole life, and she could not understand the sudden change in him. Only moments before he had been tender and loving, but now he was acting as if they were strangers.

'Come on,' he said hoarsely. 'Get yourself dressed an' I'll see you across to the homestead. And Kitty – it might be best if you don't come here again.'

'But why? I love yer, Robbie, an' I ain't ashamed o' what we just did,' she said, hoarse with shock.

'There can never be anything between us,' he told her in a voice that brooked no argument. 'Now do as you are told, please.' And with that he strode from the room as she somehow got off the bed and began to drag her clothes back on. She felt as if the bottom had dropped out of her world but nevertheless she did as she was told. When she joined him, he was standing at the open front door puffing on his pipe, and as she walked towards him he stepped out into the night air: she had no choice but to follow him. Once within sight of the homestead he nodded towards her curtly then turned and went back the way he had come without so much as another word.

When she entered the house, Maria immediately noted the girl's red eyes and was alarmed. 'Why, Kitty,' she asked, 'whatever is the matter?'

Unable to speak, Kitty bunched her long drab skirts into her fists and fled to the sanctuary of her room as Josh and Maria looked on in confusion.

'I wonder if she and Robbie have had a misunderstanding?'

Josh commented, but Maria shook her head, saying, 'Surely not. Kitty hangs on his every word.'

Even so, it was more than evident that something was amiss. Kitty was usually such a cheerful little soul but if she wasn't prepared to tell her what was wrong, there wasn't much that Maria could do to help her. Shrugging, she returned her attention to Faith who was beginning to stir. It was time for her feed again, and soon Kitty's upset was pushed to the back of her mind for now as she saw to the child's needs.

It was early the following afternoon when Josh suggested, 'How about we visit the ranch and Esperanza can find you an outfit for Saturday night?'

Maria paused. She had been on the way to take a bundle of Faith's clean clothes to her room, but now she dithered. It was weeks since she had ventured out, and although the suggestion was appealing she was concerned about leaving Faith.

'I can look after the little 'un while yer gone, Maria,' Kitty informed her. She was at the deep stone sink with her hands immersed in water as she scrubbed the dinner pots, but still Maria havered. Kitty hadn't been herself all morning and had said barely a word.

'I'm more than capable,' Kitty said haughtily, sensing Maria's indecision.

'Very well then – if you're quite sure,' Maria agreed, then to Josh, 'But I don't want to be gone for too long. I think Faith has a slight temperature.'

He crossed to the crib and gazed down on his niece. 'Then may I suggest you remove a few layers of clothes or blankets. I'm amazed the child can breathe with all that lot on.'

'I'm afraid of her catching a chill,' Maria responded defensively and then as she too peeped at Faith she admitted, 'I suppose I have rather overdone the wrappings,' and leaned over to remove the top two blankets.

'There you are! I'm sure I just saw her sigh with relief,' he teased and as she returned his smile their eyes met until Maria hastily looked away, saying, 'I'll just go and tidy myself up then.'

'Yes, of course – and I'll go and saddle the horses.'

Josh was back in no time astride his stallion and holding the reins of the gentle old mare that Maria favoured. She was still far from being a competent horsewoman and doubted now whether she ever would be.

Josh helped her into the saddle and they rode along in silence until eventually the ranch came into view. One of the house boys hurried out to take the horses around to the stable-block when they arrived and Josh led Maria into the ranch, where they found Esperanza sorting through a pile of gowns she had carelessly flung across the chaise longue.

'Ah, here you are,' she greeted them, then, 'I have already started to choose gowns that I think might suit you. What about this one? You like it, no?' She held up a beautiful evening gown in pale green but Maria eyed it doubtfully. It looked very low-cut. Esperanza discarded it and took up another in a cornflower-blue colour.

'Ah,' she sighed, 'this one may be even better for you, it will bring out the colour of your eyes, no?'

'Perhaps something a little plainer?' Maria said tentatively. 'It looks very daring.'

'Rubbish!' Esperanza laughed. 'It eez good to be daring. You have the figure for it. Come – let us go and try it on.'

Throwing the gown across her arm she grabbed Maria by the hand and hauled her off in the direction of the bedroom as Josh watched with amusement before striding away in search of his uncle.

When Esperanza turned Maria to look into the cheval mirror, the girl's hand rose involuntarily to her mouth. She hardly recognised herself. The dress, as she had feared, was low-cut and off the shoulder, and it made her waist look tiny before swirling out into a full skirt. The neckline was adorned with tiny crystals that danced in the light from the window. Other than that it was free of any adornment but it was the sheer simplicity of it that made it so stunning, and it fitted as if it had been made for her.

Esperanza clapped her hands with triumph. 'It eez perfect,' she declared. 'But now we must find you some shoes and a cape to go with it. It still tends to be chilly at night and it eez a good ride into Hobart.'

She began to rifle through a stack of shoes that stood on a rack inside a cupboard until she found just what she was looking for. The pumps were in a darker blue than the dress and proved to be slightly large for Maria, but even so the woman assured her that they could pad the toes out with sheep's wool to make them more comfortable.

'We 'ave no shortage of sheep's wool 'ere,' she joked before once again rifling through her wardrobe for a suitable cape. The one she chose exactly matched the shoes but then she eyed Maria's hair critically, telling her, 'I shall come personally on Saturday to dress your 'air before you go, no?'

'I wouldn't want you to go to any trouble on my behalf,' Maria objected self-consciously. 'It's quite enough that you have so kindly lent me your beautiful clothes.'

'Huh! I 'ave dozens of gowns,' Esperanza said airily. 'In fact, you can keep the whole outfit. I shall not miss it.'

'Oh no, I couldn't really.' Maria was desperately

embarrassed and could only begin to imagine what the clothes must have cost, but Esperanza waved aside her objections, telling her firmly, 'You are young and beautiful. You should 'ave nice things and some fun as poor Isabelle did before . . .' Her face became sad but then brightening again, she told her, 'You will be the belle of the ball, no? Now come, we shall go and 'ave some tea while Binda packs these things up for you, and you can tell me all about 'ow leetle Faith is coming along. Then I shall get Robbie to deliver the clothes to you later in the trap.'

Maria obediently did as she was told. It was very hard to argue with Esperanza. Despite her protestations she was secretly thrilled with the gifts that the kindly woman had bestowed on her, and now her excitement began to mount as she thought of Saturday night.

Chapter Twenty-six

'Now tell me, is she not beautiful?' Esperanza almost dragged Maria into the room and as Josh turned to look at her, his mouth gaped in amazement. He had always considered Maria to be pretty, but after Esperanza's kindly ministrations she looked positively stunning.

Esperanza had swept her fair hair high onto the top of her head then teased it into ringlets that lay across her creamy shoulders. The blue dress showed off her slim figure to perfection, and he was aware that looking as she did, she could easily have been taken as a lady of breeding.

Maria blushed as Kitty exclaimed, 'Crikey, Maria! Yer look like the gentry!' She was cradling Faith in her arms but now Maria started to fuss.

'Are you quite sure that you will manage, Kitty? You do know how she likes her milk, don't you? And you won't forget to change her bindings after her feed, will you? She should be all right for at least another couple of—'

'*Maria!*' Kitty said sternly. 'I ain't a simpleton, yer know. Now will yer just get yerself away an' enjoy yerself, please. I'm lookin' forward to havin' this little madam all to meself fer a time.'

'Yes, she eez quite right!' Esperanza exclaimed as she draped the long blue cape about Maria's shoulders. 'Now go and 'ave a good time. I shall want to 'ear all about it in the morning.'

Grinning, Josh made a great show of offering Maria his arm. He too was looking very smart in a brightly coloured waistcoat with a matching cravat over which he wore a light tailored jacket. His legs were encased in a pair of tightly fitting trousers, and the whole look was complemented by fine leather knee-high boots. Esperanza thought what a handsome couple they made as she ushered them towards the door. Soon they were seated in the trap that stood ready, and Josh took up the reins. The couple set off with Kitty and Esperanza waving until the homestead was left behind beyond the gum trees.

It was a beautiful evening and Maria could not remember ever feeling so excited. Her mood further improved when Josh told her, 'You look truly beautiful.'

'Thank you,' she answered coyly and they rattled on their way at a gentle trot.

When they finally drove into Hobart it felt strange. Maria had grown used to the solitude of ranch life and felt a little overawed at the sight of so many people. Eventually the Music Hall came into view and after drawing the horse to a halt, Josh handed the reins to a young boy, who was one of many waiting outside the Hall. Passing him a coin, he told him, 'See that he is well tended to until we come out and there will be another one of those for you.'

'Right y'are, sir.' The cheeky-faced urchin grinned as he

touched his cap and Josh helped Maria down from the trap. She suddenly felt nervous as she noted a number of finely dressed men and women heading towards the entrance. The women looked like multi-coloured butterflies in their satins and silks, but picking up on her mood Josh tucked her arm through his and told her, 'You will be the prettiest woman there, now try to relax and enjoy yourself.' And that is exactly what Maria did.

As she entered the enormous foyer, Maria felt as if she had been transported into another world. Enormous gilt-framed mirrors adorned the walls, along with bright posters showing the stars who had appeared there over the years. The floor was covered in a deep red carpet and as they moved forward Maria felt her feet sinking into it. When they entered the auditorium Josh bought them a programme and then they were led to their seats in the dress circle, where they had a bird's-eye view of the stage. Golden cherubs were set into the vast ceiling and huge scarlet drapes that matched the material on their seats concealed the stage.

'It isn't as big as the theatres in London,' Josh informed her, seeing the look of wonder on her face but Maria was too awestruck to answer. She watched as the seats below them slowly filled with people. And then suddenly the lights began to dim and the pit band started to play as the curtains slowly parted.

A small man in a bow tie and tails, and with a huge waxed moustache balancing above his top lip, walked importantly to the centre of the stage and announced the first act – The Riske Dancing Girls. Almost before he had had time to leave the stage, a group of girls in the skimpiest costumes that Maria had ever seen pranced onto the stage, their bare legs kicking in time high in the air. Maria was glad of the darkness that would hide her blushes as she wondered what her father would have thought of such apparel, but then she forgot everything as she leaned forward in her seat and became lost in the magic of the theatre. The dancers were followed by a magician who placed his female assistant in a box and sawed her in half before their very eyes, and Josh laughed aloud as he watched Maria's hand fly to her lips in horror. Eventually the assistant was helped from the box all in one piece again and Maria sighed with relief. He then produced a white rabbit from a top hat and Maria applauded loudly, along with the rest of the audience.

During the interval Josh led her to a bar where he had reserved them a table and she sat and sipped ice-cold sarsaparilla as she attracted more than a few admiring glances from some of the gentlemen present. She looked every inch the lady and just for this evening she felt it.

When they emerged some three hours later following the second half of the show, Maria's eyes were shining and her cheeks were flushed with excitement. She had watched every performer raptly and had actually cried with pure delight during the performance of one particular operatic singer who she was sure had the voice of an angel and had enthusiastically applauded the antics of the juggling troupe.

'Have you enjoyed yourself?' Josh asked unnecessarily as he helped her to fasten her cape.

'Oh yes, I don't think I shall ever forget tonight.'

He paused as his fingers slipped from her cloak and then without even thinking about it, he bent his head and kissed her there and then in the street. For a moment Maria tensed then relaxed against him. But then they suddenly remembered where they were and sprang apart just as the small boy they had employed for the night led the horse and trap towards them.

It was dark by then and Maria was glad of the fact; it would hide her confusion. Her heart was racing as the boy told them with a grin, "'E's 'ad a good drink, mister, an' I ain't took me eyes off 'im all night.'

'Good lad.' Josh fumbled in his pocket and dropped some more coins into the boy's outstretched hand and then as the lad scampered away to be lost in the crowds that were leaving the Music Hall, Josh assisted Maria up into her seat and soon they were headed for home.

Neither of them spoke until they had left the lights of the town far behind them and then Josh said tentatively, 'I hope you didn't mind me kissing you like that, Maria. I think I have wanted to do it ever since the very first time I clapped eyes on you.' He realised that he could contain his feelings no longer. The sky above was lit with stars that clearly showed them their way and now Maria chose her words carefully as she answered, 'I didn't mind exactly – but I think it might be wise if you did not do it again.'

'But why?'

She sighed into the balmy night. 'Because we both know that nothing could ever come of it, and we would be setting ourselves up for heartache. You have an intended waiting back at home for you, and your parents would never countenance a relationship between us. I am just a servant.'

'That's not true,' he said hotly. 'During the time that you spent with Isabelle, she came to look upon you as a friend. And I *certainly* don't have an intended, as you put it, waiting for me. I take it you are talking of Felicity Pettifer?'

When Maria lowered her head and nodded, he growled deep in his throat as he urged the horse along. 'Felicity and I have never been anything more than friends,' he informed her. 'It is our parents who have hoped for a match between us but truthfully I don't think Felicity is any keener on the idea than I am. We have known each other since we were children and I tend to look on her more as a sister than a wife. Felicity is a nice enough girl in her own way, a little spoiled admittedly, but then that isn't really her fault. Her parents have ruined her shamelessly, which I suppose is understandable as she is their only child. No, Maria, I shall choose my own wife when the time is right.'

'Even so, it could never be me,' she said passionately. 'As well as being a servant I was with child when we left England. How do you think your father would react to that, if he were to find out?'

'But that wasn't your fault. Lennie forced himself on you!'

'Yes, he did, but even so . . .' Maria let her voice trail away and they rode on in silence for some way until he suddenly drew the horse to a halt and reached out for her again.

'Maria,' he said with a note of desperation in his voice. 'Don't you realise that I am fond of you? More than fond, in fact. Do you feel nothing for me?'

She stared into his eyes before saying, 'Yes, I cannot lie, I *do* have feelings for you and have done for some long time, but your father would disown you if we were to come together and I could not let you sacrifice your inheritance for me.'

'Huh! What do I care for such things!' he said hotly. 'I have a more than ample allowance that was left to me by my grandmother, and added to that I could work. We would get by somehow.' It came as something of a shock to Joshua to realise that he meant every word he said. Maria would be worth making sacrifices for. He was playing with her fingers and she felt as if little shocks were rippling up her arms but still she held back.

305

'Let's just wait until we get Faith safely home and then decide what we are to do if we still feel the same way,' she suggested gently.

Knowing that what she said made sense, he sighed and nodded.

'Very well then – but make no mistake: this is not the end,' he told her, and urged the horse into a trot again.

'Is Robbie not coming in for breakfast again?' Maria asked the next morning as Kitty carried a plate of sizzling bacon to the table.

Kitty shrugged in an off-hand manner. 'Don't look like it,' she mumbled before going back to the stove for the platter of fried eggs.

Maria and Josh exchanged a glance but said nothing. During the last few days all the sparkle seemed to have gone out of Kitty and Robbie was avoiding coming by the house. Maria had made more than one attempt to get Kitty to confide what was wrong, but up until now the girl had remained tight-lipped. Until she was ready to talk, Maria felt that there was little she could do to help her. It broke her heart to see the girl so dejected, so now she suggested, 'How about we go and visit the spring later on when we have done all the chores? We haven't been there for ages – and now that the weather is so improved I've no doubt it would be lovely there.'

'What about Faith?' Kitty answered woodenly as she took a seat at the table.

'We could take her with us. The fresh air would do her good and she could lie and have a kick on the grass whilst we had a splash in the pool.'

Kitty thought about it for a moment before shaking her head. 'No, thanks. I have the washing to do today, so I doubt I'll be finished till late afternoon.'

'As you please.' Maria picked at the food on her plate. It seemed that they all had things on their mind today. She herself had lain until the early hours recalling the feel of Josh's lips on her own and the words he had said to her, but no matter how hard she tried she could see no happy ending for them, just as it seemed there was to be no happy ending for Kitty and Robbie.

Esperanza rode over to the homestead later that day to enquire how the concert had gone. She had expected Maria to be bubbling over with excitement about it and so was somewhat bewildered to find both young women in a sober mood. Josh had ridden out with his uncle to do a head-count of the sheep in the top pasture and was not expected back until much later in the day.

'You 'ad a good evening, yes?' she enquired as she crossed to glance at Faith who was lying cooing in her crib.

'Oh yes, it was wonderful.' Maria paused in the act of folding a pile of baby clothes. 'But I still think you should have your dress and things back now. I really appreciated you loaning them to me, but when will I ever get the chance to wear them again?'

'When should a woman need an excuse to wear beautiful things?' Esperanza responded, then, 'No, you must keep them. I am sure that Josh will have many more such outings in mind for you and maybe in time you will be able to bring yourself to wear some of the gowns that Isabelle left for you.'

When Maria flushed, Esperanza knew she had been right in her assumption that those two did have feelings for each other. But why were they not doing something about it? The same went for Kitty and Robbie. The big Scot had been walking about like a bear with a sore head for days, and Kitty didn't look much happier. Esperanza had a good mind to take her riding crop to the lot of them, to make them come to their senses! She bided her time until Kitty carried the next load of wet washing out to the line before saying cautiously, 'Would I be right in thinking that you care for Josh, Maria?'

Maria was shocked at the question and it showed on her face although she supposed she should be used to Esperanza's forthright ways by now.

'Yes I do – but it won't do me much good, will it?'

Esperanza raised a finely plucked eyebrow and Maria limped on, 'We are from different worlds. He is gentry and I am merely a servant.'

'Pah!' Esperanza waved her hand in the air. 'So what difference does that make? You are a woman and he is a man, no? The same could have been said for me and Frederick. In fact it was, which was why we chose to live here, away from the usual conventions. When two people love each other, they should be together – and we have done all right, no?'

'Yes, but it's different for you.'

'Oh? And why eez that then?'

Maria struggled to come up with an answer as Esperanza looked on with her eyes flashing. 'If Josh's father objected to your marriage you could come and live here,' she pointed out. 'I know that Freddie would welcome Josh with open arms. He is a hardworking boy and you have enjoyed the time you have been here, no?'

'Well, yes – yes, I have,' Maria admitted falteringly.

'Then bear that in mind,' Esperanza said as she lifted Faith from her crib. 'Some things are meant to be and life is too short for regrets.'

Maria nodded thoughtfully as she went about her chores.

Chapter Twenty-seven

It was towards the end of September 1857 when Faith thankfully seemed to turn a corner. Her tiny body suddenly began to gain weight and fill out, and she delighted them all when she began to smile at them.

Binda still came regularly to check on her and it was during one of these visits that she told them, 'I think the little one is strong enough to travel now, should you wish to take her back to England.'

Josh looked up from reading the *Mercury* newspaper.

'In that case perhaps I should write to my father and tell him that we intend to return. I could go into Hobart tomorrow and book the tickets for next month so that they will expect us.'

Kitty's hands became still in the sink full of warm water. Things had not improved between Robbie and herself, but once she set foot on the ship back to England, he would be lost to her forever. Her future suddenly stretched out before her, empty and lonely, and she knew that somehow she must make one last attempt to put things right between them.

Maria also felt a little trepidation at the thought of returning home – for what would she be going back to? There would certainly be no welcome from her father, and what would become of little Faith if her grandparents chose to disown her? And yet she knew deep down that returning was inevitable, and so she supposed that the sooner it was over with the better.

Josh wrote to his parents that very afternoon, intending to mail the letter the next day when he rode into Hobart to book their tickets.

It was after supper that evening that Kitty took her apron off and informed them, 'I'm going over to see Robbie.'

'Oh.' Maria glanced up from the tiny nightgown that she was embroidering for Faith in the light of the oil lamp. She and Josh exchanged a look as Kitty headed for the door without so much as another word.

'Let's hope they sort out their differences before it's too late,' Josh remarked and Maria nodded in agreement before turning her attention back to her sewing.

Kitty meanwhile was striding purposefully towards Robbie's cabin, but when she saw the light spilling from his window, her courage failed her and she faltered. But then, setting her shoulders, she ploughed on. The way she saw it, there was nothing to lose but everything to gain.

She threw the door back with such force that it banged into the inner wall, and Robbie was so startled that he leaped up from his chair and almost overturned it.

This was Kitty as he had never seen her before. Normally she was placid and easy to please, but the young woman in front of him now was standing with her hands on her hips, her eyes blazing.

'I reckon it's time you an' me had a little talk,' she spat.

'Very well,' Robbie said, righting the chair. 'What about?'

'*What about?*' Her eyes rolled towards the ceiling. 'About the fact that Josh is goin' into Hobart tomorrow to book us our tickets home, that's what about!'

'Oh,' he said.

'*Oh!* Is that all yer have to say on the matter?' she snarled. 'Don't it bother yer that once I'm gone we'll never see each other again? Didn't that night we spent together mean anythin' to you?'

'Of course it did,' he responded hotly.

'Then why have yer been avoidin' me?' The anger was fading now and seeing the deep hurt in her eyes he felt bitterly ashamed.

'Because what I did to you was wrong,' he muttered. 'I let my feelings get the better of me.'

'Ah, so you *do* have feelin's fer me then?' she said triumphantly.

He nodded miserably. 'Aye, lass, I do. But the thing is, I can never make an honest woman of you, so I shouldn't have taken advantage of you as I did.'

'The way I remember it, what we did was done by mutual consent,' Kitty said, then her voice softened as she asked, 'Can't yer *please* tell me what's wrong, Robbie? Yer owe me that much at least, an' once I'm gone it'll be too late.'

He seemed to be struggling with himself for some moments but then he nodded again. 'Aye, you're right. You do deserve to know the truth, then perhaps you'll understand.'

Crossing to him, she laid her hand gently on his shoulder as he began. 'The thing is . . . I can never marry you 'cos – 'cos I'm already married.'

It was as Kitty had feared, but she let him go on.

'I met my wife some years ago in Queensland, in a bar. She was a singer there and a right bonnie lass. She had the men falling at her feet, so I suppose I was flattered that she bothered wi' me. Within months we were married. That was when the problems started. Lilly was not prepared to stay at home. She liked the glamour and the excitement of singing in the bars, and for a wee while I put up with it. But then I started to hear whispers that she was going with other men behind my back, so I put my foot down and told her that I thought it was time she stayed at home and started a family. That was all I ever really wanted in life, you see, since I didn't have much of a childhood myself.'

Kitty's heart went out to him but she remained silent so he went on, 'All seemed well for a while, then one night I got home from work to find she'd gone. Took all her stuff an' left without so much as a by your leave. Huh! I rushed round to the bar where she had worked, only fer the landlord's wife to tell me Lilly'd run off with her husband. They'd taken every penny they could lay their hands on, and that was the last I ever saw of her. So you see, I could never do right by you, Kitty, not while I'm legally married to someone else. And that's the long and the short of it.'

'But if you *were* free . . . would yer marry me then?' Kitty asked tentatively. So much rested on the answer he might give.

'Had anyone asked me that question before I met you, my answer would have been no,' Robbie replied truthfully. 'Lilly tore the heart out of me when she ran away and I swore that I'd never get close enough to anyone to let them hurt me ever again. And then you came along and stole my heart. So the answer to that question is, yes, I'd gladly marry you tomorrow if I were free, Kitty.'

'Then that's good enough fer me,' Kitty told him tenderly.

'Fer I don't need no ring on me finger, Robbie. All I need is you. If you'll have me, that is.'

'Aw, lass.' He rose and drew her into his arms and she had a sense of coming home. 'But I've nothing much to offer you, just this place. I'm never going to be rich and you could do so much better for yourself.'

She shook her head. 'No, I couldn't. An' the thing is, what yer said about wantin' a family . . . well, this little 'un I'm carryin' is goin' to need a dad.'

She felt his whole body tense and then he held her at arm's length and stared at her incredulously.

'What? You mean you . . .'

She grinned. 'O' course I can't be certain yet,' she admitted. 'But I've already missed a course.' She blushed, speaking of such personal things but they needed to be said. 'An' I've been feelin' sick of a mornin' so I'm fairly certain.'

His eyes seemed to light up from inside as he asked, 'But wouldn't the shame of not being married get you down, lassie?'

She sniffed. 'Why should it? Esperanza and Freddie ain't married, are they? An' I don't see no one pointin' their fingers at them. As far as I'm concerned, we *would* be married – all but fer a piece o' paper. An' as fer this place . . .' She let her eyes wander about the small room. 'All those years I spent locked away in Hatter's Hall, I always dreamed o' havin' a home of me own, an' I can't imagine anywhere better than this.' But then there was no more time for talk, for as Robbie crushed her close against him she sighed with contentment.

When Maria entered the kitchen early the next morning with Faith in her arms she looked around in surprise at the empty room. Kitty was usually up and about and preparing the breakfast by now, but today there was no sign of her, which was strange to say the least. Laying Faith in her crib she then prodded the fire back to life and threw some logs onto it before pushing the sooty kettle into the heart of it. Perhaps Kitty was having a lie-in? Judging by how peaky she had looked for the last couple of weeks Maria thought that it might do her good so she decided not to disturb her.

She was preparing the teapot when Josh joined her, yawning and stretching his arms above his head. He now slept in the room that had been Isabelle's, and much as Maria had done he glanced about the room before commenting, 'No Kitty this morning?'

Maria shook her head as she prepared some milk for Faith. 'No. She's probably overslept so I thought I'd leave her for a little longer. She's been looking a bit tired and run down lately, don't you think?'

'Yes I do, but I reckon that's more to do with her and Robbie's estrangement than a health problem,' he replied, then seeing that she was trying to do two jobs at once he said, 'You see to the tea and the breakfast and I'll feed Faith, shall I?' Even as he spoke he lifted the infant from the crib and kissed her round cheek soundly. Maria smiled. It never failed to move her when she saw him with the baby. He was so gentle and tender with her, and she had no doubt that one day he would make a wonderful father. She fetched some bacon from the marble shelf in the larder and was just about to start frying it when the door opened and Robbie and Kitty appeared with broad smiles on their faces.

'Oh!' Maria said, putting the bacon down. 'I thought you were still in bed, Kitty. You must have been up bright and early.' Then as she saw the look that passed between the two, comprehension dawned and she felt herself blush.

'I'm glad I've caught yer, Master Josh,' Kitty said, ignoring the shocked look on Maria's face. ''Cos the thing is . . . well,

I won't be comin' back to England with yer. I'm stayin' here wi' Robbie so I won't be needin' yer to book me a passage home.'

'But that's wonderful news!' Maria exclaimed as she rushed over to hug them both. 'When will you be getting married? Oh, I just knew that you two were meant for each other and—'

'Whoa!' Kitty held her hand up and stopped Maria mid-flow before telling her with no trace of shame: 'The fact is, Robbie an' I won't be getting married 'cos we're not able to, but we'll be just as good as.'

'You . . . you mean you are going to live together?' Maria breathed.

Kitty nodded. 'That's about the long an' the short of it. But now Robbie, tell 'em what you told me an' then happen they'll understand.'

And so Robbie did just that, stuttering and stammering over his words. When he was done there was a stunned silence until Kitty asked, '*Now* do yer understand? Me an' Robbie love each other, so why shouldn't we be together? He shouldn't have to spend the rest of his life alone because of one mistake he made, an' I know we can be happy. An' let's face it, what have I got to go back to?'

Josh suddenly sprang forward and grasping Robbie's hand he began to pump it up and down, saying, 'Congratulations! I wish you all the best. Between you and me, I've thought you two were made for each other since the first time I saw you together.'

And now Maria hugged Kitty with tears in her eyes. 'I'm really thrilled for you, Kitty,' she told her, 'but I shall miss you so much.'

'I shall miss you too, but yer can always come out an' see us. I shall be right here – now and forever.' She and Robbie exchanged a loving glance, and in that moment Maria knew that Kitty had made the right decision. It seemed that there was to be a happy ending after all . . . for one of them at least.

'I think we should have a celebration,' Josh declared. Crossing to the cupboard, he began to rifle through it, murmuring, 'I'm sure I saw a couple of bottles of wine in here . . . ah, here we are. It should have been champagne really but this will have to do.'

In no time they all had a glass in their hand and raising his, Josh made a toast to the happy couple. Kitty was positively bubbling with happiness and Maria prayed that it would last. Kitty had become very dear to her and she wanted her to be happy. She had a sneaky feeling that from now on she would be, so she raised her glass too and soon their laughter was bouncing off the walls.

Robbie broke the news to Frederick and Esperanza the next morning and they too were overjoyed to learn that Kitty would be staying.

'We must have a leetle party!' Esperanza cried.

Frederick smiled indulgently. Esperanza didn't need much of an excuse for a get-together and a celebration but he thought it was a nice idea all the same. And then Binda said something that stopped them all in their tracks.

'Do they not wish to become married?'

'W-why yes, they do,' Josh flustered. 'But Robbie already has a wife somewhere.'

'It would be of no account if he'd settle for an Aboriginal marriage ceremony,' she informed him. 'The men in my tribe are allowed more than one wife. I could take them over to the village where I came from, and the Elder there would perform it. It would be as binding before the spirits as a Christian marriage, and then we could have a real party.'

'In that case I will certainly put it to them,' Josh told her enthusiastically. 'And I've no doubt they will both jump at the chance. Thank you, Binda.'

Binda smiled broadly then settling herself out on the verandah she sucked quietly on her clay pipe.

Just as he had thought, Kitty and Robbie were all for it, when Josh relayed Binda's message to them the next day.

'Of course, I'm not sure that it will be binding by law, but it might make you feel more committed.'

'I couldn't be any more committed to Robbie than I already am,' Kitty said softly. 'But it's a lovely idea all the same.'

Robbie nodded. 'It certainly is, so I'll tell Binda to go ahead an' arrange it just as soon as she likes,' he beamed.

The date was set for two weeks' time. Frederick would drive the happy couple to Binda's village and after the Elder had performed the ceremony they would return to the ranch for a small reception.

Esperanza was almost beside herself now that she had a wedding to arrange.

'We must go into Hobart and find you a suitable outfit,' she told Kitty, and the girl didn't put up much of a fight. She was quite enjoying all the attention. Once the shopping trip was over and the outfit was chosen, Kitty locked it away at the ranch, declaring that no one was to see it until the day of the wedding. Esperanza also forbade Kitty from staying with Robbie again until after the ceremony. 'A wedding is a wedding, after all, be it a Christian service or otherwise,' she told them primly. Everyone found this highly amusing, seeing as she and Frederick had lived together for all those years with no sign of a wedding ring. Even so they indulged her and before they knew it the big day was upon them.

*

Frederick arrived to take them in the carriage to Binda's village and when Kitty appeared on the verandah looking like a vision, Robbie could hardly speak. Kitty had always been beautiful to him, but today she looked breath-taking.

'Och lass,' he said chokily. 'You are as pretty as a picture. I reckon I must be the luckiest man alive.'

Esperanza beamed. She had played an enormous part in helping Kitty to choose her bridal attire and was more than pleased with the results. At first, she had tried to persuade Kitty to wear white, but Kitty had put her foot down. 'I'll not have some flimsy thing that will never see the light of day again,' she said. 'I want something more practical that I can wear again for special occasions.' And so together they had chosen a rich blue dress that was nipped in at the waist then billowed into a full skirt, with a lace collar to show off her delicate neckline. On her head she wore a jaunty little hat with a tiny veil that partially covered her face, and she was carrying a bouquet of cream orchids that Robbie had picked from the forest for her that morning. Esperanza had tied them with a blue ribbon to match her dress and Kitty felt like a queen in her bridal finery. Esperanza had pleaded for the small wedding party to be allowed to accompany the couple to Binda's village for the ceremony but on that Binda had stayed firm.

'Only the two to be bonded and the Elder are allowed to be present,' she told her mistress solemnly.

Kitty gazed at Robbie. He was dressed in his McPhee tartan kilt and looked every inch the rugged Highlander. Josh had taken him into the tailor's in Hobart for a new white shirt. He had shaved and plastered his unruly red hair with macassar oil, but already it was springing back into curls and Kitty's heart flooded with love as he helped her up into the small carriage. Esperanza and the children had decorated it with flowers and ribbons, and as the two were driven away side by side they waved from the window.

'Now we must hurry back to the ranch and put the finishing touches to the wedding feast,' Esperanza declared. 'Come Maria, get Faith and you can travel back in the trap with me.' Esperanza was a very experienced horsewoman and would normally have arrived on her beautiful spirited mare, but knowing that Maria would need to get the baby safely back to the ranch she had chosen to use the trap today.

The ranch was a hive of activity when the women got there. The house boys had arranged tables all along the length of one wall in the large main reception room and they were heaving beneath the weight of bowlsful of newly baked bread, whole legs of pork, sides of lamb and great cuts of beef, as well as a variety of pickles and assorted pies.

'Good grief,' Maria giggled. 'There's enough food here to feed the whole of Hobart! How are we ever going to eat it all?'

'Far better for there to be too much than not enough,' Esperanza responded and then she darted away to issue her last-minute orders. It would soon be time to welcome the newlyweds.

In the small village where Binda had been born and raised, Robbie and Kitty were just leaving the hut where the Elder had performed the 'bonding ceremony'. It had involved much chanting and joining of hands as the Elder called on the spirits to recognise the bond between the two, and neither of them had understood much of it, but they embraced it all the same. They were aware that the marriage would never be recognised in law, but for Kitty and Robbie it was enough.

'It is done, but he said that we wouldn't be properly bonded until after the birth of our first child,' Robbie told

Frederick as they climbed back into the gaily decorated carriage while the young Aboriginal women danced about and threw flowers at them.

'Then we shan't have to wait too long, shall we?' Kitty answered with a twinkle in her eye. Frederick then urged the horses forward and they trotted off at a smart pace to enjoy their reception.

Chapter Twenty-eight

'I can't believe that in less than a week you'll be gone,' Kitty said fretfully as she folded some more of Faith's clothes into an open trunk.

It was now early in October and Josh had secured passages on the *Sea Queen*, which would be sailing for England the following week.

'An' how are yer goin' to manage on the journey back wi' little Faith to see to, an' all the washin' an' everythin' all on yer own?' she went on.

'I'm sure that I shall manage,' Maria told her confidently. 'I'm quite capable, you know, and Josh will be there to help.'

Kitty stared at her thoughtfully before plucking up the courage to ask, 'An' what's goin' to happen wi' you an' Josh when yer get back? A blind man on a gallopin' donkey can see that yer have feelin's fer each other.'

Maria's hands became still and now she looked at Kitty and sighed. There was no denying it any longer but they had decided to wait until they got home and see what sort of a reception they might receive. Josh's parents should have received the letter informing them of the date of their arrival by the time they got back, and should be expecting them. Maria could only pray that they would welcome their grandchild – and then if they did, she and Josh might look to their own futures. And yet no matter how hard she tried to convince herself otherwise, she could never imagine them accepting her. It was different for Kitty and Robbie. Out here, no one seemed to mind whether couples were legally wed or not, but it was totally different in England. Still, she decided, she would cross that bridge when she came to it. For now, her main concern was getting the child safely home. She could remember only too well how difficult the outward voyage had been, and the loss of lives that had occurred during the journey, and part of her was dreading it. Faith was still so tiny and vulnerable. But at least this time Josh had managed to secure better cabins for them so with luck that would make a difference.

Kitty was humming softly to herself now as she continued with the packing, and as Maria looked at her she saw that the girl was positively glowing; life with Robbie obviously suited her. She had gained weight too and was very much looking forward to the birth of her child.

'We want at least six nippers,' she had told Maria cheerfully, which probably accounted for why Robbie was already adding extensions to their cabin. On the day of their wedding, as Kitty referred to it, Frederick had presented them with a deed of gift, which meant they now owned their cabin and five acres of land surrounding it. It had been the icing on the cake for Kitty, who had almost danced with excitement, for now she truly had her own home and family. She could have asked for nothing more and Maria knew that she was contented and that she need never worry about her. That would not stop her missing her though. They had become like sisters.

'We shall have to think about startin' to pack your stuff soon,' Kitty commented. 'We don't want to be leavin' everythin' till the last minute.'

Maria teased, 'It sounds like you can't wait to get rid of me. And anyway, what I have won't even fill one trunk – and that will be mostly taken up by the outfit that Esperanza gave me.'

'You know that ain't true,' Kitty pouted. 'I shall miss yer all like mad when you've gone. In fact, I don't know what I shall do wi' meself all day.'

Maria could well believe that. Every inch of Kitty's home already gleamed like a new pin.

'Yer never know, yer might get to wear yer best gown on the way back,' Kitty said excitedly. 'The *Sea Queen* is a lot posher than the ship we came on an' they have concerts aboard an' all sorts, so Josh were sayin'.'

'That's as maybe but I doubt I'll be going to any when I have a baby to care for,' Maria sensibly pointed out.

'Hmm, I hadn't thought o' that.'

They both laughed as they dragged the packed trunk into the corridor. Maria paused to wipe the sweat from her forehead and looked towards the open door. Not so long ago the land surrounding the homestead had been a mud bath, but now the grass stretched away into the trees like a lush green carpet, and it was strange to think that while those at home were preparing for winter, they were just coming into their summer here. Exotic plants and flowers were peeping through the earth in a riot of colour, and Kitty had taken to leaving out any left-over food for the kangaroos and wallabies to feast on – although she was careful never to approach them. The kangaroos looked harmless with their little Joeys tucked into their pouches, but Robbie had warned them never to approach one as they could inflict a nasty bite.

'Josh also says that the *Sea Queen* is much faster than the ship we came on,' Maria informed Kitty now. 'It docks at Portsmouth, and if we make good speed, we could well be home in time for Christmas.'

Kitty shuddered. Her previous Christmases at Hatter's Hall held no happy memories for her, but this year she would be spending it with Robbie, albeit in brilliant sunshine. It was hard to envisage, as she thought of the harsh winters back at home.

'Happen yer mam will be thrilled to have yer back,' she said now, and Maria nodded.

'Yes, I'm sure she will. I wrote to tell her our due date of return so she'll be expecting me, but I'm not so sure about my father. Between you and me, I think he was glad to see the back of me.' She had written to her mother three times during their stay but she had always had to be very careful what she wrote. She had not even dared to tell her mother about the loss of her child for fear that her father might read it.

'Huh, then he's a bigger fool than I took him for,' Kitty now retorted indignantly. She could not imagine anyone who knew her not loving Maria, let alone her own father, but then they did say there was none so strange as some folks.

'Let's not think about him for now,' she urged. 'The time is whistlin' past, an' before we know it you'll be gone so I want to make the most of every minute we have left together. What do yer say?'

'I say that's an excellent idea,' Maria agreed with a wide smile. 'I'll worry about tomorrow when it comes. Now, how about we take Faith for a little wander over to the pool? I could do with a dip to cool off. And on the way I could pick some wild orchids and put them on Isabelle's grave.' She still visited Isabelle's resting-place at least twice a week and Kitty had promised to do the same once Maria was gone.

'You're on,' Kitty answered with a cheeky grin and moments later the two young women set off to enjoy the warm afternoon in a magical setting.

Before they knew it, the day of departure was upon them. As Frederick loaded the trunks into the carriage that would take them to the ferry bound for Melbourne, Kitty clung to Maria with tears in her eyes. Robbie would be driving them there.

'Now yer will write, won't yer?' she pleaded chokily. 'Thanks to you teachin' me, I'll be able to read 'em. Robbie's givin' me some more lessons of an' evenin' so soon I'll be able to write back to you meself.'

Maria nodded numbly; too full to speak as Josh's uncle hugged her and said his goodbyes. Then it was Esperanza and the children's turn and they too were tearful. Maria kissed each of the children soundly before hugging Esperanza. As a going-away present the kindly woman had taken her into Hobart and insisted on buying her a smart costume in a fine needlecord and a very pretty blue bonnet to travel in. She looked every inch the lady as Josh helped her into the carriage before passing Faith up to her. Then Robbie urged the horses into a trot and she waved from the window.

'Remember, you will always be welcome here,' Esperanza shouted after them and Maria could suddenly not hold the tears back any longer.

When they were lost to sight, Josh handed her his clean

handkerchief and she wiped her eyes and blew her nose loudly.

'Don't be sad,' he urged her. 'Try to think of this as a new beginning.' But even as he said the words he was filled with trepidation about what the future held.

Unbeknowst to Maria, Josh's Uncle Freddie had received a letter from Charles Montgomery only days before in response to the one that Frederick had written telling him of Isabelle's death. Naturally, the man had been devastated at the loss of his daughter, but not once had he enquired about his granddaughter. He obviously believed that the child would be fostered out as had originally been planned, and now Frederick was blaming himself for not forewarning him that Josh and Maria intended to bring the child home. In his letter, Frederick had also mentioned that, during their stay, Joshua and Maria had become 'close'. Charles Montgomery had clearly been incensed by this piece of information and had urged Frederick to do everything he could to discourage their relationship. It all looked set to become very unpleasant, but for now Josh was determined to concentrate on getting Faith and Maria home to England in one piece.

When they arrived at the ferry for the first leg of their journey to the Australian mainland, Robbie heaved the trunks from the carriage and ordered a stout sailor to take them aboard as he said his goodbyes to them.

'And just remember, there'll always be a place here fer you with me and Kitty,' he told them as Maria smiled through her tears.

'You will look after her, won't you?' she asked him tremulously and he placed his hand over his heart.

'Aye, I will – always,' he vowed. 'Kitty is the most important person in my life and I'd die for her if need be. You have no cause to worry about that little lass any more.

She's my responsibility now, and I'll see that she never wants for anything.'

Maria believed him and she stood on tiptoe to kiss his blushing cheek before Josh led her and Faith up the gangplank. She stood on deck as the ship steamed out of the harbour and watched the island of Tasmania slowly recede. What did the future hold for her now? she wondered, and hoped devoutly for a good outcome for them all.

When they boarded the *Sea Queen* two days later, Maria was thrilled with their cabins. Josh had spared no expense and they were far superior to the ones they had travelled in before, as well as being a good deal larger. She and Faith would share a twin cabin whilst Josh had a single one slightly further along the passageway from them. He had even arranged for a cabin boy to bring Faith's milk at regular intervals, which was a huge relief to Maria.

Within a couple of days there was nothing but the vast expanse of ocean to be seen. Maria had spent the majority of the time in her cabin seeing to Faith's needs, but as the weather was still fair on the third day she took a stroll around the deck with Josh, who insisted on carrying Faith. The child cooed and gurgled, seemingly unperturbed at her change of routine and Maria was able to relax. Even the rolling of the ship on the gentle swell did not seem to trouble her and Maria prayed that the weather would stay fine. She could still remember the terrible storms they had sailed through on the way to Australia and the loss of life that had ensued.

'She seems to be handling the changes well,' Josh commented as he smiled down at his niece.

Maria nodded as an elderly lady shaded by a lace-trimmed parasol stopped to admire the baby.

'Your child is beautiful,' she complimented them and

Maria flushed as she realised that the woman had assumed they were a family. She opened her mouth to tell her otherwise but then closed it again.

When she had walked on, Josh grinned, saying, 'She must have thought that Faith was our baby.'

'Yes.' Maria nodded in agreement, but she was troubled. What if everyone else assumed the same thing once they returned home? It could well have been the case if she had not lost her own child on the journey to Australia. And if Josh's parents refused to accept the child, it would be very difficult to prove that Faith wasn't hers. After all, she only had Josh to tell them otherwise. Frederick and Esperanza were on the other side of the world so they would not be able to speak up for her. She pushed her fears aside again but noting her expression Josh touched her hand gently.

'Try not to worry,' he said. 'I shall make sure that both you and Faith are all right no matter what happens. I don't need to tell you that, surely? I fully intend to speak to my parents at the first opportunity and tell them that we have feelings for each other.'

'For what good it will do,' Maria answered shortly. Somehow she could not share his optimism; after all, Isabelle's father had banished his own daughter to Hatter's Hall rather than face the disgrace of an illegitimate baby – so why should he accept his son wishing to be tied to a servant? And in Charles Montgomery's eyes that's what she would always be; she was under no illusions about that. But still she had no wish to upset Joshua so she changed the subject, saying, 'Isn't that a whale over there?'

'Good grief, I believe it is!' he exclaimed as he followed her pointing finger. They had become accustomed to the dolphins that regularly swam alongside the ship but a whale was a much rarer sight, and for the next half an hour the passengers leaned over the rails and watched the whale diving, surfacing and blowing with delight.

Soon the days became shorter and the temperature dropped. The seas became rougher too, and Maria spent most of the time in her cabin with Faith. Josh's regular visits broke the days up and they grew closer and found that they could converse on almost any subject. That was one thing she had to thank her father for at least, Maria thought; he had insisted that all his children be schooled, and now that education was standing her in good stead.

And then came the news they had been dreading. The cabin boy who brought Faith's milk informed them, 'One of the deck-hands has gone down with the scarlet fever and the Captain is worried. The boy is confined to the sick bay but the Captain reckons this may well be the start of an outbreak. It'll be God help us all if it is.'

Maria sent up a prayer for Faith. The child was so vulnerable that she would stand no chance of survival should she come down with a serious illness.

'That's it then,' she told Josh firmly. 'I shan't be leaving the cabin again until we hear that the deck-hand has fully recovered.'

But the deck-hand died from the sickness and three days later he was buried at sea. It was the first fatality of the trip, but by then three more sailors had been confined to the sick bay and Maria was almost beside herself with worry.

'You must wash your hands thoroughly every time you enter the cabin,' she told Josh and the cabin boy strictly, and they were happy to comply with her wishes.

It was getting colder by the day now; even the temperature in the cabins had dropped and then they rode into rough seas and for two days solid the *Sea Queen* was tossed about like a matchstick. It was only thanks to the efficiency of the Captain that they finally sailed through it and Maria could breathe a sigh of relief and finally catch up on some sleep with Faith tucked in at the side of her.

And then during the second week of December the sound they had all been waiting for echoed around the ship. 'Land Ahoy!'

Many of the passengers hurried to the rails but it was getting dark and they could see little, apart from some very dull lights in the distance. Only the sailor up in the crow's-nest with his eyeglass could properly spy the landmass ahead.

'We may as well retire,' Josh said eventually as Maria cradled Faith to her. The baby was warmly wrapped in a shawl and fast asleep. It was only since the outbreak of scarlet fever had died away that Maria had ventured out onto the deck, and then only occasionally as she was worried about Faith catching a chill.

'If that is Portsmouth ahead we are almost home,' he went on 'but the Captain will drop anchor until the pilot is able to come out and meet us and guide us into the harbour tomorrow. Perhaps we can begin some packing?'

Maria nodded and as she looked up at him she saw that they were both thinking the same thing. *What sort of a homecoming was ahead of them?*

The next day the passengers on the *Sea Queen* awoke to frenzied activity. Just as Josh had predicted, they found themselves anchored outside the harbour. Maria asked, 'Do you think there will be anyone here to meet us?'

'It's highly unlikely,' he answered. 'I did give them the expected date of arrival, but it is only ever approximate and

I believe that we are two days late. I've no doubt we would have made it on time if we hadn't encountered that storm. However, once we get ashore I shall send a telegram and ask them to meet us from the train in Nuneaton. We should be home by tomorrow evening, all being well.'

Maria reached out then and grasping his wrist she told him quietly, 'I just want you to know that should your parents refuse to accept Faith, she will always have a home with me.'

He knew how devoted she was to the child, but assured her, 'I would never let you shoulder that responsibility on your own. And I love her too, my dear. She is my niece, and all I have left of poor Isabelle. But now let us not talk of it any longer. I can hardly wait to feel dry land beneath my feet again, can you?'

Caught up in his happy mood, she smiled and nodded in agreement.

Chapter Twenty-nine

The gangplank was lowered late that afternoon and clutching Faith tightly to her breast, Maria allowed Josh to help her disembark. She felt as if she was descending into chaos as the passengers swarmed past her and burly seamen hauled trunks and other luggage from the ship. She hastily stepped aside to prevent a large rat from running right across her foot. The usual mix of street girls had assembled, their lips and cheeks painted and their dresses cut low, eager to relieve the sailors of some of their hard-earned pay after all the weeks at sea. Seeing them, Maria clutched Faith to her all the harder, making the child whimper. She was nearly a toddler now; could crawl and was developing apace.

'You stay right here and don't move,' Josh instructed Maria. 'I'll go and find our luggage and then I'll get us a cab to a hotel for the night. It's too late for Faith to set off on another journey at this time.'

She felt a faint stirring of panic at the prospect of being

left alone, but raising her chin she managed a weak smile. He wouldn't be gone for long, after all. In seconds she had lost sight of him amongst the crowd, but then looking in the other direction she saw a face that looked vaguely familiar heading towards her.

'Miss Mundy?' asked a middle-aged man when he came abreast of her, removing his hat courteously.

'Yes.' And then she suddenly realised who he was. It was Jacobs, Josh's father's valet. Relief washed through her. Mr Montgomery must have sent the coach for them, which meant they would not have to endure another long train journey.

'I have the coach ready for you over there,' he told her.

'I have to wait for Joshua,' Maria said. 'He has gone to collect our trunks.'

Jacobs placed his hat back on, telling her genially, 'Yes, I know. His father has gone to find him and they will join us as soon as they have secured your luggage. He thought it might be best if you and the er . . . baby, waited in the carriage.'

'Oh!' Relieved to think that she would not have to stand there any longer, Maria followed him trustingly. There were dozens of horses and carriages scattered about, but Jacobs strode straight to theirs, and after opening the door he helped her inside. It was very gloomy inside, and Maria had barely sat down when she realised that she wasn't alone. There were two other people present, although she could not see who they were as yet. And then as she made out the features of the woman sitting opposite she gasped.

'Miss Belle! What are *you* doing here?' Hers was a face she had often seen in her nightmares since leaving Hatter's Hall, and it was one she had prayed she would never see in the flesh again.

'She's here to help me take you an' the brat to where yer belong!'

Maria had no need to see the face of the man who had just spoken. It was a voice she would never forget, and her blood ran cold as she swivelled in her seat to find herself face to face with Lennie.

'B-but I don't understand,' she breathed as Miss Belle leaned over to pluck Faith from her arms.

'Yer will soon enough. In fact you'll have the rest o' yer days to understand, yer filthy hoor,' Lennie cursed. And then suddenly he was leaning towards her with an evil-smelling piece of rag in his hand, and even as she reached for the door handle, he grabbed her and pressed it against her mouth and nose. She tried to fight him off.

'Josh!' she screamed, but the words had scarcely left her lips when a deeper darkness rushed towards her and in seconds she knew no more.

Josh strode towards the spot where he had left Maria, but she had vanished. Two of the crew were close on his heels, loaded down with the luggage, and now he turned to them to say, 'I'm sure that I left Miss Mundy here. Would you mind waiting whilst I have a scout around for her? She can't be far away as she's carrying the baby. I will make it worth your while.' The seamen shrugged: it was no skin off their nose. While they were standing about they could eye the doxies that were on offer and be paid for the waiting into the bargain. Josh began to methodically scan the faces of the people surrounding him before widening his search, but he could see no sign of either Maria or Faith. He began to stop people and ask them, 'Have you seen a young lady in a blue bonnet carrying a small baby?'

Eager to be away, many of the people ignored him and elbowed past him and now he began to panic. Maria must be *somewhere*! He couldn't have been gone for more than ten minutes at the very most. The thought calmed him and he took a deep breath. How far could she have gone in that time, after all? And so his search continued. After half an hour the quay was emptying and he could see that the seamen he had left guarding the luggage were growing impatient. He returned to them and tossed them both some coins, then spotting a nearby empty cab he told the driver, 'Load this lot in, would you, and wait for me? I will see you are well rewarded.'

'Right y'are, sir.' The man licked his lips greedily and began to drag the trunks towards the cab as Josh set off on his search again. After another half an hour he had to admit that she was nowhere to be seen and a cold hand closed around his heart. It was as if she and Faith had vanished off the face of the earth. And then he suddenly thought of what she had said aboard the ship: *should your parents refuse to accept Faith, she will always have a home with me.*

Could it be that she had been so afraid of them rejecting the child that she had decided to run away and keep Faith to herself?

His gut twisted in anguish. Portsmouth was such a big place, she could be anywhere by now if she had taken a cab, and trying to find her would be like looking for a needle in a haystack. The best thing he could do would be to get their luggage checked into a hotel and then resume his search. He could not keep the cabbie waiting there all night. And so he did just that, but the instant the trunks had been placed in his room he set off on his search again. By the time the clock in the market square chimed midnight he was disheartened and exhausted, and so after asking directions of a man who

335

had just tumbled out of one of the numerous inns that were dotted about the harbour he made his way to the nearest police station.

'I've come to report a young woman and a baby as missing,' he told the moustached desk sergeant.

'Oh dearie me. Had a row with the lady wife, have we, sir?' the man asked with a grin.

'No, I have *not* had a row,' Josh told him angrily. 'The young lady in question is single and we became separated on the quay after disembarking from the *Sea Queen*. We were travelling together but she has disappeared.'

'With the baby?' The desk sergeant raised his eyebrows and colour flared in Josh's cheeks as he realised that the man imagined the child was his.

'The baby was my *sister's* child,' he snapped. 'Not that this should make any difference to the fact that the little mite is now missing along with her . . .' he struggled here as he tried to decide what title to give Maria, and ended lamely, 'with her maid.'

'Hmm. So do you reckon she's going to try a little blackmail then?'

'Maria would *never* do that,' Josh answered hotly.

'Ah, so you are on close terms then. *Maria*, is it?'

Losing patience, Josh turned on his heel and strode back out into the night. The policeman was obviously not going to take him seriously, but then he supposed that in a large place like this, there must be a lot of people going missing. He would be better to continue the search himself, but not tonight. It was so dark now that he could barely see his hand in front of his face, so he wearily made his way back to the hotel for a much-needed rest, although he doubted that he would sleep.

*

Josh's search continued for two more whole days and then he had the luggage sent on to the train station and bought a ticket to return home. Perhaps Maria had thought she had lost him and decided to make her way back by herself? He could only pray that this was the case. And if she had gone on ahead of him she would no doubt have returned to her parents' cottage. The journey and the train changes seemed to take forever but at last the train pulled into Nuneaton Trent Valley station and he climbed down onto the platform. He had the trunks stored safely away in the left luggage department then climbed into a vacant cab and told the driver, 'Coleshill Road, please – the cottages there.'

The cabbie urged the horses into a trot and Josh screwed himself into a corner, wrapping his arms tightly about himself as his breath floated on the air in front of him. There was a thick hoar frost on the ground, and after being used to the heat in Tasmania he was feeling the cold more keenly than usual. The carriage rattled through the town and on up Tuttle Hill, then it was going through Chapel End and soon the cottages were in sight.

'Here will do,' Josh instructed the man as he leaned out of the window, and the cabbie drew the horse to a halt. 'Wait here for me, please.' He jumped down as the horse pawed at the ground. The poor beast was tired now and ready to return to his stable for his well-earned oats and a good rub-down.

Josh paused for a moment with his hands thrust deep into his coat pockets as he tried to remember what Maria had told him about her home. Then, striding towards the cottage that seemed to fit her description, he rapped on the front door. The room beyond was in darkness, but within seconds he saw the soft glow of an oil lamp through the window and heard the sound of bolts being drawn. When the door was opened, he found himself looking at an older version of Maria.

'Mrs Mundy?'

The woman nodded and Josh quickly introduced himself. 'I am Joshua Montgomery, ma'am. Would it be convenient to have a word?'

Her face momentarily brightened as she realised who he was and she glanced over his shoulder. Then, seeing that he was apparently alone, her face fell. Holding the door wide, she told him, 'Of course, sir. Do come in.'

Josh found himself standing in a spick and span tiny front parlour. It was sparsely furnished, but everything in it seemed to gleam in the light of the oil lamp. Quickly removing his hat now he told her, 'I have come to enquire if Maria has returned home yet?'

At this her mouth gaped open and she said worriedly, 'But I understood that Maria was to return home with you, sir . . . and the baby!' As she spoke, she looked behind her, as if she was afraid of being overheard, and he perceived that she was as nervy as a kitten.

'She did,' he answered. 'But when we docked in Portsmouth I left her alone for a few minutes while I went to find our luggage, and when I came back, she had gone. I assure you I have searched everywhere for her. I even went to the police station, then when I couldn't find a trace of her, I assumed she must have come on ahead of me.'

'Well, she didn't. I haven't seen hide nor hair of her,' Mrs Mundy told him, wringing her hands. She seemed to be studying him as if there was something more she wanted to say, and deciding that he looked like a nice young man, she eventually whispered, 'Lennie warned me that this might happen. That she might run away, I mean. He said she was mortally scared of bringing the child home now that she had refused to marry him because of what her father might say when she turned up with a flyblow. They were his exact words.'

'Lennie has been here?' Anger coursed through Joshua. It seemed that the man would stop at nothing to destroy Maria. He could only think that he must have jumped ship again once it had arrived back in England.

'It gave me a rare fright when he turned up.' She went on: 'We heard that he had been stabbed but it appears that it was some other poor soul.'

Confused now, Josh scratched his head with one hand as he held his hat respectfully in the other. 'But why would she be afraid of bringing the child back here? It isn't as if it is her baby. Faith is Isabelle's child. Sadly, my sister died giving birth to her.'

Martha's hand slowly rose to her mouth as she tried to take in what this handsome young man was saying. 'But if that is the case, where is Maria's baby? She was . . . in a delicate condition when she set sail.'

'I know all about that – and the fact that Lennie was the father,' Josh said impatiently. 'But I'm sorry to inform you that Maria miscarried her own baby during the voyage.'

'Oh!' Martha looked astounded and didn't know quite what to believe. This man seemed sincere enough but then Lennie had been very convincing too when he had paid her a visit earlier in the day. Obviously one of them was lying . . . but which one?

Josh then hurried on to tell her about the unfortunate incident that had taken place aboard ship, which had led to Lennie's flogging and the way he had then followed Maria to the homestead in Tasmania where he had again tried to rape her. And all the while Martha listened without saying a word. She *wanted* to believe him – but if what he was saying was true, then why would Maria have run away? All she would have had to do was deliver the baby to the Montgomerys and then come home to the cottage. But if on the other hand, the baby *was* hers, as Lennie had assured her it was, then perhaps she could not bear the shame of returning home to present her father with it. Not that he could have done much about it now, she thought wryly as she glanced towards the ceiling. Some months before, Edward Mundy had suffered a severe stroke and had been bedridden ever since. But of course she realised that Maria could not have known about this. She had refrained from mentioning it in the letters she had sent to the girl because she knew that she would have worried about how they were all faring – and after all, what could she have done when she was stuck on the other side of the world? Now, Martha thought that perhaps she should have told her, and then her daughter might not have been so afraid to return home.

It was too late to do anything about it now so she told Josh politely, 'I'm sure that she will come back when she's had time to think about things, and if she does I shall get word to you straight away.'

'Thank you, ma'am.' Josh bowed, his face creased with concern, and then placing his hat back on, he strode away out to the waiting cab.

As soon as the door had closed behind him, Martha leaned against it heavily, her mind whirling. Where was Maria? Did she have enough money to ensure that she and the baby were fed? And who should she believe? It was then that a dull thud came on the ceiling and sighing, she forced herself to climb the stairs, yet again, for what felt like the hundredth time that day, to see to her husband's needs. He was no easier in sickness than he was in health.

*

When the cab pulled up in front of Willow Park, Josh quickly paid the cabbie, adding a generous tip, then as the carriage rattled away he stood for some seconds gazing at the only home he had ever known. His mind was still reeling at the visit Lennie had paid to Maria's mother. He should have known when Robbie returned the man to the ship that he would be out to cause trouble, and Joshua wasn't at all sure that Maria's mother had believed him when he told her that the baby was Isabelle's. However, there was nothing that he could do about that for now, so he decided that he would go in to see what reception he might receive from his parents.

He entered the hallway without knocking and just as usual, Jennings the butler appeared out of nowhere, and as if he had only been gone for an hour enquired, 'Shall I take your coat, sir? Your parents have just retired to the drawing room. I'm afraid that dinner is over but I'm sure that Cook will get you a meal if you require one.'

'No thanks, Jennings, I'm fine. Please get my luggage brought inside.' Josh thrust his coat and hat at him. The way he was feeling at that moment, he wondered if he would ever eat again. And then he was striding down the long hallway, and when he reached the doors to the drawing room he took a deep breath to compose himself and straightened his shoulders.

He found his parents sitting at either side of the fire roaring in the ornate marble fireplace. Helena Montgomery was sipping at a small glass of sherry and his father had his customary glass of port and a cigar.

Helena instantly placed her glass onto a small side table and hurried towards him in a swish of silken skirts, her arms outstretched.

He could see at a glance that she had been crying as she hugged him and said, 'Oh, I am *so* relieved you are back

341

safely, darling. But where is Maria and . . . and the baby? We had a dreadful man come here this morning who told us some awful story that the baby was Maria's but that she was going to try and pass her off as Isabelle's child.'

Josh frowned. So Lennie had been here too dripping his poison, had he? He wasn't completely surprised. It was clear that the scoundrel was out to cause as much mischief as he could.

'Faith *is* Isabelle's child,' he declared, and it came out as more of a growl, causing Helena's eyes to well with tears again.

'B-but how can you be sure?' she asked tremulously. 'I happen to know that Maria was with child when you sailed and—'

'Maria lost her child when we were halfway through the voyage,' he informed her shortly, and all the time his father looked on through narrowed eyes although as yet he had not said a single word.

'If you don't believe me, surely you can take the word of Uncle Freddie,' Josh said. 'I know that he wrote to tell you that Isabelle had passed away following Faith's birth.'

Helena was openly crying again now as the loss of her beloved girl hit her afresh. She doubted that she would ever get over it.

'Yes, he did.' Charles finally spoke and his voice was cold. 'But how can he be sure it was Isabelle's child? He wasn't at the actual birth, was he?'

'Well, no . . .' Josh faltered. 'But I was – well, I was in the cabin at any rate and I tell you, Maria had lost her baby some months before.'

Charles's lips curled back from his teeth. 'You *would* say that,' he spat. 'Reading between the lines that Frederick and Esperanza wrote to us, it seems that you and the little slut have grown quite close, so it would suit you both to farm another man's flyblow off onto us, wouldn't it?'

'That is a disgraceful insinuation! And how dare you call Maria a slut!' Josh's temper had grown to match his father's now. It seemed that Lennie had done a good job, and had he been there, Josh would have taken great pleasure in wringing his neck.

'Please, you two, don't argue,' his mother implored. 'But where are Maria and the baby?'

'I have no idea,' Josh admitted, and suddenly his shoulders sagged as the events of the last few days caught up with him. He told his parents how Maria and Faith had disappeared from the quay.

'See?' Charles said triumphantly. 'It stands to reason that she couldn't go through with trying to trick us. She must have got cold feet at the very last minute and run away to look after her baby by herself. Had the child really been Isabelle's she would have had no compunction in delivering it to us and leaving us to face the shame of it.'

Josh's hands clenched into fists of rage and he turned without another word and left the room. He was just too tired and worried to argue any more tonight. But tomorrow was another day, and he was determined to find Maria and Faith at any cost.

Chapter Thirty

The darkness started to recede and Maria attempted a groan but the sound stayed trapped inside her. She felt as if she was caught in a thick fog but then she became aware of voices and deliberately lay as still as she could.

'She should be awake by now. 'Appen yer overdid it a bit wi' that laudanum. How much did she 'ave?'

'Only enough to keep 'er quiet durin' the journey.'

Maria recognised the last voice as Lennie's and her blood ran cold. Why was he there – and where was she? The voices continued in a faint mumble – they were obviously some way away from her now – and then she heard the sound of a door opening and shutting and a key in a lock. And then there was silence. She attempted to open her eyes, ignoring the dull ache in her head, and eventually she managed it. Then turning her head she tried to focus, and slowly the room swam into view. There were a number of metal beds, covered in thin grey blankets, all in a row, and a large window at one end of the room which was bare of curtains of any kind. The whole room appeared to be bare from what she could see of it, and she realised with sickening awareness that she was in one of the servants' rooms at Hatter's Hall.

Maria made a huge effort to rise, but managed to get her head no more than two or three inches off the pillow before she flopped back. Her arms and legs did not seem to be doing as she was telling them either and she took a deep breath as she tried to stem the panic that was threatening to overtake her. Perhaps if she just lay still for a while the dizziness would pass? But why was she here? And then it all came back to her. She had been waiting for Josh to get the luggage and Jacobs had approached her. She cursed herself for a fool for going with him and trusting him as she had. She should have waited for Josh. But where was Faith? What had they done with the baby? Tears squeezed out of the corners of her eyes and trickled down her cheeks as she thought of the child. She was so small and defenceless, and she had let her down.

Soon a tingling started in her fingers and her toes, and after a time she found that she could flex them. Very slowly the movement returned to her limbs and painfully she dragged herself to the edge of the ticking mattress. It was then that she noticed that her beautiful travelling costume, her last present from Esperanza, was gone and she was dressed in the dull grey clothing of the servants. She had given all of Isabelle's clothes to Kitty before leaving Tasmania, for she had found that she couldn't bring herself to wear them. Someone must have undressed her whilst she was unconscious. The thought made colour flood into her cheeks but that was the least of her worries for now. Somehow she had to find Faith and get out of this dreadful place.

She made a second attempt to sit, but the blood pounded

in her ears and the dizziness returned tenfold, so she closed her eyes again and clung to the edge of the bed until the nausea passed. At last she was able to stand, and wobbling dangerously on legs that felt like jelly, she made it to the window and grasped the sill. She found that she was in a room at the back of the Hall overlooking the laundry rooms. Through the windows she could see women flitting about like ants in the steamy atmosphere and her heart plummeted. It was common knowledge that many had come here as mere girls and never got out again. Many had died there, old before their time, worn out with work and the harsh treatment they had endured. What would she do if no one came to claim her? And what would happen to Faith? Would they too become victims of this dreadful place?

She was still leaning heavily on the sill when she heard the sound of the key grating in the lock again and, turning, she saw Mrs Bradshaw enter the room with a tray.

'Ah, so you're finally awake again then,' the Matron said sternly. 'I was beginning to think we were going to have to throw a bucket of water over you to rouse you.'

'What am I doing here?' Maria asked. 'And where is the baby?'

'You're here because there are those who want you to disappear,' the woman answered, jangling her big iron ring of keys. 'And as for the baby – she's up in the nursery with the other unfortunate little brats. If she's lucky we'll find a home for her. If not, she'll stay where she is till she's old enough to work here.'

Maria was appalled and it showed on her face as she looked around wildly for a way of escape.

'Don't get thinking of trying to run away again,' Mrs Bradshaw warned. 'There is no way out of this place, as many before you have discovered. You may as well make your mind up to the fact that you're here for good. But now I've brought you some food and you would do well to eat it. You'll need to get your strength up, because you'll be working tomorrow. You are not pandering to gentry this time around so you'll be treated no different from the rest of the servants.' At this she turned and left, locking the door behind her.

As Maria finally accepted what a terrible plight she was in, despair washed through her. Crossing back to the bed, she sank onto the edge of it and began to cry helplessly.

Charles and Helena were already at breakfast when Josh joined them the next morning feeling considerably refreshed after some sleep.

His mother gave him a watery smile and Josh noticed that she had barely eaten anything. In truth, his appetite had fled too but nevertheless he forced himself to fill his plate from the silver dishes on the sideboard. He needed the energy to continue his search for Maria and his niece.

'I have purchased a factory in Atherstone,' his father informed him, as if this was just an ordinary day. 'And I thought you might like to ride in with me and take a look at it this morning.'

'I'm afraid I have other plans,' Josh answered quietly as he folded a napkin across his lap.

'I hope you're not planning on going off on a wild-goose chase looking for that . . . that Mundy girl!' Charles said scathingly. 'She will no doubt be happily ensconced in some whorehouse in Portsmouth by now, selling her body to any sailor who will pay for it.'

Josh angrily pushed his plate away and stood up, ready to defend Maria's honour. Seeing that a row was about to erupt, Helena cried, 'Oh, *please* don't argue. It cannot make the situation any better.' And then turning her attention to her husband, she told him, 'I'm sure that isn't true, Charles. Maria did not seem to be that sort of girl at all. She comes from a very respectable family. Her father is the chapel preacher, for heaven's sake!'

Josh managed to remain silent as he marched out of the room, but his heart was thudding so loudly he feared that they might hear it. What if Maria *was* ensconced in some whorehouse! Not by choice – *never* by choice – but many girls had ended up in such places after being abducted against their will, and Maria was a pretty girl. Should some pimp have happened upon her while she stood waiting for him on the quay, she would have been a sitting target. And Faith – well, there were any number of moneyed folk who would buy a baby, especially one as comely as she. His heart broke at the thought and he cursed himself for ever letting them out of his sight for a second. But what was done was done, and now he was determined to find them both, even if it took to the end of his days. There was no point standing there quarrelling with his father; Lennie had obviously done a good job when he had dripped his lies into Charles Montgomery's ear.

He had gone no more than a few steps along the hallway when the dining-room door banged open and his mother came rushing after him, calling, 'Josh? Spare me a few minutes, I beg you. We can talk in here.' Taking his elbow she pushed him into the drawing room and after closing the door behind her she asked him straight out: 'Tell me truthfully, my dear boy: is the child Isabelle's or Maria's?'

He looked straight into her eye as he replied without hesitation, 'The baby is Isabelle's, Mother, and it was her last wish that Maria and I should bring her home for you to care for her.'

'Oh.' Helena chewed on her knuckle. She knew her son inside out and was convinced that he was telling the truth. Her grandchild, who was all she had left of Isabelle now, was out there somewhere, possibly in danger, and suddenly her need to find Faith was as compelling as Josh's.

'I believe you, son,' she told him. 'But why would that young man have come here yesterday with such a cock and bull story?'

'Because Maria rejected him.' A muscle in Josh's cheek twitched as his hands clenched into fists and he quickly told his mother everything.

When he was done, Helena nodded. It all made sense now. 'Then somehow we must find both the baby and Maria,' she said. Then, after a slight hesitation, 'Is it true that you have feelings for her?'

He sighed. 'Yes, it's true. I'm sorry, Mother. I know that you and Father had high hopes of me and Felicity coming together one—'

She held up her hand then and stopped him from going any further, saying, 'This is another thing that I needed to speak to you about. You see, whilst you've been away, there have been certain . . . developments.'

When he raised an eyebrow in enquiry she explained, 'I'm afraid Mrs Pettifer passed away shortly after you departed for Australia. It was not entirely unexpected, for as you know she had been an invalid for a great many years. Anyway, a couple of months after her death, Felicity met a young man from Nottingham when she had a day trip there. And to cut a long story short . . . she has married him after a rather whirlwind romance.'

'Really?' Josh whistled through his teeth. 'That couldn't have gone down very well with her old man.'

'Actually, he was very good about it,' she confided. 'As

you know, Felicity was always rather spoiled by her mother, and between you and me I think her father was just grateful to see her settled. He's bought them a small house up there by all accounts, and apparently Felicity is as happy as the day is long.'

'Then I am pleased for her,' Josh said sincerely. 'But I still can't see my father accepting Maria because she comes from a lower class than us.'

'Your father is a frightful snob; he's stuck in the past and needs to start changing with the times,' his mother answered, shocking her son to the roots. 'He was hardly born into the aristocracy himself!' And then she shocked him still further when she said, 'We *shall* find the baby and when we do, I shall bring her home and she will be brought up in her rightful place – with her family – whether your father likes it or not!'

He stared at her with his mouth hanging slackly open. Was this the same woman who had always meekly obeyed her husband? Until she had helped Isabelle to escape from Hatter's Hall he had never known his mother to say a wrong word to Charles, but now it seemed that the worm was finally turning.

'Father will never accept Faith,' he said eventually.

'Then we shall have to part, shan't we,' Helena said quietly, 'because by hook or by crook, I shall keep my daughter's child with me even if it means I have to leave this place. But now, no more talking. Where do you think we should start to look?'

'I don't know,' Josh admitted despondently.

'Then in that case may I suggest that you visit Maria's mother again. There is just a chance that Maria may have returned, and if she has, she would have gone there. If this is not the case, we should then track down the despicable Lennie Glover. I have a horrible feeling that he may know more about their disappearance than he is letting on.'

'But what about Father?'

'You leave your father to me,' she told him abruptly. 'It is high time he heard a few home truths and I have a distinct feeling that he isn't going to like it.'

'Very well.' Josh kissed his mother's cheek before hurrying away to get his coat. The sooner he could resume the search the better.

Edward plucked at the eiderdown with his good hand as Martha plumped up his pillows. He knew that there was something amiss, since he had overheard her talking to someone in the front parlour the night before. However, the stroke had robbed him of his speech and he was unable to ask her who it had been.

'There,' she said as she straightened up and looked down on him. 'You are all comfortable again for a while now.' The words were said kindly, but what she was thinking was, *How are the mighty fallen.*

Edward was a mere shadow of the man he had once been. One side of his face was drawn down, giving him a deformed appearance, and his tongue hung slackly from his mouth as it drooled onto his nightshirt. He was completely paralysed all down his left side and the right side had only limited movement, which meant she now had to see to all his bodily needs. It wouldn't have been so bad if he had shown one ounce of gratitude, but that would have been expecting too much of Edward. Even now in his weakened condition his dark eyes still glowed with malice, and more than once he had tried to hit her, or thrown his dish aside as she was trying to feed him. But Martha knew that she could have stood all this if he had just once in the time they had been together shown her a little kindness or consideration.

He had treated her as little more than a skivvy since the day they had stood before the altar, and she had accepted her lot because she had felt that she deserved no better. She had been carrying another man's child, after all, and so she had felt a measure of gratitude that Edward had consented to make an honest woman of her and give her unborn child a name.

That child had been Maria, and she had adored her from the day she drew breath whilst still trying to be a good obedient wife to Edward. But then she had discovered that Edward had been paid to take her, and from that day on she had felt belittled. He had despised Maria from the second he set eyes on her, and had made it more than apparent. And now her beloved girl was missing and Martha was almost beside herself with worry. Knowing her daughter as she did, she knew that Maria would never have willingly run away, and a sense of foreboding had settled around her like a cloud ever since Lennie Glover had come to her with his wild tales. She had been thrown into further confusion following Josh's visit, and now she felt helpless, so she was in no mood for one of Edward's tantrums.

He was waving his one weak hand at her and his mouth was working but nothing came from it but indistinguishable grunts. Normally she would have tried to understand what he wanted, but today she had no patience with him, so lifting the bowl she had just washed him in and scooping up the pile of dirty linen she had just changed from beneath him she told him, 'Get some rest now. I have things to do.'

As she made for the door the grunts became louder but she ignored them, and once out on the landing she closed the door firmly between them. It was only then that she paused to blink and stop the tears from falling. It was rarely that she allowed herself to think of Maria's father, but now she could not stop herself as memories flooded back unbidden. He had been such a kind and gentle man, and had been devastated when he discovered that she was with child, for he was in no position to marry her. But oh, how different her life could have been, had he been free! He had been the love of her life, and even now after all these years she still thought of him fondly.

Now she forced herself to move on, taking the steep rickety stairs carefully. Edward was already rapping on the floor for attention with the walking stick she always left within his reach, but she moved on and blocked her ears to the sound. Let him rap. She was bone weary and it wouldn't hurt him to lie quietly for a while.

Early the next morning, Maria was awoken by the sounds of the other girls who had joined her in the bleak dormitory the night before, getting dressed. They had said not one word to her but merely entered the room, collapsed onto their beds and instantly fallen asleep with exhaustion. But not before she had noted that all their eyes were dull and empty. They had obviously lost all hope of ever having any other way of life and accepted their lot silently. But Maria knew that while there was a breath left in her body, she would always be trying to find a way for herself and Faith to escape. But now Maria hastily joined the others as they crowded around the door, trying to tidy her hair as best she could with her fingers.

After a while the door was unlocked by a stout, stern-faced woman that Maria had not seen before, and they all trooped out into a long corridor. Maria had not slept well, partly due to the bitter cold in the dormitory and partly because her mind was full of concerns for little Faith, and she stifled a yawn as they were shown into a washroom where ice had formed in the water in the tin basins. The girls broke the ice and washed their hands and faces as best they could before drying them on their thin grey dresses. They were then allowed a few moments each to use a row of toilets set against one wall that were no more than wooden seats covering large buckets. The stench that emitted from them was appalling and Maria was humiliated at having to do her toilet in open view of everyone – but knowing that she had no choice, she hitched up her skirt and quickly relieved herself.

The girls were then marshalled along another corridor; down a steep set of concrete stairs and through what Maria realised must be a dining room for some of the inmates. Her heart ached at the sight of the poor unfortunate souls. Some of them were attempting to feed themselves whilst others were being force-fed by women who looked like prison warders. These then were the lunatics.

Another door was unlocked and they were led into a smaller room. Maria followed the other girls as they each took up a crude wooden bowl and queued at a table where a woman was slopping porridge into each dish. The girls sat down at bare wooden tables, and taking up the tin spoons placed there, they gobbled down the food as if they were starving. Maria's nose wrinkled as she looked at the greasy mess in her dish but she tried to force herself to eat a little at least. After a while as the girl sitting next to her noticed that Maria had not finished all her food, she snatched up the bowl and scraped it clean in seconds as Maria's stomach revolted. And then one by one they began to drift away from the tables and stand at the door until eventually it was opened and Mrs Bradshaw entered the room. Crooking her finger at Maria, the Matron commanded, 'Come along, you, there's work to be done.'

'Where am I to be working?' she asked as she obediently

swung her legs off the bench and Mrs Bradshaw's answer made her heart flutter.

'Up in the nursery, but only because that brat of yours has been yarking all night and keeping the rest of the babies awake. If she doesn't settle down soon, we shall have to gag her.' Mrs Bradshaw tutted. 'She must have been spoiled rotten – but that young lady will soon get used to the fact that no one comes running here when she screams!'

Maria's heart fluttered with joy at the thought of seeing Faith again and she swallowed the hasty retort that had sprung to her lips. She mustn't do anything that might jeopardise her being allowed to work in the nursery. Endless corridors and stairs later, Mrs Bradshaw stopped at a door and after selecting another key from her chatelaine she unlocked it whilst Maria wondered how she ever remembered which key was which. There were so many locked doors in this place and it did not bode well for her chances of escaping.

And then they were in an oblong room full of wooden cots that were little more than boxes, and she instantly heard Faith crying lustily. She would have recognised the sound anywhere.

'See what I mean?' Mrs Bradshaw said irritably. 'She has been carrying on like that all night.' She pointed to a table where a number of bottles were filled with milk and told Maria, 'Make sure they all get one each and you'll find their clean bindings in that box there. Throw all the soiled ones into the buckets and a laundry maid will come up to collect them later. I'll have something sent up for you to eat at dinnertime, but in the meantime stop that dratted child crying or it'll be the worse for her.' And with that the woman left, slamming the door resoundingly behind her.

Maria walked amongst the cots, her eyes settling on the emaciated little faces that stared up at her. They appeared to range in age from newborn up to one year old, and their eyes, like those of the girls with whom she had shared a dormitory, were dead and unblinking. They had long ceased to cry; they knew that no one would come to them even if they did. Maria's heart was breaking but she forced herself to get on with the job, and at last she was looking down on Faith, who was red in the face with indignation. Unlike her roommates, she had never been left to cry and she wasn't used to such treatment.

'There there then, I'm here now,' Maria soothed as she lifted the small body and rocked her to and fro. The child smelled strongly of urine and Maria guessed that it must have been many hours since she had had her bindings changed. Faith's sobs immediately dulled to whimpers at the feel of the familiar arms about her. Maria expertly changed her; horrified at the red rash that had erupted all over the tender skin of her bottom, and then crossing to the table, she lifted one of the bottles of milk. It was stone cold as was the room where the babies were kept because the fire in the grate had burned low. Faith preferred her milk slightly warmed but seeing as there was nothing she could do about it for now, Maria offered her the teat and the child began to suckle greedily. When the milk was finished the child eventually drifted off into an exhausted nap, so after laying her in her cot, Maria began to lift the other babies from their cots and one at a time she fed and changed them. Some of their bottoms were so sore from lack of being changed that there was barely any skin on them, but not one of them made any complaint as she cleaned them as gently as she could. They just stared up at her and her heart broke afresh. Somehow she had to help them!

Chapter Thirty-one

At the gentleman's club in town later that night, Robert Pettifer stared over the rim of his brandy glass and asked, 'Is there something troubling you, Charles? You seem very preoccupied this evening.'

'What?' Charles swirled the whisky in his glass before answering absently, 'Oh, nothing more than woman trouble, Robert. I'm afraid Helena is being rather difficult at present.'

'I see.' Robert stared into the fire as he thought of his own late wife. Now *she* was what one might have called difficult, right from early on in their marriage when she had taken to her sickbed until the time she passed away a few months ago. But Helena . . . well, Robert had always envied Charles his wife. She was a beautiful woman, loyal and kind, and despite the fact that they were friends, Robert had often secretly thought that Charles did not deserve her.

'Is it something you care to talk about?' he asked now and for a moment he thought that Charles was going to ignore him, but then the other man said: 'What would you have done if Felicity had informed you that she was *enceinte* before she was wed?'

Ah, so that was it, Robert thought. Gossip had a way of getting around, due mainly to the servants passing it on, and some months before it had been all around the village that Isabelle was 'in the family way'. Of course he realised that it might have all been malicious rumour and so he had never given it credence, although the girl's hasty departure to visit her uncle in the colonies had seemed rather suspect.

Now he chose his words carefully before saying, 'Well, Charles, I dare say I should have had to handle it the best way I could – the same way I had to handle Felicity suddenly introducing me to a young man out of the blue and informing me that they wished to be married.' He shook his head. 'I don't mind telling you that it came as a shock and I dread to think what her mother would have made of it, had she not passed away shortly before. And with us still in mourning too. He's a nice enough young chap admittedly, but not who I would have chosen for her, given a choice. We always thought our Felicity and your Joshua would have made a match but there you are. My son-in-law is a blacksmith, you see.' He chuckled then. 'Can you imagine what Margaret would have thought of *that*? She would have had a dickey fit! But on a more serious note and in answer to your question, I think I would have asked my daughter what she wanted to do, and if she had chosen to marry the man responsible for her condition, I would have allowed it.'

Charles looked at him aghast. 'But surely marriages between different classes are doomed to failure?'

Robert shrugged his shoulders. 'Not necessarily, old chap. Times are changing, and surely the happiness of our children is more important than what people might say?'

Charles's face suffused with anger. Robert was mirroring almost word for word what Helena had said – and it was not the answer he wanted to hear. His daughter had died giving birth to an illegitimate flyblow, and now his only son was talking of marrying a servant. It just didn't bear thinking about. Slamming his glass down, he ground out his cigar and rose from his seat, saying brusquely, 'Goodnight, Robert.'

'Goodnight, Charles.' Robert watched his friend leave and sighed. Now there was a troubled man if ever he'd seen one. And if truth be told, Robert believed that most of his troubles were of his own making. Charles Montgomery had always been a strict husband and father, with one set of rules for himself and another for his family, but now it looked like everything was collapsing, and Robert found it difficult to have any sympathy for him. It was a well-known fact that Charles had had more women than hot dinners, including a certain Mrs Elliot whom he visited on a regular basis; Robert found this difficult to comprehend when he had a lovely wife at home who clearly loved him. And then on the other hand, there was he himself, whose wife would have nothing to do with him. Whichever way you looked at it, life was a strange thing – there was no doubt about it.

Charles arrived home to find Helena waiting up for him and he immediately sensed trouble. Normally she retired to her bedchamber long before he chose to put in an appearance.

She came from the drawing room to greet him as the butler took his coat, saying, 'Would you step into the drawing room, please, Charles. I wish to speak to you.'

He nodded curtly, and the second the door had closed behind them she said, 'I believe that the child who was brought back to England is our grandchild, and I wish her to be found. And when she is, I shall expect her to take her rightful place here with us. Furthermore, Joshua has told me that he has strong feelings for Maria, and when we find her I think we should allow him to court her if he so wishes.'

'Have you taken *complete* leave of your senses, woman?' Charles shouted. His face went purple. 'You are standing there telling me that you wish to bring a flyblow into the house and let the heir to my life's work marry a *serving girl*! Why . . . we would be a laughing stock all across the county!'

'And what do *I* care what people say?' Helena stormed back in a rare show of temper. 'We have already lost Isabelle because of your foolish, arrogant pride. If you had had your way, she would have died in an asylum – had I not intervened!'

'Ah, but she died anyway, didn't she?' he shot back.

'Yes, she did, and now we may be in danger of losing our son too, for I will tell you now that he intends to have Maria with or without your blessing. And you should know that he will have mine, for I would not wish him to live in a loveless marriage as I have been forced to do all these years.'

Shock registered on his face as he blustered, 'What do you mean, *loveless*? Have I not kept you in comfort and looked after you?'

'Oh yes, you have done that,' she said bitterly. 'But that does not make up for an empty bed.'

'But I left your bed to protect you,' he protested. 'After Isabelle's birth the doctor warned us that another pregnancy could be fatal for you.'

'Yes, he did, but that did not mean that you had to shun me altogether. And don't think that I don't know about all the other women you have found solace with over the years either, Charles. I am neither blind nor deaf, but I put up with it because I loved you. Furthermore, I feel I should make it clear that if you do not accept Isabelle's child into this house, I shall move out and live somewhere else, where I can care for her myself!'

The man stared back at his wife incredulously. Helena had never spoken to him like this in their entire life together before and he wasn't at all sure what to do about it. Running his hand through his hair he turned from her and gazed towards the window, noting that the snow that had been threatening for days had finally begun to fall.

'Where is Joshua now?' he asked.

'He has retired for the night after spending the entire day searching for Maria and our granddaughter.'

Charles felt an unfamiliar pang of guilt. Isabelle's untimely death had affected them both badly – more than he cared to admit, if truth be known, but when he had placed her in Hatter's Hall he had only been doing what he had thought was for the best. And now Helena was demanding that he should accept her child. Josh was also making a stand about whom he wished to marry. Could it be that his own ideas *were* somewhat outdated, as Robert and Helena had claimed? And what would happen to the little empire he and his father had worked so hard to build, if his son walked away from it now?

Unused to confrontation, Charles went to his study and rang for the butler to bring him a brandy and soda. He had a great deal of thinking to do.

As Martha straightened the quilt over the mound that was her husband he suddenly grasped her wrist with surprising strength. Apart from feeding, changing and seeing to his bodily needs she had spent little time with Edward that day. She had not even sat after the evening meal as she normally did and read snippets from the Coventry newspaper to him.

There were other more pressing things on her mind at the moment, namely finding her daughter.

'What is it?' She tried to free her arm but he clung onto it like one of the leeches that the doctor had prescribed for him. He had been like this all day, ever since young Master Joshua had visited her that morning on the offchance that Maria might have returned. He had obviously heard the drone of their voices through the floor, as the parlour was directly below his room, and because she had not told him about the visitor, he had been agitated all day. His eyes burned into her as she became annoyed.

'Let me go, Edward,' she demanded. 'I have more to do than stand here and watch your tantrums!' But his head wagged from side to side, and she flinched. Even now in his weakened state he could strike fear into her heart. She knew full well what he wanted and so now she told him, 'If you must know, my visitor this morning was young Master Joshua Montgomery, the one that accompanied Maria and his sister to Australia. It seems that the young man is very taken with Maria and I have an idea that when he finds her, they will make a match. What do you think of that, eh? My lovely daughter will be a lady.' And then all her resentment of him surfaced as she rushed on, 'That wasn't what you wanted to hear, was it? You have hated that girl since the second she was born, and you would have had her rotting in Hatter's Hall if you had had your way. But it will be Maria who has the last laugh, you mark my words!'

His chest seemed to puff to twice its size beneath the bedclothes as he stared at her in stunned disbelief; his grip on her slackened and his face drained to a waxy yellow. But then Martha's kind heart won over her resentment and she told him, ''Tis no use fretting over it and working yourself into a lather. You know what the doctor said – you must try to stay calm. Now rest and I will go and make you a cup of tea.' She eased herself away from the bed and slowly made her way downstairs where she pushed the black-bottomed kettle onto the fire to boil.

It was almost Christmas but there was no evidence of it about the cottage as yet. Normally there would have been bowls of holly with bright red berries standing on the table and the windowsill, but she had had no time for such things this year. Martha had always been used to having to make every penny count, but since Edward's stroke things had been tighter still and she didn't know what they would have done without Henry's wages, bless him. The worst of it was that the doctor had confided that it was highly unlikely that Edward would ever again be the man he had been, and yet he could go on like this for years. She shuddered as she thought of it. Years and years stretching ahead of her caring for a man who stared at her as if he hated the sight of her every time she entered the room. Oh, she knew that she was partly to blame, for theirs had not been a love-match. She had been carrying Maria when Edward had wed her, but even so she had tried to be a good wife to him. If only he had tried a little too, she felt that she might have grown to love him in time, but it was too late now. Sighing, she went to measure the tealeaves into the teapot. There was no point in feeling sorry for herself, she just had to get on with it.

She made the tea and carried a cup up to her husband, but when she placed it on the bedside table he lashed out with his one good arm and the cup skidded across the floorboards, splattering tea all across the side of the bed.

'Now look what you have done,' Martha said wearily. 'That will be yet another load of washing I shall have to do in the morning now and it's so hard to get things dry in this weather.' She glanced towards the window where the snow was falling before hurrying across to close the curtains. 'It's evident that you didn't want a last drink,' she told him, trying hard to keep the resentment out of her voice; he was an ill man, after all. 'So I shall bid you goodnight – and don't worry, I shan't be disturbing you. I shall sleep in Emma's room tonight.'

Ignoring the grunts that were issuing from him she bent and blew out the candle and then left the room quietly, leaving him to burn his anger out alone.

After building up the fire early the next morning, Martha then prepared breakfast for Henry and Emma, and whilst they ate it she cut some thick slices of bread and cheese and loaded Henry's snap tin for him.

'Father's quiet this morning,' Henry remarked, cocking his head towards the ceiling and Martha's hands grew still as she considered his words. He was right. Usually the second that Edward heard her up and about he was banging on the ceiling for attention with his stick, but this morning there had been no sound from him.

'You're right, son. And happen I'll enjoy it while I can. I might even have a cup of tea before I take him one up.'

'You do that, Mam,' he urged. 'You look worn out. Oh, and I was thinking, I might stop off in the market after me shift today an' pick us a Christmas tree up.'

'It's a lovely thought, but I don't need to tell you that we have no money to spare for such things this year,' she said regretfully. 'Even the few pennies a tree would cost would make the difference atween us having bread on the table or not,' and her son nodded and lowered his eyes. It seemed a shame though, as little Emma usually loved Christmas.

Martha saw him on his way and helped Emma to get dressed, then just as she had said, she enjoyed a quick cup of tea before pouring one out for Edward and carrying it upstairs. This time, she hoped he drank it. The room was still dark so she placed the cup down and lit the candle before turning towards the bed. Her husband was lying very still with his fists clenched and his eyes staring sightlessly towards the ceiling – and in that moment Martha Mundy knew that he would torment her no more.

That night, as Charles entered the gentleman's club in town, the first person he encountered was Robert Pettifer and he joined him at the side of a roaring fire.

'Are you in a happier frame of mind now?' Pettifer asked bluntly as he poured Charles a brandy from a cut-glass decanter.

'Not really,' Charles confessed. Then he eyed Robert as if pondering whether to confide in him or not. Their friendship went back a long way, and Robert was one of the very few people that Charles felt he might trust.

'I fear that I may have done something dreadful,' he said eventually and Robert raised an inquisitive eyebrow.

'Would you care to enlarge on that?'

Charles rubbed a hand over his face before saying, 'I dare say you heard the rumours that were circulating about Isabelle before she went away?'

Robert nodded; he was an honest man and would not lie just to save his friend's feelings. 'I must admit that I did, but seeing as it was none of my business I chose to remain silent on the subject. I decided that if you wished to talk to me about it, you would.'

Charles took a great gulp of his drink before rushing on, 'The rumours were true.' There, it was said although the words had almost choked him.

Robert nodded, then said sympathetically, 'But it's not

the end of the world, man. Isabelle wasn't the first girl to find herself in such a position and she certainly won't be the last. But where is the child now?'

'She is in a safe place with the young maid called Maria who accompanied her to Frederick's ranch in Tasmania. Helena is saying that we must accept the child into our own home – and to make matters even worse, Josh is talking of marrying this girl Maria. Helena has even stated that if I do not accept the child, she will leave and find a place where she can care for our granddaughter herself. It's all such a deuced shambles.'

'I see.' Robert was shocked to his core. Helena had always been such an obedient, obliging wife. She must feel very strongly about the baby to threaten such a thing. But then he supposed he could understand it in a way. After all, the child was all she had left of her daughter now.

'It appears you have some difficult decisions to make, old chap.' Robert stared at him over the rim of his glass and Charles nodded miserably. He had been unable to concentrate on anything all day. Helena's stand had shaken him greatly; it had also made him realise that he still had strong feelings for her. Even so, he was a proud man and he had his standing in the community to think of. But what did he value most? he asked himself – his family or his reputation?

Chapter Thirty-two

'It's time to go down to your dormitory now,' Mrs Bradshaw informed Maria after unlocking the door and entering the nursery. Maria had no idea what time it was. The light outside had darkened hours ago. The Matron now stared about her and tried to disguise her surprise. The usually gloomy nursery looked almost cosy with the candles that Maria had lit, and the fire was burning brightly in the grate. The babies seemed to be more contented too but she didn't comment on it.

Maria was nursing Faith, and as she laid her back into the cot she asked, 'Couldn't I stay in here tonight with the little ones, Mrs Bradshaw? I don't mind sleeping in the chair.'

'Why would you want to do that?' the woman demanded. 'They're used to being on their own all night.'

'They might be, but Faith isn't.' Maria faced her squarely, her chin set with determination. 'And added to that, the little boy in the end cot has a fever. That's why I got the maid who brought my dinner up to fetch more coal. He really should see a doctor.'

'Rubbish!' Mrs Bradshaw was incensed. Just who the hell did this young woman think she was, telling her what she should and shouldn't do? She must have forgotten her station in life. All the same she walked over to the cot that Maria had pointed to and glanced inside. Grudgingly she had to admit that Maria was right. The child was burning up and his eyes were feverishly bright as he gasped for air.

'That's little Johnny,' she informed Maria coldly. 'He was born to one of the inmates shortly after she was placed here. He's always been a sickly child and I'm sure the doctor wouldn't appreciate me dragging him out on a night like this just to look at him.'

'Then let me stay here and do what I can for him,' Maria said. 'I'm sure you wouldn't want his death on your conscience if his fever gets worse during the night and he passes away.'

Mrs Bradshaw looked uncertain. 'Very well then,' she said finally. 'But you won't be very comfortable. I'll have young Dilly bring you up a blanket and something to eat, but you will have to use one of the buckets for your other needs. I won't allow you to be wandering about and I dare say after a night of being stuck in here you'll be only too glad to go back to the dormitory.' And yet deep down she doubted it, and she had to admit that Maria had worked wonders. The floors had been swept and she had obviously warmed water in the pan on the fire and washed all the babies. 'Is there anything else Madam will be needing?' she asked sarcastically, not expecting a reply, and once more to her surprise, Maria stood up for herself.

'Yes, there is, as a matter of fact. Some of these babies are far too old to be sustained by milk alone, so I would like some porridge sent up and some dishes and spoons. I can warm it for them on the fire.'

Mrs Bradshaw was so flabbergasted at the girl's cheek that she didn't even put up an argument but merely turned and left the room, locking the door securely behind her. Once on the landing she shook her head. She was a right cocky little madam, that one, that was for sure. But then her reasons for allowing Maria to stay in the nursery were not entirely unselfish. She had a new bottle of gin to look forward to that evening once all her work was done, and seeing as her room was within earshot of the nursery and Faith had kept her awake howling for half of the night before, she could enjoy it in peace now. But what was it Maria had said she wanted? Ah, porridge, that was it. She set off for the kitchen to have some sent up to her.

Two hours later, as the rest of the babies slept with full stomachs and clean bottoms for the first time in their short lives, Maria sat at the side of the fire sponging Johnny's burning little body with cool water. In fact, it was no sacrifice at all to stay in the nursery. At least it was warm there, which was more than could be said for the dormitory where she had attempted to sleep the night before. And here she could be close to Faith, should she wake too. But for now all her concerns were centred on the child in her arms. Poor little mite. He certainly hadn't had the best start in life and she wondered if his mother had ever even been allowed to see him. It was hard to judge how old he might be, although she guessed he could be anywhere from six months to a year old.

'Come on, sweetheart,' she crooned as she rocked his hot little body to and fro. 'Don't you dare go and die on me now; you have a lot of living to do.' Her eyes strayed to the metal shuttered windows again, and she saw that if anything, the snow was coming down faster than ever. Her heart sank as she realised that no one would be looking for her and Faith in such appalling conditions. Not even Josh. Just the thought of him made the colour rise up her throat and flood into her cheeks, for although she had accepted that nothing could ever come of their feelings for each other, she still loved him and knew that she always would. And she had no doubt that her mother would be frantic with concern by now too. Raising her hand, she angrily swiped a tear from her eye as she struggled to get a grip on herself. Commonsense told her that even if Mrs Bradshaw had left the door wide open there was no way she could have escaped. It would have meant leaving Faith behind, for no baby could survive the conditions outside, and she would never leave her there. So for now at least she would just have to accept her position and make the best of it – luckily for little Johnny.

When Mrs Bradshaw entered the room early the next morning she paused to stare at Maria, who had dropped into a doze by the fire with the sick baby still in her arms. She approached them quietly and was surprised to see that the child seemed to be slightly better. His breathing was a little easier and his eyes didn't seem to be so feverishly bright.

Well I'll be, she thought to herself. The night before, she wouldn't have given a penny for the child's chances – and yet here he was, apparently over the worst. She was used to seeing babies die in the nursery. The women who usually cared for them were not trained or equipped to look after children, but she had to admit that Maria was making a grand job of it – and despite herself she felt a measure of respect for the girl, especially as she was being held there against her wishes.

She cleared her throat and coughed quietly to let Maria

know that she was there and the girl's eyes instantly sprang open.

'Oh, Mrs Bradshaw, I'm so sorry, I must have dropped off.' She looked down at Johnny and after a moment she said, 'I think he's out of danger now, as long as he's well looked after until he's fully recovered. For a while I thought I was going to lose him, but the little chap has apparently had other plans.'

'Your care of him has been most commendable,' Mrs Bradshaw heard herself saying, but silently she scolded herself. *I must be going soft in the head! Happen it really is time for me to retire and go and join my sister at the coast. I'm getting too old for this!* Then, her voice sharp again, she told Maria, 'The other babies are beginning to stir. Would you like me to send someone in to them while you go and have breakfast and see to your own needs?'

'No, thank you. I shall eat in here with the babies,' Maria informed her and with a nod the older woman strode out of the room and left her to it, her head feeling woolly from all the gin she had drunk the night before.

Maria gently laid Johnny back in his cot and began to heat some milk up in the pan on the fire for the others. It looked set to be another long day.

'Did Father not come home last night?' Josh enquired that morning at breakfast.

Helena waited until the maid had left the room before replying.

'No, he didn't, but I dare say it was due to the weather.' The snow was still falling thickly. Overnight a dense white blanket had formed across the countryside and she had no doubt that some of the roads would be impassable already. 'I expect he stayed at his club,' she said then.

Or at Mrs Elliot's, Josh thought to himself, pushing his plate away. He had been making a pretence of eating but the food seemed to clog up his throat.

'It's time I got ready to go searching again,' he said.

'You can't go out in this weather,' his mother objected. 'The horse would never get through the snow.'

'I don't intend to take the horse. I shall go on foot. It isn't that far into the village and I have to find that creature Lennie before he disappears back off to sea again. I'm sure that he has something to do with Maria and Faith's disappearance,' Josh said grimly. 'And furthermore, I think Father knows more than he is letting on as well.'

Helena nodded. 'I agree with you there, and as a matter of fact, Joshua, I have given him an ultimatum. Either he lets Faith come here to live when we find her, or I shall seek other accommodation and care for her myself. I just hope he has thought on it and is willing to be more reasonable when he does return. But do be careful out there, darling. The weather conditions are downright dangerous and I don't trust that Lennie as far as I could throw him.'

'You don't need to worry about me, Mother,' Josh assured her. 'I am more than capable of handling the likes of Lennie Glover, and when I do finally find him I shall knock the truth out of him if need be.'

Helena watched him leave the room with a worried frown on her face before slowly crossing to the window to stare out at the white landscape. She wasn't happy at all about Josh going out in such weather but knew it would be useless to argue. He could be as stubborn as a mule when he set his mind to something – a trait he had inherited from his father – so all she could do for now was wait.

It was almost lunchtime when Josh once again knocked

on the door of Martha's cottage, and whilst he waited for it to be opened he noticed that all the curtains were tightly drawn all along the row. He assumed that someone must have passed away – and when Martha answered the door and ushered him inside he soon found out who it was.

'My husband died last night,' she told him in a hushed voice, and removing his hat, he quickly offered his condolences. It was more than clear that the family were as poor as church mice and he wondered how they would manage to pay for the man's funeral.

'I am very sorry to hear that, Mrs Mundy,' he told her sincerely. 'Have you instructed an undertaker to do the necessary yet?'

'No, not yet,' she said hesitantly and her answer told him all that he needed to know.

'Then please allow me to approach him for you. It's the least I can do under the circumstances. Had your daughter not accompanied my sister abroad she would be here still to help with the expenses, and there will be no cost to you, of course.'

Martha's pride reared its ugly head and she bristled as she told him primly, 'That is very kind of you but I don't accept charity.'

Henry had come to join them by then and he laid his hand on her arm, saying quietly, 'Don't throw Master Josh's kindness back in his face, Mother. Perhaps we could consider it as a loan until we are in a position to pay him back fully?'

She stared at her son as her thoughts raced. Even the cheapest coffin that Harry Boot the undertaker could supply would cost more than the meagre amount of money she had available and there would be nothing left at all for food for Christmas even though Henry was tipping up every penny of his wages, God bless him.

Seeing Martha hesitate, Josh rushed on, 'That would be most acceptable. I could call and see the undertaker now on your behalf on the way to see if I can find Lennie Glover. I only called in on the off-chance that you might have heard from Maria.'

'Very well then, I accept your offer – but only on the condition that it is a loan. Thank you kindly, sir.' The woman then told him sadly, 'And I am afraid we have heard nothing of Maria, and with every day that passes my fears are increasing. What if we never discover what has become of her and the baby?'

'We will!' Josh told her through gritted teeth. 'I won't stop searching for her until we do, I promise you.'

'And I'll come along and help,' Henry told him now. 'Just give me two minutes to get my boots and my coat on, and we'll be off.'

Josh said he'd be glad of his company, so Henry hurried away and ten minutes later the two young men were back out in the lane battling their way through the thick snow.

'We can try his mother's house again,' Josh said, 'although I have visited her countless times already and she has denied even seeing him.'

'I shouldn't take too much notice of what old Ma Glover says,' Henry panted. 'She wouldn't know the truth if it were to smack her atween the eyes. He's probably been holing up there the whole time we've been searching for him. But it occurred to me that if we're going to find him anywhere, we'll find him in the Salutation of an evening. Lennie likes his drink, so if she denies seeing him again we'll bide our time till the inn opens and try our luck there.'

'Capital idea!' called Josh, and they carried on in silence, intent on getting to the undertaker's to order a coffin for Henry's father.

*

'There is an er . . . a *gentleman* here asking to see you, sir,' Charles's valet informed him as he entered the Smoking Room. Each club member was allocated their own valet for when they were resident at the club and Dawson had looked after Charles for as long as he could remember.

'Really?' Charles placed his cigar in the ashtray. 'Did you get his name?' He had no idea who might be asking for him.

Dawson shook his head. 'He didn't say, sir, but he looks rather a rough character if I am allowed to say so. Should I send him on his way?'

'No, Dawson, I'll see him. Send him through, would you?'

'Very well, sir.' Dawson bowed stiffly and hurried away.

Charles drew on his cigar, waiting. There was a tap at the door and Lennie Glover slid into the room, his eyes darting about as he took in the luxurious surroundings.

'Oh, it's you again, is it!' Charles said impatiently. 'What do you want this time, man?'

Lennie smirked as he twisted his cap in his hands. 'Well, the thing is, guv'nor, that last bit o' cash yer gave me didn't last me long, what wi' havin' to look after me old mother an' what not – so I were wonderin' if yer could forward me a bit more.'

Dull colour crept into Charles's cheeks as he struggled to control his temper. This vile little leech was sucking the life's blood out of him and he had just about had enough. Lennie had already paid him three visits since he had assisted in the kidnap of Maria and Faith from the docks, and each time he had gone away with his pockets bulging in return for his silence, but Charles was at the end of his tether now. He was no man's fool and it was time Lennie discovered it.

'You have been handsomely paid and you have had all you are getting from me,' he said firmly.

The smile slid from Lennie's face and his expression became ugly. 'I'm very sorry to 'ear that, your worship, 'cos it 'ud be a cryin' shame should yer missus find out the hand you had to play in the babe's disappearance, wouldn't it?'

'Are you *threatening* me?' Charles hissed, but Lennie was in no way intimidated.

'I wouldn't put it quite that way,' he sneered, studying his grimy fingernails, 'but things 'ave a nasty way o' gettin' about, don't they?'

'GET OUT NOW!' Charles roared. 'Before I have you thrown out, you good-for-nothing piece of scum!'

'Oh, I'll go if that's 'ow yer feel,' Lennie retaliated. 'But afore I do, I should warn yer, yer goin' to regret this!' And with that he turned and stormed from the room, leaving Charles to clench his hands into fists of rage.

'Have my horse saddled and brought round to the front,' Charles ordered Dawson when he reappeared in answer to the bell. Charles had spent the evening at his club but sleep had eluded him and he had tossed and turned as he fought with his conscience. But now at last, after Lennie's visit, he knew what he must do and there was no time like the present. He pulled on his coat and his thick gloves.

'Are you sure it is wise to venture out on the horse, sir?' Dawson said cautiously. 'I am told the roads out of town are impassable already and—'

'Do as I say *NOW*, man!' Charles thundered and Dawson scuttled away to speak to the stable-lad. It was no skin off his nose, he thought, if the arrogant fool chose to break his neck in the drifts. He pitied the horse though.

Fifteen minutes later Charles was astride his horse. He threw the shivering stable-lad a coin for his trouble.

'Thank yer kindly, sir.' The lad doffed his cap and hurried away to the comparative warmth of the stables, clutching his coin. Prince was skittish and obviously uncomfortable with the deep snow but Charles drove his heels into his flanks and urged him slowly forward, swiping the snow from his eyes as he went.

Lennie meanwhile had taken all the shortcuts across the fields towards Charles's home. He knew the whole area like the back of his hand, and aware that Charles would try to beat him to Willow Park, he was eager for revenge. If he could get to Helena first and inform her where Maria and her grandchild were, he had no doubt that she would reward him handsomely and then he could make haste to Liverpool, slip aboard a ship – as a passenger this time – and be out of England in no time, a richer man. He would live like a king, in warmer climes.

When he came to a curve in Tuttle Hill he stopped to catch his breath in the icy air. This was the same path that Charles would take, Lennie knew – if only he could slow him down! And then an idea slowly formed in his mind . . . Taking a ball of string from his pocket, he carefully weighed it in his hand, thinking. Then he sprang into action. It took only a matter of minutes to stretch it across the path, securing it at each end, and pat the deep snow back into place to conceal it. And then he settled down behind a tree, to wait. It was bitterly cold and the light was already fast fading from the afternoon. Pulling the collar of his coat higher up his neck, he shuddered. His hands and feet were blue and he was beginning to lose the feeling in them, but he could be patient. If things went to plan, this time his prize would go beyond the sums that Charles had already paid him. He would soon have enough money to live like the toffs he envied so much.

*

'Damn weather,' Charles cursed beneath his breath as he urged his horse up the steep hill. Prince's nostrils flared as he lifted his legs high and felt for the ground underneath his hooves, but now they were on the outskirts of the town and Charles pointed him in the direction of home.

'Come on, damn you!' he shouted at the horse as the snow deepened and the animal became more skittish. He was foaming at the mouth now and tossing his splendid head from side to side, but Charles drove him on relentlessly. When he reached home he intended to admit to Helena his part in Maria and the baby's disappearance. After a lot of soul-searching he had realised that he still had strong feelings for his wife and that he had for many years behaved very selfishly, especially following the visit from Lennie. He prayed it would not be too late to make amends, even if it meant accepting his daughter's flyblow into his home and allowing his son to marry the girl of his choice. Charles was a proud man and set in his ways, so he was aware that it was not going to be easy, but if the alternative was to lose his wife, he knew now that he could not risk it. Nor could he risk Lennie blackmailing him for the rest of his life.

'Come on, Prince,' he urged. They were on Tuttle Hill now and the snow was so deep that it was hard to tell where the lane ended and the deep ditches started. Charles knew that he should really dismount and lead the horse until they came to a safer stretch, but he had never been a patient man and he had no intention of changing now. Lifting his riding crop he brought it down hard on Prince's rump and before he could stop him, the horse suddenly whinnied with terror and began to slide to the side.

Damn it, we're going into the ditch – he must have stumbled on something beneath the snow, Charles thought – and then as Prince pitched over he was flying through the

378

air and the last thing he saw was Lennie grinning at him
from the side of the lane. His head connected sickeningly
with the trunk of a thick oak tree, and then he knew no more
as he slithered down to lie in a pool of his own blood. Prince
staggered back to his feet and managed to climb from the
deep ditch then stood shivering, his reins hanging slackly
across his back.

Lennie rubbed his hands together. That should keep the
arrogant bastard quiet fer a while, he thought gleefully. He
told the horse: 'I'll go an' 'ave a few jars down at the Sally,
then I'll pay 'is missus a visit.'

Turning his back on the prone figure in the ditch and the
horse who was pawing at the ground in distress, he went on
his way whistling – but not before he had emptied Charles's
pockets of any money and his heavy gold fob-watch and
chain. The way Lennie saw it, the owner wouldn't be
needing them again any time soon.

Chapter Thirty-three

Harry Boot arrived at Martha's cottage mid-afternoon with the coffin that Josh had ordered and paid for. Edward Mundy was lifted into it and carried down the stairs to the parlour, where he would lie in the open casket until the next day. Neighbours and his parishioners would now be admitted to pay their last respects to him.

Martha watched the proceedings dully. It was a fine coffin made of solid oak with fancy brass handles, far better than anything she could have afforded. She supposed that she should be feeling upset, but she was ashamed to find that all she felt was an overpowering sense of relief. Edward had never pretended to love her, even though she had tried her best to be a good wife to him. Nor had he ever shown her one iota of kindness or consideration. But it was over now. He would never hurt her again, either physically or mentally. Tomorrow he would be buried, although Harry Boot had pointed out that it would be no easy task digging the grave in this weather. She would just be glad when it was all over.

'What yer doin' 'ere again?' Dora Glover said impatiently when she opened the door to Josh and Henry.

'The same thing as we were doing yesterday,' Josh told her. 'We have come to enquire if Lennie has put in an appearance yet.'

'Well, he ain't – so clear orf.' Dora scratched beneath her sagging bosom and Josh struggled to hide his distaste. She smelled of stale ale and cheap scent and he wondered how any man could find her attractive enough to bed her, although there were many that undoubtedly did, if the rumours were anything to go by.

'Thank you and good day, madam,' Josh answered as she slammed the door in his face.

Henry stared at him dejectedly. 'So what do we do now? I can't think of anywhere else to try.'

'I think we should get out of the cold for a while.' Josh stamped his feet and rubbed his gloved hands together, then as a thought occurred to him he said, 'I know – we'll go to my father's club and have a meal. I don't know about you, but I could do with something to warm me up and there's nothing much we can do until the inn opens. What do you say?'

Henry looked uncomfortable as he shuffled from foot to foot. 'But won't that be expensive?'

'Not at all. You will come as my guest. But first we shall have to get into town and it looks like we're going to have to walk.'

'It's only a couple o' miles.' Henry would have walked ten if there had been a good hot meal at the end of it so they set off.

It was way past lunchtime by the time they stepped into the gentleman's club that Josh's father favoured and as Dawson helped them off with their coats Josh asked, 'Is my father here, Dawson?'

'He was, sir, but he left for home earlier this afternoon.'

Josh nodded. 'Then could I order a roast meal with all the trimmings for myself and my friend here, please? We shall be in the bar if you'd like to call us through to the dining room when it's ready.'

'Of course, sir.' Dawson glanced at Henry's rough work clothes, bringing the colour flooding into Henry's cheeks before turning and hurrying away.

'I'm not so sure that this was such a good idea,' Henry said bashfully, feeling totally out of place. He was acutely aware that he was attracting more than a few curious glances, and was deeply embarrassed.

'Nonsense. You are my guest,' Josh assured him, taking him firmly by the elbow and leading him towards the bar. 'Now then, how about a drop of brandy to warm us up, eh? It's just what the doctor ordered on a day like this.'

Henry had never even tasted brandy, nor any other alcoholic drink in his life before for that matter, because of his father's strict religious beliefs but he nodded numbly as Josh pushed a glass across the highly polished bar to him.

'We'll sit over there by the fire, shall we, whilst we wait to be called?'

When Henry found himself seated in a fine leather Chesterfield chair, he felt as if he had stepped into another world. The amount of coal on the fire would have lasted his mother a week, and beneath his feet was a deep pile carpet that stretched from wall to wall. Patterned wallpaper adorned the walls and small tables were dotted about where the men could place their drinks and cigars.

He gulped at his drink then went into a paroxysm of coughing as Josh laughed and pounded his back.

'You're meant to sip at it, man,' he chuckled.

Josh tried to nod as he gasped for air. His throat felt as if it was on fire but he had to admit it had warmed him through – a little too much, if he were to be truthful.

The meal left Henry speechless as one delicious course followed another, and he ate so much that he feared he would burst. Martha had always managed to put nourishing meals on the table with the meagre supplies she could afford, but he had never tasted anything like this and it made him realise how the other half lived.

'That was absolutely delicious,' he told Josh as he finally laid down his knife and fork. Josh smiled. He had enjoyed seeing Henry tuck into his food and thought what a thoroughly nice young man he was. It was no wonder that Maria thought so highly of him. Thinking of her made the smile die on his face. It felt like an age since he had seen her, even though it had only been a matter of days. Somehow he would have to find her, because he realised now that it would be impossible to live without her.

'Right, if you're ready I think we should be making our way back, don't you?' Josh suggested.

Henry nodded and soon they were back out on the darkening pavements, not relishing the journey ahead of them one little bit. They hastened through the town centre, past the empty pens in the cattle-market and along Queens Road, then after taking a right turn they came to Tuttle Hill and started the steep climb, passing the odd cottage whose curtains were already tightly drawn against the fast-darkening night.

'Phew, it fair takes it out of you, this deep snow, doesn't it?' Henry commented as they approached a copse. At least the leafless trees formed a canopy here and stopped the snow from falling quite so quickly.

'Did you hear something then?' Josh suddenly asked, pausing to draw breath and listen.

Henry stopped too and strained his ears into the darkness before answering, 'I think I did. It sounded like a horse neighing.'

They moved on – and Prince loomed up out of the darkness ahead of them.

'Why, this is my father's horse.' Josh took the reins and whispered soothingly to the distressed creature as his eyes cast about for a sign of his master. 'But where is my father? He would never just leave him here in the middle of nowhere. Prince is a thoroughbred and Papa prizes him highly.'

They began to look about and it was Henry who finally shouted, 'Over here, Master Josh! I reckon there's someone down in the ditch.'

In no time at all they had scrambled down the bank. 'It's my father,' Josh said in horror. He turned him over gently and groaned deep in his throat as he saw the blood that had caked across his face. 'Is he alive?' he asked fearfully and Henry thrust his hand beneath Charles's thick overcoat and felt for a heartbeat.

'I can't be sure but I reckon he is, although his heartbeat is very slow,' he answered. Then looking about wildly he said, 'He won't be alive for much longer though if we don't get him into the warm. Come on, Josh. There's no time to go for help. We'll have to somehow lift him onto the horse and get him some of the way back. We'll stop at the first cottage we come to. Happen they'll have something we can lay him on and then we can carry him the rest of the way. Let's get him up the bank.'

It proved to be no easy task. Charles was a large man and they had to manhandle his dead weight as best they could, but at last they had him on the path. It was then that Henry, kneeling, put his hand out to lean against the trunk of the tree while he got his breath back and it came into contact with something tied about it, a few inches above the ground.

'Look at this,' he said angrily as his hand followed the string beneath the snow. 'Someone has tied this across the path, from one tree to another. It must have been that which Prince stumbled on. But who would do such a thing? Both the horse and the rider could have been killed.' Henry always carried a penknife. Taking it from his pocket he cut the string and wedged it into his pocket before telling Josh, 'There's no time to lose. Let's get your father up onto the horse.'

Eventually they managed it, then whilst Henry took the reins and led the horse, Josh walked alongside, keeping his father's limp body from falling off again. But the thought in both their minds as they made their slow way home was: would they be returning a living man or a corpse?

Chapter Thirty-four

Maria yawned as she tucked the thin blanket about Faith and went to check on Johnny. All the children were sleeping contentedly again now with full bellies. The pan of porridge that had been sent up from the kitchen had been cold and greasy, but she had managed to mash it to a suitable consistency with milk she had warmed on the fire and the older babies had gobbled it down. She just wished that she could have encouraged Johnny to try a little, but despite her best efforts he had refused to take even a drop of milk, although he did seem to be much cooler, for which she was thankful.

Now she leaned over him, and it was as she was tucking the blanket about his scrawny little body that the most amazing thing happened, for as he looked up at her, his thin little face suddenly broke into the most wonderful smile and he held his arms out to her.

'Oh, my darling,' Maria crooned as she gently lifted

him and cuddled her to him. She had thought that none of the babies in this awful place were capable of smiling. The poor mites had had little enough to smile at during their short lives, but Johnny had just proved her wrong – and all the long sleepless hours she had spent tending him were suddenly worth every minute.

'I'm going to get you out of here by hook or by crook,' she whispered into his downy hair. 'And you're going to grow up to be a big strong man.'

She cuddled him until his eyelids began to droop then gently laid him back into his cot. Perhaps now she might catch a nap while all the babies were content. She had been so busy that she had barely had time to think of anything other than the infants all day, but now tears clogged her throat. She had expected to be spending Christmas with her mother, but now she would be here in this godforsaken place, although she had no doubt that Josh would be searching for her. She made up the fire then dropped heavily into the chair and before she knew it, was fast asleep.

The man in the cottage at Chapel End where Josh and Henry stopped to ask for help could not have been more helpful. Within minutes he had produced not only a door to use as a stretcher, but warm blankets in which to swaddle Charles for the rest of his journey. He and his neighbour then insisted on helping to carry Charles the rest of the way, and so with a man on each corner of the door and another man dispatched to tell the doctor that he would be needed at Willow Park, they struggled on. There was no chance of getting a cart through the drifts so this was the only option left open to them.

They were all drooping with weariness as they finally climbed the steps to the heavy oak doors, and when

Jennings opened it to them, Josh was sure he had never been so pleased to see him in his life before.

'Goodness me, sir! Is that the master you have there? Bring him into the warm quickly. I'll summon the mistress and order hot water and towels.'

As the men gently laid the door down, Helena rushed down the hallway, her silken skirts rustling about her. When she saw Charles, her hand flew to her mouth but then quickly taking control she ordered them, 'Bring him into the drawing room and put him on the sofa. Whatever has happened?' Jennings meanwhile had ordered a stable-lad to fetch Prince and rub him down and see to his needs.

Maids were hurrying to and fro, bringing bowls of hot water and towels, and whilst the helpers were led away to the kitchen for food and a warm drink, Josh and Henry followed Helena into the drawing room. Once Charles's prostrate body had been transferred to the velvet sofa, Josh began to explain what had happened.

'It seems that someone strung a line across the path, tripping the horse, and Father must have been thrown.'

Helena dabbed gently at the caked blood on her husband's face. 'But why would anyone do such a terrible thing?' she asked, and both of the young men shook their heads. They had no answer.

'The doctor should be on his way,' Josh told her. 'That's if he can get through the snow.'

'Well, in the meantime we have to take these wet clothes off him,' Helena said, swallowing her tears. Now was not the time for crying. There would be plenty of time for that later, when she had done all she could for her husband.

The two young men stepped forward and in seconds had divested Charles of his clothes. They then wrapped him in warm blankets and placed the hot bricks that one of the maids had brought from the oven by his feet, whilst Helena tried to rub some warmth into his stiff cold fingers. He was a terrible ghastly grey colour, and she feared the worst, but while there was life there was hope, and she worked on, sponging him with warm water and rubbing his limbs.

'You two go and get a hot drink,' she said eventually. 'I can look after him until the doctor arrives and you both look fit to drop. Get out of those wet clothes too, Josh, and make sure that Henry has some dry clothes as well or you'll both catch your deaths.'

Josh and Henry left the room and now that she was alone with her husband, Helena began to talk to him even though she had no idea if he could hear her or not.

'You *must* get well,' she said. 'I know our life together hasn't been ideal for some time, but I have never stopped loving you. I want you to know that.'

Feeling a slight movement in his fingers she looked towards his face and was shocked to see he was staring at her. The deep wound on his forehead had opened up again and was leaking blood down his cheek, and she pressed a cloth to it as she told him, 'Don't try to talk, my darling. The doctor is on his way and he will help you. He has to.'

The grip on her fingers increased and his mouth worked soundlessly. Realising that he was trying to tell her something, she leaned closer.

'I . . . I'm sorry.'

'Shush,' she urged but he went on.

'I locked Maria and the baby away. I – I'm so sorry. I . . . love you.'

The breath caught in her throat but she forced herself to ask, 'Where, Charles? *Where* are Maria and the baby?'

His eyes were beginning to glaze over now and she began to panic, but before she could say anything else he muttered,

'*L-Lennie,*' and then drew a shuddering breath and became still. Sobbing, she laid her head on his chest. She needed no doctor to tell her that he was dead.

'Your father told me that *he* had had Maria and the baby locked away,' she told Josh. Her son was holding her hand and trying to comfort her while dealing with his own profound sense of shock at the death of his father. 'But when I asked him where they were, he only said one word, or should I say name? He said "Lennie". Isn't that the young man who came here to tell us that the child was Maria's?'

'Yes, it is.' Josh made a huge attempt to control his feelings at this news. 'Can you manage here on your own for a while, Mother? I hate to leave you at such a time but there is nothing we can do for Father now, so it's imperative that Henry and I find Lennie and track down Maria and Faith.'

'Of course I can,' Helena answered brokenly. It felt as if her whole world was falling apart, but Josh was quite right. If this Lennie knew where her granddaughter was, then they must waste no time in finding him. However, before Josh had a chance to take leave of her, the butler hurried towards them with a worried look on his face. The staff were creeping about the house like mice in respect for the master, and normally Jennings would have turned any visitors away at such a time, but he had a feeling that the mistress might well want to see this one.

'There is someone here asking to see you, ma'am,' he told her quietly. 'I have shown him into the day room. It's a Mr Glover.'

Josh's eyes almost popped from his head. 'Thank you, Jennings,' he said. 'Tell him we shall be along to see him shortly.'

*

A log cracking on the fire made Maria's eyes spring open, and glancing towards the window she was shocked to see that it was pitch black outside. Goodness, I must have been asleep for hours, she thought as she yawned and stretched. The babies were still quiet, although some of them were stirring now, so she hastily threw another log on the fire then set about lighting the candles that were placed around the room. The whole place instantly looked cosier as the flickering lights chased the shadows away. She put some milk to heat on the flames before going from one cot to another, smiling comfortingly at the tiny occupants. Faith gave her a gummy grin as Maria leaned over her, and she tickled her under the chin as she promised, 'You'll be having some nice warm milk soon, darling.' The child cooed in response, and happy that she was content for now, Maria hurried on to Johnny's cot. The instant she gazed in at him she had a terrible sense of foreboding. He was lying very still with his long eyelashes curled on his pale little cheeks. Too still, she found herself thinking as she reached down to touch his tiny hand. Her own recoiled as she realised that he was icy cold. But he shouldn't be, surely? She had insisted that she had enough fuel for the fire to keep the room warm. Taking a deep breath, she began to lift him from his cot and as his little head lolled to one side, a strangled sob caught in her throat.

'Oh Johnny, no, you can't be dead,' she muttered broken-heartedly. 'I thought you were over the worst.' It was then that the smell of burning pervaded the room as the milk bubbled over onto the logs, and with Johnny still clutched to her she crossed to the fire and kicked the pan onto the floor with her foot as tears bubbled out of her eyes. As if picking up on her distress, the rest of the babies began to whimper. They had soon discovered that she went to them if they did, but for now Maria was so distressed that she was deaf to them.

Mrs Bradshaw found her still standing there in the middle of the room ten minutes later, and at a glance she guessed what had happened. Even she felt the sting of tears as she saw how upset Maria was.

'Give him to me, lass,' she whispered. 'There's nothing more you can do for this one now, but the rest of the babies need you. Go on, go and see to them. I'll make sure that little Johnny is properly buried.'

For a moment, Maria resisted as Mrs Bradshaw tried to take the child from her arms, but then she relented and handed him over. As the woman had said, Johnny was beyond help now. The thought of his tiny body being buried in the earth would haunt her for the rest of her days, and she would always wonder if there was anything more she might have done to save him.

As if she could read her thoughts Mrs Bradshaw told her, 'Don't go whipping yourself over this. You couldn't have done any more than you did. Between you and me, I didn't think he'd make it. I've seen this happen too many times before.' She turned to leave then, the chatelaine containing the many keys clanking about her waist. Maria heard the key turn in the lock and suddenly her hands clenched into fists as she shouted, 'I can't bear it! It's not fair! He was just a baby!'

The infants' whimpers progressed to wails, so after pulling herself together with a great effort she swiped the tears away with the back of her hand and quickly tipped some more milk into the pan then placed it back on the fire. Deep inside she was thinking, *I have to get out of here!* Now more than ever, she knew that if she didn't, she would end up as insane as some of the residents.

*

'Right, Mother, now just leave the talking up to me,' Josh warned Helena as they stood outside the door of the day room. She nodded mutely and after a glance at Henry, Josh pushed the door open and strode into the room with the other two following close on his heels.

A fire was burning brightly in the grate and by the light of the oil lamps they saw that Lennie was standing in front of the fire warming his backside as if he owned the place.

He flashed a smarmy smile at them as Josh said curtly, 'I believe you wanted to see us?'

Lennie had been hoping to see Helena alone, but deciding to brazen it out he said, 'Actually, I reckon it's you as might want to see *me*. I've got some news yer might be interested in, see, regardin' the missin' babby an' the maid.'

'Oh yes, and what would that be then?' Josh was outwardly calm but inside he was battling to stop himself from crossing to this lowlife and throttling him.

'Ah, now that's the problem, see. Information the likes o' what I 'ave don't come cheap.' Lennie smirked and Helena laid a restraining hand on her son's arm as she saw him bristle. 'The thing is, I 'appen to know where they are, an' that's got to be worth sommat, ain't it?'

'And where are they?'

'First things first. What's this information worth to yer?'

'Name your price,' Josh said through gritted teeth and Lennie cocked his head to one side as if he was considering it.

'Well, I reckon it's gotta be in the 'undreds, don't you?'

'Yes I do,' Helena said quickly, terrified that Josh might erupt at any minute. 'How about two hundred pounds?'

'Is that all a granddaughter is worth to yer?' Lennie jeered. 'Double it an' we might 'ave a deal.'

'May I just remind you that on your last visit you told us

393

that the baby *wasn't* my granddaughter,' Helena reminded him.

Lennie shrugged. 'We can all make mistakes, can't we?'

'Very well, you can have the money. But I'm afraid we don't keep that sort of cash in the house,' she told him now. 'I shall probably have up to two hundred in the safe but you will have to come back for the rest of the money tomorrow.'

When he frowned doubtfully she told him icily, 'I assure you, Mr Glover. My word is my bond. Now tell me where my granddaughter and Maria are.'

'Not till I've seen the first lot o' cash,' he answered sulkily as he twisted his cap in his hands.

Helena turned abruptly and swept from the room in a swish of silken skirts, returning some minutes later with a bundle of notes in her hand.

'Now tell me where they are,' she demanded as she held the notes out to him and he licked his lips as he eyed the money greedily.

'You'll find 'em both in Hatter's Hall where they were placed on your 'usband's instructions.' He reached out to snatch the money, but as he did so his jacket gaped partially open and Josh saw a flash of gold chain hanging against his grimy waistcoat.

'What's this then?' he cried as he sprang forward, and before Lennie could stop him, he had pulled the gold watch that the chain was attached to from Lennie's pocket. At the same time a small roll of string rolled out onto the carpet and Lennie paled to the colour of putty.

'Why . . . this is my father's watch,' Josh gasped, and then as his eyes settled on the string he asked Henry, 'And isn't that the same sort of string that was tied across the path to trip my father's horse?'

Henry pulled the string from the pocket of the clean

trousers he had borrowed and they saw that the string was identical – and in that moment, everything became clear.

'Why, it was *you* who caused my father's accident,' Josh cried with rage. 'That must have been when you stole his watch before leaving the poor man for dead.'

'I did no such thing,' Lennie blustered as he inched towards the door.

'So how do you explain this then?' Josh shook the ball of string in his face. 'And how do explain the fact that you have my father's watch in your possession?'

Realising that the game was up, Lennie turned to run but Henry put his foot out and Lennie sprawled across the floor as panic enveloped him.

'You murdering swine!' Josh roared.

Henry hauled Lennie none too gently to his feet and shook him like a dog shakes a rat until his teeth rattled.

'I didn't kill no one,' Lennie whined. 'I just wanted to slow 'im down, like!'

'Well, you did a bit more than that. My father passed away shortly after being carried home,' Josh ground out. Hearing the commotion, some of the male staff had entered the room now, and Josh told them: 'Get this murderer locked up in the cellar then tell one of the stable-lads to go for the Constable. This is the man who killed your master.'

'But I never meant to!' Lennie protested, as he looked longingly at the bundle of notes that were now scattered about the floor.

'Perhaps you'll remember that when you're dangling at the end of a rope,' Josh spat as the men hauled him away.

He then crossed to his mother, who was sobbing uncontrollably, and wrapping his arms about her they stood drawing comfort from each other as Henry stole from the room, leaving them to grieve in private.

Chapter Thirty-Five

'I really don't know what you are talking about. I assure you that Maria Mundy and the baby are not here, madam,' Miss Belle informed Helena and Josh imperiously.

It was now fast approaching midnight and it had taken the carriage hours to reach Hatter's Hall, with the men regularly having to climb down and shovel a way through the snow for the horses. Now that she was here, Helena had no intention of leaving without her granddaughter and Maria, for despite what Miss Belle had said, she truly believed that they were there. However, should the Housekeeper continue to deny it, Helena knew that it might take hours to locate them. Hatter's Hall was an enormous place.

Her patience had already been stretched to the limit.

'I happen to *know* that they are here, Miss Belle, so why don't you just take me to them and save us all a lot of time and unpleasantness?' she told the woman. 'I am aware that you are probably afraid of repercussions from my husband, but you should know that he told me himself he had had them sent here earlier this evening just before he died, so from now on it will be me you are dealing with – and I should warn you, should you cross me I shall make things very uncomfortable for you.'

'Mr Montgomery is *dead*!' Miss Belle's hand flew to her mouth in shock.

'I am afraid he is,' Helena answered heavily, taking a deep breath to control her emotions. 'And his murderer is now under lock and key at the police station, so as you can imagine I am in no mood for games.'

At that moment Mrs Bradshaw bore down on them like a large black crow, and ignoring the Housekeeper, she told Helena, 'I know where they are, ma'am. Would you like to follow me and I'll take you to them right away.'

'Mrs Bradshaw, think what you are doing!' Miss Belle appealed.

'I know exactly what I am doing. And by the way, I shall be leaving this place just as soon as I can get my bags packed,' the Matron answered, looking the other woman straight in the eye as she stood, hands on her hips. 'I am sick and tired of seeing the unnecessary suffering that goes on in this place so I have decided to retire and go and live with my sister. But before I go, I want to see that young Maria Mundy is out of here too. She doesn't deserve what's happened to her.' Then, turning towards Helena and Josh, she repeated courteously, 'Would you care to follow me?'

Helena cast a scathing glance in Miss Belle's direction before turning about and following Mrs Bradshaw through the lengthy corridors. Her emotions were in a whirl. She had just lost her husband and apprehended his murderer, and now she was about to meet her grandchild for the first time. It was certainly turning out to be a day she would never forget.

When they eventually reached the door to the nursery, Mrs Bradshaw paused to tell them, 'You will find that Maria is very upset. One of the babies she has been caring for passed away today. Even so, I have no doubt she will be thrilled to see you and escape this place.'

She then selected a key from the heavy bunch swinging about her waist and unlocked the door. Throwing it open, she ushered them inside, telling them, 'I shall leave you now to go and begin my packing, but I wish you all the best.' Then before they could answer her, she was gone.

Helena and Josh looked at each other, then taking her elbow, Josh led his mother into the room.

The light from the candles was dim, but as his eyes adjusted to it, Josh saw Maria sleeping in the chair at the side of the fire and his heart soared.

'Maria, Maria . . . wake up, darling,' he said softly as he stroked her arm. 'We've come to take you home.'

Her eyes fluttered open and as they settled on him she blinked, thinking that she must be dreaming. But no, he was really there – and for a moment she dared not allow herself to believe it. And then he was pulling her to her feet, and when his arms went about her she knew that her prayers had been answered. She was about to speak when she noticed Helena and she abruptly clamped her mouth shut as she self-consciously ran her hands down the sides of the faded grey dress. What would the woman think of her? Maria was only too well aware that she must look a complete mess. She didn't smell very nice either if it came to that, but surprisingly the woman seemed almost as pleased to see her as Josh was.

'I am so grateful that you are safe, dear,' Helena told her and then, unable to contain herself for a moment longer, she asked, 'Which of these babies is Isabelle's daughter?'

Maria led her to the crib where Faith lay sleeping, and as Helena looked down on her, her eyes filled with tears. 'She looks just like Isabelle did at that age,' she whispered. Then, drawing herself upright, she told Maria, 'Wrap her up as warmly as you can, my dear, and follow me. It's time we got you both home. We have much to tell you.'

Slightly bewildered, Maria frowned. 'But what will happen to the babies if I go? I have been caring for them.'

'Don't you get worrying about these little souls,' Helena said firmly as she looked about. 'I shall be the main benefactor of this establishment from now on, and I intend to see that some drastic changes for the better take place, with effect from today.'

Maria swaddled Faith in one of the thin blankets, then with Josh's arm tight about her waist she left the room and followed Helena down to the foyer, where Miss Belle was still waiting for them.

'A word, if you please,' Helena ordered, and as Josh led Maria out to the waiting carriage Helena began to lay down the law. By the time she left some minutes later, Miss Belle was in no doubt where she stood, and she scuttled away to get one of the better maids to spend the rest of the night in the nursery. Helena had informed her that she personally would be coming to inspect the place the very next day – and that if she did not find the conditions vastly improved for the babies and the inmates, then Miss Belle would have to start looking for another job.

In the carriage on the way back to Willow Park, Josh braced himself to tell Maria of her father's death. The news came as a shock, but she wasn't distressed. Despite his Christian beliefs, Edward Mundy had never shown her, or her mother for that matter, an ounce of charity or kindness for as far back as she could remember; all she could feel was a deep sense of relief, tempered with guilt. Josh then went on to tell her of his own father's death, and of Lennie's part in it.

She could hardly take it all in. 'Will he be locked away?' she asked tremulously, and Josh's lips set in a grim line.

'More likely he'll be hanged,' he answered. 'And good riddance to bad rubbish, that's what I say. He will never bother you again now, Maria, so you have no need to fear him any longer.'

The carriage lurched across the snowy roads, until at last they arrived back at Willow Park, where the servants were still up, waiting for them. They were ushered into the drawing room, where a tray of hot chocolate shortly appeared, and as Helena took Faith from Maria's arms, Josh passed her a cup. She sipped at it gratefully, still scarcely able to believe that she was free.

She was relieved to see that Helena seemed to be very taken with Faith, and although her heart ached at the thought of handing over the care of her, she knew that it was for the best. Faith belonged with her family; it was what Isabelle had hoped for.

After a time she said tentatively, 'I could stay here and act as a nanny to Faith, if it would help, Mrs Montgomery, until you have time to appoint one. Faith knows me and it might be less upsetting for her.'

'Thank you, my dear, that's very thoughtful of you,' Helena responded. 'But I rather think Josh has another role in mind for you, as his wife.'

Acutely embarrassed, Maria answered, 'Josh pays me a great compliment, ma'am. But I am more than aware that it would not be suitable for him to wed someone from my class.'

'But Maria,' Josh began to object. 'You know how I feel—'

Maria raised her hand and stopped him mid-sentence. 'And *you* know how *I* feel. We have had this conversation before and I am still of the same mind as I was then. You must marry someone more suitable.'

A maid knocked and entered the room then to tell Helena, 'The nursery has been prepared for the baby, ma'am. Would you like me to take her up?'

'Yes, Ruby, thank you. But Maria will stay in there with her for tonight. See that she has all she needs and then we will all talk some more in the morning. I'm afraid it has been a very long day.'

Helena's face was drawn with the strain of the last few hours, but she kissed the baby gently before handing her to Ruby, and Maria rose to follow her.

'Maria, I think we should talk,' Josh said urgently and she paused to smile at him sadly.

'I think I have said all that needs to be said,' she answered, 'and I will not change my mind. I shall stay here and care for Faith for the time being with your mother's permission, but once a replacement for me has been found, I shall return home.' Turning to Mrs Montgomery, she politely wished her goodnight and quietly followed Ruby from the room.

'Eeh, what a day it's been,' the plump little maid commented as she carried Faith up the sweeping staircase. 'First we lose the master then we find this little mite. They say births and deaths come together, don't they?'

Maria nodded as she tried to take in the luxurious surroundings. Oil paintings of previous Montgomerys were placed all the way up the staircase, and a huge, glittering chandelier dangled down into the stairwell. It was certainly a far cry from the austere rooms in Hatter's Hall, but she told herself that she must put all this behind her now and get on with her life, even though her heart was aching. Once she left here she would probably never see Josh again – and the thought was almost more than she could bear.

The nursery turned out to be a delightful room with a huge fire roaring in the grate and thick curtains hanging at the windows.

'I'm told Miss Isabelle, God rest her soul, and Master Josh slept here when they were nippers,' Ruby informed Maria as she saw her looking around. 'That were long before my time, but I reckon you'll be comfy in 'ere.'

'Thank you, Ruby. I'm sure we will,' Maria said.

Ruby peeped at her from the corner of her eye. It was hard to believe that the young master actually wanted to wed this bedraggled-looking wench. But he did – Ruby had heard him say it with her own ears. The staff downstairs would be agog when she passed the gossip on, which Ruby had every intention of doing at the first opportunity. Maria spoke correctly enough, admittedly, but with her hair all rats' tails and smelling none too sweet in the drab uniform of the workhouse, she couldn't hold a candle to Miss Felicity Pettifer, whom everyone had expected him to wed. Still, as Ruby's mother had always been fond of telling her, you could never tell where love might strike. It was just a shame this young woman didn't feel the same for Master Josh from where Ruby was standing.

Once Faith was bathed and settled, Ruby led Maria to a bathroom further along the corridor where she found a steaming bath waiting for her.

'The mistress thought as yer might appreciate a good soak an' some clean clothes,' Ruby informed her kindly. 'I took the liberty of unpackin' yer trunk an' I've put yer nightclothes on that chair over there. Master Josh brought it back wi' him when you an' the little 'un went missin'. I hope yer don't mind?'

'It was very kind of you, Ruby,' Maria assured her. 'And it looks like heaven to me at the moment. I've almost forgotten what it feels like to be clean.'

'Well, take as long as yer like,' Ruby told her. 'I shan't leave the little 'un till yer get back, an' while yer gone I'll organise some milk fer her, shall I?'

'Thank you.' Maria waited until Ruby had gone then after locking the door she stripped off her clothes and dropped them in a pile onto the floor before sliding into the hot water and sighing with contentment. She washed her hair and every inch of herself thoroughly with lavender-perfumed soap, then after climbing from the bath she rubbed her clean hair with the soft towels Ruby had provided and donned the linen nightgown that Isabelle had bought her on their shopping trip before they sailed for Australia. It all seemed like a lifetime ago now. So much had happened since then, but soon she would return to her mother and somehow life would have to go on without Josh. It was a daunting thought, and as she made her way back to the nursery, her heart was heavy.

The next morning, later than usual due to the disturbed night, Ruby carried a tray of breakfast up to the nursery, only to find Maria already up and dressed and giving Faith a bottle. The girl was shocked to see that, dressed in respectable clothes and with her hair shining, Maria was actually a very attractive young lady. Setting the tray down, Ruby crossed to stare down at the baby.

'By, she's a little beauty, ain't she?' she sighed. 'Everyone below stairs is made up at the thought o' havin' a little one about the house again. I've no doubt she's goin' to be spoiled rotten. But while I remember, I must pass on a message from the mistress. She says to tell yer that a carriage will take yer to visit yer mother as soon as you've a mind to go. I shall watch Faith till yer get back, an' I'll take good care of her, I promise.'

Maria chewed her lip. Of course, she was longing to see her family again but she was sure that Josh had said her father was to be buried that morning.

'Thank you, Ruby. Perhaps you could arrange for me to go as soon as possible then? I believe my father's funeral is to take place this morning and I ought to attend.'

Ruby nodded understandingly as she made for the door, telling her, 'O' course yer should. I'll order the carriage to be brought round to the front in ten minutes, miss. But while I do that, eat some o' that breakfast. You ain't as far through as a broom handle.'

Maria smiled as she laid Faith back in her crib although she wasn't looking forward to the ordeal ahead at all.

She picked at the food, then after making sure that Faith was sleeping soundly, she put her cloak on and hurried down to the entrance hall, where Jennings told her, 'The carriage is all ready for you, Miss Mundy. Good luck.'

Maria thanked him. Jennings obviously knew about the funeral and now she just wanted to go and get it over with. It was then that Josh appeared from the dining room to ask her, 'Would you like me to come with you, Maria?'

Her heart pounded at the sight of him but she shook her head.

'Thank you for offering, but no. I'd like some time alone with my mother before we go to the church.'

'Of course.' He stood uncertainly for a moment. There was so much more he wanted to say to her. They hadn't had a second alone together since he had rescued her from

Hatter's Hall, but in the end he merely turned and walked away as Maria went out to the waiting carriage.

Thankfully the snow had stopped falling during the night. It was still bitterly cold, with a threat in the sky of more to come, but at last the carriage pulled up in front of Maria's home and the driver helped her alight saying, 'I've been told to take you an' yer family to the church whenever yer ready, miss. Take your time and just give us a shout when yer want to go.'

'Thank you,' she told him, then walking to the familiar door she pushed it open and there was her family. There had been times over the last months when she had thought she would never see them again, and now the tears in her throat threatened to choke her; she could not speak a word as her mother and Emma rushed over to envelop her in a hug, whilst Henry looked on with a broad smile on his face.

'Eeh lass, you'll never know how much I've missed you,' Martha told her as she drew her towards a chair, and then suddenly they were talking ten to the dozen as they caught up on all that had been happening to them. Aware of the man left out in the cold, Maria ensured that everyone was ready to leave shortly. The time seemed to fly by, but eventually they heard the hearse that Josh had ordered to take Edward's body to the church draw up outside and the undertaker entered to nail down the coffin lid.

'Your father is in the parlour. Would you like to go in and pay your last respects?' Martha asked quietly.

Maria nodded. She supposed she should; it was her duty to say goodbye to him. As she stared down at his face, stern even in death, a tear trickled from the corner of her eyes for all that should have been. He had been her father, after all, and she would have liked to have been a normal loving daughter to him, but for some reason Edward had always

Rosie Goodwin

held her at arm's length. And now it was too late to change
anything.

'Goodbye, Father, I hope you rest in peace,' she muttered,
and she then left the room to allow Mr Boot to do his job.

Chapter Thirty-six

'It was a good turnout, wasn't it?' Maria said on the way back from the church following the burial.

'Yes, it was,' Martha said as she stared from the window of the carriage. 'But then your father was a well-respected man.'

'Only because people didn't know him as we did,' Maria said before she could stop herself.

'It's wrong to speak ill of the dead.' Martha frowned at her as she held tight to Emma's small hand. 'Especially so soon after their death.'

'But I'm only speaking the truth, Mother.' Maria's chin lifted in defiance. She could not be a hypocrite and pretend to be sad at her father's passing, especially as there were more pressing things on her mind. She hadn't wished to raise them before the service but now she said tentatively, 'Wasn't the cottage tied to Father's job?'

Martha sighed. 'Yes, it was, and the landlord has already

been to see me. He intimated that as soon as another preacher is instructed to take your father's place, he will be entitled to move into the cottage.'

'And how long will that be?'

Martha shrugged, trying to hide her deep concern. 'I don't know, dear. But I shouldn't think it will take the chapel authorities long to find a replacement.' In actual fact she had lain awake all night worrying about it.

'And where will we all live then?' asked Emma, looking scared. She had been crying, and there were tear-tracks running down her face.

'I have no idea,' Martha said, 'but I've no doubt something will turn up, although it will be difficult to find anywhere as cheap. It's hard enough as it is with only Henry's wage coming in, and it's the wrong time of the year to take in any more washing. It's so difficult to get it all dry. I'm sure that having wet washing strung about the kitchen all the time isn't helping your chest, pet, but what else can I do?'

'Well, I can help out now that I'm back,' Maria assured her. 'I'm sure Mrs Montgomery will give me a wage for looking after Faith until she employs a proper nanny, and then I can get another position.'

'Don't you get fretting about us. I'm just happy to have you back safe and sound,' Martha told her affectionately as she took both her daughters' hands. 'You know what they say: when one door shuts another door opens, so let's just wait and see, eh?' But despite her brave words she was worried sick. She had seen too many people end up in the workhouse, and the thought of her youngest daughter having to live there if she could not provide for her, filled Martha with dread. It was different for Henry and Maria: they were so much older and capable of taking care of themselves if need be, but Emma, who had been left in the care of a neighbour, was still so young.

Changing the subject, Martha said, 'But what about young Master Josh then, Maria? I'm not blind and it's more than obvious that he cares for you. Do you not care for him?'

The colour that flooded into Maria's cheeks was her answer.

'So if you care for him too, what is to stop you coming together?'

'The difference in our classes,' Maria said shortly. 'I would drag him down were I to marry him, Mother. You know that his kind would never accept me.'

A pain seared through Martha's heart as she looked deep into this beloved girl's eyes, and not for the first time she was sorely tempted to take her aside later and tell her the secret she had been forced to keep for so many years. But would Maria thank her for knowing the truth, or would she despise her? Somehow, Martha knew that she was not strong enough to risk that right now. There was so much going on in their lives, so once again she remained silent. *But one day*, she promised herself, *one day I will tell her and pray that she will forgive me*. One lapse had resulted in a lifetime of heartbreak, and all she could do now was pray that the same fate was not destined for her dear girl.

'Will you come in for some tea before you go back to Willow Park?' she asked when the carriage drew up outside the cottage. There would be no funeral tea for Edward Mundy; there were no spare funds for such luxuries.

'I'll see you safely inside but then I ought to be going,' Maria answered. 'Mrs Montgomery will be expecting me back and I wouldn't like to take advantage of her good nature.'

'I understand.' Martha, Emma and Henry climbed down from the carriage, closely followed by Maria. It was as

Martha was about to put the key in the lock that she noticed a large brown envelope that had been hidden behind the old barrel that stood by the cottage door and in which she planted pansies in the spring. Pulling it out, and brushing the snow off it, she said, 'I wonder what this could be?'

Martha entered the kitchen and placed the envelope on the table whilst she removed her Sunday-best bonnet and her cloak. She had trimmed the bonnet with black ribbon as a token of mourning. Lifting the envelope again she slit it open, and as the contents spilled onto the table they all gasped. It was full of banknotes.

Henry pounced on them, his eyes almost popping from his head. 'Good Lord, there must be hundreds of pounds here,' he breathed. 'But who could it be from? Is there a letter with it?'

Her hands shaking, Martha peered into the envelope. 'Nothing at all,' she choked. 'But the envelope is clearly addressed to me. What can it mean?'

'It means that someone has given you a very generous donation,' Henry whooped. Suddenly it seemed that all their troubles were over. 'It was probably one of Father's better-off parishioners.'

'But I can't think of anyone who would have this much money,' Martha stated as she eyed the pile in stunned disbelief. 'The congregation at chapel are mostly as poor as us. How much is there, Henry?'

With Maria's help her son began to count it and when they were done he told her, 'There's three hundred pounds here.'

Martha clutched at her heart; it was more money than she had ever seen or dreamed of in the whole of her downtrodden life.

'Do you realise what this means?' Henry crowed

delightedly. Then before anyone could answer him he rushed on, 'It means that we won't have to worry about where we are going to live, ever again. In fact, we can afford to buy that cottage in Ridge Lane that I was telling you about – and still have enough money to spare to last us for years if we're careful.' He took Emma by the arms and danced about the kitchen with her until they were both breathless.

'Stop that, the pair of you! Henry, put the money back in the envelope,' his mother told him. 'I cannot accept it without knowing where it came from.'

'I think I may know who gave it to you,' Maria said. It must be from Josh – it was the kind of generous thing he would do. 'Just keep it somewhere very safe while I make a few enquiries,' she ordered Henry, but Martha was obdurate.

'No, my dear. If you think you know who it belongs to, you must return it to them for me. Give them my heartfelt thanks, but tell them that I could not accept such a sum.'

'But—'

Martha held up her hand as Henry began to object and he clamped his mouth shut, although he did not at all agree with his mother's decision. This was like looking a gift horse in the mouth as far as he was concerned – the answer to all their prayers – but knowing how stubborn and proud his mother could be, he accepted that it was useless to argue. Shuffling the money back into a pile, he then rammed it back into the envelope and passed it begrudgingly to Maria, who bent to kiss her mother's pale cheek before saying, 'I shall see that it is returned, if you are sure that is what you want, and I shall try to get back to see you later today if it's at all possible.'

Martha nodded numbly, so with a quick hug of her brother and sister, Maria then turned and hurried out to the waiting carriage.

*

When Maria entered the hall of Willow Park a short time later, she found Josh waiting for her. He helped her off with her cape, asking, 'How did the funeral go?'

'As well as could be expected. The church was full,' she told him, then added, 'Thank you so much for paying the expenses. We will reimburse you, of course, as soon as possible.'

He waved her thanks aside, telling her, 'It was the very least I could do after all you have done for Isabelle and Faith. But please, come into the drawing room. I took the liberty of ordering some tea when I saw the carriage approaching and I'm sure you must be ready for some refreshment after such a distressing morning.'

Maria hesitated, but then clutching her bag containing the money, she followed him along the hallway. It might be as well to return it now and get it over and done with.

They had barely entered the room when there was a tap at the door and a maid wheeled in a trolley containing tea and pastries. Once she was gone, Josh began to pour it out as Maria took the envelope from her bag and said quietly, 'This was yet another very kind gesture on your part, Josh. But I am afraid my mother is already indebted to you and therefore she does not feel that she can accept it.'

He frowned in bewilderment as he paused to ask, 'Accept what?'

She thrust the envelope towards him and, once he had glanced inside, he said: 'I'm afraid I don't understand. What is this?'

'It's the money you left for my mother whilst we were at the church.'

'I assure you *I* didn't leave it,' he answered firmly. 'The name on the envelope isn't even in my handwriting.'

Now it was her turn to look bewildered as she spluttered, 'But if *you* didn't leave it, then who *did*?'

'I have absolutely no idea, but I promise you it wasn't me, so I suggest you return it to your mother as soon as possible. Someone obviously intended her to have it.'

Stunned, Maria returned the envelope to her bag and accepted the tea he held out to her, but Josh did not give her long to ponder on it because then he asked, 'What are we going to do, Maria? About us, I mean. You know that I love you and I believe that you love me too. Surely you are not willing to throw that away?'

Her lips set in a prim line, she said, 'I can see no point in going over this again. Your family would be the laughing stock of the county, should word get out that you were going to marry someone from my background. Especially as your mother has just accepted her illegitimate grandchild into her home. Think of what people would say.'

'I don't give a cuss about what people will say.' Josh glared at her as he slammed his cup down on a small occasional table, sending tea spraying all over the fine Turkish carpet. 'Surely we can rise above a bit of local gossip?'

'I think that it would amount to much more than a little gossip,' Maria said sensibly.

'All right then – but at least answer me one question truthfully, please. Do you have any tenderness for me, Maria, or have I imagined it?'

She wrestled with her conscience, which was screaming at her to tell him that she didn't. And yet she found that she could not lie to him so she nodded miserably.

'I have very deep feelings for you, and had we been born of the same class I would have been proud to be your wife. But I cannot allow you to be shunned by your own kind because of me. And anyway, my mother is going to need all

413

the help she can get now, and once I leave here I intend to see that she receives it.'

'Oh, don't make your mother an excuse,' Josh said angrily. 'I would be more than happy to ensure that she and your family never went without anything. But you have made up your mind, haven't you, so it appears there is no more to be said on the subject. I will not bother you again, Maria.' And with that he strode straight-backed from the room as hot tears welled in Maria's eyes.

In the day room, Helena was listening open-mouthed to the tale that Robert Pettifer was telling her, and trying to take it all in. She had known Robert for more years than she cared to remember and trusted him implicitly, but even so she was reeling from the shock of what he had just revealed to her. He had called at Willow Park to offer his condolences on the death of her husband, but when she told him about Josh and Maria, and the reason why the girl had rejected him, he had confessed to her his secret.

'And so you see, if what you are saying is right, I *have* to talk to them,' he ended. 'I owe them that much at least. I will never be able to live with my conscience again if I don't do the right thing. Neither you nor I had the happiest of marriages unfortunately, but it could be different for them. You do understand, don't you, Helena?'

'Yes, I do,' she answered softly. 'And there is no time like the present. I shall ask the maid to fetch them both in here and then I shall leave whilst you speak to them.'

'There is no need for you to leave,' he told her as he looked at this dear woman he had secretly admired for years. There had been so much heartbreak but his love for the village girl who had borne his first child had never died. He wondered if she might ever be able to return the feelings he still had for her. Of course, it would have to be some long time before he revealed how he felt. Her husband had only just been laid to rest and there would have to be the usual period of mourning following his funeral, but then . . . perhaps? He stopped his mind from going any further. It might be best to tackle one thing at a time at present.

Epilogue

''Scuse me, miss. Sorry to disturb you but the mistress would like to see you in the day room.'

'Oh, er . . . thank you.' Maria surreptiously dried her eyes then sedately followed the young maid from the room wondering what Mrs Montgomery might want her for.

Josh was dressed for outdoors when the maid summoned him too. He was not in the best of humours and he scowled at Maria as they entered the day room to find Helena and Robert Pettifer waiting for them.

'Yes?' Josh said shortly, still stinging from Maria's final rejection. He had been hoping to go for a gallop on his horse to clear his head.

'Ah, Josh, Maria,' his mother said. 'Thank you for coming. Robert has something that he needs to explain to Maria, and he thought that you should be present to hear it too, darling.'

Josh noted that his mother appeared to be highly agitated,

but then he supposed that was to be expected, given all that had gone on in the last couple of days. Flicking his coat-tails aside, he sat down and crossed his arms as Maria eyed Robert warily.

Despite not being in the first flush of youth, Robert was still a fine-looking man, and on the odd occasion when their paths had crossed, he had always had a smile and a kind word for her. However, she had no idea why he might want to talk to her now and was intrigued.

He marched up and down the room for a few moments, his hands clasped behind his back, as if he was trying to decide how to begin but then after taking a deep breath he addressed Maria, saying, 'My dear. I fear that what I am about to tell you may cause you distress, so I apologise for that in advance. Even so, I would ask that you hear me out before you pass judgement on me. Do you think you could do that?'

'Y-yes, sir,' Maria stuttered as she clutched her hands together for comfort.

Coming to a stop in front of her and looking her directly in the face, he began, 'I wish to tell you a story. When I was a young man I resided in the family home with my parents and my sisters. Of course, when I was old enough my father sent me away to be schooled and I am ashamed to admit I was a bit of a lad, always up to some mischief or another.'

He sighed ruefully as he remembered then went on, 'Eventually I returned home and went into the family business as was expected of me. I'm afraid I had always had hopes of becoming a barrister, but being the eldest son I bowed to my parents' wishes. After all, I knew that one day I would inherit the family business as well as the house when my parents died. During this time they introduced me to the woman who would become my wife. I feel no shame in admitting that ours was not a love-match. Our fathers knew that both their businesses would be enhanced by our union and so we went along with it as was expected of us. It was whilst we were betrothed that I met a young woman from a neighbouring village, and I'm afraid I fell in love with her – and, I like to think, she with me.'

He gazed towards the window with a faraway look in his eyes, but then pulled himself together and continued, 'We would meet each other whenever we could, and after some time and shortly before I was due to be married, the girl informed me that she was with child. I was full of foolish ideals back then so I went to my father and told him about the situation and said that I was going to marry her. My father was incensed, but I was sure that I was doing the right thing. And then suddenly she disappeared. My father told me that she had come to him asking for money so that she might go away to have the child, and so he had paid her off. I was heartbroken and found it hard to believe, so I searched for her. Of course I didn't find her, so my wedding went ahead as planned, and I am not ashamed to say that I have barely known a happy day since. The only good thing to come from my marriage was Felicity, and when she was born I swore that she would be allowed to marry for love. Anyway, some years later I was riding through Chapel End when I saw the girl again, leading a little blonde-haired child by the hand.'

Mr Pettifer stopped for a moment to collect himself. He cleared his throat. 'I reined my horse in, and I don't mind telling you that it would have been hard to say who was the more shocked. I asked her why she had run away, said that I had searched for her, and she explained that my father had visited her, telling her that I wanted nothing more to do with her, and that he had found a man who was willing to marry her for a price and bring up my child as his own. Seeing no other option open to her, she had agreed to it.'

Robert took a handkerchief from his breast pocket and mopped his brow before telling Maria: 'That girl was your mother, my dear . . . which means that you are my daughter.'

Maria felt her legs buckle beneath her, and had it not been for Josh rushing across to take a firm grip of her elbow, she was sure that she would have dropped to the floor there and then. The silence was all-enveloping as she tried to take in what Robert had just told her, but then things began to fit together like pieces of a jigsaw puzzle. The way her father had always treated her differently from Henry and Emma. The way he had treated her mother; more as a servant than a wife.

'I realise that this must come as a tremendous shock to you,' Robert told her contritely. 'I know that I do not deserve your forgiveness, but what I will tell you is that when I found your mother again I begged her to let me help her, financially at least. It broke my heart to know that I had a daughter whom I could not recognise. But your mother is a fine, proud woman, and she told me that we had missed our chance and that we were both wed to other people now. She felt that she owed it to your father to stay with him, and so we agreed that we would go on as before. But now your father and my wife are dead, so I think you deserve to know who you truly are, my dear. Furthermore, I have left a sum of money to ensure that your mother and her family need not suffer financially, and should she ever, at any time in the future, need any more help she has only to ask. That is the very least I can do for her.'

'So it was *you* who left the envelope,' Maria breathed, feeling as if she were caught up in some sort of a dream.

Robert nodded. 'Yes, it was, and please do not think of trying to return it, for I shall not accept it. You are a fine, principled girl, just like your mother, but I must insist on this.'

The silence returned again then until Josh suddenly said, 'Do you realise what this means, Maria?'

Bewildered, she shook her head, then looked up at him to see a broad smile on his face.

'It means that you are the daughter of gentry. Don't you see? Robert is your father and the preacher Edward Mundy was nothing to do with you. So tell me . . . what stands between us now? If Robert is prepared to acknowledge you as his daughter, we are on a level.'

Maria swayed as his words struck home. From now on, her mother need never work again and the family would be well provided for, and as for herself . . .

'Do you think you might ever find it in your heart to forgive me?' Robert asked humbly and Maria stared at her real father for a moment with a sense of coming home before saying, 'Of course. It appears that what happened was not your fault and I thank you for the help you have given to my mother.'

'But what about *us*?' Josh persisted, taking her hand, and now as she looked up at him again, a radiant smile lit up her face.

'Well, given these revelations I suppose I shall have no option but to marry you,' she said teasingly.

As Josh took her tenderly in his arms, Robert led Helena from the room, whispering, 'Come, let's find some fresh tea and leave the lovebirds to plan their wedding, shall we?

Then we'll go to the nursery and check on that beautiful granddaughter of yours.'

Helena looked back up at him with a twinkle in her eye before answering, 'I think that is a very good idea, sir!'

Acknowledgements

Thanks to the wonderful team at Constable & Robinson; to my great editor, Victoria; my lovely PR Laura Sherlock; the wonderful Joan Deitch, my copyeditor; and of course my brilliant agent, Sheila Crowley. Many thanks to you all for your support and encouragement.

Don't let the story stop here

Join
ROSIE
GOODWIN
and her readers

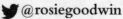